C0-ASZ-603

Oakland Community College
Orchard Ridge Campus Library
27055 Orchard Lake Road
Farmington Hills, MI 48018

ML 60 .T666
Tovey, Donald Francis
The main stream of music,
and other essays

occOR Aug-23-1990 13:28

FEB 2 6 1994

Oakland Community College
Orchard Ridge Campus Library
27055 Orchard Lake Road
Farmington Hills, MI 48018

DEMCO

THE MAIN STREAM OF MUSIC
AND OTHER ESSAYS

THE
MAIN STREAM
OF MUSIC
AND
OTHER ESSAYS

DONALD FRANCIS TOVEY

SOMETIME REID PROFESSOR OF MUSIC
IN THE UNIVERSITY OF EDINBURGH

Collected, with an Introduction,
by HUBERT FOSS

Geoffrey Cumberlege
OXFORD UNIVERSITY PRESS
NEW YORK
1949

ML
60
.T666

OR 11/90

First printed in England in 1949 under
the title *Essays and Lectures on Music*

Printed in Great Britain by
Western Printing Services Ltd., Bristol

CONTENTS

INTRODUCTION

'IT was one of my naïve undergraduate ambitions to make a contribution to aesthetic philosophy by a systematic review of music.' So writes Donald Francis Tovey in the lecture printed on pp. 160–182 of this book. He continues: 'Forty years on, I come to you with empty hands.' That is not a wholly true statement. That 'systematic review' which he discussed with the writer and others over so many years was, indeed, never written. But despite the fact that only one of his books was (so to say) *durchcomponirt*,[1] Tovey was in practice a voluminous writer. He wrote when occasion called him, and in that busy life of practical music-making, of playing, conducting, and lecturing, occasion called him very frequently. The philosophy expressed in those sixteen volumes that stand massively on our shelves may not be 'systematic' nor expressed in the form of argued review, but it is consistent, of the widest possible reference, developed, and positive. It has the added advantage of being expressed in a prose that it is a pleasure to read for its own artistry.

In this volume, a companion to the other sixteen, are gathered the larger part of Donald Tovey's writings that have not already been garnered into sheaves. Completeness has been neither aimed at nor attained. Of the few deliberate omissions, one essay (a contribution to a volume long out of print) was not thought suitable for inclusion: of the first series of Cramb lectures, no complete copy has yet been found, and, if it were, the difficulty would arise in reprinting the lectures that they were copiously illustrated at the piano. For the same reason, the broadcast scripts cannot be sensibly reproduced. Only those who knew Tovey personally are aware of how readily and continuously he illustrated his seemingly incessant flow of talk with passages at the piano. I was not present in person at Lady Margaret Hall on 4 June 1934, when he gave the Philip Maurice Deneke Lecture, but I am as certain as if I were hearing it now that he sang 'the text of that Sweelinck Psalm' (see p. 177 of this volume) 'to its proper tune of the "Old Hundredth"'. But though the rigours of print and its metal must to some extent clip the eagle's wings, I venture to express the opinion that he 'soars the morning clouds above' at an altitude unattained by contemporary writers on music.

[1] *A Companion to 'The Art of Fugue'* (Oxford, 1931).

vii

A collection of scattered writings cannot avoid the dangers of the miscellany, which, too, has its pleasures. There is varied fare in these pages, essays that are wide and general in their approach to the subject, others that are severely technical and analytical. I repeat with warm agreement the words of Dr. Ernest Walker in his preface to *A Musician Talks*:

'It is by these many hundreds of pages that he has achieved a world reputation; and, indeed, there is nothing like it at all in English nor, so far as I know, in any other language. Perhaps we see the quintessence of his thought most completely in . . . "Musical Form and Matter"' (p. 160 of this volume).

Here, then, are Tovey's scattered 'hundreds of pages' collected into one accessible volume. Every word contained herein has been printed before, but for the most part those words are inaccessible outside the major libraries, and some had only the ephemeral life of the periodical. It may thus be realized that Tovey himself read all the proofs of these essays and lectures, and in presenting his text anew I have had occasion to make only the most trivial corrections and to add a reference to an example or a page here and there. But, final though this reprinted form is, we must not take it that it represents more than what the author decided at that moment of proof-correcting. It is, in my view, not unlikely that that great reviser would have desired (even if he had not been allowed) to make many changes.

On p. 168 *et seq.* there occurs an interesting and pertinent reference to Tovey's own methods and experience of composition, and 'A Note on Opera' (p. 353) is the essay which he wrote to introduce his opera *The Bride of Dionysus*. They give us a timely reminder of Tovey the composer, too soon neglected and now almost forgotten, though I do not myself believe that his music will long endure this oblivion.

The problem of indexing this allusive, talkative prose style is no easy one; the indexer is racked with constant tortures of indecision, of over-fulness, repentant excision, and a nervous final jump to what he hopes is safe ground. For the adoption of an entirely arbitrary plan, I am solely responsible, and would apologize in advance for those omissions which each reader will observe and those redundancies which, no doubt, will irritate many. I am responsible, too, for the text as definitively printed. But I record here my great gratitude to those who read the first proofs, and who indeed assisted me in the task of gathering together the material:

I refer, of course, to those indefatigable workers in the Tovey cause, Dr. Mary Grierson, Dr. Ernest Walker, and Mr. R. C. Trevelyan. The debt to them cannot be paid.

It may be expected that no more words from Tovey's pen will ever be published, save only the letters which he wrote so fully and entertainingly. Dr. Mary Grierson's forthcoming biography will give the world, I have no doubt, a taste of that banquet of wit and wisdom with which, in his letters, Tovey regaled his friends.

HUBERT FOSS

March 1949

HAYDN'S CHAMBER MUSIC[1]

In the history of music no chapter is more important than that filled by the life-work of Joseph Haydn. He effected a revolution in musical thought hardly less far-reaching than that effected at the close of the sixteenth century by the monodists who wrote the earliest operas, and supplanted the pure vocal polyphony of Palestrina by the new art of supporting solo voices on instrumental chords. But whereas the monodic revolution destroyed a great art so effectively that there is a gap of a century between Palestrina and the new polyphony of Bach and Handel, the revolution effected by Haydn has its only immature phases in unpretending tuneful efforts within the lifetime of Handel, whose art-forms Haydn supplants, not by destruction, but by reabsorption into his own new musical life as soon as this has firmly established its independent basis.

Before it is possible to measure Haydn's achievement it must be realized that his conscious musical culture rested on a music much older than that of the generation before him; and that, except in so far as his music is derived literally from the streets, its foundations are not in Bach and Handel, but in Palestrina. When the young Haydn came to Vienna, Fux, the court organist, had not long been dead, and Fux's *Gradus ad Parnassum* was more important to him than victuals for his body and fuel for his garret in mid-winter. Fux's Church music, which is still drawn upon by serious Roman Catholic choir-masters, is genuinely masterly work by an eighteenth-century composer who prefers to write in pure sixteenth-century style. To Fux, if to nobody else at the time, that style was still a living language; and even if it could be proved that Haydn knew nothing nearer to Palestrina than Fux, the fact would remain that he educated himself with a sixteenth-century musical culture. In his old age he even lent his name to a project for publishing the archaic works of Obrecht.

Now the pure polyphony of the Golden Age had solved for all time the central problems of vocal harmony. Its medium was the unaccompanied chorus of voices producing a mass of harmony by singing independent melodies; and its grammatical laws (surviving for the vexation of students to-day in the form of garbled and

[1] An article published in Cobbett's *Cyclopedic Survey of Chamber Music* (Oxford University Press), 1929.

arbitrary rules for exercises that exist only on paper and represent no musical language) were essentially practical rules of instrumentation. For not only was the chorus the only instrument seriously cultivated, but no other instrument had familiarized the ear with any complete ideas that the voice could not spontaneously express. The great monodic revolution at the beginning of the seventeenth century is far too complex a process to sum up in a phrase, or even in a volume; into the world of Palestrina it opened out the aspirations of Wagner, and provided no technical experience for the equipment of its pioneers. After Bach and Handel had closed their epoch, the latter half of the eighteenth century still found need for a fuller solution of what might be supposed to be the simplest musical problem of the seventeenth century—that of producing an instrumental harmony not less complete and satisfactory than a purely polyphonic chorus. It is vain to regard viol music as in any line of ancestry to the string quartet. The viols merely played vocal music which was enjoyed for the sake of the vocal sense, and hardly, if at all, for the tone of the viols. As the word 'monody' implies, the revolutionary composers of the early seventeenth century directed their attention to the solo voice; and their first urgent practical question was how to organize a harmonic accompaniment for the supporting instruments. Within a surprisingly short time they developed the art of playing a semi-extempore accompaniment from a figured bass on a keyboard instrument. At the same time the violin and its family were ousting the flat-backed, husky-toned viols, and were raising more important new issues by flying and diving into regions far beyond the compass of human voices.

Thus at the outset of the seventeenth century the two problems of the solo performer and the instrumental accompaniment were already defined. Uncharted difficulties remained in the special techniques of the various instruments, and contrasting and blending their tones in a mass of harmony. A full century passed before these difficulties were artistically solved; and the solution as achieved by Bach and Handel is so remote from the aesthetic system of even Haydn's and Mozart's orchestra that it is only now beginning to be realized that it is a genuine solution, and that to dismiss Bach's and Handel's orchestral intentions as primitive is as Philistine as to modernize Palestrina's modal harmony. The life-work of Haydn effected the whole transition from the aesthetic system of Bach to that which is common to all instrumental music from Haydn to Brahms; and it effected it by no destructive revolution, but in an orderly progress of works full of promise at the outset and culminating in a long series of masterpieces.

Haydn's culture in the Palestrina style remained a fundamental, though undisplayed, element throughout his art; but the hypothesis of Bach's and Handel's instrumentation was immediately and irretrievably abolished by him in his earliest instrumental works. Yet on that hypothesis every musician in Haydn's young days was trained, and there was no definite period in Haydn's long life at which the hypothesis was consciously abandoned. The hypothesis still depended on the monodists' device of the continuo. Carl Philipp Emanuel Bach, the most famous of Bach's sons, and the master whose clavier works and treatise on clavier-playing were appearing as a revelation to the boy Haydn in his Vienna garret, protested bitterly against the growing neglect to provide a con-tinuo for performances of oratorios and orchestral music. The hypothesis of the continuo is based on a truth which is as important to-day as it was in the time of Bach; for neither practically nor ideally does the orchestra produce a homogeneous mass of har-mony like a chorus endowed with instrumental powers. The con-trast between background and foreground is involved in the nature of all instrumental combinations, and is only artificially imported into pure vocal polyphony. If a composer writes choral harmony according to certain old grammatical rules, without troubling to imagine the effect, he will never be disappointed with the result, for the rules are absolutely safe, and the composer who writes cor-rectly, without using his mental ear, is unlikely to appreciate any-thing better even when he hears it. But with all instrumental combinations the limits within which vocal rules apply are soon reached; and the composer who writes concerted music without using his mental ear is quickly brought to his senses by defects obvious to everybody as soon as he ventures beyond vocal idioms. The pioneers of instrumental music in the years 1600–20 showed an accurate instinct by promptly treating all groups of instruments as consisting of a firm bass and a florid treble, held together by an unobtrusive mass of harmony in the middle. Up to the death of Handel and beyond, throughout Haydn's boyhood, this harmonic welding was entrusted to the continuo player, and nobody ever supposed that the polyphony of the 'real' orchestral parts could, except accidentally or by way of relief, sound well without this supplement. The written instrumental parts are an aristocracy for whom the problems of domestic service are perfectly solved by that most learned and most modest of artists, the continuo player, who was, in the best performances, generally the composer himself.

It is not too much to say that one half of the problems of instrumentation, both in chamber music and in the orchestra, since Haydn began to work, up to the present day, lies in the distribution of the continuo-function among all the instruments. But, for Haydn, most of the other half of the problem arose from a feature in early eighteenth-century music which concerns only the keyboard instruments and which leaves no trace in the written record of compositions. Hence its existence is often overlooked, though the modern art of instrumentation has to replace it besides the continuo. In the early eighteenth century, everybody who played upon keyboard instruments (that is to say, every educated musician) was brought into constant contact with the power of the organ and the harpsichord to double in higher or lower octaves whatever was played upon them. One obvious result of this is that good counterpoint in two or three parts need never sound thin, for, by merely pulling out a stop, it becomes a mass of sounds which would require four or six vocal parts to produce, but which adds nothing more than a quality of timbre, much as if the upper partials of each 'clang' were heard through a set of Helmholtz resonators. And there is no more striking illustration of the correct instincts of medieval musicians than the fact that one of the most ancient devices of the organ is the use of 'mixtures' extending to the whole first six overtones, thus anticipating Helmholtz's theory of timbre by half a millennium.

With these facts in mind it is more easily understood that, when Haydn began his work, his auditory imagination was fed on experiences fundamentally opposed to the whole hypothesis of future chamber music—the hypothesis that the written notes completely define the composition. How could the string quartet develop in a musical world where necessary harmonic filling-out was always left to be extemporized, and where a single written note might sound in three different octaves at once? There were string quartets before Haydn, but nobody troubles to revive them. In his later years Haydn was indignant at the suggestion that he owed anything to the quartets of Gluck's master Sammartini, saying that he had indeed heard them in his youth, but that 'Sammartini was a dauber' (*Schmierer* or 'greaser'). Haydn's own first quartets were commissioned by a patron in whose house quartet-playing was an established custom. The date given by early accounts is 1750, the year of Bach's death; but Pohl assigns Haydn's first quartets to 1755, partly for vague biographical reasons and partly because he considers the technique too advanced to have been achieved without long study and leisure. The growth of ideas and style in Haydn's first eighteen quartets (opp. 1, 2, 3) is so fascinating that Pohl may be forgiven for overrating their artistic value; but there is really nothing in the first eighteen quartets which is technically beyond the power of a talented young musician between 1750 and 1760; some features (e.g. the structure of the finale of op. 1, no. 6) could hardly have survived any study at all; and the merits of the works are not accountable for by study, for the whole significance of Haydn's development is that it took a direction which no other composer before Mozart ever suspected or even recognized when it became manifest.

There was, at the outset, no clear distinction between a string quartet and a string orchestra. The fifth quartet is undoubtedly Haydn's first symphony, though it is at least four (if not more) years earlier than the work that has been catalogued as such by all authorities, including Haydn himself. Authentic wind-parts have been found for this 'quartet'; and here the point is not merely that it is indistinguishable from orchestral music, but that Haydn never objected to its inclusion among his published quartets, though he omits it in his own MS. catalogue. In external form it differs from the quartets, and conforms to the first two acknowledged symphonies, inasmuch as it has no minuets and its three movements are occupied with formulas and argumentative sequences to the exclusion of anything like a tune. The first eleven real quartets, on the other hand, have five movements, including two minuets, one on each side of the middle movement; and the other three movements often combine tunefulness with a certain tendency at first hardly distinguishable from awkward irregularity, but already urging towards the quality by which Haydn's life-work was to effect a Copernican revolution in musical form.

Though all the important chamber music before Haydn was designed on the continuo hypothesis, it would be a mistake to suppose that Haydn started without experience of what could be done by instruments unsupported by keyboard harmony. Such experience was familiar to him in the music of—the streets. Serenading was a favourite pastime, enjoyed as much by listeners as by players. One of Haydn's boyish practical jokes consisted in arranging for several serenade parties to perform different music in earshot of

each other, to the annoyance, not only of a respectable neighbour-
hood, but of an adjoining police station. Serenade music consisted
naturally of dance tunes, marches, and lyric ariosos. By the time of
Mozart it had developed into works longer, if lighter, than symphonies, the typical serenade becoming in fact a cheerful six-
movement symphony, with two slow movements alternating with
two minuets. If the combination of instruments was solo rather
than orchestral, the composition would be called a divertimento;
and the remaining name for such works, 'cassation', is a corruption
of *Gassaden*, which means music of the *Gassen* or back-streets.
And just as Hans Sachs was accused by Beckmesser (or by more
historical persons) of writing *Gassenhauer*, so Haydn, whose first
quartets became rapidly and widely popular, was frowned upon by
this and that preserver of the official dignity of music who could
predict no good from such vulgar beginnings; nor was Haydn ever
spared the charge of rowdiness even in his ripest works.

For the purposes of a catalogue it may be important to distinguish between quartets, divertimenti, and symphonies; but for
aesthetic purposes the distinction emerges only gradually as the
works improve, each in their own direction. Haydn's first twelve
quartets are moving cautiously from the style of the *Gassaden* to
that of the future symphonic sonata-forms. The movement towards
a genuine quartet style can be traced only with reference to what
was present to Haydn's auditory imagination at the time. Of street
music one thing is certain, that it never sounds well. The sound
may be romantically suggestive, the occasion gratifying to the
listener, and the performance perfect; but suggestiveness is almost
all that is left of the actual body of sound, the finer nuances of performance are lost, and the rest is all moonshine. The development
of Haydn's auditory imagination will depend upon the use he makes
of the experience of hearing, writing, and playing music unsupported by the continuo, within four walls and a ceiling. And for
pioneer work, a fastidious taste in performance is both an obstacle
to enterprise and a necessity to progress. On the whole it is more
of a necessity than an obstacle.

Haydn himself knew the technique of several different instruments, but was, he confesses, 'no conjurer on any of them'. Composers' playing is proverbially bad; since not only is the composer
unlikely to devote his time to acquiring the technique of a conjurer,
but he is of all persons the most capable of imagining desirable
qualities without needing to supply them himself. Only when he

takes up the conductor's baton do conditions naturally awaken in him a present sense of what a performance should be. It is accordingly significant that Haydn's achievement in his first twelve, or even his first eighteen, quartets is no fruit of his experience under the stimulating conditions as conductor of Prince Esterhazy's private orchestra, but is rather a demonstration of his eminent fitness for that post four or perhaps nine years before it was offered him. It is significant that there is no sign of the need for a continuo in the general conception of these earliest quartets. Here and there one finds Haydn insensitive to the baldness of a progression which long habit of reliance on the continuo had completely submerged below the composer's consciousness; and thus, even as late as 1769, in a quartet otherwise astonishingly mature (op. 9, no. 4), Haydn not only leaves a blank space for a cadenza at the end of a slow movement, but represents its conventional 6/4 chord by a bare fourth.

Ex.1 *Adagio cantabile*

Even in his old age, Haydn's pen is liable to small habitual slips, which, like all such lapses, should reveal to the psychologist how far the mind has travelled, instead of suggesting dismal broodings on squalid origins. It will save space to deal with these lapses here. The fact that Haydn's fifth quartet was actually a symphony raises the question whether throughout opp. 1 and 2 his 'cello part was not supported, or even (as many years later in Mozart's ripest divertimenti for strings and horns) replaced, by a double-bass. Aesthetically the question is more open than it might appear to a fastidious taste in mature chamber music. Long after Haydn's and

Mozart's quartets had set the standard of style for all educated musicians, Onslow, having found the double-bass an unexpectedly good substitute for a missing 'cello, proceeded to write several very decent quintets for strings with double-bass.

The double-bass is unthinkable in Haydn's quartets, from op. 9 onwards; and yet he is never quite sure of his octave when, without using the tenor clef, he writes his 'cello above the viola. Even after Mozart's artistic debt to Haydn appears repaid with compound interest, there is an astonishing miscalculation throughout six bars of the development of one of Haydn's greatest first movements, that of the Quartet in E flat, op. 71, no. 3 (bars 20–6 from the double-bar).

and so on for
another four bars

The passage is not, like other accidents of the kind, to be remedied by putting the 'cello part an octave lower (as with an incident in one of the last six quartets, op. 76, no. 4, where the use of the treble clef at its proper pitch may have caused confusion), for Haydn is evidently thinking of the tone of the A string. And in a later passage of the same movement the viola and 'cello are found crossing each other with exquisite adroitness, the lowest note at each moment being the real bass (Ex. 3).

Where Haydn miscalculates in these mature works, the error really lies in the viola part. Thus, in Ex. 2, the one possible and perfectly satisfactory correction consists in substituting a rest for the first quaver in each bar of the viola part. There is a more special significance of such oversights in Haydn's viola parts; but for the present it is important to realize that they originated in the habit of thinking of the 'cello as supported by a double-bass.

The double-bass was not the only cause of ambiguity as to the octave in which passages of early chamber music are conceived; and Haydn's first quartets, no less than his symphonies, show certain uses of octaves which suggest the mutation-stops of the organ and harpsichord. It is possible to watch the process by which these uses, beginning in habit, awakened Haydn's consciousness to their actual sound when transferred from the automatic action of a stop on the organ or harpsichord to the efforts of four living players on

Ex. 3

four instruments. In orchestral music the young Haydn agreed with his contemporaries in finding two-part harmony more satisfactory to the ear when merely 'registered' in several octaves than when filled out with a viola part which, like those of Bach and Handel, makes no attempt to usurp the function of the continuo. Where Haydn from the outset differed from almost all his contemporaries was just in the excellence of his two parts. And in his quartets he startled his listeners by doubling the melody in octaves as well as the bass. Accurate discrimination is needed in comparing his early procedure in quartets with that in his orchestral music; it must suffice here to summarize the result by stating that Haydn's use of octaves in his first quartets is far more a matter of conscious art than in any but his ripest symphonies. He can hardly have needed to wait for practical experience to tell him how successfully he had imagined the effect of the second minuet in the Quartet, op. 1, no. 1.

There is nothing in the scoring of this spirited little movement which Haydn would have thought necessary to alter at any period of his life, though the viola has only four bars in which it is not in

Ex. 4 MENUETTO

octaves with the 'cello. The fact that this bold and bleak doubled two-part harmony is common in the first eighteen quartets and rare in the later ones must not be allowed to hide the more important facts that it startled his contemporaries and that it is an effect as genuinely imagined in op. 1 as in the wonderful canonic *Hexen-Menuett* in op. 76, no. 2.

Ex. 5

MENUETTO *Allegro ma non troppo*

His imagination has promptly grasped the vital difference between octaves produced by a mechanical coupler and octaves played by two living players on separate instruments. Moreover, it has grasped the more delicate but equally vital difference between octaves in the orchestra and octaves in the string quartet. In spite of all ambiguities, Haydn's earliest efforts are distinctly more effective as the string quartets they purport to be, than as the semi-orchestral works with which publishers continued to confuse them as late as 1784.

Haydn's chamber music may now be profitably surveyed in approximate chronological order from the first quartet, op. 1, no. 1, to the unfinished quartet, op. 103, his last composition. As to the chronology of the quartets, the order of opus numbers given in the familiar *Payne's Miniature Scores*[1] is fairly accurate; though Haydn's opus numbers were in an unholy muddle in the editions of his lifetime. The whole extant collection will thus consist of the following sets, six quartets in each opus: opp. 1, 2, 3, 9, 17, 20, 33; a single quartet, op. 42; six in op. 50; three each in opp. 54, 55; six in op. 64; three each in opp. 71, 74; six in op. 76; two each in op. 77; and the unfinished last quartet, op. 103. The quartet arrangement of that curious work, *The Seven Last Words* (a series of orchestral adagios composed for a Good Friday service in the Cathedral of Cadiz, and afterwards expanded into a choral work), shows no technical detail beyond the capacity of a copyist, though it was, strange to say, admitted into the collection of quartets as op. 51 by Haydn himself. This collection of seventy-six quartets, equal in bulk to quite a large proportion of the most experienced quartet-party's classical and modern repertory, is probably nearly complete. Quite complete it certainly is not,[2] but it contains no spurious works. At the time of writing, the great critical edition of Haydn's complete works (Breitkopf & Härtel) has not yet sorted out the chamber music, and a survey of what is commonly known must therefore suffice. But in Haydn's lifetime Breitkopf & Härtel used to publish an annual catalogue of works in stock, both manuscript and printed, and by good luck the Reid Library in the University of Edinburgh possesses this catalogue from the year 1762 to 1784. Here are found sporadic evidences of what was attracting attention among lovers of orchestral and chamber music and solos, from Haydn's op. 1 (which first appears in 1765) to some *Variations da Louis van Betthoven* (sic), *âgé de dix ans*, in the single part dated 1782-3-4. The Haydn entries include all the quartets from op. 1 to op. 33, besides four unpublished works, one of which is vouched for by Haydn's mention of it in a catalogue drawn up by himself. Most of the quartets in opp. 1 and 2 are first announced as divertimenti; two of these, op. 2, no. 3 (E flat) and op. 2, no. 5, appear as sextets with two horns. Throughout the catalogue, B (for basso)

---

[1] Now known as the 'Eulenburg Miniature Scores', the Leipzig firm of Eulenburg having purchased the edition from A. H. Payne, the founder, in the late nineteenth century. They are now published by W. Paxton & Co. Ltd., Dean St., London, W.1.

[2] At the date when this article was written, Miss Marion Scott's critical edition of Haydn's actual first quartet (earlier than that usually known as op. 1, no. 1), had not appeared. Tovey makes a reference to this 'historical document' in *Essays in Musical Analysis*, vol. vi, p. 135.

stands for double-bass or continuo as well as for 'cello, which seldom appears in its own name. The mature set of quartets, op. 33, also appears under the alternative title of divertimenti; and the quartets are outnumbered by the scherzandi, cassations, or notturni for all manner of semi-orchestral and solo combinations. The symphony, op. 1, no. 5, does not appear among the first quartet entries, but is incorporated later. According to Pohl, the sextet versions of the quartets, op. 2, nos. 3 and 5, are original, and Haydn afterwards reduced them to quartets. Pohl further tells us that in the D major quartet, op. 3, no. 5, the viola and second violin represent the original horns in the trio of the second minuet. This awakens attention to several horn passages traceable in op. 2, no. 3; especially the so-called 'variation 1' in the second minuet, where again it is the viola that chiefly represents the horn.

Ex. 6

The old Breitkopf catalogue bristles with evidences of Haydn's early and growing popularity. Early works, like the quartet-sextet-divertimento, op. 2, no. 3, continue to appear when the mature styles of Haydn and Mozart were already in favour, in spite of controversy. There is no means of distinguishing the genuine chamber music from the orchestral, or from that in which 'basso' implies the continuo hypothesis. Pohl sums up the situation by remarking that the term 'symphony' was freely applied to compositions for any number of instruments exceeding three. Many of the divertimenti and scherzandi may, for all we can tell, be as valuable as the quartets in op. 33, and may have become neglected because of the extreme difficulty of Haydn's horn-writing, or the obsolescence of certain instruments. Trios for two violins (or other soprano instruments) with 'basso' may be suspected of being a survival of the continuo hypothesis; and into his piano trios Haydn poured a stream of his finest music—early, middle, and late—without once justifying the use of the 'cello or scrupling to make the piano double the violin part during whole sections. But trios for violin, viola, and 'cello are a serious matter; and in 1772 the catalogue announces the six quartets of op. 17, and a set of six genuine string trios by Haydn. If these trios can be supposed to be of anything like the calibre of his quartets in opp. 9 and 17, the set would be an achievement even more important than these quartets. Haydn is, however, known to have written trios at the earliest period; and the themes here quoted do not (as such quotations once in a while may do) happen to indicate whether the works are early or not.

A divertimento in A seems to be a string quintet (2 violas); though it has been denied that Joseph Haydn wrote any quintets, the one in C, ascribed to him as op. 88, being by Michael Haydn. The appearance of a set of six unknown quartets by Giorgio Hayden, op. xviii, in Paris, is thrilling, but the name Giorgio (unknown in Haydn's family) is a warning against disappointment. The persistent spelling of the surname with an E is probably right for the first time in the catalogue; in which case the author of these quartets will be George Hayden, organist of St. Mary Magdalen, Bermondsey, and composer of the two-part song, 'As I saw fair Clara walk alone'. Other confusions are suggested by the statement that certain of Haydn's duets for two violins '*laufen im MS. unter dem Namen* Kammel'. The critical edition of Haydn's works now in progress has already disentangled Haydn's symphonies from the divertimenti and from spurious works, with the result that 104 symphonies are known to be genuine; thirty-eight known to be spurious; and thirty-six are doubtful. The chamber music is probably in no better case. Haydn and Mozart were popular enough for erroneous attributions to be profitable, in one direction; and it may be doubted whether the error would be so readily acknowledged if Kammel's works were to '*laufen im MS. unter dem Namen*' Hayden.

No doubt later volumes of the catalogue would give further matter for thought; but it seems likely that, after the appearance of op. 33, Haydn's published works were settling down into more or less the condition in which they are known. Evidently the quartets have survived in a far more complete and orderly corpus than the rest of Haydn's works; and this fact is itself a proof of the early and permanent ascendancy which they attained over the minds of musicians.

In the five-movement divertimenti which constitute opp. 1 and 2 of Haydn's quartets, the first movements and finales seem hardly more developed than what may aptly be termed the *melodic* range of form such as is found in a good-sized allemande or gigue in a

Bach suite. But the development of Haydn's sonata style is a matter neither of length nor of diversity of theme; and its dramatic tendency asserted itself in his earliest works.

On comparing the first movement of Haydn's op. 1, no. 1, with a typical Bach gigue, the first observation will probably be that, whereas Bach's texture is polyphonic, Haydn's is not, and the second 'observation' (if the observer ceases to observe and begins to quote books) will be that Bach has only one theme whereas Haydn has a definite second subject. This term 'second subject' is the most misleading in the whole of musical terminology; the German term *Seitensatz* is correct enough, for *Satz* may mean clause, sentence, paragraph, or a whole musical movement; but the wretched word 'subject' is always taken to mean 'theme', with results equally confusing both to criticism and musical education. If the practice of Haydn, Mozart, and Beethoven be taken as a guide (and who shall be preferred to them?), the discoverable rules of sonata form are definite as to distribution of keys, and utterly indefinite as to the number and distribution of themes in these keys.

The matter may be tested by comparing the first movement of Haydn's op. 1, no. 1, with the gigue of Bach's C major 'cello Suite, which, being unaccompanied, cannot be polyphonic, and which happens to have a very distinct second subject, if by that term is meant a second theme. That feature is by no means rare in Bach; dance movements with four themes might be cited from his par-titas. Whatever progress Haydn's first movement shows is not on text-book lines. As to themes, it has either none, or as many as it has two-bar phrases, omitting repetitions; the second part contains no more development than the second part of Bach's gigue; and though the substance that was in the dominant at the end of the first part is faithfully recapitulated in the tonic at the end of the second part, the formal effect is less enjoyable than in Bach's gigue in proportion to the insignificance of the material. Artistically Bach's gigue is obviously of the highest order, while Haydn's pre-sent effort is negligible. Yet within the first four bars Haydn shows that his work is of a new epoch, anticipated in Bach's time only by the harpsichord music of that elvish freak, Domenico Scarlatti. Bach's C major gigue, in spite of its contrasted second theme and its enforced lack of polyphony, is of uniform texture. Its limits are those of an idealized dance tune, which actually does nothing which would throw a troupe of dancers out of step. Within such limits Bach's art depends on the distinction of his melodic invention.

But to Haydn it is permissible to use the merest fanfare for his first theme, because his essential idea is to alternate the fanfare with a figure equally commonplace but of contrasted texture, throwing the four instruments at once into dialogue, *p*, after the *f* opening. And he is not going to keep up this alternation as a pattern throughout the movement. As soon as it has made its point, other changes of texture appear; and the phrases, apart from their texture, soon show an irregularity which in these earliest works appears like an expression of class prejudice against the imperturbable aristocratic symmetry of older music.

Before Haydn there is nothing like this irregularity, nor in any of his contemporaries. The only approach to it was a single recipe made fashionable all over Europe by composers of the Neapolitan school. It consisted in making a four-bar or two-bar phrase repeat itself or its latter half, and then, as it were, tie a knot by making a firmer cadence of the last echo. A careful note must be made of this Neapolitan rhythmic formula, which will be illustrated by Ex. 13. It is a cliché for producing irregular rhythm without accepting the responsibility of making the music genuinely dramatic; and its presence in anything of Haydn's is a mark of early date. Otherwise, in these first quartets, Haydn, alone in a crowd, cares not what awkwardness or abruptness he admits in his first movements and finales, if only he can prevent the music from settling down to the comfortable ambling gait with which the best chamber music of the rising generation was rocking the listener to sleep. The comic opening of the finale of op. 1, no. 1 is already worlds away from such decorum.

Ex. 7 Presto

Its six-bar opening would already sound irregular, even if it played out the sixth bar instead of stopping in the middle. And there is no intention of making this opening a pattern for the rest. The hearer's sense of design must be satisfied with its return in the recapitulatory part of the movement, with all or most of the other bits of coloured glass in Haydn's kaleidoscope; the only pattern and the only congruity lies in the whole. In virtue of this it is still felt that the dramatic style has not exceeded the limits of melodic form; the listener has merely enjoyed a certain bulk of lyric melody distributed in witty dialogue and stated more in terms of fiddles and fingers than of song.

The slow movement of op. 1, no. 1 has four bars of solemn sustained harmonies by way of prelude, which are expanded into six bars as a postlude. This is all that gives distinction to a poor and pompous specimen of a Neapolitan aria in which the first violin is a tragedy queen singing an appeal to generations of ancestral Caesars, and accompanying with superb gestures her famous display of *Treffsicherheit* in leaping from deep contralto notes to high soprano and back. The other instruments devoutly accompany, in humble throbbing chords which are allowed to be heard in solemn approving cadence when her tragic majesty has paused for breath. From this type of slow movement Haydn advances in three directions, of which only two are distinctly seen in the first twelve quartets. First, then, he can improve the type of melody, in which case he will underline its form by drawing a double-bar with repeat marks after its main close in the dominant, so that his slow movement becomes formally identifiable with a first movement. This is the case with op. 1, nos. 2, 4, and 6; and with op. 2, nos. 1, 3, 4, and 5. Secondly, he can improve the accompaniment; and in this respect no two of these early slow movements are exactly alike. But though this arioso type of adagio may become a duet, as in op. 1, no. 3 (which begins with the slow movement), and op. 1, no. 4, and though all manner of colour-schemes may be used in the accompaniment, e.g. pizzicato as a background to the muted first violin, as in op. 1, no. 6, and in the famous serenade in op. 3, no. 5; yet none of these devices will carry him a step forward in the direction of the true quartet style; for they are merely decorative, and, far from contributing to dramatic motion, fix the pattern and metre throughout the whole movement in which they are used.

Chronology is better in disproof than in constructive argument, otherwise it might be tempting to draw *a priori* conclusions from the fact that Haydn's early work coincides with the full influence of Gluck's reform of opera. But, strange to say, the peculiar dramatic force of Haydn's mature style owed nothing to Gluck, and was, indeed, hopelessly paralysed when he wrote for the stage. For Haydn's dramatic movement is the tersest thing in the fine arts; it is the movement of the short story. Gluck's reform of opera did, as he claimed for it, sweep away nuisances; but he was not more careful to avoid interrupting the action than to avoid hurrying it, and to impress upon his librettist the necessity of reducing it to the simplest and broadest issues. The finale of any of Haydn's greatest symphonies would explode its whole three-act comedy of manners in the listener's face before Gluck's Admetus could, in a single heart-rending scene, wring from Alceste the admission that she was the victim who had offered her life for his. The only part of Gluck's reforms which touches Haydn's art is that which Gluck expressed when, in his famous preface to *Alceste*, he wrote, 'I conceived . . . that the grouping (*concerto*) of instruments should be managed with regard to [dramatic] interests and passions'. It was this sentence that meant death to the old art of scoring decoratively and architecturally; and its implications have little dependence on the material resources of the orchestra. Many luxurious possibilities of texture in the string quartet would have been an actual danger to Haydn's progress if he had developed them. The warning is exemplified by Haydn's enthusiastic admirer Boccherini, who wrote literally hundreds of quartets and quintets. The quintet published in *Payne's Miniature Scores* will do for an example; it was made more famous than the rest by its celebrated minuet, which, though extraordinarily pretty in scoring, is by no means its only remarkable feature. As regards string-colour, this quintet is a casket of jewels more gorgeous than anything Haydn ever aspired to. But a casket of jewels will have to be stolen before it contributes anything to the progress of a drama. The listener may be surprised at the brilliance of the inner parts in Boccherini's quintet. But, alas! this is an illusion fatal to Boccherini's own progress. It means merely that he played the 'cello himself and that his innumerable quintets are accordingly written with two 'cellos, who take it in turns to supply the bass and to warble in high positions. We shall find more and more reason to admire Haydn's concentration on the essentials of quartet style and his rejection of all tempting hindrances.

In the slow movement of the symphony-quartet, op. 1, no. 5, Haydn abandons the arioso style, and works on the lines of his first movements and finales. Poor and blustering as the whole of this primitive symphony is, its peculiarities show that in the rest of opp. 1 and 2 Haydn was deliberately confining himself to the style of the divertimento, and was actually trying to restrain his first movements and finales from seriously outweighing his minuets.

C

Otherwise, no doubt, passages like that hereafter quoted from op. 2, no. 4 would have been less exceptional.

It is natural that by far the ripest things in these quartets should be the minuets. They already show Haydn's boundless capacity for inventing tunes and for making the most irregular rhythms convincing by sheer effrontery. While the minuets of opp. 1 and 2 are distinctly what the naïve listener would call tunes, and never more tuneful than where the rhythm is irregular, the tendency of the trios is to build themselves up into regular structures by means of sequences. The trios of Haydn's later works tell a very different tale. But it would be rash to assert of many of his earliest minuet tunes that they could not have been written with zest at any later period of his art.

What has been said of op. 1, no. 1 will cover the remaining ground of opp. 1 and 2. Two quartets begin with slow movements; op. 1, no. 3, in D (beginning with an arioso duet), and op. 2, no. 6, in B flat (beginning with an air and variations). These accordingly have a presto middle movement, of the same size as a minuet and trio, instead of another slow movement. In later works Haydn finds no difficulty in making his third movement slow when he has opened with an andante con variazioni.

Though the quartets of op. 2 show no general advance on op. 1, they contain significant features. The second minuet of op. 2, no. 3 (E flat) is mysterious inasmuch as its trio is followed by three sections called variations. But variations these sections are certainly not, for they follow the lines neither of the minuet nor of the trio. They do not even follow one another's lines. Perhaps Haydn has simply strung a row of actual dances together, and the publisher has tried to explain them by calling them variations. The fact that they and the trio happen, unlike the minuet, to be in regular four-bar rhythm would fit with their being practical dance music. A sight of the original divertimento version with its two horns might explain much. The slow movement of op. 2, no. 4 (F minor) is Haydn's first sustained effort in a minor key, and it achieves a tragic note which would have enhanced and prolonged the reputation of any of Haydn's contemporaries. But the most significant thing in this quartet is the development of its first movement, where, perhaps for the first time in musical history (except for some Arabian-Night incidents in Domenico Scarlatti), the true dramatic notion of sonata development is realized. A short quotation can show the first dramatic stroke, but the consequences are followed up in a series of better and better strokes for another twenty-four bars, right into the heart of the recapitulation.

In op. 2, no. 5, there is another incident of historical importance, the interrupted cadence into B flat where the hearer would expect D major, in the slow movement (bars 17–21).

Regard these bars with reverence; they are the source of all the purple patches in Mozart's, Haydn's, and Beethoven's 'second subjects', of all Beethoven's wonderful themes that pack two profoundly contrasted keys into one clause, and of all Schubert's enormous digressions in this part of a movement. How such modulations bulked in the imagination of Haydn's best contemporaries may be realized by looking at the change from B flat to G flat in Dittersdorf's Quartet in E flat, a work not unknown to modern quartet players, and easily accessible, with five others of its set, in *Payne's Miniature Scores* (Ex. 10). In the recapitulation Dittersdorf shows further insight by making the foreign key C major instead of C flat; and his quartets show in other positive merits that it was not

by accident that he became a successful composer of comic operas.
But nowhere is he like Haydn in the capacity, predicated of genius
by Keats, to 'walk the empyrean and not be intoxicated'.

Ex.10

In op. 2, no. 6, it is surprising to find Haydn's technique in
ornamental melodic variations already so ripe. Trivial as the problem seems, and poor as is some of Haydn's and much of Mozart's
later work in this fashionable eighteenth-century form, it is needful
to look carefully at contemporary examples before one can realize
the boundless opportunities of going pointlessly wrong where Haydn
and Mozart know of nothing but what is inevitably right. And the
very composers who have gone farthest in the basing of variations
on deeper rhythmic and harmonic factors have shown an unex-
hausted interest in the simplest melodic embroidery. Beethoven's
purely melodic variations in the slow movement and choral finale
of the Ninth Symphony are to him as important as the deepest
mysteries of the Diabelli Variations; and Brahms's views on this
matter were equally shocking to the Superior Person.

If Pohl demands a post-dating of five years for study preparatory
to Haydn's op. 1, it is strange that he should not demand another
five years to account for the great progress made between op. 2
and op. 3; a progress which makes it impossible to put the first
eighteen quartets into one group. The difference is obvious to
practical musicians and the general public; for with op. 3, Haydn
enters into the public repertory of modern quartet-players. Pohl
cites the case of a famous quartet-party that used to substitute the
delightful *Dudelsack* minuet of op. 3, no. 3 for the minuet of one
of the finest later quartets; and the whole of op. 3, no. 5, with its
well-known and irresistible serenade (a title applied to its andante),
has been chosen by the Busch Quartet for a gramophone record.
The *Dudelsack* minuet, the serenade, and its twin brother the
andante of op. 3, no. 1, are examples of luxury-scoring, contributing, with all their charm, no more than the art of Boccherini to the
development of quartet style and dramatic sonata-activity. They

are not out of place in the works as wholes, for everything that
enlarges the range of contrast between the middle and outer movements is a contribution to sonata style. And, in the four normal
cases, the outer movements of op. 3 are firmly established on
Haydn's early symphonic scale. Haydn no longer finds it necessary,
though he may still find it amusing, to use irregular rhythms in
order to enforce dramatic movement; and so op. 3, no. 1 (E major),
can afford to begin by trotting along in four-bar phrases without
fear that the motion may degenerate into somnolent carriage-
exercise. Before the double-bar the crescendo in syncopated
crotchets and dotted quavers will have roused the hearer's mental
muscles quite satisfactorily, without spoiling the placid character
of the whole. With the minuet it may be noted that the trio is not
a sequential structure, but a specially tuneful contrast, enhanced by
its being in the same key. The andantino grazioso is not inferior to
its twin brother, the famous serenade in op. 3, no. 5. In fact we
are emerging from the regions of progressive musical history into
those of permanent beauty, though we are not yet under its full
sway. The finale is a freak; Haydn marks it 'presto'; begins with
twelve introductory bars of minims and crotchets, then proceeds to
give a binary dance tune, 16 + 32 bars, writing the repeats in full
in order to change the scoring, which does not become lively till
the repetition of the last sixteen bars. Then the finale concludes
with its twelve introductory bars. As for any sense of pace, Haydn
might just as well have used bars of double length with quavers and
semiquavers and called it andante. This is the first and perhaps
the last occasion when his sense of tempo fails him.

Op. 3, no. 2 (C major), begins with an excellent little set of
variations on a theme which it is extremely unlikely that Clara
Wieck knew when she invented the similar tune on which Schumann wrote his Impromptus, op. 5. With the ensuing minuet it
is certain that beauty has dawned; it pervades the sound as well
as the sense; and the beauty of sound is not achieved by anything
like luxury-scoring. The finale (there are only three movements)
is another freak, a genuine presto this time, but sprawling in long,
loose phrases which unfold themselves in a symphonic sonata-form
without repeat marks. When this is finished in 228 bars (twice the
length of Haydn's largest earlier finales), there is a sort of trio consisting of a decidedly sentimental binary tune, mainly in crotchets,
eighteen bars plus thirty-four, with repeats. After which the listener
is asked to hear the former 228 bars da capo! Perhaps the

movement (and hence the rest of the quartet) might be presentable if the da capo were started from its recapitulation at bar 135.

Op. 3, no. 3 (G major) is remarkable chiefly for the *Dudelsack* minuet. In its largo Haydn fully replaced the lyric arioso manner by a genuine symphonic sonata-style. This largo would pass muster, with less suspicion than the *Dudelsack* minuet, in a much later quartet, though it would not be its most attractive feature. The finale is also an advanced specimen of sonata form.

Of all Haydn's accessible works, op. 3, no. 4 is the most unaccountable. It consists of two movements which not only fail to make a whole, but which manifestly cannot belong to the same work. Both are sprawling, long-limbed sonata-form movements, with some half a dozen agreeable themes, and a perfunctory and primitive passage of goose-step on the dominant to serve for development. One movement is in B flat; the other, a shorter movement with a recurring slow introduction, is in E flat. It is a mystery how anybody could suppose that they belonged together.

Op. 3, no. 5 (F major), has been proved to be a work of art acceptable to the general public. The first movement carries the hearer along in full tide, and as to development, nothing could be more convincing than the imbroglio Haydn produces from an episodic figure which he then drops for some fifteen bars, in order that it may then clinch matters by leading back to the recapitulation. Then comes the famous serenade. The minuet and the finale (called scherzando) show no falling off.

The quick movements of op. 3, no. 6 (A major) are equally successful; but the slow movement relapses heavily and at great length into the old arioso style, with elaborations and dramatic pauses in the accompaniment which contribute historical interest without achieving permanent artistic power. Haydn was loth to part company with the arioso slow movement; which indeed has continued to be rediscovered by great composers, from Mozart to Dvořák, whenever luxury-scoring and homogeneous textures are admissible.

Then comes a great gap. This interval, between opp. 3 and 9, is approximately filled by the first forty symphonies, and Pohl knows how many cassations, divertimenti, sonatas; trios for two violins and bass (i.e. continuo) and for two flutes and bass; pieces for Prince Esterhazy's queer kind of gamba, the baryton; and operatic and vocal works galore. Of the divertimenti, the writer has seen the autograph of one in the possession of [the late] Mr.

Edward Speyer, a trio for horn, violin, and 'cello. It consists of
three tiny movements, of which one is a set of variations containing
horn-passages which make Bach's most appalling flights appear
almost easy. There are other evidences that the principal horn-
players at Esterház had a technique that was demoralizing to the
composer's artistic economy. Among the divertimenti advertised
in that old Breitkopf & Härtel catalogue, I suspect, and Pohl confirms me, that one of those for two oboes, two horns, three bassoons,
and serpent contains one of the greatest melodies in the world, the
theme entitled *Corale St. Antoni*, on which Brahms wrote his
orchestral variations. If a contrafagotto be used for the third bassoon and serpent, the instruments given in the catalogue correspond
to the scoring of most of that theme.

One of Haydn's works for wind instruments is accessible in a
modern score, the little Octet in F published by C. F. Kahnt,
Leipzig. In his old age Haydn expressed regret that he must soon
die, just as he had found out how to write for wind instruments.
Slight as this octet is, it shows that by the time Haydn wrote it he
could die in peace, if the handling of wind instruments was his
only anxiety. While the definitive edition of Haydn's complete
works remains in its present merely initial stage (1928), no systematic discussion of his less-known chamber music is possible;
and it will save interruption at a less opportune point if his treatment of wind instruments is dealt with here. This octet shows the
profound influence of Mozart's finest wind-band serenades, with
the addition of Haydn's independent thought. Mozart's technique
is shown first in the deliberate choice of chord-formulas and other
severely schematic types of theme which may serve to concentrate
the listener's attention on the tone-colours for their own sake;
secondly, in the sympathetic treatment of the clarinets; thirdly, in
the absence of the flute, which, as Mozart realized, stands to the
rest of the band as water-colour to oil paint; and lastly, in the perfect and normal balance of the chords, a matter in which Haydn in
all his music often attains perfection, but seldom achieves it by
normality. (Even here the bassoon occasionally shows Haydn's inveterate confusion between bass and double-bass.) His independent
thought is shown in several features, notably the difficult but not
reckless G minor horn solo in the third variation of the slow movement; the fourth variation, with the melody as bass for the two
bassoons in unison; and the effective way in which, near the end
of the finale, the first oboe is screwed up to its top F, a detail

Haydn may have learnt from Mozart's masterly little Quartet for oboe and strings (K. 370). The maturity of this tiny octet shows, by comparison with Haydn's treatment of wind instruments elsewhere, that in saying that he had only just learnt in old age how to write for them there was no more affectation in his modesty than boastfulness in his claim. It would be interesting to obtain sight of the early works for wind instruments mentioned in old catalogues; e.g. trios for clarinet, violin, and bassoon: for Haydn's treatment of the clarinet in the orchestra is primitive until those crowning works *The Creation* and *The Seasons*. The oboe and bassoon Haydn always understood. The 'Great Bassoon Joke' is the smallest, though the most obvious, item in his exhaustive knowledge of the capacities, poetic more than comic, of that important and long-suffering bass of the wood-wind. The flute represents one of the most curious problems in Haydn's aesthetic system. It is very important in his mature orchestral works; and at all periods he was ready to write for it in chamber music. Three of the thirty-one piano trios now in print (Edition Peters, Nos. 29, in F; 30, in D; and 31, in G) are with flute, and cannot be early works—they would fall into line soon after the quartets of op. 33. The writer does not find them, and did not expect to find them, in the old Breitkopf catalogue of works in stock up to 1782. Then there is a musically very great sonata with piano in G, which, with the addition of a minuet as large and powerful as a mid-Beethoven scherzo, was afterwards rewritten as one of the last and greatest of the string quartets. Haydn seems in sympathy with the soul of the flute, or with its Undine-like aspirations towards a soul, and he appreciates its April-rain translucency. But he never seems to realize that its lower octave, which was excellent under the conditions of the continuo period, is powerless under those of his own art; and in an orchestral tutti or the final tonic-and-dominant scrimmage of a sonata he will set the flute to puff its low notes away in a futile nominal fortissimo calculated rather to damage the dignity of the performer than to attract the ear of the listener.

A more important moral is pointed by Haydn's treatment of the horn. During his long tenure of office at Esterház he took full advantage of the presence of horn-players who must have had the most enormous technique ever achieved on that acoustically interesting but most hazardous instrument. But sharp disillusionment evidently awaited him when he left the shelter of Esterház and came to deal with European orchestras at large. He promptly ceased to take risks; and when in a mature symphony some exceptional high or low note for the horn is found, it is always so covered that failure will not be noticed. More important is the occasional prominence of some passage which text-books will assert to be impossible; e.g. the low staccato rapid quaver octaves in the finale of the 'Oxford' Symphony; but *solvitur ambulando*, for it proves to be a knack. Apart from knacks, however, the moral is that a composer cannot learn much from generous young virtuoso-players with a formidable technique. Generous veterans have learnt fastidiousness as part of their wisdom; and they demand that all technical difficulties shall serve two purposes only, to reveal the nature of the instrument and the ideas of the composer. The young virtuoso is apt to make it a point of honour to prove that nothing can be difficult for him. Thus it is by no means clear that Haydn's duties at Esterház were stimulating to his own line of progress, in either orchestral or chamber music. We should be glad of an opportunity for studying his music for Prince Esterhazy's favourite instrument, the baryton. But when one is told, first that it was considered impossible to use it in more than one key; secondly, that Haydn set about learning it in order to prove that it could be used in various keys; thirdly, that Prince Esterhazy did not relish Haydn's success, but merely said, 'Well, it's your business to play better than I'; and lastly, that Haydn saw that such efforts were a waste of his time—it is hardly necessary to study the actual baryton music before risking the guess that it belongs to the region of *tours de force*; and this may be suspected of some proportion of the chamber music for curious combinations. With the first forty symphonies the facts can be measured by observation. Their many interesting features disguise the fact that the fortieth symphony is on the same plane of orchestral thought as the first; for most of the special orchestral effects consist essentially of solo combinations and *tours de force* against a background of primitive orchestration. In form and range of contrast there are significant events; and the First Symphony (not counting op. 1, no. 5) represents more nearly the level of the quartets in op. 3 than that of opp. 1 and 2. But the advance from op. 2 to op. 3 is far more decided than the subsequent advance from Symphony no. 1 to Symphony no. 40. And, with all their interest, there is no such progress in these forty symphonies as can explain or illustrate the advance made from the quartets of op. 3 to those of op. 9, which now claim attention. While none of the first forty symphonies is known to the public of to-day, the quartets of op. 9, written in the same year as the fortieth symphony, belong to the presentable Haydn repertory. Haydn himself requested the publisher, Artaria, to put them forward as the first quartets, and to ignore all his earlier ones. Beauty, which was dawning in op. 3, shines in full daylight here. They are not yet among the infinities of art where comparisons are meaningless; but they are beyond the regions of historical patronage. What is right for one work is irrelevant and therefore wrong for another, and there is seldom anything wrong in the particular work in hand. The technique is not that of later works. Enormous progress remained for Haydn yet to accomplish, if by progress is meant a process of enlarging the range of ideas in successive works of art. But if 'progress towards perfection' is meant, we are chasing rainbows, and the centre of the rainbow is perfection and is here: here as the quality of the artist's mind, not as the actual finished execution of his designs; here as in Shakespeare and Handel, not as in Milton and Bach. We shall find inequalities, such as the bad lapse already quoted (in Ex. 1). And the style of op. 9 is perhaps better suited to an audience of connoisseurs than to the general public; though the writer well remembers the impression made by the D minor Quartet, op. 9, no. 4, at the 'Pops' in 1887, at a time when Wagnerians tolerated Haydn and Mozart mainly from charity towards the feelings of children and dotards.

In four of these quartets the first movement is in a tempo of peculiar significance, a moderato or allegro moderato distinctly slow for counting four in a bar, and consequently with plenty of room for triplet semiquavers or even for demisemiquavers. This indicates an ornate style, and is Boccherini's favourite tempo. But it also permits of a thoughtful style, and Haydn knows how to prevent it from ambling monotonously. It is no imperfection in the style that the part of the first violin is full of brilliant features which the other instruments cannot share. The other instruments are perfectly happy in their place, and there is not a dull or useless note. In the presence of such art it seems as unmannerly to point out lapses like Ex. 1, or places where the 'cello has forgotten that it is not a double-bass, as to call attention to a cough or a sneeze. History and progress are forgotten while one listens and enjoys.

Of the six quartets in op. 9, no. 1 in C major has a noble first movement very sonorously scored; a graceful minuet with a sly abrupt end (the eternal joke of ending with one's initial phrase), and a glum little trio, the second part of which does not finish, but leads back to the minuet; an indolently sweet and simple slow movement in sonata form; and a finale which is reminiscent of earlier examples in its nervous abruptness. But the quartet-writing throughout is such as can only be heard with the ears and fed on by the imagination. Even such a simple-seeming melody as the theme of the slow movement can express the most intimate secrets of the violin, with its legato rising tenth at the end of the first bar. No. 2, in E flat, less attractive in appearance, is well in step with its companions; and the development of the first movement might serve as a *locus classicus* for its function. The minuet is one of Haydn's loveliest melodies, and he liked it well enough to write a pretty little set of piano variations on it; which, however, are no such work of art as it makes with its trio (in the same key) in this quartet. With the slow movement we encounter the only art-form Haydn owes to Bach (C. P. E.). The movement (in C minor) has a slow recitative-like introduction in common time, seven bars long; after which it proceeds in an arioso in 3/4 time. When this has come to the close of its first part in the relative major, the first part is repeated; but the repeat is written out in full, in order that the ornaments of the melody may be varied. The second part, which Haydn cuts down to perfunctoriness, is not repeated, but a blank space is left (over the usual 6/4 chord) for a cadenza before the end.

Now this idea of writing out a repeat in full (instead of using repeat-marks), in order to vary or add to the ornaments, was the special invention of Philipp Emanuel Bach's later years, and was highly prized by him. Not only had he a great and inspiring influence on the young Haydn (clearly discernible in Haydn's piano style), but, when Haydn's early piano sonatas appeared, Bach sent him a message to say that nobody else had understood him so completely. In the face of such testimony it must seem unreasonable to dispute the accepted opinion that C. P. E. Bach is the founder of the sonata style, and the man to whom Haydn owed the possibility of his own work. And yet the very facts before us point to a different conclusion.

Without claiming a knowledge of C. P. E. Bach's complete works, one may be justified in drawing one's own inferences from the study of some eighty sonatas, besides many rondos and fantasias, ranging from the year in which Sebastian Bach wrote the B minor Mass to the year in which Mozart produced *Don Giovanni*. After perusing these sonatas with a zest that would cheerfully burn all the 'progressive' matter in all the fine arts for the sake of preserving

one example of permanent beauty, one is forced to conclude that
C. P. E. Bach never shows an inkling of the special idea of 'development' in sonata style. As an art-form apart from the sonata
he invented a special type of rondo, utterly unlike anything in
earlier music. In these rondos he digresses wildly and at absurd
length, bringing his beautiful main theme back in the most unexpected keys and expanding it in passionate modulating sequences.
It is in these rondos alone that he shows the idea of development;
but the only trace of their influence upon Haydn is to be found in
two splendid and obviously late piano pieces, Haydn's Fantasia
in C and Capriccio in G. In both of these Haydn enjoys all the
sense of adventure in C. P. E. Bach's rondos; but the quality which
he emphatically does not owe to them is that by which these two
pieces live, a sense of climax and finality. The long passages of
unsupported runs and light arpeggios, which are a common feature
in Haydn's ripest sonatas and are freely translated into the language
of the violin in his quartets, may again, together with the whole
range of his piano style, be traced to C. P. E. Bach. Not so, however,
the fact that from the outset (e.g. in the quartets of op. 17, where,
mutatis mutandis, they first appear) Haydn presents in them a perfect study in the psychology of dramatic suspense, whereas the
immediate effect of nearly all C. P. E. Bach's digressions is to cause
the friendliest critic to exclaim 'This won't do!'

Not only is the notion of development absent from C. P. E.
Bach's sonatas; but this late and highly prized invention of the
veränderte Reprise (repeat with alterations), which Haydn now
adopted, is radically hostile to it. Can anything be conceived more
incompatible with the dramatic activities of a true sonata-develop-
ment than that the repetition of both parts of a binary movement
should be written out in full, in order that the *ornaments* should be
varied? This can imply nothing else than that the whole attention
is fixed on an uninterrupted flow of lyric melody: which is precisely
C. P. E. Bach's intention, and which is Haydn's reason for confining the device to slow movements.

What, then, is Haydn's real debt to C. P. E. Bach? It is a pity
that the word 'rhetoric' has been degraded to a term of abuse, for
it means an art the perfection of which is as noble as the noblest
cause in which it can be used. Rhetoric is what Haydn learnt from
C. P. E. Bach: a singularly beautiful and pure rhetoric, tender,
romantic, anything but severe, yet never inflated. This great and
comprehensive gift is independent of all reform or progress. The

example of Bach's chaotically wild rondos and fantasias may have been necessary in order to stimulate Haydn's far more realistic sense of adventure. But of art-forms, the only thing that Haydn adopted from C. P. E. Bach was this device of the *veränderte Reprise*. Its original motive arose from the fact that in any movement, sections marked to be repeated were in fact often varied by the performer on repetition, the repeats being, indeed, supposed to be prescribed for that purpose. The real aesthetic function of repeat lies deeper than this hypothesis; and the view taken of it by Haydn, Mozart, and Beethoven is, of all points in their art, the most remote from the habits of modern listeners. It is evident, from the way in which C. P. E. Bach carries out his invention, that, with or without variation, the repeats were actually executed wherever they were marked. And while unwritten variation is unthinkable with Haydn, Mozart, and Beethoven, the juncture of the repeat is, as late as Beethoven's last quartet (op. 135), often so subtle that a fine point is missed when the repeat is omitted, though the length of the section to be repeated is formidable.

Now, how does Haydn treat Bach's reprise device? Besides restricting its use to lyric slow movements, he shows none of the patience which enabled C. P. E. Bach to write out an ornamental repeat of both parts. In the final recapitulatory stage of his movement the ornaments will combine both versions of the exposition or will otherwise throw appropriate light on it. The reprise movements in Haydn's quartets are the slow movements of op. 9, no. 2; op. 9, no. 4; op. 20, no. 6; and op. 33, no. 3: with which the history of this art-form closes, to be reopened only once, many years later, in the most original and exquisite masterpiece of orchestration Haydn ever achieved, the slow movement of the ninth 'London' Symphony, in B flat, in which the repeat of the first part is written out, in order to alter, not the ornaments, but the scoring. There is another version of this movement in a piano trio in F sharp minor. As Haydn's trios give no scope for changes of scoring, this version has no repeat at all.

The survey of the individual quartets can now be resumed. To an audience of connoisseurs, op. 9, no. 3 (G major) should prove a convincing masterpiece. The first movement is spirited and sonorous, and the minuet epigrammatic and witty. One should make no hasty judgement about the slow movement. The sight of two blank spaces for cadenzas, one at the end of each part, is apt to provoke a comment on the lines of Dr. Johnson's summary of the effect of mythological machinery in English poetry. 'The attention retires from the transactions of' the virtuoso violinist when the fatal 6/4 chord has wound him up and released the clutch. But if the attention will consent to fix itself on the largo of op. 9, no. 3, from the outset of a devout performance in adequately broad tempo, it will find itself rewarded by music too great to be destroyed even by bad cadenzas, and quite unharmed by suitable ones. The resemblance of the opening, with its broken rhythms and long measured pauses, to that of the largo of Beethoven's Sonata, op. 7, is probably accidental, but is not superficial. Haydn is ornate where Beethoven is laconic; Haydn's gravity is meditative, and grows upon one as the music settles into a long sustained flow, whereas Beethoven instantly inspires awe, and allows his largo only just as much uninterrupted flow as will carry the listener across its many abrupt unfathomable depths. But if there is any earlier movement in Haydn that so comprehensively foreshadows Beethoven's most solemn moods, it has not yet been printed.

The finale is, as usual, lively and witty, the wittiest device being a surprising joint across the dividing line at the repeats.

Op. 9, no. 4, in D minor, is, as we have seen, a work that is sometimes heard in public. One effect of making its acquaintance is that Mozart's great D minor Quartet becomes inseparably associated with its sombre first movement. The minuet is one of Haydn's largest, and is full of vehement passion, though its tempo is, if anything, slower than his minuets have hitherto been. Up to this point the tempo of a Haydn minuet is the same as with Sebastian Bach; a three-in-the-bar at a smart stride, too fast for the stately dance of the *Don Giovanni* minuet, but making no approach to the one-in-a-bar rhythm of a scherzo. The trio of this D minor minuet is a suave melody in the major, and is literally a trio in the long-forgotten sense of being in three-part harmony. But Haydn has amused himself and the leader of the quartet by writing it as a duet for the violins, the first violin playing in double stops.

The slow movement is on the reprise lines, but the alterations in the ornaments are much slighter than those in the accompaniment, which is extensively rewritten. Could anything better indicate Haydn's tendency towards the deeper issues of whatever art-form he presses into the service of instrumental music? Yet it is in this beautiful movement that the lapse quoted in Ex. 1 occurs.

The finale is a masterpiece so concentrated on the idea of de-

velopment that it would be an ideal example to set beside the
largest possible polyphonic gigue. It makes a spirited end to a
work unquestionably great as a whole.

Op. 9, no. 5 (B flat), begins with an andante theme with variations; a form in which, as we have seen, Haydn already knew in
op. 2, no. 6 all that was as yet to be known. It is not until the
middle of his whole series of quartets that he enlarged the scope of
his variations by inventing a new form on a pair of alternating
themes. The minuet is a little faster than previous examples, and
is as gracefully witty as usual. The slow movement is a fine, serious,
and mature composition in sonata form with repeats (not *veränderte
Reprisen*) and without pauses or cadenzas. The finale is a presto
with long-limbed, slightly sprawling phrase-rhythms, the successful
handling of which contributes to the progress of Haydn's technique.

Op. 9, no. 6 (A major) begins with a first-rate presto, full of
picturesque passages and lively (not luxurious) scoring. The freedom of its recapitulation shows a tendency which will eventually
necessitate a discussion of the vast subject of Haydn's mature
sonata-form. The minuet is in the old tempo, and has a pensive
trio in the minor. The slow movement is an arioso with repeats,
and, but for a certain breadth and simplicity, would have attracted
little notice if it had occurred in op. 2. It has a blank space for a
cadenza at the end. The finale begins as if it were going to be an
energetic rondo (a thing that has not yet appeared in these quartets).
After its first phrase, one listens with interest to an expanding
middle phrase and a return, and to several cumulative afterthoughts,
tapering away to an emphatic close. This is repeated from the middle
phrase onwards. But that is all! Though inadequate, its effect is
not as absurd as the description sounds; but this quartet undeniably
collapses after two movements well worthy of the rest of the set in
which Haydn first knew himself. There is only one more such
collapse in the whole series.

The quartets of op. 17 are on a larger scale. The first movement
of no. 1 (E major) is a moderato (the characteristic tempo of this
period) with a grass-green theme that is already the quintessence
of Haydn. The rhetoric is highly strung, and the first violin begins
to display itself more extensively than in op. 9. A remarkable
feature in the development section is the return of the main theme
in the tonic a little before it seems due, whereupon, however, its
second bar expands into a fine vista of sequences before the theme
is allowed to return again and follow its normal course. The

minuet is very fine, and on a large scale. The slow movement, in
E minor, is in broad sonata form without repeats; flowing, symmetrical, and pleasantly pathetic. One interesting turn of harmony,
in the recapitulation (bar 68), is actually Wagnerian in principle.

Ex. 11 *Adagio*

It is by no means out of place, though the style of the movement
no more resembles Wagner than lemonade resembles wine. The
finale is the subtlest part of the work, the final results of a passage
in the subdominant near the beginning being a stroke of genius at
the end. The development section begins with no less than the
first eighteen bars of the movement in the tonic before it strikes
out elsewhither. The effect will be excellent if Haydn's repeat
marks are disregarded, and disastrous if the repeats are played.
The tempo must be very fast to bring out the coherence of Haydn's
lanky phrasing. He is in about the stage of experience in handling
form that Mozart reached in his 'Paris' Symphony. He wants
plenty of elbow-room.

Op. 17, no. 2 (F) begins with a fine specimen of Haydn's early
ornate rhetoric. The short minuet (distinctly faster than Bach's
tempo, but not hasty) is splendid both in sound and in sense. Its
quiet trio in the relative minor does not finish, but pauses on its
dominant in order that the minuet may re-enter more splendidly
than ever. The slow movement is a placid adagio in sonata form,
bordering on the arioso style. With the aid of op. 2, no. 5, it enables
us to clear up a point that sometimes mystifies players, viz. the
use of alla breve time signature ₵ for slow movements, as here. It
obviously cannot mean two in a bar. But Haydn actually entitled
the slow movement of op. 2, no. 5 'largo alla breve'; and it happens
that in both these movements the eye is not distracted by any
demisemiquaver passages that would make them look like other
slow movements. Thus the ₵ signature means 'take your time at
about half the value you would give to most adagios'.

The finale of op. 17, no. 2 is a sprawling allegro di molto. The
effect of the joint from the end of the second part to the beginning

of the development is the best stroke in the movement, and, if this quartet is to be heard at all, leisure and patience will be needed for once to listen to what perhaps no living concert-goer has ever heard, the repeat of the second part of a long binary movement.

Op. 17, no. 3 (E flat), begins with a set of variations. Advance is shown in the ripe Haydnesque beauty of the second part of the theme, a thing he could not have achieved earlier. But the main advance in this quartet is shown by the minuet, which would be thought remarkable if met with in op. 76. Its trio is an intensely original tune, scored in a way that would be as surprising in a quartet of Dvořák as it is here.

Ex.12 *Allegretto*

The slow movement, in A flat, is nobly serious and mellow in sound, and has a rich digression of harmonies in its broad transition passage to the dominant. There are several pauses, but they are for reflection, not for cadenzas. The finale is terse, and more in the best style of op. 9.

Op. 17, no. 4 (C minor), is full of subtle points. Its first two notes (E flat G/C) being unaccompanied, the key of C minor is revealed only when the other instruments enter in the second bar. The two notes can accordingly modulate in other contexts to E flat and elsewhere. They pervade the inner parts, and seem prophetic of a renascence of polyphony. The movement, and indeed the whole quartet, is in a passionate vein not far from tragedy. In this context we first experience the most heavenly type of Haydn's favourite contrasts. The minuet is in the major (distinctly faster than hitherto), and begins with childlike consolation. Its trio is plaintive and thoughtful in the minor mode. Here, again, it would be impossible to rule out the latest date for this movement, if we

D

did not know when it was written. The slow movement is in the reprise form. In spite of fine points, its length weighs the quartet down. One is glad that C. P. E. Bach's procedure did not impel Haydn to carry out the reprise of both parts. The finale is in a blustering temper, and has a theme suggestive of more polyphonic treatment than it actually receives. The first violin has many rather difficult double-stops and other brilliant features. After the recapitulation there is a fine coda, short but dramatic. With consummate playing this quartet might make a considerable impression on connoisseurs.

Ex.13   *Allegro*

Op. 17, no. 5 (G major), has established itself in concert repertories. The first theme gives an opportunity of seeing how Haydn's brother Michael handles it; for he used it in one of his four duets for violin and viola, to which Mozart added two to complete the contract for six which illness prevented Michael from finishing. Michael's four have recently been republished, and are quite pretty; but he shows no more capacity than Boccherini to vary the pace of whatever amble his first theme sets. And so it happens that where he and Joseph hit upon the same theme, five bars of the one against eight of the other will show that Joseph is an inveterate comedian whose first eight bars are no multiple of two, but already contain

rhythmic contrasts that will have unpredictable but inevitable consequences throughout the movement; whereas Michael would feel
that the smallest deviation into the unexpected created a situation
beyond the resources of his tact, his five bars owing their irregularity to their fashionable Neapolitan 'quite so' cadence (Ex. 13).

Every phrase, taken in its context, in this thoroughly normal
example of Joseph Haydn's sonata form is a lesson in the highest
art of composition.

Ex.14 *Moderato*

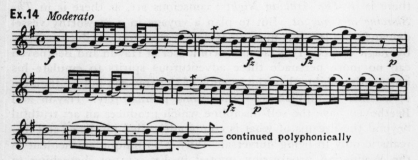

continued polyphonically

Perhaps the *locus classicus* is to be found at the end of the development.

Ex.15

eight more
bars

Brilliance is the last word to apply to so meditative a passage,
but its function of dramatic suspense is essentially that of the most
brilliant fireworks in Haydn's piano music; and it is fair to remind
oneself that these were suggested by those in the rondos and fantasias of C. P. E. Bach. But discoveries must not be transferred
from those who achieve them to those who did not understand the
drift of their own suggestions. The slow movement of this quartet
is a test of the musical historian's sense of proportion. It is a scena
in operatic recitative, such as may suggest to one kind of enthusiast
a prophecy of Beethoven's arioso dolente in the Sonata, op. 110;
while another kind of enthusiast will trace it back to sonatas written by C. P. E. Bach before Sebastian Bach had begun the *Christmas Oratorio*. Which of the three recitatives will have the most
wonderful modulations—the recitative of 1740, of 1770, or of 1822?

The modulations of C. P. E. Bach are beyond all comparison the most remarkable. Those in Beethoven's op. 110 are within the simplest harmonic range of Corelli or Handel, but the key of A flat happens to be so situated that the familiar modulation to its flat submediant (F♭ = E♮) seems to require a complicated change of notation.

Now there is no disputing that C. P. E. Bach's modulations are wonderful flights of imagination. There is high art in them, as there is in *The Arabian Nights*; conscious art, as there is in *The Shaving of Shagpat*. But to plan a voyage in a seaworthy vessel demands not less but more imagination than to describe a journey by magic carpet. This favourite composer of Haydn and Beethoven can no more persuade these adventurous spirits to emulate his imaginative flights than the legends of alchemy can induce the man of science to publish his conclusions prematurely. Haydn and Beethoven have the self-discipline which produces an art truthful beyond the dreams of what is commonly called idealism, and unrealistic only in being universal. Why is so unique an incident as the Wagnerian progression quoted in Ex. 11 not disturbing to Haydn's aesthetic system? Precisely because the progression is actually Wagnerian; that is to say, a typically rationalistic device by which a couple of passing notes are dwelt upon long enough to suggest to the ear that they are a complete chord in some impossibly remote key, after which suggestion they explain themselves away. Thus the incident is within the range of that sense of probability which governs Haydn's pathos and humour from first to last; and his self-discipline is even more strikingly shown in his not founding upon this highly convincing effect a style which would have been (*pace* Reger) irrelevant to the key-system of sonata form, than in his abstention from the higher imaginative flights of his beloved C. P. E. Bach. As to the recitative movement in op. 17, no. 5, it proves that the sonata style has little more difficulty in digesting operatic recitative than in digesting the operatic aria.

The movement is thus merely an extreme case of the arioso-adagio, and, *mutatis mutandis*, foreshadows the discovery, made by Spohr in 1820, that a violin concerto could be designed on the lines of an operatic scena. On the other hand, there is no warrant for connecting Haydn's instrumental recitatives in any such way with Beethoven's, even though, as will be found in Haydn's op. 20, the operatic impulse coincides (as in Beethoven) with a reaction to the other extreme, the style and form of the fugue. Beethoven, it is true, retained to the last his early love of C. P. E. Bach; but his instrumental recitatives are no echo of his childhood. Haydn's recitative in op. 17, no. 5, and the dramatic fantasia (not in recitative but nearly allied thereto) in op. 20, no. 2, are the last of their line because to him they are already becoming old-fashioned. They belong to a music which has not yet risen beyond the scope of the stage: whereas Beethoven can at a sublime crisis recall the ancient dramatic tropes and gestures as things heard and seen in an ecstasy.

The finale of Haydn's op. 17, no. 5, is, like the minuet (which precedes the slow movement), worthy of its position. Its device of ending comically with its initial phrase is on the way to becoming standardized for larger movements in both Haydn and Mozart. One more point of historical and aesthetic importance in op. 17, no. 5, is the brilliant passage of double stops for the first violin in the 'second subject' of the first movement.

This brings to a crisis a tendency which if carried farther would have threatened one of the vital criteria of quartet style. Only a killjoy criticism could object to it here, for no unbiased listener can find the passage less enjoyable to hear than the violinist finds it to master and to play. Dangerous shoals await the critic who sails rashly into the channels of these early quartets, secure in his two criteria, that a string quartet must not be orchestral, and that it must not be a 'first-violin' quartet. Every individual work of art exists in its own right, and has nothing to fear from any developments except those within its own form and matter. Now these two criteria of quartet style involve an evolutionary process; they are applicable only in the degree suited to the development attained by each individual work.

There is, of course, a primitive stage below which a quartet style cannot exist; and with Haydn opp. 1 and 2 are evidently below the line, and op. 3 is evidently rising above it. But the health of his work depends on its progress in all directions; and a developed quartet style with an undeveloped sonata form would be a monstrosity. As to orchestral style, Haydn's quartets have already completely parted from it in the first bars of op. 9, no. 1, if not already in op. 3, no. 5. This criterion is, even then, not easy to handle; for each practical way of organizing musical instruments will aim straightforwardly at producing music, and will not deviate to avoid resemblances to other musical organizations. A string quartet is to blame, not when it sounds like orchestral music, but when it fails in an effort to do so. It has a right to succeed in that effort if it can; and its best condition for success is that it shall remain the music of four players. Haydn's illusions with double stops in opp. 9 and 17 are carried far enough to enhance instead of destroying our sense and his own that we are listening to a string quartet and not to organ music cleverly spread over sixteen fiddle-strings. As to the brilliance of the first violin, Spohr himself hardly carries it as far as Haydn in op. 17, and actually writes more interesting parts than Haydn's for the other instruments on the whole. But his point of view is fatally wrong; his work reveals a later stage of development; the positive merits of his accessory parts condemn him for leaving them as they are while his first violin has all the melody; and the whole scale of his work purports to be as large as that of Beethoven's, while his form cautiously follows one single procedure generalized from the inexhaustibly various Mozart. Spohr actually told Joachim that he wished some day to produce 'a set of quartets in the true strict form—i.e. with the cadences ending with a trill'. This inculcates as a criterion of string-quartet style that the first violin shall sit upon the safety-valve! Turn from this to Haydn's indiscreet fireworks in op. 17, and see how efficiently they contribute to open up the texture. Why does he give them to the first violin? Because he is writing music in which the normal place for melody is on the top. Had he been a 'cellist like Boccherini, he might have been tempted to give the fireworks to the 'cello. Meanwhile, whether the violin rule or not, music is not, even in string quartets, going to reconcile its dramatic growth with the cultivation of quadruple counterpoint until Beethoven has attained his last phase. (And yet quadruple counterpoint appears in Haydn's next opus!)

Haydn's criteria, though evolutionary, are already positive and severe in op. 17. That a work of art belongs to an early stage of evolution is not an excuse for its failing to satisfy its own implications. Op. 17, no. 6, in D major, opens with a presto which puts to admirable use a theme feebly treated in variation form (perhaps about the same date or earlier) in one of Haydn's queer violin sonatas, about which a word must be said hereafter. In this quartet the plunging of the 'second subject' into C major where A major is expected is a Beethoven-Schubert device executed quite broadly. The minuet contrasts well with this lively hunting-scene, and should be taken at a statelier moderato than is by this time usual in Haydn. Now comes a disconcerting surprise. The largo is an arioso of the most archaic type, and would produce no comment in a quartet from op. 1. In times and places where classical revivals are matters of fashion rather than of popularity, it is impossible to say what styles may be thought interesting so long as they are at least partially unconvincing to the naïve listener; and so perhaps Haydn's op. 17, no. 6, might now be revived as it stands without anybody noticing that its largo is a relapse into an obsolete style, and a dull specimen at that. The distinguished quartet-party mentioned by Pohl that rescued the *Dudelsack* minuet from op. 3, no. 3, at the expense of the minuet of a later quartet committed an outrage not justified by the rescue, for no minuet of Haydn, early or late, is without its proper effect in its own place. But it would be a real charity to replace the largo of op. 17, no. 6, by one of the best of the slow movements buried in the archaic quartets. Two keys are possible, without violating the limits of Haydn's range in op. 17: the present subdominant key of G, and A major, the dominant. In G we could use Pohl's favourite movement from op. 1, no. 6 ('a serenade such as the rosiest child could not wish more beautiful'), or the less attractive largo cantabile alla breve from op. 2, no. 5, which, otherwise nearly as archaic as the present largo, has the modulation quoted in Ex. 9, which would bring it into line with the harmonic range of op. 17, while its archaic language would exactly carry out Haydn's present intention without dullness. In A major one might enjoy the exquisite andante of op. 3, no. 1, a quartet which, unlike op. 3, no. 5, with its famous serenade, has failed to live as a whole. If one of these experiments be tried on op. 17, no. 6, a first-rate and flawless work will be obtained, with a witty finale surpassing all Haydn's earlier finales as an intellectual masterpiece of concentrated development of a single theme, admirable in sound and sense.

The next set of quartets was known to contemporaries by two titles: *die Grossen Quartette* and *die Sonnen-Quartette*. Great they are and, even after op. 17, a sunrise over the domain of sonata style as well as of quartets in particular. Every page of the six quartets of op. 20 is of historic and aesthetic importance; and though the total results still leave Haydn with a long road to travel, there is perhaps no single or sextuple opus in the history of instrumental music which has achieved so much or achieved it so quietly.

Imagine that one has listened with attention, keen and duly rested
and refreshed, to all the quartets from op. 1, no. 1, to this point.
A deep, quiet chuckle from the 'cello at the end of the fourth bar
of op. 20, no. 1, then comes as a warning that a new element is
entering into Haydn's quartet style; and eight bars have not passed
before the 'cello is singing in its tenor regions, not as a solo, nor with
any new technique, but nevertheless with an effect which instantly
shows that Haydn's imagination has now awakened to the tone of
the 'cello as something more than a mere amenable bass to the
harmony. This awakening, which freshens the tone-colour of all
four instruments from now onwards, leaves Haydn as liable as ever
to his habitual quasi-clerical errors as to the octave of his bass notes.
But perhaps another explanation of these errors may now be found.
The startling example already quoted (Ex. 2) from op. 71, no. 3,
showed that the fault and its easy correction lay in the viola part,
and not in the 'cello. And after studying all Haydn's quartets from
op. 1 to op. 103, the surprising fact emerges that his imagination
hardly ever awoke to the sound of the viola as it is found in op. 20
awakening to the sound of the 'cello. Of course there is no passage
in which, except in these slips of the pen, the viola sounds bad;
nor is Haydn ignorant of its peculiar tone; it has already been seen
that in op. 2, nos. 3 and 5, he recognizes that it is better suited
than the violin to replace a melody originally conceived for the
horn. But he shows no further interest in its quality; and there are
few passages in his later quartets where the sound of his viola is as
characteristic as it already is in the little-known quartets which
Mozart at the age of seventeen was writing, at about the period of
Haydn's opp. 20 and 33. Haydn's quartet style, then, attains
maturity without asserting the special character of the viola, but
by no means without giving it a satisfactory place in the scheme.

Taking the quartets of op. 20 in order, we find in no. 1 a quiet
first movement admirable in every respect of its technique, with a
peculiarly Haydnesque piece of audacity in form at the beginning
of the development, where the first theme calmly returns in the
tonic before three bars have elapsed, of course only to strike out
in vigorous real development immediately afterwards. The full
effect is felt only if the previous repeat has been played, as otherwise
the first false start of the development will sound merely like a
prolonged lead-back to the beginning. The next movement fulfils,
as always, Haydn's wish that 'somebody would write a new minuet';
and its thoughtful abruptly broken-off trio returns to the minuet in

an unexpected way. The slow movement (affettuoso e sostenuto) is an utterance of such quiet gravity that consummate playing is needed to do it justice. Unquestionably it must have been in Mozart's mind when he wrote the andante of his E flat Quartet (K. 428) in the set dedicated to Haydn as the master from whom he had learnt quartet-writing. The finale glides quickly along, with lively moments, but on the whole as quietly as the rest of the quartet. Perhaps there are not more people who can appreciate this work than there are connoisseurs of T'ang china. Music of this quality would draw crowds if it could be priced like ceramic art.

Op. 20, no. 2, is also unknown to concert-goers, but it is one of Haydn's finest works. It begins with a cantabile for the 'cello which tersely achieves a fine spaciousness by the way in which it repeats its figures and adds a 'dying fall', which latter strain, repeated, gains energy to move to the dominant, in which key the violin takes up the theme. But for the translucent string-quartet tone, such an opening might not have been inconceivable in the old Neapolitan music; yet here there is no reversion to an old style, but the rediscovery of ancient truth in a modern light. And this opening is no mere case of a 'cello solo; the discovery that the instrument can warble away in the tenor clef is not more important than the discovery that its fourth string can, with good economy, sound unfathomably deep, and that a not too rapid arpeggio ranging over all four strings *pesante* is one of the most sonorous possibilities of quartet style. Note the significant fact that Haydn, Mozart, and Beethoven refrained from the more brilliant kinds of arpeggio, long known to string players and usually indicated by abbreviations, as in J. S. Bach's *Chaconne*. In the classical quartet style there is no place for a technique that is not, as it were, pure draughtsmanship. This restraint is unknown to Boccherini, as the rondo of his E major Quintet (with the celebrated minuet) shows; and the coda of the first movement of Beethoven's 'Harp' Quartet, op. 74, gloriously approaches without violating the limit. Severe critics who scruple to enjoy the brilliant violin passage in op. 17, no. 5, would find less danger in the not less rich and sonorous violin arpeggio at the beginning of the development of the first movement of op. 20, no. 2, inasmuch as the figure is not only an accompaniment to a dialogue on the main theme, but is given to the second violin. Among all these luxurious effects, the quieter passages stand out in exquisite relief, especially the purple patch of the modulation from G to its flat submediant (E flat) in the course

of the 'second subject', an effect which has been traced from its
dawn in the slow movement of op. 2, no. 5, and which is now fairly
on the way to becoming standardized. It is treated here exactly as
it would be treated by Beethoven. In this wonderful piece of
quartet-writing even the viola, besides having a vote (as it has had
from op. 9, no. 1, onwards), actually achieves a maiden speech in
the parliament of four, at bar 61, a single bar in which one feels that
Haydn's imagination has for once heard the querulous tone of the
high-lying viola as he now hears the cantabile of the 'cello.

Yet, as will be seen, this movement, so rich and so uniquely
romantic in sound, does not represent Haydn's final solution of the
quartet problem. Perfect in itself, it is not normal; it is a striking
success, and one can imagine how, under modern commercial conditions, strong pressure might have been brought on the artist to
devote the rest of his days to making imitations of it; just as, under
good business management, Beethoven ought to have written nothing but 'Kreutzer' sonatas from op. 47 to op. 135, and Mr.
Arnold Bennett's Priam Farll ought to have painted nothing but
policemen. Haydn teaches a stern lesson; this movement is without
sin or blemish; yet he never scored so gorgeously for string quartet
again! With the slow movement of op. 20, no. 2, Haydn takes a
lingering farewell of all operatic idioms in a grand fantasia beginning with a noble, tragic unison theme which moves in vast
sequences, expanding now and then into ruminating and declamatory passages for the first violin, shared in due course by the other
instruments. This plan is nobly conceived, and executed with
accurate dramatic sense; with the result that when eventually a
pause on the dominant, *pp*, is reached, one is prepared for some
such event as the opening of a lively or impassioned finale. What
happens instead is a continuation of the adagio in a stream of con-
soling melody in the relative major. Familiar in its Neapolitan
style, the simple pathos need not fear comparison with that of
Gluck's Elysian music in *Orfeo*. As to form, Haydn shows here
that he has clearly grasped the principles of composition on a larger
scale than sonata form permits: it is manifestly inconceivable that
this cantabile should behave as a 'second subject', or that the first
theme ever had any intention of confining itself to the function of
a 'first subject'. It would take twenty minutes to work the material
out in that way, and then there would be no sense of freedom and
expansion. But Haydn is here able to make his melody ruminate
and rhapsodize, to interpolate several ominous interruptions in the

former tragic style, and finally to drift, in three solemn steps of gigantic sequence, down once more to the dominant of C. And now, in C major, the minuet begins, in a hesitating syncopated rhythm, like an awakening gaze dazzled by the daylight—after which all is sunshine, with just the right shadow in the trio. Haydn shows in this pair of movements what Mozart showed later in his C minor Fantasia (K. 475), that if composition within the time-scale of the sonata had not absorbed his interest, he could easily have produced a music that moved like a modern symphonic poem. His art of composition is a general power which creates art-forms, not a routine derived from the practice of *a priori* schemes.

Not even in this unique fantasia is his freedom better shown than in the finales of four quartets: of this one, of op. 20, nos. 5 and 6, and op. 50, no. 4. These four finales are fugues, and nothing but fugues. Now it was not from J. S. Bach that Haydn derived his ideas of fugue. His traditions in this art were Italian, and the old text-books will not help one to understand his fugue forms; while later treatises, from Cherubini onwards, bewilder us by flying in the face of every fact in Bach's works (including his didactic last opus, *Die Kunst der Fuge*) without throwing light on any other composer. The fact is that the later text-books are trying to lay down laws of form for an art whose rules define nothing but a tex-ture. It would be a correct use of language to speak of certain kinds of music being 'written in fugue', as certain kinds of poetry are written in blank verse; and Cherubini's rules for compositions written entirely in fugue are true only in so far as they concern matters of texture. Their authority on matters of form may be gauged by the fact that though J. S. Bach's last work, *Die Kunst der Fuge*, is an explicit demonstration of all kinds of fugue in the abstract, classified in a progressive system and all written on the same subject, yet Bach shows the same shocking ignorance of the rules here as he showed in fugues written at large. Now the mys-tery is, where Cherubini found his rules of fugue form. Cherubini, though out of favour at present, was near enough to greatness as a composer for us to find Beethoven's enormous admiration of him not inexplicable, in the light of Beethoven's reverence for all that was austerely firm of purpose. Now, one of the formative events in Cherubini's career was the occasion when he first heard a Haydn symphony. It moved him to tears. Perhaps this fact becomes easier to reconcile with the sour martinet portrayed even by friendlier witnesses than Berlioz, when we note that the only classical fugues that faintly adumbrate Cherubini's scheme of fugue form are these quartet fugues of Haydn, and a few in Mozart's Masses, together with two in some early quartets he wrote possibly already under the influence of Haydn's op. 20. The point in which they agree with Cherubini's rules is that they tend to save up the stretto (where subject and answer are to overlap in closer and closer combination) until the end, actually separating it off by a pause on the dominant. As a fixed rule this notion is, on the face of it, unclassical. It implies that the devices of a fugue stretto are inherently surprising; whereas they were matters of course to any composer to whom fugue texture was a normal language. A more serious objection to such a rule is that it excludes all fugue subjects that are not capable of stretto, thus extinguishing some ninety per cent. of Bach's fugues at large, besides thirty-five of the 'Forty-eight' and (as to treatment of subject) at least six of the *Kunst der Fuge*.

But if a fugue is going to be a rare and conscious essay in a form romantically or solemnly imported from an older world, it will tend to include everything that is characteristic of all the most brilliant ancient examples taken together, and will, moreover, choose old subjects markedly unlike those of more modern art-forms. Now a school of criticism may or may not like the fugues of Haydn, Mozart, and Beethoven; but whether it likes any fugues or none, it cannot dismiss those examples with facile man-of-the-world patronage as deviations into scholasticism. The aesthetics of sonata fugues are no more scholastic than the aesthetics of a play within a play, such as the Murder of Gonzago in *Hamlet*. Here are dramatic conditions in which common sense demands the use of an evidently old-world language; and it is no accident that even Haydn has, in the quartets of op. 20, a hint of the emotional and dramatic impulse which became so volcanic in Beethoven's fugues.

Of Haydn's four quartet fugues, two represent a sublimation of an emotion of almost tragic pathos, the F minor in op. 20, no. 5, and the F sharp minor in op. 54, no. 3. The C major in op. 20, no. 2, is, as we have seen, the finale of an extraordinarily romantic work. Only the A major fugue in op. 20, no. 6, can be said to be written for pure fun. All four fugues are directed to be played *sotto voce* until, at or near the end, a sudden *forte* winds them up in a coda which more or less abandons fugal polyphony so as to end the work in sonata style. The counterpoint is of the highest and smoothest order, a fact all the more remarkable as Haydn is elsewhere anything but an academic writer, far less scrupulous about grammatical purity than Beethoven, to say nothing of the immaculate Mozart. Haydn calls his fugues '*a quattro soggetti*'—'*a tre soggetti*'—as the case may be, according to the number of permanent countersubjects accompanying his main subject, whether one or more of these is announced simultaneously with the main subject or introduced only as accompaniment to its answer. Cherubini would have called all except the main theme countersubjects. The fugue in op. 20, no. 2, is *a quattro soggetti*, two of which are announced together; as in the case of the fugue *a tre soggetti* in op. 20, no. 6. That in op. 20, no. 5, is *a due soggetti*, announced simultaneously, and both consisting of well-known ancient formulas. The fugue in op. 50 in F sharp minor, though it has a not negligible countersubject, is not labelled by Haydn as double. It is one of his most deeply felt utterances, and will demand quotation in due course.

Enormous importance lies in these fugues. Besides achieving in themselves the violent reconquest of the ancient kingdom of polyphony for the string quartet, they effectively establish fugue texture from henceforth as a normal resource of sonata style. Here and hereafter Haydn knows not only how to write a whole fugue for instruments, but how to let a fugue passage break out in a sonata movement and boil over quickly enough to accomplish dramatic action instead of obstructing it. A mere revival of the old polyphony would have been as wide of the purpose as the introduction of Greek choruses, even in Miltonic verse, into *Hamlet* instead of the Murder of Gonzago. But, apart from its value as a means of development, fugue texture is a most important resource as a type of instrumentation. Obviously it solves the problem of equality in quartet-writing by a drastic return to Nature, and puts the four instruments where four voices were when all harmony was counterpoint. But the very nature of contrapuntal harmony is impartially friendly to all instruments that can sing. And all instruments try to sing as well as they can, except those whose normal functions are thrumming and drumming. Hence, when the texture of the music is contrapuntal, the listener's attention is no longer concentrated on the instruments in themselves; within reasonable limits good counterpoint sounds well whatever group of instruments plays it. An endless variety of new tone-colours becomes possible, simply because the admissible range is no longer restricted to those effects on which the ear would dwell for their own sake. The interplay between the polyphonically interesting and the acoustically

euphonious puts an end to monotony and to the temptation to
develop luxury-scoring at the expense of dramatic vigour. We
must not be misled by the common allegation that the fugue style
lends itself to silly ingenuity; what is wrong with bad fugue passages is what is wrong with all bad composition and bad scoring.
Contrapuntal combinations as such are not very difficult; the
materials will either combine or not. The only effect of ingenuity
is to make the combinations smooth, or, if smoothness be not
desired, to give a convincing meaning to harshness, as is Beethoven's
intention in his rough-hewn counterpoint, and Mozart's indisputable achievement in the introduction to his C major Quartet (K.
465). At first one is inclined to say that Haydn is never harsh; but
the exceptions are even more remarkable than in Mozart, for they

are in passages which are not contrapuntal at all. In the peaceful
slow movement of the F minor Quartet, op. 20, no. 5, a ruminating
passage at the end of the development (compare the similar incident cited from the first movement of op. 17, no. 5) is inscribed by
Haydn *'per figuram retardationis'*.

The writer well remembers Joachim's answer when, in 1888, a
bewildered small boy asked him about this passage. 'It means that
the figures of the violin are always a step behind the chords; it must
be played dreamily and tenderly, not stiffly and coldly.' With this
passage Haydn completes his resources of harmony.

Op. 20, no. 3, in G minor, begins with a fiery and passionate first
movement, with several of Haydn's most spirited themes. A certain agitated passage in the 'second subject' is expanded in the
recapitulation to a climax with a freedom which anticipates Haydn's
later treatment of sonata form. The note is almost tragic, and is
well maintained in the minuet, with its trio that leads so romantically back to the da capo. This minuet and the still more impassioned
and sombre minuet of the F minor Quartet, op. 20, no. 5, are
probably the sources of Mozart's inspiration in the most passionate
of all his minuets, that in the great G minor Quintet. The finale
of op. 20, no. 3, is in sonata form, but with a polyphony as close as
any fugue. With its liveliness and energy its quiet end is nearer
to tragedy than to comedy. The whole work would certainly have
found a position in concert programmes but for its slow movement,
which has a breadth not easily distinguished from length by spoilt
modern audiences; and Haydn almost admits this when he calls it
'poco adagio', which shows that it will not bear dragging. The
grand possibilities revealed by the largo of op. 9, no. 3, are not easy
even for Haydn to follow up, and of the four sonata-form slow
movements in op. 20, only that undiscovered little violet in op. 20,
no. 1, is terse enough to achieve breadth without length. Perhaps
this explains how the D major Quartet, op. 20, no. 4, has met with
more public recognition than the other five; for not only are its
first movement and finale in Haydn's most comic vein, but its only
melancholy part, the slow movement, consists of a pathetic theme
(un poco adagio affettuoso) with four variations ending with an
admirable coda, and thus avoiding the difficulties of designing a
big adagio in sonata form on the scale of these quartets.

No. 5, in F minor, is the most nearly tragic work Haydn ever
wrote; its first movement being of astonishing depth of thought,
with quite a big coda containing a new *ff* climax of its own,

followed by a pathetic collapse. The other movements have already
been described.

No. 6, in A major, is a graceful comedy, in which the adagio
cantabile, in C. P. E. Bach's reprise form, is the only part that can
be said by severe criticism to drag. The neglect of this quartet can
hardly be due to any other cause; and perhaps, as with the rest of
op. 20, we may nowadays expect a public appreciation of Haydn
less patronizingly fastidious and more appreciative of subtleties than
that which has dictated the survival of the more brilliant and comic
works at the expense of the more reflective.

It is interesting to compare the remarkable modulating opening
of the 'second subject' in the first movement of op. 20, no. 6,

with that in the first movement of Beethoven's sonata, op. 2, no. 1.

What Haydn thought of a young man who could have the effrontery
to dedicate to him a work in which a 'second subject' starting in
E minor modulates to B flat, has not been recorded; but he was
presumably clever enough to see that Beethoven's modulations are
the by-products of an irresistible steady upward-movement of his
bass, whereas Haydn's, in op. 20, no. 6, are an improvisatorial

adventure undertaken for relaxation, and controlled by the unaided power of its melody.

With op. 20 the historical development of Haydn's quartets reaches its goal; and further progress is not progress in any historical sense, but simply the difference between one masterpiece and the next. Not all the later works are equally valuable; inequalities of value are relatively more rather than less noticeable, and no later set of six quartets, not even op. 76, is, on its own plane, so uniformly weighty and so varied in substance as op. 20. If Haydn's career had ended there, nobody could have guessed which of some half-dozen different lines he would have followed up: the line of Beethovenish tragedy foreshadowed in the F minor Quartet; the Wilhelm Rust line suggested by the fantasia in the C major; a return to fugal polyphony as the main interest; the further development of the comic vein of the D major; the higher and non-farcical comedy of the A major; and the development of (or subsidence into) luxury-scoring.

Something different happened. The 'Russian' Quartets, op. 33, are the lightest of all Haydn's mature comedies. In one place in the old Breitkopf catalogue the opus appears with the alternative title of Divertimenti; and it is also known as *Gli Scherzi*, from the fact that its minuet movements (which are in a quicker tempo than hitherto) are entitled by Haydn himself either scherzo or scherzando. This title Beethoven borrowed for his great satiric movements; but these little scherzi of Haydn's are, except in their quick tempo, nothing like as near to Beethoven's scherzi as the larger minuets, sometimes even marked presto, in which Haydn was in later works to encroach upon the style and scale of Beethoven's second period.

Op. 33, no. 1, often figures in catalogues as in D major. But though it begins with a D major chord, it is really in B minor, and half the point of the opening consists in its effect when resumed in repeating the exposition which, of course, has closed in D. In Haydn's only other quartet in B minor, the same point is made. Haydn got it from a sonata by C. P. E. Bach, also in B minor. In the same key the same idea, elevated from wit to sublime pathos, inspires the opening of Brahms's Clarinet Quintet, the point here also fully revealing itself only when the repeat is begun. Other instances of this device, with bolder key-relations, are to be found in C. P. E. Bach and in works of this date by the eighteen-year-old Mozart. The musicians who were shocked at Beethoven's begin-

E

ning his First Symphony in the subdominant must have been of an uncultured class if they did not know that the composers whom they already revered as classics had gone much farther in this matter.

The slow movement of op. 33, no. 1, conceals behind its formal opening a wealth of quaint beauty, notably its 'second subject' (Ex. 20),

Ex.20 *Andante*

and contributes perhaps more than the slow movement of op. 20, no. 1, to the andante of Mozart's E flat Quartet. The finale is full of energy, and is the only sonata-form finale in this set. For in the other quartets of op. 33 we encounter not only the new title of scherzo for the otherwise unchanged minuet and trio, but the essentially new element of finales in lighter rondo and variation forms. All the six first movements of op. 33 steadily maintain a high level of thought; and of the slow movements it may be affirmed that Haydn has now completely solved the problems of all kinds of form in a slow tempo. The principle of his solution is well seen in the 'second subject' of the slow movement of op. 33, no. 3, an adagio in which Haydn manages to make the reprise device compatible with a sense of sonata activity.

Ex.21 *Adagio*

The secret (which may also be found in the largo sostenuto of op. 33, no. 2) lies in the composer's realizing that a bar of slow music is not a bar of quick music played slowly, but an altogether bigger thing. In music slowness either means bigness, or it means emptiness. And to express action in a slow tempo demands the power of executing a plan in less than a quarter of the number of notes reasonably required in a quick tempo. Nor does it make any difference if any part of an adagio breaks out in demisemiquavers; a run can effect no more dramatic action than the changes of its underlying harmonies. From op. 33 onwards we may be certain that no slow movement of Haydn, however unimportant, will stagnate.

In the largo cantabile of op. 33, no. 5, Haydn shows us what can be done with the old arioso, punctuated by an ominous figure:

Ex. 22

For the middle section he deliberately uses a cliché which is found in Gluck's *Orfeo*; while the cadenza is the finest climax of a highly organized composition, and all the instruments take part in it. The result is a fine movement, contrasted on one side with one of Haydn's largest and most humorous first movements, and on the other with the most comic of the six little scherzi. The finale, however, shows that the revival of the divertimento style, though adding important new resources to the string quartet, has its dangers. Three melodic variations and a runaway coda do not make an adequate finale to a quartet with so important a first movement; and the prettiness of Haydn's Siciliana theme is extinguished by comparison with the poetry of that of the finale of Mozart's D minor Quartet, a comparison it has the misfortune to suggest. Another variation finale, in op. 33, no. 6, is more fortunate, and introduces us to a form peculiar to Haydn and already used by him in piano works. Whether or not he was anticipated by some other composer is a matter for statisticians; the solitary specimen the writer has found in C. P. E. Bach might possibly be later than Haydn's first example. Anyhow, in the record of permanent works of art, Haydn is the master who created delightful sets of variations on a pair of themes, one in the major and the other in the minor;

and nobody has followed up this idea except Beethoven, at the height of his second period, with the solitary example of the Haydnesque allegretto in C major and minor in his great E flat Trio, op. 70, no. 2. The examples of this form in Haydn's quartets are the finale of op. 33, no. 6; the first movement of the *Rasirmesser* Quartet, op. 55, no. 2 (F minor); and the slow movements of the quartets, op. 50, no. 3 (E flat), op. 50, no. 4 (F sharp minor), and op. 71, no. 3 (E flat). Except in the *Rasirmesser* Quartet and in op. 71, no. 3, the form is not seen at its best in Haydn's string quartets; his full enjoyment of it is shown in piano music, especially in the later trios where he pours out some of his greatest themes, using the alternating variation form without scruple for a first movement, a middle movement, or a finale.

The remaining three finales in op. 33 are rondos; a form which, with rare exceptions, is wholly different in Haydn from the form standardized by Mozart. In op. 33, no. 4 (B flat), it is a mere dance, the main theme alternating with several square-cut other tunes, and facetiously varied whenever it returns. The final pizzicato joke is good, and is introduced with just enough composition to provide a *locus in quo dulce desipere sit*. The finale of the otherwise meditative and mellow quartet in E flat, op. 33, no. 2, is known *par excellence* as 'The Joke'. It is a rondo with one episode, and a trailing coda to do duty for the other episodes; and the joke consists in Haydn's winning, by grossly sharp practice, his wager that 'the ladies will always begin talking before the music is finished'. His ridiculous theme consists, as to its first strain, of four two-bar clauses. At the end of the work, after a solemn adagio warning, the strain is played with two-bar pauses between its clauses. When the fourth clause has been played, the music is morally over; and if Haydn chooses to indicate another four bars' rest and repeat the first clause again, he ought to lose his wager.

The rondo of op. 33, no. 3 (C major), is one of Haydn's most comic utterances, but is (like the first movement of op. 33, no. 5) none the less a vital item in the record of his art, and well worthy of its place in the only quartet in this opus that has been often taken up by concert-players. One would like to think that the delicious effect of its opening on a six-four chord was not a consequence of the usual oversight about the octave of the 'cello.

All six quartets are important in their first movements. In the smallest of the six quartets (no. 6, in D) the first movement is important as in the other five, but the unpretending arioso slow movement, while turning the long *messa di voce* of the first violin into an occasion for fine polyphonic organization of the other parts, actually leaves a blank space for a cadenza at the end; for the last time in Haydn's works.

The whole opus gravitates round Joachim's favourite C major Quartet (no. 3), which remains one of Haydn's profoundest studies in childhood, trailing clouds of glory at any and every moment. Its tiny scherzando, with the contrast between its tenderly grave melody on the fourth string and the bird-like duet which does duty for trio (whence the title *Vogel-Quartett*), has always been a popular feature. The first movement is at once the quietest and the greatest Haydn had so far achieved, and it sounds most spacious if played without either repeat. It is time that musicians and music-lovers paid attention to the B minor Quartet, a not less thoughtful work and equally perfect in every way. Nor is there more gain than loss in refinement of taste by neglect of the rest of this opus.

The isolated quartet in D minor, op. 42, occupies a central position in Haydn's art. Pohl, puzzled by its astonishing terseness, and faced with the undoubted fact that it was published after op. 33, conjectures, on no ground whatever but his failure to see anything in it, that it was written about the same time as opp. 1, 2, and 3. This is even more absurd than to suppose that Beethoven's F sharp major Sonata, op. 78, might have been written before he left Bonn because it is so short. Haydn's D minor Quartet, op. 42, is to his art very much what the F sharp major Sonata is to Beethoven's. The slow movement is, as Pohl says, *anspruchslos*; and this unpretentious movement will do as well as any other part of the quartet to prove that Haydn could not have written it any earlier than the date of its publication. If he had only had the luck or cunning to call it a cavatina, nobody would have failed to see the point of this melody without development, without a contrasting second theme or middle section, without sign of dramatic action, extending itself before us till we note, first, that it is not going to be a mere theme for variations; secondly, that it is becoming broader than any melody that we have ever heard worked into larger designs with other themes; finally, that it is rounding itself towards a conclusion, and is sufficient in itself, and justified by sheer contrast for its position in a work of dramatic action. The rest of the quartet (even the tiny four-bar-rhythmed minuet) is a lesson in composition such as would have puzzled the Haydn of 1765 almost as much as it puzzled Pohl, and for very different reasons. In 1765 Haydn could not have written eight bars of andante or adagio without more ornament than suffices for the whole of op. 42. Even in opp. 9, 17, and 20, the moderato tempo of his first movements is not the same thing as the 'andante ed innocente' of op. 42, which is a real andante moving with such economy of action as to accomplish without haste all that sonata form can do, both architecturally and dramatically. The moderato tempo in his earlier first movements has the purpose of crowding as much movement as possible into comfortably long bars; the slow tempo in the first movement of op. 42 has the purpose of spreading few notes over a large space. Finally, Haydn here follows up a point already noticed in the first movement of op. 20, no. 3, and works up part of his recapitulation to a passionate climax in no way anticipated by the original state-ment. This climax brings to maturity the peculiar freedom of form which is to be a leading feature in Haydn's works from now on-wards. In conclusion, if there were any doubt about the date of op. 42, no date within Haydn's lifetime would be too late, and the actual date of publication is the earliest which is technically possible.

From this point onwards Haydn and Mozart converge; they were soon to meet in person, and Haydn's quartets of opp. 20 and 33 were probably among those that had inspired Mozart in his own great set of six dedicated to Haydn. At this point it will be con-venient to consider how Haydn's art-forms, after influencing those of Mozart, diverge in spite of the obvious returning influence of Mozart's style.

Up to op. 42 Haydn's treatment of sonata form, though urgently dramatic, lays a decided stress upon symmetry. A normal first movement (and up till now the same form is adopted for slow movements, with the rare exception of themes with variations) con-sists of a group of material clearly in the main key, leading in a well-organized transition passage to another group of material in the complementary key (the dominant in a major movement, the mediant major, or rarely the dominant minor, in a minor move-ment). This second group (so misleadingly called 'second subject') comes to a definite end, and leads back to the repetition of the whole exposition, and, after repetition, forward to a development which travels, unlike the exposition, freely through many keys until its course brings it back to the tonic. Here the whole material of the exposition is recapitulated, the second group being now in the tonic as well as the first; and its end often suffices for the end of the whole movement. This description has avoided all assertions as to how many themes there are, and how they are distributed; and by this reticence it contrives to be true of Haydn's procedure so far, and of Mozart's and Beethoven's *passim*. But we have now reached the point where it will no longer be a trustworthy guide to Haydn's first movements. His recapitulations have already begun to expand conspicuously: the term 'second subject' as implying a different theme opposed to a single 'first subject' never was applicable to Haydn except in cases which, counted up statistically, are as individual as the cases of many unclassified procedures; nothing could be clearer than the 'second subjects' of op. 33, nos. 3 and 5; and nothing could be more parenthetic than the only discoverable new figures in the corresponding regions of op. 33, nos. 1, 2, and 4. But as to the recapitulation, the very idea utterly breaks down already in op. 33, no. 4; there is instead a brilliant peroration, and this is also the case in op. 33, no. 5, in spite of its clear 'second subject'. From the earliest works to the latest, nothing can be firmer than Haydn's distribution of keys; and nothing can be more dramatic than his later indications of return to his tonic: but beyond this all *a priori* assertion must cease. Pitiful will be the subterfuges of the teacher or student who succeeds in making out that the first movement of our next quartet, op. 50, no. 1 (B flat), has a 'second subject' and a recapitulation; nor will orthodoxy be saved by saying 'this is form in the making, before these things were differentiated'. It is form in the highest state of efficiency, freedom, and terseness, long after every element has been differentiated. From op. 50 onwards there is no dealing with Haydn's first movements except by individual analysis.

His finales remain more often amenable to rule; a symmetrical recapitulation is a useful thing in finales because the end of a work requires more perspicuity than the beginning, and (even in sonatas, where the necessity is not that of the logic of concrete events) its function is to satisfy expectation rather than to raise doubt. Though an individual analysis of each case is the only means of obtaining even a roughly correct idea of Haydn's mature sonata forms, it is fortunately possible to sum up his main resources by the single general statement that 'Haydn invented a brilliant type of coda *à la* Beethoven, and used fully developed codas instead of recapitulations'. From op. 33 onwards one of his strongest impulses was towards terseness, and it was balanced by an equally strong impulse towards expansion. Outward symmetry was for him an obstacle to the reconciling of these two opposite impulses; and the reconcilia-

tion of such opposites is a fundamental condition of art. Mozart
reconciled them by working on a larger scale, where outward symmetry was a necessity. Hence Mozart lays stress on his recapitulation, is usually terse and mono-thematic in his developments, and
seldom has a large coda. The freedom of his form, vital as Haydn's,
is to be sought in fine detail; and in fact the *entasis* of the Parthenon
is not more suitable and accurate than Mozart's handling of his
apparently so symmetrical recapitulations. Beethoven, writing on a
scale initially larger than Mozart's, and expanding to a totally different order and range, adopted as a matter of course the recapitulation of Mozart together with the peroration of Haydn. And Haydn
himself, in the first movement of one of his most famous quartets
('The Lark', op. 64, no. 5), has casually tucked a fairly complete
recapitulation of his complementary-key material into one of his
most brilliant perorations, with an effect like neither Mozart's nor
Beethoven's forms. With this conception of the procedure of the
three masters, we can trace the forms of Haydn's later works without difficulty; with the commonly accepted doctrine of sonata form
the task is hopeless.

Before following Haydn to the end of the various threads he has
now gathered up, we must note a detail of instrumentation which
raises general principles, and gives occasion to discuss Haydn's
other chamber music as far as it is in print to-day. Note the case of
the adagio cantabile of one of the greatest quartets, op. 64, no. 5.

Ex. 23

Here there is unmistakable evidence that the piano was more of a
hindrance than a help to the formation of Haydn's chamber-music
style, even when he was already a veteran. It is, of course, pedantic

to object to a simple musical formula that it can be played as well by a piano as by two violins; and the critic would forget that instruments were made for music and not vice versa, if he sought to damage Haydn's last and greatest complete quartets (the two in op. 77) by pointing out that they were first written as sonatas for piano and violin (or flute). So elaborate an instrument as the piano would be a strange ineptitude if, with the aid of another instrument, it could not give a tolerable account of most things likely to happen in a string quartet in Haydn's musical language. This, however, does not justify Haydn in condemning a violin and viola to spend two-thirds of an adagio in playing an accompaniment which is actually better on a piano, since half the notes of one of the two stringed instruments are redundant where they meet between the beats. It is a forlorn hope to call this a special effect; it is nothing but a lapse in Haydn's imagination, more serious as such than as a sacrifice of the inner parts to mere accompaniment. Contrast the sound of this with that of the accompaniment to a similar but less inspired melody in the curious adagio finale of Haydn's C major Quartet, op. 54, no. 2, where the slow creeping arpeggios of the 'cello rise from the depths right into the region of the melody, combining with the simple repeated chords of the accompaniment in one of the finest tone-colours in any quartet (Ex. 24, overleaf). ('Da hab' ich mir Mühe gegeben,' said Hausmann, when the effect was admired.)

Haydn used to compose at the piano; and the example from op. 64 is the only passage in all his string quartets where we may trace any harm to this habit. It evidently did not limit his powers of phrasing, as it does with weaker musical heads. What it did unequivocally ruin for him was all possibility of working out the combination of the piano with other instruments. Haydn, enjoying himself on the piano with C. P. E. Bach's technique (filled out where necessary), simply 'could not keep a dog without doing the barking himself'; with the result that all his magnificent piano trios are just what his favourite pupil Pleyel called them when, having gone into business as a publisher in Paris, he produced a *Collection complette des Sonates d'Haydn pour Forte-Piano*. You may play unsuspectingly through a magnificent sonata in this edition until you are brought to a stand by a long passage of mere accompaniment, with no melody; and then you will find, on looking at the index, that the work is 'avec accompagnement de Violon et Basse'. You will never have suspected the slightest need for the

Ex.24

basse, though when you try the work with the violin you will see that where it is playing an inner part Haydn wants 'cello tone to complete it, though the piano is already playing the necessary notes. But you may play many of these sonatas without missing anything at all, even though the index tells you that they are 'avec accompagnement de Violon'. Some of these are known nowadays as piano sonatas; and though the new critical edition of Haydn's complete works has not as yet (1928) begun to clear up the chamber music, it has already eliminated all but three of the so-called violin sonatas by publishing them as the piano solo sonatas which Haydn intended them to be.

The trios are in a different case. All the thirty-one now in print require the violin (or, in three cases, the flute) to play important themes; and in accompanying passages they further require the 'cello to support the violin, though hardly for a dozen notes in the whole collection is it allowed to diverge from the bass of the piano. The only movement in real trio-writing in the whole thirty-one works is the adagio at the beginning of the two-movement work in A major, no. xv in Breitkopf & Härtel's edition. For the rest, the musical contents of these trios are, with a few early exceptions, glorious; and the works cover Haydn's whole career, and are far richer than the quartets in fine specimens of his smaller forms, such as alternating variations, sectional rondos, lyric A-B-A- slow movements, and, above all, movements breaking off and leading into finales, a dramatic event that only twice happens in the quartets, but always coincides with Haydn's finest imagination in these smaller works. It is not difficult to place the trios in approximate chronological order among the quartets. The main thing to bear in mind is that Haydn takes the view that a quartet is a symphony, whereas a piano trio is an accompanied solo. Consequently a slight finale, such as a merely sectional rondo, or an unpretending movement in any position, is no evidence of early date. The famous 'Gipsy' Rondo, for instance, belongs to one of the last trios (which of course figures in no. 1 in current editions; they always put the ripest works first)—and that trio begins with a set of rondo variations (i.e. variations with divers episodes instead of a second theme), and has a middle movement in simple A-B-A- form; so that this most famous among Haydn's trios contains no sonata form at all. It is none the less mature for that. No trio contains four movements; the presto that follows the splendid alternating variations in the G minor trio, no. 17, is itself an expanded variation of the second theme. Some of the sonata-form first movements are in Haydn's greatest style, e.g. trios nos. 3 (a work to which occasionally 'cellists have sacrificed themselves in public), 6, 8, 13, and 23, and so are some of the finales, whether developed rondos or sonata movements; e.g. in trios nos. 3, 5, 8, 13, 17, and 23. All the double-variation and rondo-variation movements are great; and some of the smaller finales are intensely poetic; e.g. the gentle consolatory allegro ma dolce, which, after a deeply pathetic fragmentary andante intermezzo, brings the great D major trio, no. 6, to an abrupt end; and perhaps most of all the melancholy tempo di menuetto of the quite late trio in F sharp minor. One of the earliest trios, in G minor, in the style of op. 9 or earlier, is as beautiful as any. Two other early works (no. 12 in C and no. 27 in F) sprawl with a gawkiness compared with which that queer couple of fragments known as the quartets op. 3, no. 4, is graceful and terse. Trio no. 27, however, is the more presentable of the two. The flute trios, nos. 29, 30, and 31, are easy-going, early-middle Haydn.

Trio 18, in E flat minor, is one of Haydn's last compositions, and consists of the most pathetic of all sets of rondo variations, followed by a subtle and pensive finale in the major, allegro ben moderato. Many other trios claim attention; but we must now deal with the remaining quartets.

Op. 50 consists of six quartets (B flat, C, E flat, F sharp minor, F, and D). The F sharp minor Quartet is a great work. It shows for the first time Haydn's definite renunciation of tragic ends to sonata movements, and his now typical association of the minor mode with a passionate, somewhat blustering temper, ending with a recapitulation (in these circumstances regular) in the tonic major, so that everything turns out well. As he said of himself, 'Anybody can see that I'm a good-natured fellow'. It is a pity that he did not think fit to provide the variations of his andante with at least a few bars of coda; the contrast between the two themes is grand, but the

impression left by the unexpanded end of the whole is perfunctory. In striking contrast to the happy end of the first movement, the final fugue, quietest and deepest of all the few instrumental fugues since Bach, strikes a note so tragic that Beethoven's C sharp minor Quartet is the first thing that one can connect with it (Ex. 25). Op. 50, no. 5, F major, in exquisite childlike happiness from beginning to end, is one of the most perfect and subtly proportioned of all Haydn's works. Its poco adagio is known as *Le Rêve*.

Op. 50, no. 6 (D major), begins as if in the middle of a sentence and is broadly designed. It is known as *Der Frosch*, from the froglike effect of the theme of its finale, which plays across open strings and their unisons. Op. 54 contains three of the most brilliant quartets. Brilliance is the note of the opening of no. 1 (G major), which has for slow movement a wonderful quiet allegretto in sonata form with profound modulations. No. 2 (C), a great favourite with Joachim, has the biggest and most symphonic first movement so far. The astonishing adagio consists of a sepulchral melody with a wild, florid counterpoint for the first violin, all *per figuram retardationis*, as we saw in op. 20, no. 5 (Ex. 17). It leads into the minuet, which has a very remarkable trio. The finale is a freak, already cited for its scoring. It is a lyric adagio, with an introduction and one short presto episode. No. 3 (E) is one of Haydn's greatest works, and should be better known. Equally great is the first of the three quartets of op. 55; in A major, with an adagio in rondo form (a very difficult thing to handle with Haydnesque breadth), a remarkable use of the extreme heights of the violin in the trio of the minuet, again exploited in op. 64, no. 6, and a finale which begins like a rondo, and runs away in an excellent (unofficial) double fugue.

Op. 55, no. 2, is the *Rasirmesser* Quartet, so called because Haydn's host overheard him exclaiming, under the torture of shaving, 'I'd give my best quartet for a new razor'. The wish was fulfilled, and the vow redeemed with this F minor Quartet. In its opening double variations Haydn wallows in the sentiment evoked by the heavenly contrast between its passionate minor and consolatory major theme. A proved personal friend of Haydn's whole family of a thousand sonata movements might venture to ask Haydn's permission, at the second (i.e. last) variation of the major theme, to omit the unvaried first statement of its first eight bars, and begin it immediately with the fresh tone of the 'cello. This would lose nothing, and would save the movement from

dragging. The rest of the quartet is among Haydn's most intellectual works, and its neglect is due to the fact that, besides being
subtle, it is by no means easy. Let no musician call it ineffective if
he would escape the shame of the fox in that affair of the grapes.

Now that we are sure of Haydn's methods and mastery, op. 55,
no. 3 need not detain us; nor need op. 64, no. 1. But the other five
of op. 64 are of the highest importance. The thoughtful B minor,
no. 2, with its replica of the D major ambiguity of op. 33, no. 1,
and its humorous ethereal end in B major, is a great work unduly
neglected. Not so the remaining four (B flat, G, D, and E flat),
which are among the most constantly played of Haydn's works,
nos. 5 and 6 being specially popular. The common new feature in
these four quartets is the appearance of lyric slow movements in
the form of a broad melody, a minor middle section, and an ornamental da capo. This form had already appeared in the great E
major Quartet, op. 54, no. 3, but in a more ornate and less idyllic
style. Op. 64, no. 5, called 'The Lark', from the entry of the first
violin warbling in the heights, after a staccato opening theme by
the other instruments, is famous for its little *perpetuum mobile*
finale. Op. 64 as a group has some resemblance to op. 33. On the
basis of longer experience, it gloriously develops the lighter side of
Haydn's art-forms.

The remaining complete quartets (opp. 71 (3), 74 (3), 76 (6),
and 72 (2)) are all on the largest symphonic scale, and so doubtless
would the wonderful fragment, op. 103, have been if Haydn had
had the strength to write a first movement and finale for it. Of the

Ex. 26 *Andante con moto*

three neglected masterpieces in op. 71 (B flat, D, E flat), the third is the greatest and most perfect. Two passages have already been quoted in connexion with the viola-below-'cello problem (Exx. 2 and 3); another quotation from the exquisite rondo-variation slow movement will show a new tone-colour (Ex. 26).

The D major Quartet (no. 2) is the only quartet with a slow introduction; a fact curiously in contrast with the custom Haydn had long since come to establish in his symphonies. The finale of that neglected quartet has one of the loveliest themes of his special later kittenish type.

Op. 74 begins with a glorious work in C major, taken up with enthusiasm by Joachim in his last years. For the first time we encounter a feature by which a work of Haydn's may be surely recognized as a work of his latest period. The trio of the minuet is in A, a key only remotely connected (through its tonic minor) with C, the key of the movement. The choice of these keys for sections not continuously linked up in a flowing structure (e.g. in trios of minuets and as keys for middle movements) is Haydn's contribution to the scheme of tonality which Beethoven, Schubert, Brahms, and (*mutatis mutandis* for the conditions of the music drama) Wagner were to develop into so mighty a resource. Haydn's insight is shown in his abstention from explanatory or miraculous modulations where these key-relations are concerned. His beloved C. P. E. Bach was always treating remote modulations as things to declaim upon; Haydn puts the contrasted keys in plain juxtaposition; for which he would assuredly get no marks in our Mus. Bac. modulation questions. And so his key contrasts shine out like the colours of a sunset. You will find them in most of the later trios (Breitkopf nos. 1, 3, 5, 8, 9, 11, and 23); though of course their absence will not prove an earlier date.

Op. 74, no. 2, F major, is another neglected masterpiece. No. 3, in G minor, on the other hand (called *Rittquartett* from the prancing rhythm that pervades its first movement), is a great favourite, with its blustering tragic first movement and finale, both ending happily like 'the good-natured fellow I am', and its specially solemn largo in the remote key of E major.

The six quartets in opp. 71 and 74 have, with op. 76, no. 1, the common feature of beginning with some introductory gesture or phrase.

In op. 76, nos. 1 and 3, Haydn presents a feature imitated only by Mendelssohn in his 'Italian' Symphony and Brahms in his First Violin Sonata, B major Trio, and F major Symphony. Although each of these works is in a major key, the finale is in the minor. The reverse relation is, of course, not uncommon. As usual, Haydn's two blustering finales end happily in the major; but not without some downright solemn thoughts in their development. The intellectual depths and the freedom of form in the last twenty quartets are among the inexhaustible experiences of art; and Brahms's friends need never have been surprised to find him absorbed in the study of a Haydn quartet. Only once, towards the end, does the work seem a little too easy; the graceful ingenuities of op. 76, no. 6 (E flat), roll away like the process of peeling an onion; the fantasia, which is the slow movement, seems more arbitrary than free; and actually the most beautiful part of the quartet is the trio of the minuet, which consists wholly of the scale of E flat in iambic rhythm, descending and ascending with counterpoints as multitudinous and heavenly as the angels on Jacob's ladder.

But the rest of op. 76 is beyond description. No. 2, in D minor, with a powerful first movement unique in its concentration on its first theme of four notes, has the most imaginative minuet (the *Hexen-Menuett*) before Schubert. No. 3, in C major, nearly as great, is famous for its variations on Haydn's Austrian Hymn. These, which simply pass the unadorned melody from one instrument to the other, are not as great as their tune, but can be made to sound very spiritual. No. 4, in B flat, is known as 'The Sunrise', from its remarkable sustained opening. One of the most glorious of Haydn's tunes is that of the anomalous first movement of op. 76, no. 5, which is followed by the great largo in F sharp major which has given this quartet its title in the catalogues. Beside these melodies, we may place the theme of the andante of the last complete quartet, op. 77, no. 2 (the whole quartet is perhaps Haydn's greatest instrumental composition, with two of the last symphonies to bracket with it); and, finally, the deeply touching andante theme of his last composition, the fragment, op. 103. With this Haydn bids us farewell, not in terms of the quotation from his part-song, *Der Greis*, which he issued as a visiting-card, complaining of age and weakness, but rather in terms of the end of that song, which says, 'Thanks to Heaven, a harmonious song was the course of my life'. Power and eternal youth remained in these last and gentlest strains that the venerable creator of the sonata style allowed his pen to record. That power we can feel; in that eternal youth we can rejoice; and we may be satisfied to seek out what Haydn has done for us without more than a mystic notion of how he did it.

CHRISTOPHER WILLIBALD GLUCK (1714–87) AND THE MUSICAL REVOLUTION OF THE EIGHTEENTH CENTURY[1]

THERE are five great composers who have become the special property of the non-musician. This is not an unmixed advantage, either to the reputation and preservation of the music or to the non-musician's understanding of it. The layman's approach to other arts lies through many normal experiences which are much more closely related to these arts than to music. It is only in recent times that pictures have been held to be the worse for having subjects that are describable in literary terms; and poetry itself is not wholly unapproachable through literature. But there are notorious disadvantages in approaching music through literature: indeed, it is a pity that the disadvantages are not more notorious than they are. The non-musician's composer gains a large measure of his popularity at the expense of his musical qualities. The purely literary critic seldom knows anything about the literary side of the musician's work, and therefore sheds no expert light upon it. Histories of English literature are not thought defective if they omit all mention of Purcell and Handel, who gave new values, both classical and popular, to the poetry of Milton, Dryden, Pope, and the Authorized Version, besides immortalizing humbler writers from Nahum Tate downwards; while even in the case of Metastasio, every line of whose work was written for music, the orthodox encyclopedist is content to tell us that his works were too poetical for music and too musical for poetry. Meanwhile, the composers tend to become represented by such works and features of style as can be described without any commitments of musical judgement. Performances and editions of their works are undertaken by enthusiasts whose knowledge is weakest on the musical side; and isolated fragments obtain, by some accident of effective performance or popular fancy, an extraordinary vogue. Then comes the more expert musical showman, who dresses up these items or whole works in a tasty modern confection with selected quaintnesses from the style of several centuries; and the public and critics rejoice in the ever-fresh appeal of the grand old pioneer with his naïve sincerity.

The most famous sufferer from this fate is, of course, Handel;

[1] From *The Heritage of Music*, vol. ii (Oxford University Press), 1934.

the most dangerous of all composers; the most industrious and un-scrupulous in writing himself down; but, when he chose, exactly what Beethoven called him, the 'master of all masters, and capable as no one else of producing the greatest effects with the simplest means'. Less than one-twentieth of Handel's work is known to the public, and most of what is known is buried in a debris of moderni-zation which the *Musikgelehrte* of the present day removes often to create worse confusion by failure to include common sense and general musicianship as elements of scholarship.

Berlioz is another non-musician's musician. His French prose is far less amateurish than his music, though few men of letters except W. E. Henley have taken notice of it. But his music is saved from its own amateurishness, and from amateurish production and interference, by the fact that he is a pioneer of the modern orchestra. Inextricably mixed with his curious ineptitudes, there is an astound-ing intuitive grasp of certain principles, not only of orchestration, but of composition on a very large scale. He is a master of vast exordiums and perorations, and also of sky-vault heights and infer-nal depths. Neither in time nor in harmonic space has he any material for middle regions; but the very hollows reverberate im-pressively, and he is even less amenable to correction than Gluck.

At the opposite extreme we have Chopin, with vision strictly confined to the pianoforte, but with perceptions in form and har-mony so deep as to transcend equally the comprehension of the admirers and the detractors of his fame as a writer of salon music. His music, again, is to some extent protected from misrepresenta-tion by the fact that it is difficult enough for those who murder it to feel conscious of their barbarity.

The most fortunate of non-musician's composers is Wagner. Amateur productions of his works are obviously impracticable, and the mastery of his mature style is beyond the cavil of any musician who knows enough to have the slightest fear of giving himself away.

A defective technique is a grave disadvantage to the non-musi-cian's great composer. To the interesting or charming historical figure it does not matter. No musician with a sense of humour nowadays wishes to correct Domenico Scarlatti. Bülow had a sense of humour, and did, nevertheless, correct Scarlatti; but Bülow's habits of tidying up were an anachronism even in his own eccentric personality. With composers of the calibre of Gluck or Berlioz a bad technique is a great bar to their intelligibility. It aggravates the controversies which must in any case arise between the musician and the non-musician. The musician's criticisms are not easily presented in a better light than that of pedantic objections irrelevant to the pioneer's or reformer's vast and noble aims; and the non-musician merely loses his temper at such cavils, helplessly, but with popular sympathy on his side. What the general reader is seldom told about the controversies is that for the most part the musician has the advantage of talking not only about music, but about this music in particular: whereas every word that the non-musical enthusiast has to say can be said, and has been said, of any number of other composers known only by name to readers of books on musical history. Performances of the works under discussion will not always help matters. The technical defects of the composer do, in fact, require some intervention on the part of the conductor or editor; and the minimum intervention is the thin end of a wedge which usually leads, as we have already noted, to the dispersal of the composer's style through the idioms of two and a half centuries. Then we have the purists and the modernizers at each other hammer and tongs, with amateur incompetence evenly divided between them, both in fact and in imputation.

Gluck is perhaps the most interesting of all composers who are in this predicament. The literature about him is enormous, and for the most part very readable. He is in touch with interesting people throughout his career, including the French *encyclopédistes*. By far the most readable essay that could be written about Gluck would consist mainly of extracts from the correspondence, private and journalistic, that raged around him throughout his life. I confess myself quite incompetent for such a task; but any temptation I might have for adding to the volumes of Gluck literature from this point of view would be annihilated by one simple reflection: it does not matter a brass farthing what contemporary musical name you substitute for Gluck in the whole of such literature, as far as the music is concerned. It would not be true to say that there was no trace of a musical judgement in the whole of that literature, but it is quite fair to say that it contains few statements, however many there be that seem shrewd and discriminating in form, that you can trust to retain a discoverable meaning when confronted with the music.

An eminent critic has recently quoted with approval a remark of Fétis, that in order to appreciate a symphony of Haydn you should listen to symphonies by Stamitz and Vanhal, so as to measure the immense progress that Haydn's work represents. It has been suggested that we should follow this advice in public concerts. But I am afraid that the result would convey nothing, except to musicians who could have attained it with much less time and trouble by a glance at the works of Stamitz and Vanhal in a good musical library; and that the effect of a public performance would only be to set going the usual outburst of enthusiasm from people who have no sense of composition, who recognize styles merely by tags, if at all, and who think that anything contemporary with Haydn and Mozart must be worth reviving so long as it is not by either of those masters. Where such enthusiasms are genuine the enthusiasts are probably quite right about the qualities they see in their hobbies. Their one mistake is that these are the only qualities they can see in all art and life. That is why we may at any moment find ourselves attacked by new Piccinnists at the expense of Gluck. Their appreciation of music quite possibly will not even go far enough to do justice to Piccinni, who was himself an out-and-out Gluckist. I have often envied the connoisseurship of a philatelist, but nobody wants to know what it feels like to have a mind that has never contemplated a larger field than that of a postage-stamp. The brutal truth is that the great masters and the Interesting Historical Figures differ in the fact that the great masters can compose and the I.H.F.s cannot. The general public has, if it is given a chance, some feeling for composition, though it is easily taken in by patchwork. But most of the discussions that rage around the composers of what has, more by its misfortune than its fault, become literary music, are discussions that have nothing to do with musical composition at all; and for the purpose of such discussions the compiler of shreds, patches, and clichés is quite as useful a topic as a real composer.

If the reader who has borne with me so far will bear with me a considerable way farther, I hope to arrive in this essay at some estimate of Gluck as a composer. But a large dump of literary debris remains to be cleared away before we can get an unobstructed view of his music.

The worst of musical history is that when the history is interesting the music is often disappointing without it, and when the music is great it often has no describable history. But there are a few composers whose work has made history and also become immortal on its own merits. In such cases we do not need the history to explain the music; on the contrary, we read the history in the light of the permanent value of the music, and produce an official legend that is much too good to be true. Such is the legend of Palestrina as a reformer of Church music; and such is the legend of Gluck as a reformer of opera. Palestrina did reform Church music, and Gluck did reform opera; but neither the corruptions nor the reforms were quite the obvious affairs which legend has made of them. In order to measure Gluck's achievement it is necessary to understand not merely the outward forms of opera in his day, but the whole nature of the change that was revolutionizing music, both instrumental and vocal, independently of the theatre.

Gluck was born in 1714 and was producing operas in London in 1745, five years before the death of Bach and fourteen before the death of Handel. Yet we rightly think of Gluck as belonging to a later period than the age of Bach and Handel. Our chief mistake is in thinking that the age of Bach and Handel regarded those composers as its representatives. Aesthetically, our estimate of that age is a fairly just verdict of history. If all the music of other composers contemporary with Bach and Handel were annihilated, we should miss the equivalent of museums full of china-ware, and should still have the musical equivalent of all the great sculpture and architecture of a Golden Age. But to the music-lovers of 1740 the annihilation of Bach and Handel would have meant the disappearance of Bononcini's successful rival and of an obscure scholar locally famous in Leipzig. The rhymester would still have sung:

> Strange that such difference there should be
> 'Twixt Tweedledum and Tweedledee.

For there were dozens of Tweedledums waiting to contend with Bononcini. When we associate the first half of the eighteenth century with the music of Bach and Handel, we naturally think that the period is one of classical polyphony; but it is no way to be compared with the 'Golden Age' of the sixteenth century. The contemporaries of Palestrina certainly thought that they were witnessing the culmination of pure polyphony; and we agree with them. The polyphony of Bach and Handel is the art of a musical renascence; its principles are not those of the pure vocal art of the sixteenth century, but are profoundly and organically modified by an equally classical sense of the properties of instruments in themselves and in their effect upon voices. This renascence art not only culminates in Bach and Handel, but reaches in those masters the only maturity which interests us. To their contemporaries, this renascence was old-fashioned. Latin could still be quoted in Parliament, and fugues could still be written in oratorios; but in the drawing-room Latin was hardly more out of place than fugues. It was still possible to adumbrate fugues after the fashion of a parliamentary quotation; and if the subject was lively and repeated itself with an echoing tag, a composer like Vanhal could, even in a later generation, write fugues that were amusing enough to be considered elegant. But the pages of Burney show again and again that he had witnessed in his youth the production of Handel's later works, enjoyed the personal acquaintance of Gluck and Philipp Emanuel Bach, watched with disapproval the prodigious career of the young Mozart, and brought his *History of Music* to a conclusion in 1789, all without the slightest idea that Handel's immortality lay in his choruses, that contemporary polyphony was anything but pedantry, and that any more important revolution had taken place in music beyond the 'new ways of taking appoggiaturas and notes of taste'.

In his contempt of polyphony Burney voiced the best opinion of his day. Handel himself, before he finally deserted the glories of Italian opera for the less fashionable 'good works' of oratorio, had made the texture of his later operas more and more like that of the works of his illustrious contemporary Hasse, whose wife, Faustina, he succeeded in getting to sing in the same opera with a rival prima donna, Cuzzoni. A contemporary writer of sonatas, Alberti, who died in 1744, ought to rank as one of the greatest composers in musical history, if the highest art were not to conceal but to avoid art. He invented the 'Alberti bass'; or, if he did not invent it, at all events made it his own, and, like the famous grimy writer of a testimonial to a famous soap, having used it in his first works, used no other for the rest of his life. Hasse's favourite texture consisted of chords repeated in quavers, a device which saves even more labour than the Alberti bass. It is not to be confused with the tremolo, which, limited to measured semiquavers, Handel uses often enough, but never without imagination. Neither it, nor any similar apparently worthless formula, is a resource to be despised by dramatic reformers. But we shall never understand Gluck's early environment until we realize that such resources were already in full use, and that the age of Bach and Handel was an age in which those masters stood (except for occasional freaks of art elsewhere) alone in all the qualities that we admire in Handel, and in every aspect of Bach's art. The age was one in which, to a contemporary, the renascence of polyphony had long spent its force. To a mind less complacent than Burney's it was an age of decadence; for there was little chance for the ordinary observer to guess that in a future century Johann Sebastian Bach would be discovered as a supreme master, and that Handel himself would join the ranks of the immortals on the strength of works written after he had twice become bankrupt as a producer of operas. The present-day worshippers of the later phases of Russian ballet are not more hostile to Brahms than the musical fashions of 1745 were to Bach.

In this period of Alberti basses and vocal acrobatics, Gluck began to make his mark in Italy as a fairly successful writer of Italian opera. We shall do his early works no injustice by inferring their character from collateral and subsequent events. They succeeded well enough in Italy to cause Gluck to be invited to London to compose for the Haymarket in 1745. Here he made little impression; the works were severely trounced by the critics; and Handel pronounced on Gluck his famous judgement that 'he knows no more counterpoint than my cook'. In this early visit to England Gluck made a better impression by his performances on the 'musical glasses', for which he wrote a concerto. The instrument was not the nerve-racking system of bowls revolving on a spindle and played by moistened finger-tips for which Mozart wrote, some thirty years afterwards. It was a more primitive affair struck with some kind of soft hammer; and the vogue of Gluck's performance on it is in all probability commemorated in the phrase 'Shakespeare and the musical glasses'. Indeed, unless the phrase can be discovered to be used before 1745, no other origin for it seems possible.

We are told that Gluck's first impulse towards reform of opera rose from the failure of a pasticcio which, in accordance with a common-sense custom of the day, had been made out of the most applauded numbers of his other operas. Let us take that legend at its face value and note what it means. In the first place it implies that pasticcios did not often fail; in the second place the cause of this failure was ascribed to the fact that the music fitted the words in the original operas but did not fit those in the pasticcio. Now this is remarkable, for it implies that Gluck's music had become essentially dramatic long before he had any idea of reforming opera. Probably if we could get at the music and texts both of the originals and the pasticcio, we should find that the facts were not quite so simple; that, for example, when Handel made a pasticcio, his librettist made a better job of the text than Gluck's librettist; or that Handel's arias are too effective to be ruined by literary causes to which nobody paid any attention, whereas the success of Gluck's early music was at best a trembling in the balance. Still, the legend is significant; and we must not too hastily assume the unimportance of Gluck's early music. Handel himself was not more reluctant than Gluck to write a new piece when an old one could serve; and the greatest of Gluck's works live as unscrupulously as Handel's, by taking in not only each other's washing, but the washing of operas which the historians tell us relapsed into the bad old style which Gluck so drastically reformed. In short, it is quite possible that the chief merit of the works which Gluck produced in London in 1745 was a new kind of dramatic fitness, and that when this disappeared in the adaptation to a new text the other merits proved insufficient.

If this new kind of dramatic fitness was anything like an adumbration of Gluck's mature style, we need inquire no farther as to the nature of its importance. But we must not suppose it to have been the only kind of dramatic fitness that existed. Nowadays, great if sporadic efforts are made to revive Handel's operas; and the propagandists in such revivals always claim that Handel is a genuinely dramatic composer. In the performances less is spent on spectacle and costume while more attention is paid to stage-management and gesture than was perhaps usual in Handel's time; and the arias, especially those with much coloratura, are cut down, sometimes considerably below the limits of musical coherence. Enough beautiful music remains to entertain the listener; and as Handel is a consummate rhetorician whose music is connected with the words in a not wholly accidental fashion, the result is remarkably like an opera. But before we acquiesce in the enthusiastic opinion that Handelian opera should have made Gluck's reforms unnecessary, we should do well to realize that this result has been obtained by cutting out the elements on which Handel chiefly relied; and that if such a production of his operas had been offered him, he would have flung his wig at the producers, and good Princess Caroline would have had to say, 'Hush! hush! Handel is angry'.

How much counterpoint did Handel's cook know? This is a fundamental point in the case for reform of opera. Handel's cook was Mr. Walz, a singer with an excellent bass voice, on whom Handel relied for small roles in his operas. It is quite possible that Mr. Walz could have written a tolerable thorough-bass to an air of his own composition. Clarissa Harlowe is supposed to have had this much accomplishment, and Richardson even contrived with the aid of a clerical friend to give the music of a song she wrote, figured bass and all. In a polite age the horror of pedantry is itself a scholarly instinct; and the object of contrapuntal skill was then, as always, not to display erudition, but to move easily and gracefully. The good contrapuntists, Handel, Hasse, Graun, and other masters of the time, all yielded more or less to the temptation to write flimsily; but the Alberti bass itself moves better under the guidance of a contrapuntist than under that of a writer who really knows no higher art of accompaniment. We need not impute to Handel the stupidity of complaining that Gluck did not write fugues. Handel himself seldom carries a fugue out to completion even in his most serious works; and the fugues in his opera-overtures coalesce into the diddle-diddle of the cat and the fiddle as soon as the third voice has entered with the theme. But the contrapuntist guides Handel's harmonies and basses as surely as a draughtsman may guide the scene-painter splashing his colours out of a pail. Handel was quite right in saying that Gluck lacked counterpoint. The criticism was relevant, and the difficulty contributed far more than dramatic immaturity to the failure of Gluck's early operas. It was never entirely repaired. In moments of inspiration all difficulties vanish; and in Gluck's greatest works inspiration is present almost throughout. But large and elaborate works cannot depend upon the highest and most impulsive inspirations from beginning to end. They need a considerable bulk of matter that may be characterized as 'business'; and the 'business' needs resources that can obviously be classed as technique. In the last resort the artist with a brilliant technique finds inspiration for the 'business' as well as for the supreme moments of his work. He attends to everything in its proper place; his brilliant handling of the 'business' does not interfere with the grand simplicities of the main inspirations, and the main inspirations are recorded by methods which do not make the adjustment of details impossible when their time comes. Gluck did not attain any such balance of power. His routine technique was and remained poor. It is interesting, by the way, to note that Verdi, also (as he himself admitted) an unlearned but a very experienced composer, never could quite understand why Gluck ranks so high in musical history. His dramatic merits Verdi took for granted; his imperfect musicianship offended, as showing the very difficulties from which Verdi had set himself free with mighty struggles. A lack of counterpoint is a very serious handicap to the designer of large musical works, even if he never wishes to combine his themes at all.

There are two ways, and two only, out of the difficulties resulting from this lack. The drastic and thorough way is Beethoven's. Finding polyphony as necessary to his music as air to his lungs, Beethoven forced himself to become a contrapuntist in spite of all obstacles. The natural contrapuntal styles of Bach, Handel, Haydn, and Mozart were beyond his reach. To him they were like ideal instruments; and he had to use the imperfect instrument of his own style. The only difference between it and other imperfect instruments, such as the pianoforte and the instruments of the orchestra, is that its imperfection is not that of a material object. Nevertheless, Beethoven transcends it exactly as great·artists transcend the imperfections of material instruments; the difficulties are deliberately turned into qualities. Or we may compare the style with a language rather than with a material instrument. For no two artists use quite the same language; and genius may force an exquisite precision out of an uncouth language, thereby expressing subtleties beyond the reach of smoother tongues.

Gluck has another way out of the difficulties of his imperfect technique. It is an infallible way only under favourable circumstances; in other circumstances it is not available at all. It amounts simply to this; get your librettist to devise the simplest possible dramatic situations of sublime emotion, and become inspired by them yourself. In such situations a small technical apparatus in the hands of an inspired composer may achieve the same result that would have been achieved by a larger technical apparatus in the hands of a master who prunes away superfluities. Handel is a master with a large technical apparatus which he hardly ever puts into operation. When he is inspired there is no ready means of distinguishing his technique from that of his laziest work. It is his rhetoric, not his counterpoint, that you must study in order to see where the mastery lies; and then you will find that in essentials it is very like Gluck's. Such a masterpiece as Stanford's favourite illustration, the air 'Total eclipse' in Handel's *Samson*, is not a thing in which a note could conceivably be altered; and if Gluck had been given the task of expressing the situation of the blind and captive Samson, he would have been glad enough to achieve an air on exactly Handel's lines. To the inspired composer such problems solve themselves. A good school of melodic rhetoric comprises all that is needed for their technique.

Unfortunately, dramas cannot be constructed entirely on a sequence of beautiful emotions without a rational sequence of events to connect them. Two of Gluck's greatest operas, *Orfeo* and

Alceste, were designed by their enthusiastic librettist Calzabigi to realize as nearly as possible this agreeable consummation. No account of Gluck's operatic reforms is honest unless it faces the fact that in the two works in which this reform was accomplished Gluck and his librettist simplified the dramatic problem almost out of existence. But here the word 'almost' is the key to the situation. There is drama both in *Orfeo* and in *Alceste*; and it demands an inveterately dramatic music. But in *Orfeo* there is practically no 'business'; and in *Alceste* the need for a certain amount of dramatic 'business' has wrecked the original Italian third act and caused such changes and interferences in the later Paris version that the supreme action of Alceste's return from the underworld is badly patched up by another hand. In his last works Gluck handles more complicated libretti; and we recognize more clearly in them where the composer finds no inspiration and the craftsman falls back upon doctrinaire mannerisms.

Before dealing with Gluck's greater works in detail, let us continue to investigate the legend. Accepting Handel's judgement that Gluck had never learnt counterpoint, let us ask what he had learnt. His master Sammartini (or San Martini) was an excellent contrapuntist. But his vogue was that of a writer of operas and concertos and chamber music. Haydn was said to have come under his influence, but was by no means gratified by that report, which he indignantly denied, saying that Sammartini was a 'dauber'. Let us thank Haydn for this admirable word, which so exactly describes the essential quality of musical scene-painting from the point of view of a master of genuine chamber music. From Sammartini the non-contrapuntal Gluck could learn to daub, and to use with a sense of dramatic fitness the various forms of tremolo, including such as he could afterwards invent for himself or pick up in the theatre orchestras of Paris. Besides picking up these useful and splashy accomplishments, a pupil of Sammartini was in the position of an apprentice in a painter's atelier; he was allowed to complete the less important parts of his master's works. We hear much of the plagiarisms of Handel and of other masters of the eighteenth century; but it would be interesting to know whether an eighteenth-century composer was allowed during the lifetime of his master to claim his share in the works that went under the older master's name. Many charges of plagiarism were brought against Gluck in later years, sometimes interesting, sometimes merely comic; and, as has already been mentioned, all Gluck's works lived by taking in each other's washing. But it might be worth while to discover what early arias of Gluck's pass under the name of Sammartini. Not only the splashy theatrical texture, but also the larger aspects of Gluck's musical form owe much to Sammartini. The sonata style of Haydn and Mozart is inveterately dramatic, to an extent of which its reputed pioneer Philipp Emanuel Bach had no conception. But it is not through the sonata forms that Gluck arrived at his dramatic style. The instrumental forms of Sammartini are, like the textures associated with them, degenerated from the style of the concerto grosso. In the greatest examples of the genuine style, such as Bach's Third Brandenburg Concerto, we shall find large stretches in homophonic vibration, by way of relief, or even as a means of bringing more highly organized textures to a climax. Gluck's overtures to *Alceste* and *Iphigénie en Aulide* are as intimately connected with the operas as any Wagner *Vorspiel*; and their orchestration is wonderfully satisfactory to modern ears and was quite acceptable to Mozart. But such resemblance as they have to the sonata style is rather deceptive: their material and contrasts are conceived far more on the lines of the concerto grosso. Strange to say, the classical symphony itself was an offshoot from operatic overtures in this style and did not immediately coalesce into the genuine sonata forms. Philipp Emmanuel Bach was a lyric rhetorician whose style grew steadily more aloof from dramatic action; yet the first movements of his symphonies are not in line with his sonatas, but with Gluck's overtures.

But these are matters of musical form which belong to a later stage of the present discussion. It is futile to discuss the problem of opera as if it were primarily musical. At least four-fifths of the problem is centred in the libretto. An opera may be a concert on the stage; and this was, if only for financial reasons, its main purpose and the main cause of its vogue before Gluck. The performances of great singers were ruinously expensive, and it was well to provide some four hours' entertainment for the cost. Expensive dresses and expensive scenery entertained the eye, and so relieved what would otherwise have been a strain on the attention of the ear. An opera with a simple plot would not employ enough singers, nor could it give its few characters enough material for the required thirty-odd arias with which to fill out the four hours' entertainment. When Handel deals with the subject of Alceste, the title of the opera is *Admeto* and the story has a counterplot. What the counterplot is, I frankly own I have forgotten, if I ever knew; and those who know it know something that Handel's audiences never thought about. To the best of my recollection all the plots of Handel's operas are complicated. Seven characters are almost obligatory in normal circumstances. In special circumstances, special measures are needed. Thus when Handel induced the rival prima donnas Cuzzoni and Faustina to sing in the same opera, it was necessary to design two imperial roles, one that of the tragedy-queen, the other that of the bride or bride-elect of the conquering Alexander. The two queens first entered together singing in thirds. In writing the score, it is necessary to write one part under the other. Handel was careful to put the higher notes on the lower stave at the outset. In their second duet the queens exchanged relative positions, both on the stave and in pitch; and probably a more minute statistical examination than I have the patience to undertake would show that neither of them had a single quaver's cause for jealousy. Handel's diplomacy was for several nights quite successful, and the two prima donnas bristled with beautiful modesty. Unfortunately the public began to take sides. If it is almost certain that 'Shakespeare and the musical glasses' dates from Gluck's visit to England, we may perhaps conjecture that the phrase 'this beats cock-fighting' dates from the rivalry of Cuzzoni and Faustina. At all events the phrase became appropriate enough when the public had decided to spoil Handel's game.

Apart from its comic aspect the game is interesting for this reason, that it concerned the librettist quite as much as the composer. The revivers of Handel's operas tell us with enthusiasm that he was a bold innovator. The Cuzzoni-Faustina hen-fight was one of his innovations. The opera *Teseo* embodies two other innovations, inasmuch as it is in five acts instead of the customary three, and its arias are allotted to the characters in pairs. The dramatic value of these daring innovations is not obvious, and they must have been accomplished by the librettist before a note of the music was written. We can base a better case for Handel as a dramatic composer on the masterpieces of rhetoric which are perhaps as frequent in the operas as in the oratorios. But the operatic master-pieces are for the most part happier out of their context than in it. Perhaps the great scene of madness at the end of the second act of *Orlando* has something to gain from the drama that leads up to it; and there is much in the rest of *Orlando* that would have interested Gluck, who was only prevented by Piccinni from treating the same subject. But even here Handel would not have been able to write a scena of unprecedented range if his librettist had not laid out the text accordingly.

The problem of the libretto must be solved as to its general principles before the composer can even begin to theorize about operatic reform or operatic ideals. We may neglect the theories of the fact-proof egotist who would like to write the music first and get a libretto fitted to it afterwards. Hardly less negligible is the view of the professional hack-writer for music, and of the kind of composer for whom he caters. The ideal music-drama will not be based on a low estimate of the subtleties and resources of music, and will contrive to move at the pace of the music without sacrificing literary qualities. Weber, in the course of nine revisions of the hopelessly tangled libretto of his greatest work, *Euryanthe*, exclaimed 'You don't suppose a musician allows a libretto to be put into his hand like an apple!' But he also said, 'Give me all the strange rhythms and inversions you can think of; nothing stimulates the composer's invention more'. The composer of operas cannot help sometimes wishing that he could take an extant stage play more or less as it stands, and set it to music with the minimum of alteration. Since Wagner achieved complete continuity in a music that moves at the same pace as the drama, this ideal is no longer remote. Oscar Wilde's *Salome*, Hofmannsthal's *Elektra*, and Maeterlinck's *Pelléas et Mélisande* had made their mark as plays before they became operas; but it is not too much to say that the consummate art of Strauss's and Debussy's timing ensures that they are better acted as operas than they have ever been as plays. If the composer's traditions and musical apparatus are simpler than Wagner's and the drama older, more adjustment is needed; and Boito had to go to great lengths in simplifying Shakespeare before the *Otello* and *Falstaff* of Verdi could come into being. One of the most remarkable facts in Gluck's achievement is that after effecting once for all the reform of opera in two works with libretti purposely designed with extreme simplicity, he was able to continue by setting the classical dramas of French literature in fairly recognizable shapes.

If we neglect the views of the hack-writer of verse for music, we lose nothing valuable either in music or literature. But it is unfortunate that so many of the greatest poets have happened to be unmusical. Goethe, though he once tried to conduct an amateur choral society, had no gift for music and knew better than to trust his own judgement about it. Unfortunately he preferred a musical adviser who would not venture to argue with him. And the spectacle of Goethe led in musical matters by Zelter is like a vision of Messrs. Shaw, Chesterton, and Belloc trying to keep up with science by studying Jules Verne. Stanford threw himself at Tennyson's feet in generous youthful adoration, and probably saved that poet from one or two blunders in musical matters. Browning talks cryptically and suggestively about music, but it was almost a feature of his style to call everything by the wrong name if he possibly could. In Shakespeare almost the only passage that uses musical terminology without something wrong or hopelessly obscure is the gamut of Hortensio in *The Taming of the Shrew.* Only in Milton and Bridges can the student of English literature find positive statements about music that the musician can follow up in the certain hope that the meaning is worth finding out. It would ill become a musician to compare musical culture with so vast a field as that of letters. But it may safely be said that no musician has ever ventured to remain so ignorant of the national literature, and of all that has been made international by translation, as most persons of literary culture are content to remain ignorant of music.

This was not so in England in the days of the Tudors, nor at the period of the Restoration. Nor was it so in Italy during the seventeenth and eighteenth centuries while opera was taking shape. The humblest writer of words for composers could not consider himself a hack-worker when one of the leading poets of his age and country devoted the whole of a long life and a personality of princely bearing to writing words exclusively for music. Such was the lifework of Metastasio (1698–1782). If you want a fair estimate of Metastasio's art you must turn to the historians of literature, who are somewhat puzzled to describe a poetry so exclusively designed for a kind of music that is no longer studied even by musicians. From musical historians Metastasio gets nothing but abuse. Brilliant debating points are made out of such a fact as that he 'expired in a canzona', extemporizing in neat verse on the occasion of receiving extreme unction. It is not clear why this should be more ridiculous than the fact that Bach on his death-bed dictated a figured chorale in fugue by contrary motion. The main difference in the two cases is that Metastasio wrote poetry which was set to music by composers whose works have perished with them, whereas Bach has written music that endures. There is also a spiritual difference between Metastasio and Bach which makes it seem trivial to bully poor Metastasio with a gibe. But two facts remain: first that Metastasio's poetry is still read for its own sake by students of Italian literature, and secondly that Metastasio was continually vexed at the way in which his operas were set to music. What he achieved in his dramas was a very rational musical scheme, according to which each situation was arrived at by a natural and smooth progress of dialogue and action, in order to be marked at every emotional crisis or possible point of repose by a tableau during which the emotion could be expressed in an aria set to a few lines of pregnant poetry so designed that the words would bear repetition with good rhetorical effect in a musical scheme. There is no essential difference between this and ordinary drama; indeed it reduces the conflict between music and action to the constant element of conflict between lyric poetry and action in all drama. The Metastasio formula was doomed from the outset, not because it was irrational, but because it was too easy. Hasse, who wrote operas literally by the hundred, could not remember whether he had set some of Metastasio's dramas three times or only twice. The essential tragedy of Metastasio's long career is that his operas were never once set by a great musician until Mozart himself, desperately driven under the pressure of more important works, hurriedly executed a commission for the wedding festivities of the Austrian Emperor and set *La Clemenza di Tito* in a style suitable to the occasion. The play has been said to be one of Metastasio's best. To the modern Philistine its moral seems to be 'Why cannot a hard-working Roman Emperor have three wives?' And the new Empress graciously characterized Mozart's music as *una porcheria tedesca*. But there is nothing in the structure of the play to prevent Mozart from making a fine thing of it if he could have felt a little more sympathy for the intrigues of persons with a reversionary interest in Titus's dilemmas. Otherwise there is no discoverable reason why the Metastasio plays should not have been set by great composers. The poet's only faults are those of an inveterate improviser; and for the musician these are not faults at all. Perhaps one of the most momentous disappointments in musical history was that of the child Mozart, when at the age of twelve he was not allowed to have a libretto by Metastasio for the opera he was to produce at Milan. An alliance between Metastasio and that amazing child might have grown into a greater partnership than that of Gluck and Calzabigi. If only Metastasio instead of Varesco had written *Idomeneo*!

Raniero Calzabigi was an enthusiastic poet whose ideas on operatic reform were highly congenial to Gluck. It is quite likely that the poet induced Gluck to cross his Rubicon sooner than he might have done without prompting from a person who had original ideas as to the construction of libretti; but Calzabigi was a simple soul and betrayed a certain inflation of the head when he afterwards claimed that he taught Gluck the proper rise and fall of melody in the setting of his words. He is supposed to have been a violent opponent of Metastasio; but if this is so he must have been in disagreement with his own family, for Metastasio's favourite edition of his own works was edited by a Calzabigi. Be this as it may, Raniero Calzabigi encountered Gluck at the right moment for both of them. Gluck could no more reform opera on Metastasio's lines than he could walk up a mountain of glass. There was no need for reform. Anybody could set Metastasio to music, and everybody did. There was no aesthetic reason why Metastasio's drama should not provide a large number of characters and a complicated plot, and there were many financial and practical reasons why it should. Calzabigi attacked the problem by striking at vested interests. The subjects of serious opera were invariably classical, or at least concerned with the decline of the Roman Empire, though one of Handel's librettists once ventured as far as Richard Coeur-de-Lion. Calzabigi and Gluck stuck to Greek legend but reduced it to a more than Greek simplicity.

The plot of *Orfeo* is as follows: Act I presents Orpheus and the chorus mourning at the grave of Eurydice. Orpheus asks to be left alone with his grief: he communes with the echo, and resolves to kill himself. Enter Eros or Cupid, called Amor by the poet. He tells Orpheus that the gods, touched by his grief, will allow him to visit the underworld and bring back Eurydice on condition that he does not look upon her face until he reaches the light of day. Orpheus resolves upon this enterprise. The second act begins in the underworld with a chorus and dance of the Furies. They are interrupted by the sound of Orpheus's lyre. He pleads with them, and at last they yield him passage. The scene changes to the Elysian fields. The happy shades are enjoying their quiet songs and dances. Orpheus enters and asks for his Eurydice. His prayer is granted, and, keeping his face averted, he leads her away. In Act III Eurydice is following Orpheus to the upper world. They are still among the underground rocks, and Eurydice is distressed because Orpheus will not look at her. Apparently he understands that he is forbidden not only to look at her but to explain why he cannot. At last, tormented by her jealousy, he gives way and turns

G

towards her. She falls dead, and he is in despair again. Amor returns and, stating that the gods are satisfied after all, revives Eurydice, and the scene changes to his temple, where his triumph and the happiness of Orpheus and Eurydice are celebrated with ballet and chorus.

Already the first pioneers of opera in 1600 had found that in a musical setting the pathos of the Orpheus legend becomes intolerable unless a happy ending is provided. Music concentrates its emotional effects so powerfully that either a considerable intellectual apparatus or a melodramatic callousness is necessary to make a tragic end tolerable. Thus when later Italian opera became tragic it became eminently blood-and-thunder. The story of *Il Trovatore* is gruesome; but a critic has not ineptly observed that nobody ever risked sitting down in the trunk-hose of the gipsy's foster-son. And, by the time libretti had become so tragic, music had learnt to provide common dance-rhythms for the most solemn occasions. But there is something very different from conventionality in the refusal of earlier musicians to face tragic issues in music. Their art recaptured the emotional values of childhood; and to the normal child a story that ends sadly is an outrage. That criticism is altogether too easy which condemns the recapture of the child's instincts. Nobody need trouble to justify the mechanism by which happy endings are secured, unless on these grounds, that the cruder the device the more honest is what Scots law would call the confession and avoidance. Alike in primitive, unreformed, and reformed opera, the composer was dealing with a musical apparatus that contained few elements which appeal primarily to the intellect. Beauty of musical design, beauty of harmony and tone, immediate emotional expression, these things may be directed by genius to results in which the intellect may find inexhaustible enjoyment. But they are not primarily addressed to the faculty of conscious reason. A fugue instantly draws attention to the interplay of its voices: a sonata presupposes that you will recognize its themes when they recur: a drama with an elaborate plot demands your attention to the course of events. All such apparatuses may be used to heighten the total power of emotion, but they invariably reduce its immediate shock. There is evidently nothing to reduce the shock of emotion in Gluck's *Orfeo*; and its effect is incredibly moving. Indeed, its most famous (though not really its greatest) achievement in pathos is the aria 'Che farò senza Euridice', which comes after Eurydice's annoying behaviour, and might have been expected to alienate the sympathy of any listener who had not given a holiday to the faculty of reason.

Ignore Euripides when you approach Gluck's *Alceste*. Verrall has shown that the Brownings were too literal-minded for the ironies of Euripides' satiric drama; but if Verrall is ten times as subtle as Balaustion, that interpreter is twenty times subtler than Calzabigi. The whole opera has precisely this and no more connexion with the Greek drama: that it concerns a king at the point of death, whose life can be purchased by the willing sacrifice of some other life, and is so purchased by that of his wife, who is finally brought back from death by superhuman means. Every vestige of a problem is removed from the treatment of this story. The devotion of the people to their king and their grief at his impending death are the dominant notes of the first act; and the difficulty of finding a willing sacrifice is not stressed. Admetus is horrified at the idea that anyone should be sacrificed for him, and the chief tragic moment is that in which his wife confesses to him that she is the sacrifice. Thus Calzabigi secures two acts full of intense emotion without any occasion for doubt or analysis of motives. In the third act he encountered problems of dramatic 'business', and here he failed conspicuously. When the opera was remodelled for the Parisian stage the third act ruined its effect. Gluck exclaimed 'Alceste est tombée', to which Rousseau replied, 'Oui, mais elle est tombée du ciel'. The rest of the opera was so impressive that the rescue of its third act was thought worth the trouble. A new part was created for Hercules, who had not appeared in Calzabigi's libretto at all. Thus, instead of Calzabigi's Apollo *ex machina*, it is now Hercules who, as in the Greek story, plunges into the underworld and rescues Alceste. Unfortunately not only the whole role of Hercules, but the supreme crisis of his conquest of the underworld were composed, while Gluck was away in Vienna, by a certain Gossec whom musical historians mention with a respect by no means justified by the ridiculous effect of his stiff little phrases and jejune harmonies in the midst of Gluck's greatest music. Gluck seems to write badly enough when he is not inspired; but his feeblest stuff would put Gossec to shame. And the four leaves containing Gluck's own handling of the climax are lost! The original Italian version cannot help us here; for throughout the opera Gluck's reconstructions are so extensive that, in re-adapting the Paris version to Italian words, not one line of Calzabigi's text can remain. And, on the whole, the Paris version is incomparably finer, to an extent which can be measured already at the rise of the curtain, where the overture leads to a mighty outcry of the populace instead of dying away almost formally as in the original.

Yet there is much to be said for taking the Italian rather than the French version of *Alceste* as the basis of modern performances of the work. There is no reason why the manifest improvements of detail in the French version should not be grafted on the original Italian form in such a manner as to leave the third act unencumbered by any foreign matter whatever. The French alterations have to some extent affected the plot; and, no doubt, if we could recover the missing passage in Gluck's French third act it would prove to be finer than anything in the Italian version. But Gossec's Hercules and his music for the combat between Hercules and the Infernal Deities simply will not do. When one is not in the act of enjoying Gluck's music one recollects him as an unlearned composer whose crudeness needs some indulgence; but if we want to see how illusory such after-impressions can be, we have only to contemplate the harmonies and rhythms which Gossec thinks impressive enough for the Infernal Deities in the act of yielding to Hercules. I forbear to give a musical example, but the reader should be warned that most of the printed vocal scores give Gossec's rubbish without the slightest hint that it is not by Gluck. Apart from internal evidence it may be easily distinguished by the fact that it all belongs to the role of Hercules and that its choral portion is in C major.

The Italian *Alceste* contains several beautiful numbers that are not in the French version; and the French version contains, besides an enormous amount of ballet, several new arias which show the growing complexity and subtlety of Gluck's rhetoric. In the Italian *Alceste* the air 'Non vi turbate' has become almost unrecognizable in its French form 'Ah! Divinités implacables', though a close examination shows the French version to be a bar-for-bar variation of the Italian. But meanwhile the Italian version has become known as an Andantino in E flat for pianoforte by Mozart, because he copied it on pianoforte staves for some unknown purpose, possibly as theme for a set of variations. Such a work would have made an agreeably serious companion to the excellent comic variations on Gluck's *Unser dumme Pöbel meint*. The influence of Gluck on Mozart is deeper than we are ready to suppose; and in *Idomeneo* the oracle scene and the ballet music pay tribute to Gluck that amounts to something like explicit quotation. Throughout Mozart's works there are certain pathetic turns of phrase that are more probably to be derived from Gluck than from any less important maker of the musical language of the eighteenth century. Here is a 'conflation' of one of the Gluck-Mozart idioms. Mozart often uses the chromatic version (*b*) which is not in Gluck's vocabulary; but Mozart by no means neglects the severer form (*a*).

Ex.1

At this point it becomes interesting to inquire why *Idomeneo* is the only work in which Mozart shows the dramatic influence of Gluck in any obvious way. It is an insufficient answer that Mozart's lines of progress lay in comic opera where Gluck's contribution was insignificant: we want to know why the musical power shown in the tragic grandeur of *Idomeneo* did not improve upon this opening, developing the manifestly congenial dramatic aspect of it, and automatically extruding with growing taste the anti-dramatic elements of coloratura singing and redundant symmetry which spoilt *Idomeneo*. In his later works there are no limits to the dramatic sensibility Mozart shows when he chooses; and there are plenty of points in *Idomeneo* itself that are considerably more dramatic in Mozart's hand than the librettist Varesco had any reason to expect. But the first thing that is obvious about Mozart is that he is very fond of music. He could never have approved of Gluck's avowal in the dedicatory letter of *Alceste* that the composer's aim should be 'to restrict music to its proper function of rendering service to poetry and dramatic situations as colour and chiaroscuro serve the purpose of a well-composed picture'; and Gluck's own achievement was not to restrict but to enlarge music 'to its proper function'.

It never became self-evident to Mozart that any musical resource was necessarily undramatic. His whole development, alike in instrumental and stage music, might be traced in terms of his growing insight into the dramatic meaning of any and every musical resource. In the last resort he would probably have come to consider an undramatic libretto as unmusical, though his life was not nearly long enough for him to outgrow a readiness to irrigate Saharas with his flow of musical inspiration. Even as it was, Mozart became a dramatic reformer of opera over a much wider area than Gluck could command. But to Gluck belongs the supreme credit not only of displaying genuinely dramatic music on the stage, but of creating such music at all. We only weaken the resources of language by applying the epithet dramatic to all forms of rhetoric. We may agree with Macaulay that some dialogues in *Paradise Lost* would make excellent drama, and we may remind ourselves that Demosthenes said that the three essentials of rhetoric are 'action, action, and action'; but we shall get an inadequate meaning from the word dramatic as applied to music unless we restrict it to actions less static than those of the orator, and changes of situation capable of interrupting the flow of Milton's finest dialogue.

Now we have seen that in *Orfeo* and *Alceste* Calzabigi had simplified the dramatic problem of opera almost out of existence. And there is much to be said for the view that the critical atmosphere of Paris enlarged Gluck's sense of the theatre and set him free from what might have become cramping in Calzabigi's doctrine. But this brings us to another distinction that might form the subject of a useful essay which to the best of my belief has not yet been written. Is the sense of the theatre co-extensive with the sense of drama? The history of opera in France shows that it is manifestly nothing of the kind. Every time a foreign composer has brought dramatic music into France he has encountered criticism which, whether it exasperates or pleases him, profoundly affects his style for the rest of his life. Few tendencies in musical history have been so conspicuous and so unmistakable as the vitalizing effect of French criticism upon writers of opera. And yet, who are the great classics of French opera? Lulli, an Italian; Rameau; Gluck, an Austrian; and Meyerbeer, a German Jew, the Barnum of opera; and aloof and austere, but a teacher of several famous if recalcitrant pupils, the Italian Cherubini, influenced against his masterful will by both Gluck and Beethoven. With the pupils of that much abused martinet the history of French opera becomes more obviously the history of French composers, and also passes into a very much lighter phase. But the curious thing about the classical history, whether it be French or foreign, is that with few exceptions its masterpieces have not been particularly dramatic, and have, indeed, for the most part, fallen into a respectful neglect for that very reason. The 'sense of the theatre' which they show is a sense of entries, exits, and groupings.

Before Gluck came to Paris his two great 'reformed' works, *Orfeo* and *Alceste*, contained a few ballets to make appropriate resting-places in the very simple action of these works. He found that performance was out of the question in Paris unless there was at least an hour's bulk of ballet music distributed over each opera. To this we owe large masses of instrumental music in which Gluck rises to incomparably greater heights than in his few and unimportant symphonic efforts apart from the stage; and it is to this that we owe, a century later, that Wagner grafted on to the crudeness of his *Tannhäuser* a good half-hour's bulk of music in his ripest and most brilliant orchestral style. But it is quite clear that in neither case is such music a contribution to the reform of opera. It almost seems as if the arbiters of taste whose dictates were followed by the composers of French opera regarded dramatic action as a thing subversive of the art of the theatre. Perhaps this is why *Orfeo* was received in Paris with almost universal approval, while *Alceste* (having more action in it) at first failed. The few who complained of the insufficiency of action in *Orfeo* admitted in the same breath that the music carried the spectator over that defect.

Gluck did not find it necessary to reconstruct *Orfeo* to anything like the extent that the Parisian stage required for *Alceste*. The two works present widely different problems for modern performance. An entirely new opera would have cost Gluck little more labour than his revision of *Alceste*. Yet we may perform the original Italian version with the certainty that we are dealing with Gluck's own first inspiration in every detail, and without much difficulty in grafting upon it those features of the second *Alceste* which are real improvements. If, on the other hand, we base our performance on the French *Alceste*, we must find some scholarly substitute for Gossec's stuff. With *Orfeo* the case is different. Where the French version differs from the original Italian in musical content and declamation, it is so incomparably finer that no sensitive judgement could abandon it. The Italian version has recently been published in vocal score and presumably adopted as the basis of performance, but none of its unfamiliar details will bear comparison with the sublime style of what may be conveniently called the authorized version. This criticism is no mere result of custom. The effect of a return to the Italian version is by no means that of a return to something more severe. In one of the greatest passages of all, the entry of Orpheus into the Elysian fields, the Italian orchestration is actually more elaborate than the French, and a glance is enough to show that Gluck has here removed superfluities. All the new French details represent quite obviously a deepening and purifying of

Gluck's style. Yet, as a whole, the authentic French version, in the form given in the monumental Pelletan-Damcke edition, is intolerable almost from beginning to end, inasmuch as the whole part of Orpheus was transposed by Gluck from an alto to a high tenor voice; with the result, among minor disadvantages, that the whole scene of Orpheus's contest with the Furies has become entirely decentralized in key, and the magnificent original plan of its modulations obliterated. The famous tenor, Le Gros, in whose interest these dreadful changes were made, must have had an unpleasantly high voice, and he could sing the great Elysian recitative at its original pitch. That movement therefore remains untransposed; but the shrill tenor is quite subversive of the deep calm that Gluck originally intended for this most wonderful of accompanied recitatives.

We may take it, then, that every adequate modern performance of *Orfeo* will consist of the French scoring grafted on to the Italian plan of keys and voice. Neither by this means nor by returning to the pure Italian version shall we recover exactly what Gluck intended; and this is just as well. Scholarship itself is not obliged to insist on the restoration of conditions that ought never to have existed. We may sing the cantatas of Bach nowadays without following the precedents of the *Thomasschule* under Bach himself by giving the choir a well-deserved flogging afterwards. In graver mood we may hope that Western civilization will never again allow the voice of the *castrato* to be heard. Let us stick to our modern innovation of giving the part of Orfeo to a woman with a contralto voice, and let us have the benefit of Gluck's most inspired final touches on the undamaged fabric of his first and freshest essay in music-drama. It is ridiculous to suppose that the glorious voices and noble persons of Amalia Joachim and Giulia Ravogli produced a less natural and classical representation of Gluck's Orpheus than the eunuchs of the eighteenth century.

Gluck had not settled in Paris long before the French recognized in him a glorious opportunity for the development of musical party politics. Paris had not yet forgotten the great war between the Buffonistes and the Antibuffonistes. But that was a mere matter of fine art, though it established the triumph of comic opera as represented by Pergolese's *La Serva Padrona*. The arrival of Gluck gave occasion for something much more exciting, a contest of personalities. The French operatic stage was already showing hospitality to another foreigner, Piccinni, and here was a glorious opportunity for setting up a rivalry between masters of two different schools. The wars between the Gluckistes and the Piccinnistes filled the feuilletons of the day with volumes of quite interesting literature. But Gluck's victory was decisive at the time and annihilating for the future. Nowadays, even if we take the trouble to read the contemporary literature on the subject, we have not the slightest idea what the Piccinnistes were talking about; nor shall we find that the literature becomes more intelligible in the light of Piccinni's music. None of the literature, even when it is by as good a musician as Rousseau, comes to grips with music as music at all. Rousseau was a composer, though a very poor one; but when he begins to explain the subtleties of Gluck's chorus of Furies in *Orfée* he flies in a thoroughly amateurish way to extremes of pedantry in theorizing about an enharmonic modulation which he reads into his text by mistake, and which, even if his account were correct, would have about the same aesthetic value as Virgil's masterly use of the ablative absolute. What emerges from all the literature, even before we take the trouble to consult the music, is that the whole controversy was a quarrel between the supporters of French music and the supporters of Italian music, in which the French partisans were so patriotic as to choose an Austrian champion.

In looking at Piccinni's music the first thing that is manifest is that that amiable artist has an admiration for Gluck and is working his hardest to imitate him in every particular, not always stopping short of plagiarism. I regret that I have not had an opportunity of reading Piccinni's *Iphigénie en Tauride*. Obviously the first document to consult is Piccinni's execution of the work which the Parisians arranged that both composers should set in rivalry. On the other hand, I have picked up the score of Piccinni's *Roland*, a later work, the libretto of which Gluck refused to set when he heard that it had been given to Piccinni. The subject is that of Handel's *Orlando*; but Handel's treatment is at least as dramatic. Piccinni's is well worth reading, but not worth reviving. To revive Handel's *Orlando* would be to produce some thirty pieces of music that never fail individually to move with an admirable circulation within the limits of static musical forms, and which moreover sometimes show thrilling signs of a larger dramatic life in development and juxtaposition, though the whole does not profess to cohere. Against this it is vain to urge the superior claims of a music-drama that achieves coherence for three and a half hours with a uniformly sluggish circulation and no remarkable features of composition. Coherence is not enough; the composer who wishes to fill hours with one piece instead of thirty must show power and momentum. Yet Piccinni's *Roland* quite justifies the Piccinnistes for existing. All music, great and small, would soon come to an end if it were the invariable fate of musicians as good as Piccinni to starve.

He was a considerable master of melody and had other attractive features in his style. His instrumentation is defective in its technique, and sugary in its merits. The sugary qualities no doubt helped his vogue. The defects are different from those of Gluck, but it is hard to say that they are more serious; and in any case there is no evidence that even the most learned musicians of Paris at the time were better judges of instrumentation. As has been said above, Gluck's escape from technical difficulties depends upon inspiration; and the short and sufficient description of the difference between Gluck and Piccinni is the old critical evasion that Gluck is inspired and Piccinni is not. Fortunately, criticism need not so completely abdicate as to leave the matter here. Inspiration is not a *chimaera bombinans in vacuo*, and even the most dramatic music of the most drastic reformer of opera does not attempt its task without being musical. In the last resort the greatness of Gluck reveals itself conclusively as the greatness of a composer. If this were not so, the whole business of reforming opera might as well have been left to Calzabigi and the journalists. Now it so happens that composition is an aspect of music which is never dealt with in musical literature. In this matter the technical treatises are even more to seek than the journalists; for they, one and all, take the fatal line of substituting generalizations from complete works of art for the methods by which works of art are really produced by masters.

The art of composition in music is essentially the same as the art of composition in prose and poetry, and the worst possible way to learn it is by setting up a large art-form as if it were a scenario and trying to fill it out. A composer should learn all forms of musical texture as he would learn a language, and he should then find out by experience what each kind of texture is good for. A composer as respectable as Piccinni can trust his music to proceed at a comfortable amble without breaking down. If he is more learned than Piccinni his musical textures will be richer and more interesting; but if he is a genius his music will not amble uniformly, but will show a momentum that carries everything before it, whether the intellectual and material apparatus be as primitive as Gluck's or as complex and luxurious as Wagner's. The external art-forms are the results of the various powers of movement which the composer of genius sets to work. Certain kinds of music can fill a given time with certain ranges of contrast and certain musical evolutions. For the composer of opera the times to be filled up and the ranges and evolutions to be accomplished within them depend upon the libretto, and if he is not his own librettist some of the merits of his art-forms manifestly belong to the poet. To Calzabigi, and to the collaborators who adapted Quinault and Racine to Gluck's purposes, we must give credit for a leading feature in Gluck's operatic schemes —the building-up of a long scene to a fine architectural design by means of a recurring chorus or recurring movements, such as the funeral choruses and the echo songs which constitute the main bulk of the first act of *Orfeo*, and the choruses of the grief-stricken populace in the first act of *Alceste*. But the merit of the librettist would have availed little if the composer had not transcended it.

When the producer wishes to treat the composer with the contempt due to all who approach the stage otherwise than by the orthodox progress from call-boy to actor-manager, his first procedure is to find any two passages which repeat the same phrase or arrive at the same chord, and then to cut out everything which occurs between them, in accordance with the axiom that any cut, however nonsensical, is better than any music or any argument, however necessary. There are works where this axiom is of some practical use, but with Gluck it is conspicuously untrue. I should be surprised to learn that the most Philistine of producers ever even thought of cutting down the three statements of Orpheus's lament to the echoes, with the three recitatives that alternate with them. There are cases where Gluck has used in a later work a shortened form of an earlier piece of music. I believe that the longer form will invariably prove to be the better. Dramatic cogency seldom enters into the question, because, as we have seen, Gluck's reform of opera owes most of its cogency to its having got rid of almost all action except an emotional tension which has more to gain than to lose by spreading itself over a long time. For the purposes of Gluck's reforms music did not require to be speeded up and compressed. It did, indeed, demand release from the imperturbable amble of the da capo aria, and the da capo itself was a repetition which achieved a fool-proof symmetry by a stroke of the pen and prolonged every pause in the action by some five minutes without contributing any architectural quality to a scene as a whole. The mere getting rid of this convention is in itself a speeding-up; but the total effect of Gluck's methods is not a compression, but an expansion, of music. In modern performances we are not obliged to agree with the eighteenth-century Parisian in demanding a whole hour of ballet music, nor would Gluck have provided so much ballet to suit his own taste; but the last things that you need to cut out from Gluck are his repetitions and expansions. It is precisely in these that his power of climax is a musical resource epoch-making in its own day and true for all time. Music had to learn to expand with the kind of expansion that does not arise from the working out of a polyphonic argument. Gluck's power in that matter is one of the reasons why his music is not easy to illustrate by short quotations. This difficulty is a constant source of mis-understanding in books on musical history, and the only possible safeguard against it would be to compel every musical historian to produce a volume of whole compositions illustrating his points. In every art there will always be literally hundreds of artists who can say a good thing here and there, for one who can produce a whole work of art that has more momentum than that of a safe amble.

Let us see whether it is possible to indicate Gluck's power of composition by illustrations that, without ruinous expense, may show the scale on which he can work. Fortunately, there is an example in *Iphigénie en Aulide* which can be summarized in a few musical staves; it consists almost wholly of elements inconceivable to Bach and Handel, and is on a time-scale which would not be felt to be in adequate in Wagner's mature style (Ex. 2). Agamemnon is protesting that the gods cannot expect him to obey the command to sacrifice his daughter. He has twice sung in the plain abrupt rhythm of the words: 'Je n'obéirai point à cet ordre inhumain'. This takes five bars punctuated by pauses. Then he breaks into a cantabile: 'J'entends retentir dans mon sein le cri plaintif de la nature; elle parle à mon cœur, et sa voix est plus sûre que les oracles du destin'. This takes twenty-seven bars, with no repeti-tion of words except 'que les oracles du destin'. Here is the ground-plan of the whole procedure. The appoggiatura of the oboe is only approximately a crotchet, being written as a grace-note which may be treated with some freedom, here preferably on the slow side.

Nothing like this had ever been written before, and it is one of the things that cannot be surpassed by anything later. The tempo is, so far as a metronome can measure it, the same in the rhetorical passage as in the abrupt declamations: a good conductor and a good singer will take care that there is no substantial change, otherwise we should only lose the fact that the music is now moving at least

Ex. 2

four times as slowly. In terms of an earlier static music, 'le cri plaintif de la nature' would have been present throughout the whole aria in the form of a more or less florid oboe solo, if the composer happened to be using Gluck's group of instruments. A later composer might have localized 'le cri', putting it once just before the utterance of the words, or oftener, according as he chose to repeat the words. The classical procedure for musical illustration is to put the illustration first and let the words explain it afterwards. This is proof against disappointment, for if the illustration does not seem apt to the listener he will not associate it with the words at all, whereas if the words are put forward first the composer challenges criticism. At the outset Gluck obeys this rule: the audience and Agamemnon himself hear the cry of the oboe before it is identified with 'le cri plaintif de la nature'; but it does not remain a local illustration, though the words are not repeated; nor, on the other hand, does it explain itself away as a decorative scheme. It rises at long but equal intervals for no less than nine steps, to which it adds four more declining over the dominant and establishing it; after which Agamemnon resumes his short protest: 'Je n'obéirai point à cet ordre inhumain', and ends abruptly.

The accompaniment to 'le cri plaintif' consists of repeated quavers in the middle of the harmony, and of pizzicato basses once in two bars alternating with the cry of the oboe and giving rise to faint sustained notes of a bassoon. To the eye of a reader accustomed to enjoy polyphonic scores there is nothing to distinguish the appearance of this page from that of absolute rubbish; but with an experienced ear the score-reader will recognize that the quality of tone in the whole vast expanse is Wagnerian in depth and perfection, and the composition will overawe anybody who can feel the difference between living form and patchwork. The repeated quavers throb with a human emotion which not even our modern experience of the vibrato of the cinema organ can defile; though, as Gluck shows us all modes of instrumental vibration in their original full health, the cinema organ translates them into the now more familiar terms of every disease from which instruments and voices can suffer. The pizzicato notes of the basses, with their faint prolongation in the sighs of the bassoon, have the exact emotional value of sobs.

The whole passage is nevertheless marked by the highest qualities of Greek art and is eminently what is commonly, but misleadingly, called reserved. The term is misleading because it implies that something is withheld. This is not the case: nothing is withheld, but nothing is in excess. The simplicity is Greek, and so is the subtlety. The four last steps about the dominant of C minor are the consummation of architectural and emotional perfection. Their chief point is musical, and it would be far-fetched to find rhetoric or irony in the fact that the last clause of the words is repeated. So far as the voice part is concerned, it is a more remarkable achievement that in the whole passage the words have not been repeated before. It is no part of Gluck's aesthetic system that repetitions of words should be avoided, nor did the poets of the eighteenth century, whether they wrote specially for music or not, expect that their words could be sung without repetitions.

For my other illustration I select the substance of one of Berlioz's letters. The whole of this letter consists of a quotation not quite co-extensive with mine, and commented upon solely by four notes of exclamation. To that admirable comment I will add that this melody shows, as my phrase-numerals indicate, one symptom of Gluck's power of movement and composition in the irregularity and overlapping of its rhythm. The quotation is from *Iphigénie en Tauride*, Act II, No. 17 (Ex. 3 overleaf).

This quotation seems to lose interest as it continues, though the intention to express emotion by high notes and minor chords is manifest. But this is just where short and sketchy quotations of dramatic music become misleading. The very features which here look weak are the signs of a constant increase of power; and even the magnificent first phrase gives little warning of the cumulative effect of the whole composition. Gluck is not only never stiff; the amblers manage to get through their works without manifest signs of rheumatism; but Gluck's movement, his momentum, whether in slow or quick tempo, is always powerful. The accompaniment of this wonderful air is a little more elaborate than that of 'le cri plaintif de la nature', and quite different in effect, though it has in common the throbbing quaver-movement and the deep pizzicato basses, with what one might call harmonics for a couple of horns several octaves higher. The movement is kept up for no less than 112 bars, broken by two pauses only in the last line but three; the singer is Iphigénie, joined towards the end by her fellow-priestesses of Tauris. Note that as in the previous quotation, and in 'Che farò' and the echo songs in the first act of *Orfeo*, Gluck's highest pathos is expressed in the major mode. He uses the minor mode

Ex. 3

chiefly to express protest or energy, and sometimes for picturesqueness or variety with no set purpose at all. The study of Gluck's
most serious melody is a useful method of shaking modern criticism
out of its conventional values.

Both these illustrations are in a slow tempo; an illustration of
Gluck's power of movement in a quicker tempo would need more
room than can be afforded. I must leave, therefore, in a dogmatic
form, the statement that Gluck never fails to convey a sense of
speed when he wishes. In point of fact, there is more of quick than
of slow tempo in his representative works. Young composers used
to be told that slow movements were the acid test of a composer's
power, and that it was there that the young were most liable to fail.
I have never found this to be the case. In the days when that
advice was orthodox, a young composer generally made a fool of
himself over scherzos and showed his best talent when his tempo
was slow. The usual failure of composers at the present day, and
at all times, has been in maintaining a quick movement. Modern
civilization is said to worship pace, but this does not often express
itself effectively in music. You can sleep more easily in a train
going at sixty miles an hour on a good line than in a Bath chair. If
you transcribe a slow movement, changing the notation so that
demisemiquavers are represented by minims and slower notes by
semibreves tied to other notes in due proportion, you will have to
bar it in alla breve bars and call it prestissimo, with semibreves at
208 of the metronome; but it will remain a slow movement in spite
of the notation and the convulsions forced thereby upon the conductor. It is astonishing how few composers show a grasp of this
fact; and I have not yet seen the text-book on composition which
attempts to bring home to the student that if a phrase of given
length be played twice, first in a quick tempo, and secondly in a
tempo four times as slow, the slow rendering will take four times as
long.

I cannot recall any passage in Gluck which does not 'go'; though
there are plenty of passages where inspiration fails him. 'Les
mouvements des monstres' in Armida's garden cannot in the best
of productions be much more awe-inspiring than the usual pantomime dragons, and Gluck's music for them is neither better nor
worse than the music Handel wrote in *Rinaldo* for the same situation, as an accompaniment to those fights between Signor Nicolini
and the lion at which Addison pokes fun in the *Spectator*. But
whether Gluck is moving on a small scale or large, he never breaks

H

down, nor at his dullest or most doctrinaire does his rhythm become stodgy. I have already remarked upon the ineptitude of Gossec's intervention in *Alceste*. It is like hearing a small schoolboy interrupt with his construe a recital by Gilbert Murray. 'These are indeed circumstances in which a man saying "Ah!" would speak correctly.'

Thanks largely to Berlioz, Gluck enjoys a popular fame as one of the pioneers of orchestration. It is a remarkable fact in the style of a composer who really was not a contrapuntist that Gluck's accompaniments, basses, and inner parts are never tiresome, and are almost always beautiful and thrilling in colour. Such qualities they maintain in spite of an often exasperating liability to grammatical mistakes. These, however, are often difficult to correct without removing something essential to the style. A curious case is the grammatical blunder of giving a chorus of female voices the upper fourths of a series of chords of the sixth, leaving the bass to the orchestra, as in the famous Hymn of the Priestesses in *Iphigénie en Tauride*, 'Chaste fille de Latone'. Critics will never agree whether this is a mere error; or whether Gevaert is right in thinking it a trait of genius, showing a scholarly sense of austere primitive Greek music. Both views contain some truth. Gluck never had a scholarly sense of any kind, and his genius was as triumphant as the British Constitution or the Light Brigade in blundering from precedent to precedent. Parry, whose general admiration for Gluck would almost satisfy Berlioz, deplores most of Gluck's choruses, and explains them by saying that in that department he was brought up in a bad school. The bad school was certainly not that of Gluck's Italian apprenticeship, where the choral traditions were excellent; but there is no denying that the choral traditions of the French theatre constituted a thoroughly bad influence. Yet on the whole the truth seems to be on the side of the patriotic French, to whom Gluck's choruses are the *ne plus ultra* of efficiency and point. They ought no doubt to be very bad, but they happen to be for the most part astonishingly good. And before the Furies in *Orfeo* and *Iphigénie en Tauride* criticism becomes silent reverence.

I have purposely selected details from Gluck that have not been made famous in literature. The more famous achievements of Gluck's dramatic rhetoric are neither greater than nor inferior to my illustrations. They are very much finer than the literary description of them manages to indicate, because they would all remain great music if the things they illustrated were removed without trace. They would, of course, suffer from the substitution of things they were manifestly not meant to illustrate; but it is no fair test of music to distract the listener's attention. Hence, no doubt, the failure of Gluck's early pasticcio. But when Orestes says 'le calme rentre dans mon cœur' and the violas belie him with their syncopated monotone:

Ex. 4

the tragic irony is terrible. But the prose writer who can describe this rhetorical point might possibly have conceived it himself without being a greater musician than Rousseau.

My own experience of such interesting details in musical history leads me to have the profoundest distrust of all such descriptions when they are attached to the works of an unknown or neglected composer. This particular passage is a conspicuous item in the architecture of one of Gluck's grandest achievements; and it depends, like all of them, on the elementary fact that, though he could talk about music in a very interesting way, he composed infinitely better than he talked. His instrumentation, primitive though it looks, contains so many strokes of genius that it supplies almost a majority of the quotations in Berlioz's treatise on that art. But here again its isolated points, impressive though they may be in themselves, have a far deeper meaning and effect as manifestations of his general power of composition. His tone-colours owe quite as much of their value to how long they last and at what moment they change as to any intrinsic quality that can impress the mind at once. Gluck summarized his own principles in the famous letter which dedicates the Italian *Alceste* to the Duke of Tuscany. He touches upon the abuses of the old opera, especially the da capo aria which often concludes the da capo where the words do not make sense, and which holds up the action in order to give the singer time to extemporize four different ways of ornamenting the same phrase, &c., &c. But the most important part of his letter is a sentence which has attracted less attention than the rest. He says that the combinations of instruments should be controlled by the passion of the situation.

This is, so far as I am aware, the only statement about instrumentation made in the eighteenth century which shows a consciousness that that art had undergone a total revolution from the aesthetic systems of Bach and Handel. It means two things: first, that the scheme of orchestration was no longer a decorative pattern, uniform and unchangeable for each movement; secondly, though in practical use no visible change was made, it implies the abolition of the continuo, the system by which the domestic service of filling out the harmony in the background was entrusted to a gentleman at the harpsichord or pianoforte, while the instruments of the orchestra proper were free to make their own patterns. One of the many interesting tendencies in modern music is that of groups of musicians who, sometimes in different countries and independently of each other, aspire to return to Bach and to write musical textures in which every note has the necessity of a main or coequal part in a polyphonic design. Some of the modern aspirants to this consummation undoubtedly fail to realize that Bach himself would have been extremely discontented with the tubby thinness of those modern performances of his works that are given by unscholarly purists who make no attempt to produce his continuo, and who do not realize that the harpsichord itself produced by means of octave registers often twice, and sometimes three times, as many notes as those written. Continuo music, and harpsichord music with its faculty of mechanical doublings, made up a very aristocratic art, but had essentially the advantages, if not the disadvantages, of a civilization that relies upon slavery. The stupendous revolution that was accomplished by the art of Haydn and Mozart is not, as some of our neo-classics are inclined to think, a decadence and extravagance, but perhaps the severest and strongest economy that music has yet achieved. It means that the orchestra and the inner parts of all written music perform their own domestic service and are content to use humble formulas (suggestive, if you will, of scrubbing-brushes and pails of water) at any moment, without loss —but on the contrary with much gain—to their dignity. Gluck is far more than a pioneer of opera. He is a pioneer, and a great one, in the whole of that noble musical revolution. Haydn and Mozart seem to have achieved their task in complete independence of Gluck, but it is probable that the enormous impression made by Gluck upon dramatic music contributed more than anybody at the time was aware of to the capacity of the public to appreciate Haydn's and Mozart's purely instrumental art.

The works of Gluck which concern the present discussion are:

I. *Orfeo*, which exists ideally and practically in the grafting of the improvements of the Paris version (without the dislocations) upon the original vocal pitch and key-system of the Italian version. In this form it is perhaps the most perfect and certainly the most moving of all Gluck's works; and the scene in which Orpheus conquers the Furies is one of the supreme achievements in music-drama.

II. *Alceste*, the Italian version of which is prefaced by Gluck's famous manifesto of his principles in the dedicatory letter. The French version is in every respect finer, except for the deplorable loss of Gluck's own climax in the third act. *Alceste* is on a larger scale than *Orfeo* and, as far as mature perfections can be compared, may be said to mark an advance in power of handling musical form in grand proportions.

The libretti of *Orfeo* and *Alceste* are by Calzabigi, as also that of another important work:

III. *Paride et Elena*, of which I have never succeeded in obtaining a full score. Gluck in pianoforte score is not an attractive spectacle to anyone who has once enjoyed the touching vitality of even the most primitive features of his orchestration.

IV. *Iphigénie en Aulide*, written in official rivalry with Piccinni's work on the same subject. This work again shows 'progress', if that is the proper term for increase of range. On the other hand, the doctrinaire has to come to the rescue of the composer when he passes from Calzabigi's unmixed personified emotions to the maternal and priestly conflicts and stratagems of Clytemnestra, Calchas, and the other diplomatists of Racine's stage.

V. *Iphigénie en Tauride*, perhaps one of the most spiritual, as well as one of the most picturesque, works ever put upon the operatic stage.

Both the *Iphigénies* owe something, though not as much as has been supposed, to Racine, whose phrases are sometimes distinctly traceable in *Iphigénie en Aulide*, and whose scenario has been followed in both operas.

VI. *Armide*, derived, like Handel's *Rinaldo* and Sacchini's *Renaud*, from an episode in Tasso's *Gerusalemme Liberata*, is the last of Gluck's great works and the one of which he said that he could wish it to finish his career. The libretto, by Quinault, had been set by Lulli ninety years earlier. With a composer of Gluck's power it was a foregone conclusion that the character and style of Armida would not remain confined to that of an enchantress who produced choruses of birds warbling in a magic garden, like the 'rainbow-dyed sparrows for the opera' which Addison encountered being carried in a large cage down the Haymarket for a rehearsal of Handel's *Rinaldo*. It is not surprising that the critics accused Gluck of giving the enchantress the task of a monotonous and tiresome caterwauling; and Gluck's replies to his critics anticipated the best vitriol of Wagner's prose. Though its subject is best suited neither to Gluck nor to modern taste, *Armide* remains a work which, with pious and tactful production, is very impressive. Gluck's full power is shown in the scene where Armida summons the Spirit of Hate to extirpate from her heart her love of Rinaldo, but her courage fails her and she dismisses the wrathful spirit with her purpose unaccomplished.

After *Armide*, Gluck finished another large work, *Écho et Narcisse*. The title is enough to show that here Gluck is cramped with the limits of prettiness; and this cramping is fatal to him. Under stress of emotion he can be recklessly pretty; or rather, the beauty of his pathetic melodies has an exquisite tenderness which seems to be the inspiring source of every pretty thing that has since been achieved by lyric composers at the height of their powers. But Gluck confined to prettiness is a sad and dried-up creature, and I, who have a sinful appetite for prettiness, have never been able to take a large dose of *Écho et Narcisse*.

Gluck died before he had finished another work, *Les Danaïdes*, which was finished for him by Salieri, if I recollect rightly. Here, again, we may doubt whether the subject could have inspired him.

The five great works, including *Armide*, are manifestly majestic in their scope; and, once we become absorbed in them, all inequalities and faults of style become swept away in the essential grandeur, nobility, and adequacy of the composer's powers.

FRANZ SCHUBERT[1]
(1797–1828)

FRANZ SCHUBERT, the youngest of five survivors of the fourteen children of a parish schoolmaster, was born at Vienna on 31 January 1797, and died there on 19 November 1828. It is not plausible to write optimistically of a life thus cut short before its struggles with poverty have achieved more than moments of present success and remote hopes of future security. And musical biographies are specially intractable material for writers and readers who wish to take a view of life which is neither dismal nor patronizing. The musician is usually quite as sociable as most artists; but his art is more of a mystery to the world at large, even where it is most praised, than any other art; and the biographer finds singularly little help from the musician's contact with other interesting people. In the vast scheme of Goethe's general culture, music had as high a place as a man with no ear for anything but verse could be expected to give it; but the one famous meeting between Beethoven and Goethe reveals nothing except that Goethe disliked Beethoven's manners nearly as much as Lord Chesterfield disliked Johnson's, and that Beethoven more than suspected Goethe of being a snob. Beethoven is easily the most interesting personality in purely musical biography; nor perhaps need he be denied that supremacy even if we regard Wagner as a mere musician. Schubert, Beethoven's junior by seventeen years, was a shy man, and almost every anecdote that is told of him shows him in some pathetic position of failure to make his way.

Let me tell a new one. There is a curious English musical dictionary, published in 1827, which may sometimes be found in the fourpenny box outside a second-hand bookshop; and in this dictionary Beethoven is given one of the largest articles and treated as unquestionably the greatest composer of the day (though on the evidence only of his less dangerous works). Such was Beethoven's fame in the year of his death. Schubert died in the next year. There are five Schuberts in this dictionary, but Franz Schubert is not among them. When I showed this dictionary to Joachim he remarked that it was a pity that there was not a Franz Schubert in it; because as a matter of fact there was another Franz Schubert

---

[1] From *The Heritage of Music*, vol. i (Oxford University Press), 1927.

early in the nineteenth century, whose publisher once wrote to him
enclosing a song that had just been issued by another firm, as being
by Franz Schubert, which, if true, constituted a breach of agreement which the publisher was the less ready to credit since the song
was not only marked as Opus 1, but entirely lacked the smoothness
of Herr Schubert's accomplished and esteemed pen. Herr Schubert replied with some stiffness that he was glad his publisher did
not feel ready to impute to him the authorship of this wretched
production. The '*Machwerk*' in question was Schubert's *Erlkönig*.

From such portents it is easy to infer a tragic picture of neglected
and hopeless genius. But these are accidents, thrown into undue
prominence by the crowning accident of early death from typhus
fever in poor circumstances. Modern sanitation, to say nothing of
modern medicine, has made typhus fever a rare cause of death.
But we are unduly optimistic if we imagine that a musical genius
of Schubert's calibre has a better chance of success before thirty-one
at the present day. When we are invited to show indignation at the
barbarity of an age which made Schubert consent to part with a
dozen of his finest songs at a *krone* apiece, and with his great E flat
Trio for about seventeen shillings and sixpence, we may as well
begin by asking the Carnegie Trustees what their experience shows
them as to the modern composer's opportunities for getting his
works published at all. Schubert's early death during a struggle
with poverty is too sad for us to waste our emotion on details which
indicate, if they indicate anything, that he lived at a period of
exceptional opportunities for young and obscure men of musical
genius. In literary biography a brave standard of tragic and moral
values was established, at all events for English readers, by the
giant who in his own person brought forth the exodus of literature
from Grub Street and gave the death-blow to the system of patronage. Musical biography did not begin to attract the attention of
otherwise cultured people until the dogmas of the Eccentricity of
Genius and the Virtues of the Deserving Poor had brought into our
moral currency a new kind of patronage, equally remote from good
breeding and good science.

Biography is not to the purpose of the present essay; and in any
case a musician's work is, more than that of most artists, far more
important than the events of his life. All the more necessary, then,
is it to dismiss from our minds certain prepossessions which originated at a time when music, not being taken seriously by the educated Englishman, was alternately revered as a religious mystery and

set forth biographically and historically as a charitable investigation in slum-life. If Forster had written his *Life and Times of Goldsmith* on the lines that have determined popular notions of the lives of Beethoven and Schubert, he would have produced one of the dismallest books in the English language. The bare facts of that delightful biography amount to a career far more miserable than the facts about Schubert. Sir George Grove played a distinguished part collecting both the works and the biographical records of Schubert; and his article in the *Dictionary of Music and Musicians* is, with all its indignation at Schubert's fate, such a summary of Schubert's friendships, hopes, interests, and activities as can leave the careful reader no excuse for imagining that the pathos of Schubert's life was the pathos of misery. But Grove's enthusiasm in his researches left him no leisure to realize the need of warning the general reader explicitly against the prevalent dismal tone of early nineteenth-century musical biographies; and in any short biographical survey the heart-rending facts about the deaths of Mozart, Beethoven, and Schubert inevitably dominate the narrative. On the other hand, works on a larger scale, which might restore the balance by a fuller record of the composer's conversation and daily life, find no John-sonian club-records to help them. It is remarkable that within the compass of his dictionary article Grove has achieved an attractive picture of Schubert incessantly composing; the acknowledged tyrant of a host of adoring friends; hopeless and helpless in argument, but the possessor of the glorious nickname of 'Kanevas', since his invariable question about any prospective new acquaintance was, 'Kann er was?' or 'What's he good at?'[1]

On the other hand, Schubert presented an elusive problem to the enlightened and musical Viennese aristocracy that did so well by Beethoven. In Beethoven's republican pride Archdukes could recognize the call of *noblesse oblige* without the need of his superb gesture when (being questioned in the law-courts as to the prefix 'van' in his name) he pointed to his head and heart, saying 'My nobility is *here* and *here*'. But the difficulty with Schubert was that he evidently preferred the servants' hall, where he, the son of a parish schoolmaster and sometime schoolmaster himself, could be at friendly ease with everybody, to the drawing-room of Count Johann Esterhazy at Zselesz, where 'no one cares for true art, unless

---

[1] This, though not a literal translation, is the only idiomatic English I can find for a locution in which 'Können', the ability, is intimately linked with 'Kennen', the knowledge.

now and again the Countess'. It is the more necessary to take warning against indulging in too miserable a view of Schubert's struggle with poverty, since Grove himself is stung by the tragedy of the end into an outburst of anger at Schubert's friends. The anger is not ungenerous, and nobody will wish to minimize the tragedy. But *is* it clear that 'with his astonishing power of production the commonest care would have ensured him a good living'— even in those days when a publisher could actually be found for a setting of the *Erlkönig* with an accompaniment which the finest pianists of to-day cannot master without either long practice or some way of evading its difficulties? The worst of this angry view of Schubert's outward circumstances is that it proceeds from and fosters an unwarrantable optimism as to the conditions of modern musical life. There will never be many Schuberts, even among men of genius; but in all the arts there have been, before and since, and there are now and will be in future, many worse tragedies. The conclusion, then, remains that there is not the slightest reason to hope that, now or in future, a genius of Schubert's calibre will have any better chance of recognition before the age of thirty-one. Even in Utopia there will be room for accidents.

In approaching Schubert's work something has been gained when we have discarded notions that confuse pathos with misery and mischance with culpable neglect. But more serious difficulties await us in the criteria of form and style by which his work has been judged. Here, again, it would be as misleading a paradox to assert that Schubert was a perfect master of musical form as to assert that his career was prosperous; but we have also here to deal with the current errors far more radical and definite than the vague false proportions of a biographic treatment true as to fact, the result of patient research, and mistaken only in the inexperienced emotional tone of a more comfortable phase of life and culture.

Certain criteria of musical form have been fixed with an illusory decision by the extraordinary number and perfection of a series of instrumental compositions by three great masters whose lives overlapped each other, and whose mature works were all produced within the eighty years beginning at the middle of the eighteenth century. No great misunderstanding need have arisen from thus basing our laws of musical form on the works of the Haydn-Mozart-Beethoven triumvirate (as we base the laws of Greek tragedy on what we know of Aeschylus, Sophocles, and Euripides), if it were not for the fact that purely musical phenomena are difficult to describe in any but technical words. The description of a developed musical form is, even with the aid of technical terms, a bulky statement which fills the mind to repletion without giving much real information. When we say that the ground-plan of most cathedrals is cruciform, nobody imagines that the statement is either abstruse or indicative of a large number of conventional rules and restraints on the architect's liberty. Add to it the mention of a spire, dome, or towers, and specify the aisles, and still you will have nothing which anybody supposes to be profoundly technical. Even the orientation of the building raises no question greatly beyond the intelligence of a child who knows his right hand from his left. But these architectural facts already amount to notions fully as definite as all that musical text-books have ever inculcated as to sonata form. If elementary architectural concepts were definable only in mathematical terms, we might over-estimate their artificiality as grossly as we at present over-estimate the rigidity of the art-forms of classical music. But in reality the sense of key-relationship in music is on the same level of thought as the elementary topographical sense that enables us to enjoy the symmetries of architecture. The method and scope change from age to age; an ancient Greek would be even more shocked than an eighteenth-century Englishman of 'classical' taste at the barbarities of Gothic architecture; and Palestrina would, on first acquaintance, find the harmonic banality and coarseness of Mozart and of all classical instrumental music so shocking that he would hardly notice that Beethoven, Schubert, or even Wagner could aggravate or modify the anarchy. Such is the normal first impression of the art of a later period as seen from the point of view of an earlier period. It is thus no question here of 'immutable laws of art'; but it is a question of permanent categories. If these categories are describable only in such untranslated technical terms as *counterpoint* and *tonality*, and if such vernacular words as *harmony*, *rhythm*, and *form* develop technical meanings which are at once narrow and ill-defined, who shall set limits to the possibilities of plausible nonsense in musical history and education?

Schubert's masters at the *Convict*, or court-chapel choir-school, have been severely blamed for neglecting his education and allowing him to compose without restraint. One of these masters left on record the honest remark that when he tried to teach Schubert anything, he found the boy knew it already. It is evidently dangerous to leave such remarks lying about where the directors of later institutes of musical education can get at them. But we are not justified in inferring that the master really taught Schubert nothing. And there is abundant evidence that the child taught himself with remarkable concentration, if not with severity. One of the most trying tasks ever imposed on a young musician is that still recommended by some very high authorities, which consists of composing an instrumental movement that follows, phrase by phrase, the proportions and modulations of a selected classical model. It might be objected to this exercise that it is unlikely to reveal the inner necessity of the original form of a purely instrumental piece; but this objection would lose force if the exercise were ever applied to vocal, and especially to dramatic, music, with its cogent outward necessities. Now the earliest song of Schubert that we possess is *Hagar's Klage*, an enormous rigmarole with at least twelve movements and innumerable changes of key; evidently (one would guess) a typical example of childish diffuseness. It turns out, however, to be accurately modelled, modulations and all, on a setting of the same poem by Zumsteeg, a composer of some historical importance as a pioneer in the art of setting dramatic narrative for voice with pianoforte accompaniment. The same is the case with several other songs; and Mandyczewski has printed three of Zumsteeg's original settings in his complete edition of Schubert's songs, so that we can see how this child of thirteen was spending his time. Zumsteeg, by the way, was no fool. Yet even within the limits of *Hagar's Klage* Schubert makes decisive progress, beginning by following his model closely until about the middle of the work. At this point Zumsteeg's energy begins to flag, and the child's energy begins to rise. Schubert's declamation improves, and before he has finished his long task he has achieved a sense of climax and a rounding-off which Zumsteeg hardly seems to have imagined possible. Song-writing, whether on a large or a small scale, was still in its infancy. A few masterpieces appear sporadically among the experiments, themselves few and heterogeneous, of Haydn, Mozart, and Beethoven. The real development of the art-forms of song was worked out by the child Schubert with the same fierce concentration as that with which the child Mozart laid the foundations of his sonata forms.

Within four years from this first attempt to 'play the sedulous ape', Schubert had written three stout volumes of songs of all shapes and sizes, besides a still larger quantity of instrumental music. A professional copyist might wonder how the bulk was achieved by one penman within the time. And as the songs lead up to and include *Gretchen am Spinnrade* and *Erlkönig*, it seems futile to blame Schubert's teachers for not teaching him more before he was seventeen. The maturity of this famous couple of masterpieces remains as miraculous when we know the mass of work by which the boy trained himself for them as when we know them only in isolation. *Gretchen am Spinnrade*, the earlier of the two, is an even more astonishing achievement than *Erlkönig*. There is no difficulty in understanding how the possibilities of *Erlkönig* would fire the imagination of any boy, though only a genius could control to artistic form the imagination thus fired. Schubert's *Erlkönig* is as eminently a masterpiece in musical form as in powerful illustration of the poem. It has the singular luck to be rivalled, and to some tastes surpassed, by Loewe's setting, a work not much later in date but more in touch with modern methods. Loewe brings out the rationalistic vein of Goethe's ballad by setting the Erl-king's words to a mere ghostly bugle-call which never leaves the notes of its one chord. Schubert uses melodies as pretty as the Erl-king's promises. In other words, Loewe's point of view is that of the father assuring the fever-stricken child that the Erl-king, with his daughter and his whisperings, is nothing but the marsh-mists and the wind in the trees; while Schubert, like the child, remains unconvinced by the explanation. His terror is the child's; Loewe's terror is the father's. Schubert has already, at the age of seventeen, mastered one of his cardinal principles of song-writing, which is that wherever some permanent feature can be found in the background of the poem, that feature shall dominate the background of the music. The result is that, after all, he naïvely achieves a more complete setting of the poem with his purely musical apparatus than Loewe with his rational adroitness. Loewe has almost forgotten that the father, with his child in his arms, is riding at full gallop in the hope of reaching shelter before the marsh-fever takes its toll. Schubert, composing, like Homer, 'with his eye on the object', represents the outward and visible situation by means of an 'accompaniment' the adequate performance of which is one of the rarest *tours de force* in pianoforte-playing. (Liszt's transcription of *Erlkönig* as a concert-solo is far easier, for the added fireworks give relief to the player's wrists.) But Schubert's accompaniment also realizes the inward and spiritual situation. With the Erl-king's speeches the accompaniment, while still maintaining its pace, takes forms which instantly transfer the sense of movement from that of a thing seen by the spectator to that of the dazed and frightened child in the rider's arms. To some critics this may seem a small point; but it is decisive, not of the superiority of one version over the other, but of the completeness of Schubert's view. Against it all cavil at the 'prettiness' of the Erl-king's melodies is as futile as a cavil against the prettiness of the Erl-king's words. Schubert at seventeen is a mature master of the ironies of tragedy and of nature. He is also a better realist than Loewe. The change in the point of view at the Erl-king's speeches is a matter of fact; nobody but the child heard them, and only the father or the narrator could have recognized that they had no more substance than can be musically represented by Loewe's chord of G major. This does not dispose of Loewe's achievement as a work of genius on lines inadequately recognized until recent times; but it shows the futility of attacking a great composer like Schubert on the *a priori* assumption that the declamation and illustration of words is at variance with the claims of purely musical form. When we have got rid of this assumption we shall be in a better position to see the true origins of the classical forms of music, and, incidentally, to follow the methods by which Schubert provided himself with a musical education.

Gretchen am Spinnrade is a far more astonishing achievement for a boy of seventeen than *Erlkönig*. If, for the sake of argument, we summon up the naïve impertinence to ask where this shy choir-boy, absorbed incessantly in writing and only just out of school, could have obtained the experience, not of Faust, but of the victim of Faust and Mephistopheles, the answer is not easily guessed; for *Faust*, though published, had not yet been presented on the stage. But plenty of good drama was cultivated in Viennese theatres, and we need not suppose that Schubert avoided it. He kept then his eye on the object, in this case the spinning-wheel. And he knew, as Parry has admirably pointed out in *The Art of Music*, not only that the climax comes at the words 'Und ach! sein Kuss!' but that with that climax the spinning is interrupted, and resumed only with difficulty. With these points settled, all that remains to be postulated is the possession of a noble and totally unsophisticated style, together with some individual power of modulation to secure variety in simplicity throughout a song which is too dramatic to be set to repetitions of a single strophic melody. The style Schubert already had; the individual power of modulation shows itself at the third line of the poem. Before Schubert, only Beethoven would have thought of moving from D minor to C major and straight back again without treating C as the dominant of F. This modulation is here entirely Schubert's own, for the influence of Beethoven on Schubert had not at this time produced in him any direct result beyond a decided opinion that Beethoven was responsible for the 'bizarrerie' of most contemporary music. Beethoven and Schubert were, in fact, developing the resources of key-relationship on identical principles; but this fact is not one that ever appears in the guise of any external points of their styles. Schubert's idolatry at this time was devoted to Mozart; and in the art-forms of song there was even less room for Mozart's style than for Beethoven's. With the forms of opera and of instrumental music the position was very different; and, now that we have illustrated Schubert's amazing early maturity in the pioneer work of the song with pianoforte accompaniment, it is time to direct our attention to his work in other and older art-forms.

If one half of the six hundred-odd songs of Schubert's whole life's work are to be regarded as waste products, then Schubert, as a song-writer, must rank as an economical and concentrated artist. To estimate the wastage as high as one half is the limit of severity. By this I do not mean to imply that three hundred of Schubert's songs are masterpieces. In all such matters the fruitful criterion is not perfection but intrinsic significance; and certainly at least three hundred of Schubert's songs have intrinsic significance. Most of the waste products have, on the other hand, historic significance, as we have seen in the case of *Hagar's Klage*. What, then, is the position of the equally vast bulk of Schubert's juvenile work in larger and older forms?

Here, if anywhere, we may suspect, as Schubert's contemporaries already complained, that Schubert would have been the better for a firmer guiding hand. But it is no easy matter to name anybody who could have done better for Schubert than his adoring and bewildered masters at the *Convict*. It is a great mistake to suppose that any master living in 1810 could teach a young composer of instrumental music the genuine art-forms of Haydn and Mozart. There was Beethoven, who was enormously expanding and apparently revolutionizing those forms; there was Mozart's best pupil Hummel, who was inflating certain safe and imitable procedures of Mozart's by means of a pianoforte technique far too brilliant for anything those procedures had in purpose; and there was Spohr, who was doing much the same thing far better than Hummel by means of a really beautiful violin technique as yet unspoilt by his cloying later mannerisms. These were, to all appearance, the great masters in such forms; and they are, in fact, almost the only names prominent enough for modern criticism to scoff at. The great Cherubini was totally outside the classical tradition of instrumental music; Clementi had already retired to London in 1810, and was probably remembered in Vienna mainly by the hard brilliance of his technique in the days of his 'tournament' with Mozart in 1781. On what lines were the art-forms of instrumental music taught in Schubert's boyhood? I have never seen this question asked, and do not expect to see it answered. All I know is that to this day it would be invidious to specify the few text-books on these forms that do not consist mainly of platitudes deviating only into such misstatements as must make the book demoralizing to any observant child who tries to learn from it. In Schubert's day there was certainly no more a received method of teaching the art-forms of Mozart than there is to-day a received method of teaching those of Wagner and Richard Strauss. The only item of musical education which Beethoven's teacher, Albrechtsberger, called 'composition' was what is now called 'counterpoint'; it was not as yet in the shocking tangle of arbitrary and unenlightened rule-of-thumb to which it degenerated during the later nineteenth century; but it was already dangerously remote from its original living sixteenth-century practice, no less than from the art-language of instrumental music. Sir George Grove is very angry with one of Schubert's older friends for encouraging his larger efforts when 'he had better have taught him some counterpoint'. Later on, Grove very rightly draws attention to the magnificence of Schubert's basses. That settles the question: a composer whose basses are magnificent is a great contrapuntist, even if (like Wagner) he never published a fugue in his life. Nor is the case weakened by Schubert's producing some obviously unsuccessful fugues towards the end of his short career; and still less is it weakened by the fact of the awakening which the reading of the works of Handel effected in him, and the resulting determination to go through a course of counterpoint with Sechter, a project frustrated by Schubert's own untimely death. The grammatical exercise nowadays called counterpoint contributes nothing beyond brick-making towards the architecture of a fugue; and the text-book rules of fugue as an art-form are usually based on a scheme, best known in the form drawn up by Cherubini in his text-book, which completely ignores both Handel (who has, in fact, no scheme that could be generalized) and Bach, whose last work, *Die Kunst der Fuge*, was a series of scientifically classified fugues. Doubtless in Schubert's days at the *Convict* 'counterpoint' was among the things which his honest teachers 'found he knew already'. From Sechter he hoped to get something very different from a belated filling-up of gaps in his primary schooling. Sechter was a researching scholar who knew his sixteenth century. Even Beethoven was attracted by him, long after he had, for somewhat similar reasons, left Haydn for the more painstaking and systematic Albrechtsberger, who, being neither a genius nor sympathetic to Beethoven, nevertheless knew how to explain matters of scholarship. It may surprise some readers to know that within living memory Brahms, whose early works already show him to be easily the greatest contrapuntist since Mozart, took keen pleasure, after he was fifty, in working at counterpoint with Nottebohm, the scholar to whom we owe the deciphering of Beethoven's sketch-books. Real scholarship will always attract men of genius; but it is almost as rare as genius itself. The sanity of true genius may, as often as not, rightly revolt against tradition; but there is no revolting against knowledge.

Now, just as Schubert's juvenile work in song-writing culminates at seventeen in *Gretchen am Spinnrade* and *Erlkönig*, so does the equally huge pile of work in larger forms culminate, at the same age, in the Mass in F. The doyen of English theorists, the late Ebenezer Prout, has called this work the most remarkable first mass next to the first mass of Beethoven; thereby paying a pious tribute to the greatest of musical names; for the most remarkable thing about Beethoven's first mass is that Beethoven, entering on the full swing of his 'second period', should have spared the energy to finish a work which contains hardly a feature that expresses anything but inhibitions. Schubert's first mass is, in its way, a not less astonishing phenomenon than *Erlkönig*; and it is far more perfect in form, and even in style, than the ambitious efforts of his later years, the Masses in A flat and E flat. Prout quotes one of the fugues *in extenso*, and dubs it a very creditable performance, open to no criticism except that the voices are too low at the opening. I am not acquainted with any models Schubert can have had for the very definite style of church music he here achieves. Possibly he had heard a mass or two by Cherubini, whom Beethoven considered the greatest composer of the age, who visited Vienna in the train of Napoleon, and whose church music is the only first-rate work of

I

the period that shows the faintest resemblance to the peculiar fragrant piety of Schubert's masses. There is nothing remotely like it in the church music of either Mozart or Haydn. The triumphant performance of this important choral and orchestral work by the choir of Schubert's school was an experience such as very few modern conservatoire students can obtain at the age of seventeen. A year afterwards Schubert wrote a more 'effective' *Dona Nobis* in the form of a vigorous final fugue. In the same way English Doctors of Music have been known to spoil a poetically conceived oratorio or cantata by a final fugue, in order to satisfy the examiners. In the critical edition of Schubert's complete works this second *Dona Nobis* is rightly relegated to the appendix.

We must return to Schubert's masses later. Some readers may be surprised to hear that the next topic that concerns us with Schubert at seventeen is his operas. His first, *Des Teufels Lustschloss*, is historically more important than appearances might indicate. The libretto seems hopelessly silly, but it stands under the name of Kotzebue, who was a writer of quite clever comedies which Jane Austen would have enjoyed; and its idea is traceable back to *The Castle of Otranto*, much as parts of *Northanger Abbey* are traceable to *The Mysteries of Udolpho*. Kotzebue, however, has here failed to show any of his sense of humour, and Schubert never attempted burlesque; his slightly later imitations of Rossini (the overtures 'in Italian style') developing into sincere flattery rather than caricature. But the interesting thing about the music of *Des Teufels Lustschloss*, apart from one or two successful passages, is that the young Schubert took the trouble to revise it and to go to Salieri for lessons in Italian operatic style and method. Herein he followed the example of Beethoven, who had gone to Salieri for the same purpose some twenty years earlier, and who, while grumbling that Haydn had taught him nothing, took pride and pleasure in calling himself Salieri's pupil. No view of either Beethoven's or Schubert's development can be trustworthy which fails to account for the zest with which these mighty men of genius put themselves into Salieri's hands. Salieri had the misfortune to have shown jealousy of Mozart; and it seems certain that at a time when a word from him to the Emperor might have improved Mozart's position, Salieri not only missed the opportunity but intrigued against him. Be this as it may, his retribution was appalling. Mozart died young and in straitened circumstances, and gossip said that Salieri had poisoned him. This was a wild slander; but even within living memory

Rimsky-Korsakov wrote an opera, *Mozart and Salieri*, which I do not know except in very charming quotations, but which only the vainest of hopes could expect to deal with anything so dramatically ineffective as a refutation of the slander. On Salieri himself the slander must have weighed cruelly; for when he was dying he sent for Moscheles in order to say these words—'I did not poison Mozart.' So even the friendship of Beethoven and Schubert, both of whom must have heard and contemptuously ignored this inhuman gossip, did not avail to bring peace to the old man's mind. Now, what was it that Salieri could teach these great composers? Here the significant point in Salieri's history is that when Gluck, at the end of his life, found himself unable to carry out his last project, an opera entitled *Les Danaïdes*, he handed the task over to Salieri. This proves that he could trust Salieri to set dramatic situations as well as words. And the reader may verify this without taking the trouble to investigate Salieri's own work further than by playing the theme of one of the best of Beethoven's early sets of variations, those upon 'La stessa, la stessissima', from Salieri's *Falstaff*. Any opera on the subject of Falstaff must take its plot from *The Merry Wives of Windsor*; for no coherent story can be made from the genuine Falstaff of the two parts of *King Henry the Fourth*, though it may be possible to transfer his best speeches to the perfunctory dupe of the merry wives, as we may learn from Boito and Verdi. Now, the first situation in *The Merry Wives of Windsor* is the meeting of Mrs. Ford and Mrs. Page after they have received identical love-letters from Falstaff. 'La stessa, la stessissima'— here you see them comparing notes ('the same, the very same!') in Salieri's theme as recorded in simple pianoforte terms by Beethoven. You can see them pointing from one letter to the other in symmetrical phrases; and in the disruption of symmetry with the truncated second part of the tune you can identify the burst of laughter, the quick scolding phrase in which vengeance is vowed, and the derisive triumphant gesture with which the letters are flourished in the air. You can see also that though Salieri shows no profound musical invention in this trivial affair, he is no formalist. To Beethoven and Schubert it was unimportant that Salieri was jealous of the brilliance of Mozart and warned his pupils against the poetry of Goethe. In these high matters they could take care of themselves; Salieri was neither a preoccupied man of genius nor a pedant, but a clever and highly cultured Italian musician with the will and the power to give practical and interesting information.

The fruit of Salieri's teaching is clearly shown in Schubert's early operas. The outward course of events is that the operatic stage had a fascination for Schubert, which grew in proportion to the disappointments it brought on him. As his talent for work on a large scale matured, so did his grasp of dramatic movement in theatre-music weaken, and the only operas which it has recently been found possible to rescue from the wreckage of his fourteen efforts in this art-form are the one-act *Der Vierjährige Posten*, written soon after the Mass in F, and *Die Verschworenen*, written in 1820 and showing how he applied his riper musical style to the technique of Salieri. We must return to the operas and their grave defects later; at present our concern is to note that while Schubert's whole development and the mightiest influences of his time drew him steadily and fatally away from the solution of the problem of dramatic movement in stage-music, he had nevertheless as a mere boy eagerly and successfully learnt from Salieri an admirable light theatrical style; a thing totally different from the style of his songs. He could not set an action to music; but he could set a dialogue. His own contemporaries said of him that he could set an advertisement to music; and the statement has a higher truth than the implication that words did not matter to him. It means that he had exhaustively mastered the inwardness of musical symbolism; and Salieri was the last teacher of the great Italian tradition that had steadily viewed music from that centre ever since the time of Palestrina and earlier. Pseudo-classicism, opposing itself to helpless experiment and *a priori* theory, occupied the whole field of musical education as soon as teachers formed the futile ambition to teach 'composition' in larger and more abstract senses than that of musical rhetoric.

Schubert's boyhood, then, culminated in two of his most powerful songs, a uniquely charming piece of church music, and an almost equally pretty one-act opera (*Der Vierjährige Posten*). In his early instrumental music there is nothing so important, though the quantity is not less enormous. The earliest pieces, including the earliest string quartets, are fantasies of such ubiquitous rambling that the catalogue-maker cannot specify their keys. Some of them may possibly be regarded as Zumsteeg ballads without words; but why should we allow the young Schubert no child's-play at all? Music paper was always as necessary to him as food and coals; the *Convict* afforded very insufficient supplies of all three. The mastery he so early attained in vocal music already stultifies all aspersions on his early training; and his early instrumental works do not alter the case. We are right in thinking that his maturest works in large instrumental forms are diffuse and inconsistent; but, apart from the earliest child's-play, the quartets and symphonies of his adolescence show, as often as not, the opposite tendency, being for the most part stiff exercises in the outward forms of Mozart with a certain boyish charm of hero-worship in their melodies. The stiffness is anything but Mozartean; it is, in fact, the typical angularity of a conscientious student. Six symphonies, about a dozen string quartets, another dozen of pianoforte sonatas, and a vast number of fragments, show him pursuing a consistent line of work, of observation and experiment; if with ideas in his head, then so much the better for the result; if without, then so much the better for the practice. It is quite a mistake to suppose that any contemporary master could have pointed out to Schubert where he went wrong. Beethoven himself, in whom Schubert's work aroused a lively interest which would assuredly have led to historic consequences if both composers had lived a few years longer, made no criticisms on points of form, though he had before him some of the larger works, on which he could and would, with time for reflection, have spoken out of the fullness of his own experience. At all events Schubert's instrumental music did not begin to go definitely 'wrong' until it began to be as definitely and prophetically right as his best songs. There is nothing of first-rate importance to mention here until we reach the work of his last nine years of life. Our discussion up to this point has aimed at removing certain grave current misconceptions and substituting for them a more reasoned account of Schubert's early development. The ground being thus cleared, we need not attempt any chronological or otherwise systematic account of the rest of Schubert's works; it will suffice to quote, for the most part from well-known masterpieces, such points as illustrate the full range of his musical thought up to the time of his death.

The first instrumental work which shows his peculiar power beginning to rise up against his greatest weakness of form is the ambitious Quintet in A major for the unusual combination of pianoforte, violin, viola, violoncello, and double-bass. It is known as the *Forellen-quintett* because the fourth of its five movements (the most perfect, though not the most important) is a set of variations on his pretty song *Die Forelle* ('The Trout'). The scherzo is another successful movement in one of those small melodic and sectional forms which nobody denies to be thoroughly within Schubert's grasp. But the important things are the first movement, the slow movement in F, and the finale. In all three cases the first half of the movement is the boldly drawn exposition of a design on the grandest scale, while the rest, with the exception of a well-managed modicum of development in the first movement, is a mere exact recapitulation of this exposition starting in such a key as to end in the tonic. In the first movement and in the finale Schubert adds insult to the crudity of this procedure by giving the usual direction that the exposition shall be repeated!

Now, the sonata forms, which are here in question, depend largely on the balance and distinction between three typical organic members; an exposition, a development, and a recapitulation. Of these, the most delicate is the recapitulation, on which the symmetry of the whole depends. In works like the *Forellen-quintett* Schubert was exhausted by the effort of his grand expositions and fell back with relief upon a mere copyist's task by way of recapitulation. This was wrong; but the *a priori* theorist is not less wrong who regards extensive recapitulation as a weakness in the classical schemes. There is no surer touchstone of Schubert's, as of Mozart's, Beethoven's, and Brahms's, treatment of form than the precise way in which their recapitulations differ from their expositions; and where Schubert is at the height of his power this difference is of classical accuracy and subtlety. Technicalities may be avoided by means of the following generalization. Whenever a composer with a true sense of form conceives anything in the nature of exposition he inevitably conceives therewith some notion of its possible effect in returning after other matters or in the course of recapitulation. The question of its return or recapitulation, whether finally answered positively or negatively, is inherent in the original idea. In the simplest typical case we may imagine the composer thinking, 'How splendid this will sound when it sails in again at another pitch and at home in the tonic!' This simple notion may become too familiar for the composer to notice it, but it will guide him even in the extreme case where an exact recapitulation is all that is required. This case actually occurs in genuine works, and is there as much the result of subtle balance as in the cases of utmost variation. Whether in exact repetition or in free variation, the true conception of this musical symmetry is thus essentially dramatic, and has nothing in common either with such effrontery as the fold-up forms of Schubert's *Forellen-quintett* or with arbitrary short cuts and divergences, attempted for the sake of variety with no clear

conviction that if the later statements are right the original statements were not wrong or superfluous. Now when Schubert is at
the height of his power in large forms we may know it by the
returns to his main themes. Two great movements notorious for
their redundancies and diffuseness are the first movement of the
String Quartet in G major and the first movement of the Pianoforte Sonata in B flat, Schubert's last composition in this form. In
both of them the whole interest converges upon the return to what is
called the 'first subject', involving the return to the main key after
the wanderings of a long and dramatic development. The method
of that return is entirely different in the two cases; both passages
may rank with the most sublime inspirations of Beethoven. In the
G major Quartet the return has an overpowering pathos, which is
the more surprising since the tone of the whole movement, though
at the acme of romance and picturesqueness, is by no means tragic.
Yet this passage is the most 'inevitable' as well as the most unexpected part of the whole design. The original first subject began
with a soft major chord which swelled out and exploded in an
energetic phrase in the minor key. The next phrase repeated this
event on the dominant. In the return, which is long expected, the
soft tonic chord is minor, and the energetic phrase is calm and in
the major key. The subsequent theme is not less wonderfully transferred in another way. In the B flat Sonata the return is more
subtle. The whole movement, as in the case of the G major Quartet, runs a course not unusual in Schubert's large designs; opening
with a sublime theme of the utmost calmness and breadth; descending, by means of a good though abrupt dramatic stroke, from the
sublime to the picturesque, and then drifting from the picturesque
through prettiness to a garrulous frivolity. But then comes medita-
tion. The frivolous theme itself begins to gather energy in the
course of the development. It originates a dramatic passage which
begins picturesquely and rises from the picturesque to the sublime.
When the calm has become ethereal a distant thunder is heard.
That thunder had been twice heard during the opening of the
movement. At present the key (D minor) is not far from the tonic.
The main theme appears softly at a high pitch, harmonized in this
neighbouring key. The distant thunder rolls again, and the harmony glides into the tonic. The theme now appears, still higher,
in the tonic. An ordinary artist would use this as the real return
and think himself clever. But Schubert's distant thunder rolls yet
again, and the harmony relapses into D minor. The tonic will have

no real weight at such a juncture until it has been adequately prepared by its dominant. The theme is resumed in D minor; the
harmony takes the necessary direction, and expectancy is now
aroused and kept duly excited, for a return to the first subject in
full. Accordingly this return is one in which transformations would
be out of place; and so Schubert's recapitulation of his first subject
is unvaried until the peculiarities of his transition themes compel
the modulations to take a new course.

At the risk of entering into further technicalities, we must now
consider Schubert's dealings with what the idiotic terminology of
sonata form calls the 'second subject'. The grounds for this term
appear to be that there are no rules whatever to determine how
many themes a sonata exposition shall contain, nor how its themes
shall be distributed; but that whatever is contained in or about the
tonic key, from the outset to the first decisive change of key, shall
be called the first subject, and that whatever is contained from that
decisive change of key to the end of the exposition shall be called
the second subject. The material that effects the decisive change of
key will obviously be called the transition. But as for what and
where the different themes are, Haydn may run a whole exposition
on one theme, Mozart may reserve one of his best themes for the
development, and Beethoven may have one-and-a-half themes in
his first subject, a very definite new theme for his transition, five-
and-a-half themes in his second subject, and still a new one in the
course of his development. And in all three composers you will
have no reason to expect any two works to be alike; and all three
composers may adopt each other's procedures.

The real fixed points in the matter are: that there is at the outset
a mass of material clearly establishing the tonic key; that there then
follows a decisive transition to another key; and that in that other
key another mass of material completes the exposition. In any case,
the exposition asserts its keys in order to maintain them.

Schubert's first subjects are generally of magnificent breadth,
and the length of his big movements is not actually greater than
their openings imply. If Beethoven had to set to work from any
one of Schubert's finest openings two things are certain: that he
would have produced quite as long a movement, and that its
materials would have been very differently distributed, especially as
regards the continuation of the second subject. Up to that point
all is well with Schubert (the present summary is no occasion to
specify the exception that might be cited). His transition is usually

an abrupt and sometimes primitive dramatic stroke; whereas with
Mozart it is, when not merely formal, an occasion of magnificent
musical draughtsmanship such as Schubert achieved for another
purpose in the passage in the B flat Sonata which we have just
discussed. Schubert, in avoiding the problems of such draughtsmanship, is only doing as Beethoven often did in his best early
works; for Beethoven, too, found it easier to be either clever or
abrupt at this juncture than to achieve Mozart's calm breadth of
transition, until his own style and scale of form had passed altogether beyond Mozart's horizon. Meanwhile, why should he or
Schubert reject more startling methods which perfectly suit the
circumstances of their early works (for Schubert did not know that
his early works were going to be his last)? An author is perfectly
justified in simply saying, 'Then a strange thing happened', on two
conditions: first, that what happens is really strange; secondly, that
the strange event is not a mere device of the author to get out of
a difficulty.

Schubert's strange event is usually the beginning of his second
subject in a quite unexpected key, remote from that in which it is
going to continue. The masterly examples are to be found in the
following first movements: the great String Quintet in C; the Symphony in C; the E flat Trio; the 'Grand Duo' for pianoforte *à
quatre mains*; and, once more, the Sonata in B flat. This last case
is on the border-line; but the device is a true art-form, widely
different from the things in Beethoven which may have suggested
it (see Beethoven's Sonatas, op. 10, no. 3, and op. 28); and Schubert's ways of bringing the unexpected key round to the orthodox
one are thoroughly masterly. The trouble begins after this problem
is solved. Then Schubert, feeling that the rest of his exposition
must not be less spacious than its enormous opening, fills up most
of what he guesses to be the required interval with a vigorous discussion of the matter already in hand. Even if the discussion does
not lead him too far afield, it inevitably tends to obliterate the vital
distinction between exposition and development, a distinction universal in the arts (at least, in all those that have time as one of their
dimensions) quite irrespective of their names and shapes. The
cruellest irony in this situation is that Schubert, whether he knew
it or not, is only following or anticipating the advice so constantly
given nowadays to orthodox young composers 'to stick to the main
themes and not dissipate energy on a multitude of new ones'.
Schubert is commonly cited as the awful example of such dissipa-

tion, which is supposed to lead to the bottomless pit of Liszt's symphonic poems. But these nefarious works are, in point of fact, fanatical efforts to evolve a new kind of music out of transformations of a single musical germ. And the first and greatest of symphonic poems on Liszt's principles happens to be Schubert's *Wanderer-Phantasie*, a masterpiece of independent form which the *Lisztianer* were desperately anxious to explain away.

The real classical procedure with the continuation of a big second subject, the procedure of Mozart and Beethoven, is to produce a series of new sentences, all conspicuously shorter than the main themes but not less sharply contrasted in length and shape among themselves. If the key of the second subject is not remote, one of these themes will probably have a strong admixture of a remote key within its own single phrase. This instantly serves all the purpose of Schubert's widest digressions. I have here sometimes called these items 'themes', and sometimes 'sentences'. It does not matter a pin whether they are new themes or old; what matters is that they have the manner of exposition and not of development. They are epigrams, not discussions. That is why they make paragraphs that will bear recapitulation in the later stages of the movement, while Schubert's expositions will not, though there is no other means of dealing with them. Schubert himself achieves the right kind of paragraph to perfection in the unique case of the 'Unfinished' Symphony; the very case which is most often quoted against him as illustrating his besetting sin of 'vain repetitions', because its admirably terse and rhythmically uneven phrases persistently recur to the same theme. But Haydn, Mozart, and Beethoven would have recognized that Schubert had in this case grasped the secret of their own technique.

So far, then, we already see that it is no mechanical matter to sift 'right' and 'wrong' from Schubert's instrumental forms, even with the earlier great masters to guide us. But when we find (as, for instance, in the first movement of the great C major Symphony) that some of the most obviously wrong digressions contain the profoundest, most beautiful, and most inevitable passages, then it is time to suspect that Schubert, like other great classics, is pressing his way towards new forms. In any case, where a work of art, or a human being, has ubiquitous great quantities together with a manifest lack of unity, there may be great difficulty (and, perhaps, small profit) in determining which of its conflicting personalities is the more real. If the progress is (as we have seen in the Sonata in

B flat) from the sublime to the garrulous, we shall naturally appeal from Schubert garrulous to Schubert sublime; but in the C major Symphony the whole tone is sublime, and nowhere more so than in the grotesque finale which fell on a blind spot in Bülow's sense of values. It is impossible in a summary non-technical statement to demonstrate what were the new forms towards which Schubert was tending; and the mechanical triviality of the accepted doctrines of sonata form makes even a detailed technical demonstration more difficult than work on an unexplored subject. I must therefore beg permission to leave this matter with the dogmatic statement that the fruition of Schubert's new instrumental forms is to be found in Brahms, especially in the group of works culminating in the Piano-forte Quintet, op. 34. Whoever has once begun to notice the profound influence of Schubert on these undisputed masterpieces, and especially on this quintet, the ripest and weightiest of the group, will be surprised at the blindness which, following the lead of Hanslick, ascribes Brahms's forms mainly to the direct influence of the last quartets of Beethoven. Of course, the influence of the later works of Beethoven is just as clearly there as the influence of Schumann is definitely not there. Schumann's interest in Brahms would have been but tepid if what Schumann saw in him had not been the very powers he felt to be lacking in his own work. These powers are characteristic of the instrumental art-forms of Haydn, Mozart, and Beethoven; and they determine the fitness of a certain range of musical thought to be cast in sonata forms, and, conversely, the fitness of sonata forms to deal with that range, or to adapt themselves to a more extended range of musical thought. Schumann soon felt a lack of these special powers, and, being a very clever man, created for his larger works a kind of mosaic style, in which he imitates sonata forms only in so far as mosaics imitate pictures. He thus creates a province for himself, and must be understood on his own terms. But Schubert's larger works belong to the main stream of musical history; their weaknesses are relaxations of their powers, and Schubert has no devices (unless we count the absurdities of the *Forellen-quintett*) for turning them into an artificial method with a point of its own. Hence it is as easy for a later master in the main stream of musical thought to absorb and develop the essentials of Schubert's ideas as it is for a poet similarly situated to absorb the essentials of Shakespeare's. Neither Shakespeare nor Schubert will ever be understood by any critic or artist who regards their weaknesses and inequalities as proof that they are artists of less than the highest rank. Even if a great artist can be 'written down by himself', one work of art cannot be written down by another; and even if the artist produces no single work without flaws, yet the highest qualities attained in important parts of a great work are as indestructible by weaknesses elsewhere as if the weaknesses were the accidents of physical ruin. I see no reason to conclude that Shakespeare had at the age of thirty-one attained either a greater mastery or a wider range than Schubert. Up to that point it seems clear to me that Shakespeare, Schubert, and Keats are artists not unlike in achievement and calibre.

Other elements in Schubert's sonata forms are in much the same condition as his expositions; a condition in which weakness in the actual context is often indistinguishable from new power in some future art. The part of a sonata movement known specially as the development is, of course, already at an almost hopeless disadvantage in Schubert because his exposition will have already digressed into developments of its own. But nothing could be wider of the mark than the orthodox statement that Schubert is weak in this part of his form. His best developments are in themselves magnificent; but he has in some four or five cases committed an indiscretion which is a characteristically youthful result of the impression made upon him by the first movement of Beethoven's 'Eroica' Symphony, the development of which produces a brilliant cumulative effect in its earlier stages by reproducing its first topic in another key after an energetic different line of argument has been worked out. This procedure Beethoven handles so tersely as to give a feeling of enormous breadth to a development elsewhere crowded with other matters; but when Schubert decides to resume his first topic in this manner, he has no room for much beyond a plain transposed reproduction of the two pages of argument it has already cost him. After thus repeating his argument he generally has in store some stroke of genius by which its end shall bring about a beautiful return to the tonic; and the most primitive of Schubert's developments is more highly organized than that of the first movement of Schumann's Quintet, in which Schubert's simplest plan is very successfully carried out in terms not so much of a mosaic as of a Dutch-tile fireplace. In this case it is so clear that to doubt Schumann's success is merely to question the whole postulate of his quintet, that we have here an interesting proof how much safer it is to yield to temptation when working on an obviously artificial basis than when working on highly organic lines. The most notorious of Schubert's developments is that in the first movement of the E flat Trio; where he goes over his argument, itself a cumulative slow crescendo, three times. When the third statement begins, its effect is, at the moment, disastrous, but it leads grandly enough to the return to the main theme in the tonic; and thus even here what is wrong is not the scheme in itself, but the impossible scale on which it is worked. In the first movement of the C major String Quintet, where the process consists of twice two stages, the one lyric and the other (on the same theme) energetic, the total impression is by no means unsuccessful, though processional rather than dramatic. There is no reason why it should not indicate a new type of form, such as Schumann actually produced, with less than his usual hardness of outline, in his D minor Symphony.

In both the E flat Trio and the String Quintet there can be no doubt as to the magnificence of the harmonies and changes of key, not only from one moment to the next, but as an entire scheme. This is still more eminently the case with the considerable number of Schubert's developments, some of them long and some short, that have no redundancy in their plan. I have already described the wonderful end of the development in Schubert's last composition in this form, the Sonata in B flat; the whole development is a masterpiece, the more remarkable in that it all arises from the weakest part of the exposition. It would be a mistake to ascribe any part of its effect to its origin in that weakness; Schubert, in the year of his death, had not yet attained the power of Shakespeare and Beethoven in blending tragedy and comedy; though he had long overcome his early resentment against Beethoven's use of that power. It is impossible to set limits to what he might have achieved in a longer life; both Beethoven and Shakespeare were older than Schubert before they could be sure of finding the right continuation and the right contrast to any note as sublime as that of Schubert's greatest openings.

At least two of Schubert's first movements may be considered flawless; at all events, that is by far the best assumption on which to interpret them. The first movement of the 'Unfinished' Symphony has already been cited; its development is in superb dramatic contrast to the exposition; and nothing can be more characteristic of the greatest composers than the subtlety, pointed out by Sir George Grove, of alluding to the syncopated accompaniment of the 'second subject' without the theme itself. The other masterpiece among Schubert's first movements is little known, and not easily accessible. It is the first movement of an unfinished pianoforte sonata in C, not included in the usual collections of his pianoforte works. Perhaps it is the most subtle thing he ever wrote. To describe it would involve a full account of Schubert's whole range of harmonic ideas, which are here sounded to their utmost depths. And these depths are not such that later artistic developments can make them seem shallow. Schubert's harmonic range is the same as Beethoven's; but his great modulations would sound as bold in a Wagner opera as in a Beethoven symphony.

We have now seen in what ways the weaknesses of Schubert's expositions and developments are intimately involved in tendencies towards new kinds of form; and it remains to consider his recapitulations and codas. When Schubert's instrumental works are at their best his handling of the recapitulation (that is to say, of what follows after his development has returned to the tonic) is of the highest order of mastery where the original material permits. He shows an acumen not less than Beethoven's in working out inevitable but unexpected results from the fact that his 'second subject' (or his transition to it) did not begin in the key in which it was destined to settle. To describe these results would be too technical a procedure; but the reader may go far to convince himself of their importance by taking the cases of the 'Unfinished' Symphony and the C major Symphony and comparing what actually happens in the recapitulation with what would have been the course of modulations with a plain transposition of the 'second subject' into such a key as would lead to the tonic automatically. The externals of these two cases are obvious enough; behind them lies an art unknown to text-books on musical form, but as vital and subtle as the *entasis* of a Greek temple, whereby every apparently straight line has its curve and every column its imperceptible narrowing towards the centre. There is nothing surprising in the fact that with Schubert such art may be found in works notorious for obvious faults of structure.

Since the indiscretions of Schubert's expositions, though they may spoil the effect of his developments, do not prevent him from almost always developing magnificently, and sometimes faultlessly, we may say that up to the end of the recapitulation Schubert's energy stands the strain of his most impracticable designs. Further it seldom goes, and the codas of his first movements, with the solitary exception of that in the C major Symphony, are all in the manner of an expiring flame, often supremely beautiful, sometimes abruptly dramatic, but never revealing new energies like the great codas of Beethoven. In the codas of finales Schubert's energy is capable of expansion, for the enormous sprawling forms of the typical Schubert finales are the outcome of a sheer irresponsibility that has involved him in little or no strain, though he often shows invention of the highest order in their main themes. Here, again, there are two exceptional masterpieces of form, in both of which the grotesque is the veil of the sublime: the finales of the String Quintet and the C major Symphony.

But the mention of Schubert's finales opens up the whole question of his range of style. In the present discussion I have been compelled to make frequent use of the word 'sublime', not by way of mere reaction against the current impression that Schubert is a composer of secondary importance in his larger works, but by way of accurate definition. The only qualification the term needs is that in Schubert it is still associated with the picturesque and the unexpected; it is, in fact, as sublime as any artist's earlier works can be. No one calls the clear night-sky picturesque; and when Beethoven was inspired by it to write the slow movement of his E minor Quartet, he was older than Schubert lived to be. It is, however, one thing to write under the direct inspiration of the night-sky, and another thing to set a description of it to music; and there is a wonderful song for tenor solo with male voice chorus and pianoforte, in which the pianoforte part, representing the innumerable multitude of stars, achieves the sublime by Schubert's characteristic picturesqueness. In the voice parts Schubert is, of course, already an older and more experienced artist; more experienced, in fact, than Beethoven; and so in this way, as in many others from *Erlkönig* onwards, the spacing of the words and the turns of melody are as severe and indistinguishable from familiar forms or formulas as the lines of a Greek temple.

Now, it is in this matter of the sublime use of formulas that we can trace gradations in Schubert's style. When he begins a big instrumental piece with a formal gesture (as in the big A major Sonata and the *Forellen-quintett*), his intention and achievement are usually grandiose; and this applies to most of his argumentative sequences and processes of development. He can seldom rise above the grandiose when either his musical forms or his verbal subjects give him a sense of responsibility. On official occasions he is rustic, if not awkward; and though the beautiful features of his last two Masses (in A flat and E flat) outweigh the clumsiness of their officially necessary fugues, it is perhaps only in the *Incarnatus* of the A flat Mass that his church music reveals the depths of the Schubert vein of imagination. In a *Kyrie* or a *Benedictus* there is a vein of beauty which rises far above, but which is not incompatible with, a vein of rather too comfortable piety prevalent in the religious poetry of the period; and we have an excellent opportunity for measuring the difference between the wrong and the right stimulus to the imagination of a rustic tone-poet by comparing Schubert's grandiose song, *Die Allmacht*, a fine opportunity for singers, with its origin, as to modulations and general aspirations, in the aria known in English as 'In native worth' in Haydn's *Creation*. Here it is Haydn, another rustic composer, who quietly reaches the sublime in describing man made in God's image; while Schubert, dealing with verses that begin with the Almighty speaking through thunderstorms and end with the heart of man, achieves Haydn's finest modulation twice in a plainly repeated passage instead of once as a divinely unexpected variation.

It is tempting, but dangerous, to draw inferences, unsupported by musical facts, from the statistics of Schubert's song-texts. Every great musician, even if he be as voluble as Wagner on matters of general culture, is quicker to seize upon a fine musical possibility in a poem than to perceive that the words which gave it to him will not bear scrutiny. For no false sentiment can deceive except by claiming to be a true sentiment. It is therefore unprofitable to draw inferences as to Schubert's limitations from the merits of the poems he set to music. His friend Mayrhofer, who was said to toss him song after song across a table to be set as fast as the next poem could be written, was no Goethe, nor does he compare with the unpretentious Wilhelm Müller; yet most of the Mayrhofer songs rank with the Goethe and Wilhelm Müller songs among the greatest of Schubert's or any musician's achievements in lyric music. At his own best Mayrhofer will 'do'; but his *Viola, eine Blumenballade*, would have had no more chance of coming within Jeffrey's notice than Macaulay's 'Tears of Sensibility', had that parody (which was plausible enough to worry his father into horrid doubts) been intended seriously. Yet *Viola* inspired Schubert at the height of his power to one of the last of his very long songs, a masterpiece of form, using every suggestion of the words to purposes of an imagination as true as Wordsworth's.

Müller, the poet of Schubert's two great song-cycles, we are in some danger of underrating; he deserves at all events full credit

for the quality ascribed by Pope to Homer and by Johnson to
Thomson, of always writing 'with his eye on the object'; and his
style is absolutely free from affectation. It is, like all German
poetry of its class, untranslatable without disastrous injustice. German poetry at the turn of the eighteenth to the nineteenth century
had the good fortune to blossom out with no Augustan tradition,
and hence with no cleavage between poetic and prose diction; with
the result that, apart from the philosophy of his nature-worship, the
propaganda of Wordsworth could have had no meaning to a German poet. A simple test case will suffice. An English composer,
Loder, happens to have produced a really beautiful setting of an
English version of *Wohin?*, one of the most typical songs of *Die
schöne Müllerin*, set by Schubert with the utmost simplicity and
continuity of flow, like that of the stream the youth is following till
it leads him to his fate. The mere fact that Loder's setting is in
9/8 time shows how the English composer is driven to an elaborate
rhythm in order to convey any acceptable degree of distinction to
a text that translates 'so wunderhell' by 'so wondrous bright'. It
is a sheer impossibility to avoid such wrong notes in any English
or French translation of Müller's poetry.

The cumulative pathos of *Die schöne Müllerin* owes its force to
the radiant happiness which culminates in the middle of the song-
cycle, when the young miller in his *Wanderjahr* is accepted by his
beloved miller's daughter, who afterwards deserts him. The story
of the *Winterreise* is as simple, but is not directly told; all we know
is that the wanderer sets forth in mid-winter to leave the town
where his beloved has jilted him, and that everything he sees re-
flects back upon lost happiness and forward to death that will not
come. The text of each song is a straightforward verse description
of some common scene of country life, but this suggests none but
misleading analogies to a student of English poetry. Crabbe, according to Macaulay, has a pathos which can make a hardened and
cynical reader cry like a child; but nobody ever thought of setting
Crabbe to music. Thomson, the pioneer of simple truth to Nature,
was so far from impressing Haydn as a kindred spirit that it was
only after a long and direct protest against the project as a prosaic
and Philistine affair that Haydn was persuaded to compose *The
Seasons*. Wordsworth's nature is a pantheism always indicated
above and behind his Lucy Grays and Alice Fells. Tennyson's
rural scenes have squirearchy around them and aristocracy above
them, through which the Higher Pantheism penetrates with diffi-

K

culty. The English reader who wishes to capture the inspiration of Schubert's overpowering pathos in *Trockne Blumen* or *Des Baches Wiegenlied* (the lullaby of the brook for the young miller who has drowned himself) will find the nearest analogy to it in Herrick's *Mad Maid's Song*. There is no room for character-drawing, no philosophy, no pantheism; but purely the presentation of a sorrow such as unhinges the reason of a young miller or a country lass, in terms of the common sights and sounds around the sufferer which assume a primitive animistic relation to the sorrow.

These two song-cycles, *Die schöne Müllerin* and *Die Winterreise*, must be taken as two single works. To regard them as forty-four single songs will only lead us to the endless shallows of a criticism occupied with questions of which is the prettiest, the most important, or the most distinguished. The prettiness and perfection of any single member does, no doubt, seem sufficient to itself, like Loder's setting of an English version of *Wohin?*: but the cumulative effect of the whole cycle is overwhelmingly greater than the sum of its parts. Even taken by itself, *Trockne Blumen* has a pathos that makes us grudge Schubert forgiveness for subsequently writing on it a set of variations, which was a bad thing to do; and writing them for flute, which was worse; and making some of them brilliant, which was blasphemous. But in its context *Trockne Blumen* is a song which many a singer has found difficult to learn because its pathos destroys all control of the voice.

The final song, *Des Baches Wiegenlied*, is not less difficult, and its supreme art lies in its being merely strophic, with melody and accompaniment unaltered throughout all its stanzas. The criticism of vocal music will never attain what should be regarded as its ordinary professional competence until it recognizes that the merely strophic song with a single melody for all stanzas is no mere labour-saving device, but, as Brahms always maintained, the highest accomplishment of the song-composer's invention, compared to which the declamatory song is child's play. Schubert himself has produced too many masterpieces of declamatory song, such as *Der Wanderer*, *Der Doppelgänger*, and *Der Tod und das Mädchen*, not to stultify any theory of song-writing that does not accept Wagner and Hugo Wolf as masters of the theory of musical declamation; but a criticism that regards that theory as constituting the whole, or even the highest, art of vocal music is fundamentally incapable of understanding verse. If Sullivan had not been a consummate craftsman, we should have had our declamatory theorists pointing out that Gilbert's metrical novelties were *a priori* incapable of any treatment more lyrical than that of *Das Rheingold*. Very different is the theory of the masters of lyric melody, whose view of declamation was not confined to prose. Weber writes to his librettist: 'Mind you give me plenty of trouble with unexpected rhythms and strange inversions; nothing so stimulates the composer's invention and drives him out of the common grooves.' Schubert had from childhood practised the musical handling of all kinds of sentence, so that, unlike Weber, he presents us with results in which it is impossible to guess the difficulties. In his six hundred songs there is, no doubt, as Brahms said, something to be learnt from each one; but it will not always be easy to learn it unless you have Brahms's knowledge to begin with. Of course, there is no more infallibility with Schubert than there is with Shakespeare; *Erlkönig* and *Gretchen am Spinnrade* stand alone in four volumes of early work; *Die Forelle*, after two strophes perfectly realizing in melody and accompaniment the picture and mood of the darting trout in the clear stream, shows none of Schubert's later skill when, in the last stanza, the music makes a perfunctory effort to follow the narrative; and even in the later years there are songs, not always despised by singers, from which Brahms himself could have learnt little but the fact that Schubert was always keeping his pen in practice, whether or not he had anything in his head at the moment. The most summary critical sifting of this material would require a volume, with an introductory essay on principles of musical word-setting that have never been formulated in text-books.

One technical principle, not difficult to understand, suffices to dispose of any *a priori* objections to what has been called the 'lazy' method of the strophic song with the same tune to all stanzas. The objection rests on an ignorant belief in the bar-stroke as a genuine and rigid musical unit, together with the idea that no other basis of accent counts. Composers with poor rhythmic invention produce melodies in accordance with these limitations; and they are rightly afraid of deviating from them, since they cannot do so with conviction. But great masters like Schubert play with all possible occasions of musical accent as great poets play with verse accent; and the various occasions of accent coincide only in order to mark special points. The first notes of the first song in *Winterreise* show the method at once. The first note is off the beat (an anacrusis); but is higher than the second. The beat comes on the second, which is an expressive discord. The height of the first note provides enough accent to fit any prosodic inversion without interrupting by declamatory pedantries the dogged march of the jilted lover as he leaves the town of his joy and sorrow. But the note is not so high as to make an accent where the iambic feet of the verse are normal. Then the sensitive discord on the first of the bar asserts itself.

Schubert is not less masterly in the handling of paragraphs as wholes. He never over-punctuates, as is the inveterate tendency of the conscientiously declamatory composers. 'Dass sie hier gewesen', a series of statements that the air, the flowers, &c., prove that the beloved has been there, is set by Schubert, strophically, to a musical paragraph beginning outside the key and corresponding in every point of musical analysis to the grammatic structure of the poem, so that it is as impossible to lose the thread of its series of dependent clauses as to misunderstand its sentiment. In the first of the *Schwanengesang* (a publisher's title for a selection of Schubert's latest songs), *Liebesbotschaft* (*Rauschendes Bächlein*), the *Bächlein* continues its movement while the thought of the beloved hanging her head in a pensive mood is expressed at a tempo twice as slow as that of the rest of the setting. In short, Schubert the songwriter is as great a master of movement (which is form) as Mozart or Beethoven. All his structural devices seem so absurdly simple, when pointed out, that only the cumulative effect of their number, variety, and efficiency will suffice to undo the injuries that our understanding of Schubert's art has suffered from over-emphasis on his incapacity to theorize in words, and from academic ignorance of the nature of musical art-forms on a large scale. Vogl, the singer who, in Schubert's own lifetime, recognized and produced his songs, spoke of his insight into poetry as 'clairvoyant'; and that praise was useful in its day. At present we cannot too strongly emphasize the fact that, clairvoyance or common sense, Schubert's mastery in his songs includes an immense technique consciously developed and polished from childhood in over six hundred extant examples, many of them several times rewritten. His inability to explain himself in verbal or analytic theory is the inability of a master to explain an art to people who, thinking they know all about it, do not, in fact, know that it exists. From Salieri Schubert learnt Italian declamation and operatic gesture with a thoroughness which, musically, stood him in good stead so long as his dramatic ambitions and his uncritical good nature to poetaster friends did not betray him into wasting precious time and fine music on hopeless blood-and-thunder like *Fierrabras* and *Alfonso und Estrella*. Zumsteeg, the pioneer of long ballads, he outpaced, as we have seen, in the very act of making a musical paraphrase as a self-taught boyish exercise. The sporadic non-operatic lyrics of Mozart and Beethoven can hardly account for any measurable fraction of Schubert's range of song-forms; you might as well try to account for Shakespeare by his parentage. It is easier to trace Schubert's emotional power to contemporary influences than so to trace his technique. Too much has been made of his adverse criticisms of Weber and Beethoven; these are the honest first impressions of a fearless young artist, shy only in the actual presence of persons formidable by position or attainment. Many an artist has spoken resentfully of things that have profoundly influenced his work even before he learnt to enjoy them. Beethoven, for his part, on his death-bed recognized Schubert as a kindred spirit; and he had no love of things incompatible with the sublime. When all the pretty and picturesque things, and even all the dramatic things, in Schubert's songs have had their due; even after *Der Doppelgänger*, which many consider the greatest of his songs, has been revered for its awful transcendence of Heine's grim pathos; still the full measure of Schubert is revealed when, unoppressed by ceremonies and official responsibilities, he joins Beethoven and Wordsworth in nature-worship. The classical interests of Goethe and Schiller contribute largely to this strain, and Schubert is magnificently himself when dealing with Greek subjects, and with 'cosmic emotion', as in Mayrhofer's *Auflösung* (a glorious opportunity for a big soprano voice, unaccountably neglected), or, in a less remote vein, the great long *Waldesnacht*.

It is in this mighty framework that the sorrows of the Miller and the banished Winter Traveller become universal; and the calm of *Du bist die Ruh* is as mystic as the glory of Beatrice's eyes which drew Dante from heaven to higher heaven.

TONALITY IN SCHUBERT[1]

TONALITY, or the harmonic perspective of music, is a subject which most writers avoid. It is not a thing which can be discussed in non-musical terms; and in calling it a perspective I have exhausted my stock of such metaphors as can bring it within the cognizance of persons of general culture. For we all know that in England a person of general culture is a person who knows nothing about music and cannot abide musical jargon.

The readers of this essay, however, may be supposed to add musical culture to their general culture. And their impatience of musical jargon will be aroused only by the sort of terminology that substitutes professional routine for first-hand artistic experience. They may even bear with a little codification of elementary principles, if thereby we can better observe so wonderful an artistic resource as Schubert's tonality.

It is high time that the facts of classical tonality were properly tabulated. We cannot go into the ultimate foundations here, but will begin, as with granted facts, by enumerating the key-centres from a major tonic; premissing that in the classical harmony which comprises Handel's and Schubert's aesthetics the key of a piece is like the point of view, or the vanishing point, of a picture. Mark Twain once defended a badly drawn 'study' by saying that the tower was drawn from below but the man on the top of it was drawn from the roof: and in the same way many unorthodox harmonic progressions are conflicts of key-perspective.

Here, then, are the key-centres of a major tonic, taken as C major. To make the scheme applicable to all major keys we have only to name the degrees of the scale. These functional names explain themselves and are easy to remember. The only ones requiring comment are the subdominant and the submediant. The supertonic is the note, or chord, above the tonic: but the subdominant should be thought of not as the note below the dominant, but as an anti-dominant having the opposite effect to the dominant, and lying a fifth below the tonic as the dominant lies a fifth above. The meaning of the term submediant then becomes clear: it is a third between tonic and subdominant, as the mediant is a third between tonic and dominant. Now represent these degrees by

[1] From *Music and Letters* (Schubert Number), vol. ix, no. 4, October 1928.

Roman numerals and you will have the advantage of being able to distinguish major chords (and keys) by capitals and minor by small figures.

Ex.1

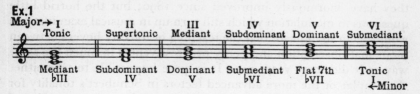

There is no common chord on the 7th degree. The basis of key-relation is that two keys are related when the tonic chord of one is among the common chords of another. A cardinal rule in key-relation is that no third tonic is involved. I am not dealing with the means of modulation, but with the basis of key-relations, however reached. Ex. 1 shows that to C major all the five keys—D minor (ii), E minor (iii), F major (IV), G major (V), and A minor (vi)—are equally related. The so-called 'relative minor' A (vi) is no more closely related than the others, and D minor and E minor owe nothing to the fact that they are the relative minors of the subdominant and dominant respectively.

If the tonic is minor its relations cannot be found by putting common chords on its scale, for the minor scale is unstable. The dominant chord must be major, or there would be no leading note for full closes; but the dominant key must be minor, or it will either be no key at all, a mere dominant chord, or too remote for direct relation. Any doubt on this point can be settled by trying to answer a minor fugue subject in the dominant major!

Ex.2

And if the dominant is minor so is its antipodal converse, the subdominant. The pathos of modulation from a minor tonic to its subdominant comes from the tragic irony of the change of the tonic chord to major, not in its own right but as dominant chord of a darker minor key.

The other relations of a minor tonic are the converse of its own relation to a major key. Below Ex. 1 the names of the relations of A minor are given.

In apology for this apparently elementary exposition, and for more words on the same plane, I must plead that it is, so far as I know, new. I am not a great reader of text-books, and I know that they have enormously improved since 1890; but the horrid little questions in modulation which still turn up in musical examinations would seem to indicate that the teaching of tonality hovers between pious mal-observation and perky progressiveness in much the same way as it did forty years ago. It is quite impossible to take either the simpler or the more advanced factors in Schubert's tonality for granted in this article, or no two readers will form the same idea of my meaning. So please bear with me while I continue to explain everything as we proceed.

In referring to 'a darker minor key' I am not describing subjective fancies. Keys in themselves are major or minor, and their other differences vary according to the techniques of instruments and not at all on voices except in pitch. That is to say, there is no difference between a song in C and the same song transposed to F sharp, except that in F sharp it will suit a totally different voice, and the colour of its accompaniment will be much lighter if the transposition is upwards and probably impossibly darker if it is downwards. (When Henschel sang *Das Wandern* he put the voice-part a major 3rd down and the pianoforte part a minor 6th up.) But there is no reason why one piece in C should not have exactly the same character as another in F sharp. Notions about the characters of keys in themselves are entirely subjective, and no agreement about them is to be expected, though doubtless their psychological statistics might be as interesting as those of 'number-forms'. But I doubt this: there happens to be another basis for these ideas of key-colour, which rather knocks the bottom out of their psychological interest.

What is not subjective at all is the effect of one key as approached from another. And as nobody can know the names of keys without knowing their distance from C, there is a strong probability that subjective ideas of key-character will be a tangle of associations with C major overlaid by recollections of the first piece that made an impression and was remembered by its key. In my own case, for instance, E flat minor, which is difficult to connect with C, has the character of Bach's E flat minor Prelude, overlaid by the sense of its extreme remoteness from C and the darkness of a modulation from C to it. On the other hand, E flat major, which is a warm dark key in relation to C, has for me overwhelmingly the character

of the 'Eroica' Symphony. And it is quite certain that no composer
with any pretensions to mastery ever allowed merely subjective
ideas of key to get in his way. When Beethoven arranged his little
E major Sonata, op. 14, no. 1, as a string quartet, he transposed it
to F without any scruples as to change of character. Yet he had
picturesque ideas about keys. B minor was 'black', and A flat,
very unlike his numerous gentle movements in that key, was
'barbarous'.

Now let us consider the functions of the key-relations exhibited
in Ex. 1. First comes the dominant. As that chord is penultimate
in every normal full close, it follows that the natural way to establish a new key is to get on to its dominant chord and stay there
long enough to rouse the expectation of a close into the new tonic.
Hence the dominant chord is the centre of activity and forward
movement in tonality. Moreover, if we alight on any major triad
and harp on it, there will arise a strong suspicion that it is a dominant chord and not a tonic. One of the most important distinctions
in all music, though I have not encountered it in books, is that
between *on* the dominant and *in* the dominant. Bülow understood
it thoroughly; but many later and plausible writers are hopelessly
at fault about it. Mozart plays upon the distinction with a power
and brilliance that has never since been equalled; for a wider
range of key is like a faster rate of travel, and lets you see less of
the country.

The subdominant, or anti-dominant, used as a penultimate chord
in the solemn ecclesiastical plagal cadence, is opposite to the dominant in function and effect. Make your first extended modulation
to the subdominant, and you deprive your movement of all forward
energy and indicate at once that your intention is lyrical and repose-
ful. The cheeky and voluminous finale of Schubert's early *Forellen-
quintett* contradicts this; but it is evidence only of its own effrontery.

It is not to the present purpose to describe those phenomena of
tonality which are common to Schubert and all classical composers;
so I will say no more at present as to his treatment of the dominant
and subdominant, but will proceed to illustrate other key-relations.
The reader must, however, beware of receiving from the sum of my
illustrations the idea that they represent the prevalent tonal colour
of Schubert. If that were so they would be mannerisms, not marvels. They do not even represent the greatest marvels, but only
such points as I have room to illustrate within any reasonable length.
When we start from a major tonic, and take the dominant and

subdominant as read, the other three related keys are minor, and are not markedly different from each other when used on a small scale. The supertonic is easily reached; Mozart slides in and out of it as in the stride of a regular melody,

Ex.3

&c.

and it is a favourite gambit in later openings, such as the Allegro of Beethoven's First Symphony, and, more melodiously and grandly, his C major Quintet, and, most grandly of all, in Schubert's C major Quintet.[1]

Now arises the question: When is a modulation not a modulation? Clearly 'key' and 'chord' are relative terms. You cannot assert a key without giving its dominant chord; and in the second bar of Ex. 3 the G sharp does give the leading note and represents the dominant chord of A minor. But the passage could have done without this; and only the chromatically gliding D sharp in the melody, which no sane person will take for a modulation to E, forces upon us the underlining of A minor as a key instead of as a plain supertonic chord. But for this underlining the previous chromatic D sharp must have borne some independent weight, whereas it now means scarcely more than the merely chromatic A sharp. Here, then, are the possibilities for many subtle masterstrokes in the draughtsmanship of harmony.

Let us see how Schubert takes advantage of them. Ex. 4 is an outline of the trio of the Scherzo of the great C major Symphony.

The key is A major, which we will take as a thing in itself, ignoring its relation to the scherzo, which is in C. The harmony moves slowly, taking sixteen of these short bars to cover the three cardinal chords of the key. In the next twenty bars the chord of the submediant almost becomes a key, but the diminished 7th in bar 25 impinges on to the dominant, and shows that we have not yet moved. But in bar 29 another diminished 7th on the same bass, and with a difference of intonation too delicate for the pianoforte to show, turns out to be quite a different chord and takes us into the key of the mediant. Is this key going to be established? Not yet; bars 37–40 oscillate between the original tonic chord and this

[1] In the finale of his last sonata he makes his theme persistently *start* in the supertonic, as Beethoven did in the finale of his Quartet, op. 130.

mediant chord, and are repeated with an ornament in bars 41–4. On your life do not play D sharp in bar 43! The whole point is that we are not in C sharp minor until bar 45 takes us there.

The second part swings lustily back to the dominant chord of our tonic and stays there for sixteen bars. The second eight of these sixteen bars repeat this in the minor mode, and another eight lead to sixteen bars in C major, which is in no direct relation to A major at all, but only to A minor. Then another eight bars lead deliber-

Ex.4 *Allegro vivace*

ately back to the dominant of A and so to a repetition of the first phrase of sixteen bars. Its counter-statement now underlines the chord of the submediant by using it as a step towards the subdominant. This would not itself amount to more than local colour but for the fact that bars 121–8, still in the stride of the melody, suddenly rise a semitone into the key of the flat supertonic, a relation which, like that of C major above, is outside the scheme covered by Ex. 1. It takes another eight bars to restore the tonic. The chromatic bass of bars 129–33 contains the only quick-moving harmonies in the whole gorgeous colour-scheme of this trio, which ends quietly with a recapitulation, in the tonic, of bars 37–48. Yes, that is what it sounds like, but the harmonies are turned round, the tonic chord being where the other chord was. On a small scale this is typical of Schubert's mature recapitulations; he knows exactly how far the true balance is to be obtained by plain recapitulation and how far the harmonies must be recast.

For reasons that will appear later, the supertonic is not a key that makes a good contrast for a section. Its converse, the flat 7th from a minor tonic, is rather vague even in local modulations; it suggests that it is not a real key but only the dominant of the more familiar so-called 'relative major'. If the composer succeeds in contradicting this construction the effect, on a small scale, suggests the Dorian mode of the sixteenth century, and on a larger scale it exactly fits Gretchen's 'ich finde sie nimmer und nimmermehr'. Nothing is more astonishing in all Schubert's development than his achieving, quietly and simply, at the age of seventeen, exactly the right modulation at the beginning of *Gretchen am Spinnrade*. The four and a half bars in C may, till the last moment, turn out to be a dominant of F, but the harmony swings back inexorably and dryly to D minor.

Ex. 5 Piano

etc. Meine Ruh ist hin, mein Herz ist schwer; ich finde ich, find - e sie nim-mer und nim - mer mehr. *etc.*

F major does not appear till Gretchen is thinking of 'Sein hoher Gang, sein' edle Gestalt', in the calm before the crisis. The other modulations in this marvellous and perfect composition carry us beyond the range of Ex. 1, and it will be convenient first to explain how that range is extended on classical lines.

First, we must not cease to give a definite meaning to the term key-relation. There are no forbidden modulations; but there are modulations which cannot be made to mean the same thing as a key-relation however much we may advance in our understanding of that almost theological dogma, 'the unity of the chromatic scale'. The advance of mathematics beyond simple arithmetic can find a use for the square root of a minus quantity, but it is not going to give a meaning to the unimpeachably grammatical statement that 'the soul is either blue or not blue'; and a modulation from C to F sharp is as easy as falling out of bed, but, however correct in grammar, it is not going to establish a key-relation.

Elsewhere in Schubert these changes from major to minor are frequent, but never facile, always beautiful, and sometimes (as in *Trockne Blumen* and the end of the theme of *Der Tod und das Mäd-chen*, as treated in the D minor Quartet) of almost unbearable pathos. One would hardly imagine the same pathos could be attained in a movement which is in a major key from the outset; but the return to the main theme of the first movement of the G major Quartet is one of the most moving passages in all music. The main theme at first arises from sustained major chords which break out into energetic minor figures.

Ex. 6

After an enormous (and very redundant) exposition and a rich and masterly development, the return of the tonic and of the main theme is prepared with great breadth and excitement.

And then the theme takes this form:

Ex.7

Now let us look at the results of treating tonic major and tonic minor as interchangeable. Calling the degrees of the first key by Roman figures, as in Ex. 1, we start with the direct relations of a major tonic, viz. ii, iii, IV, V, and vi; and those from a minor tonic, ♭VII, ♭VI, v, iv, and ♭III.

We can extend these relations in two directions, so long as, for reasons to be described later, we leave the supertonic and the flat 7th alone. With a major tonic we can change the modes of its relatives and so obtain the new harmonic colours of III, iv, v, and VI. And we can add to our major tonic the relations of its tonic minor and so obtain ♭VI, v, iv, and ♭III. It will be seen that the dominant minor and subdominant minor are reached in both ways. They are, in fact, hardly felt as remoter relations at all, and their use on an almost ordinary footing is as old as Bach and Handel. The effect of the other modulations is highly coloured, those in the forward direction (III and VI) being very bright, while their converses (♭VI and ♭III) are correspondingly dark.

The secondary relations of a minor tonic are, with the exception of the major dominant and major subdominant, also minor, and this deprives them of much of the contrast that their remoteness would otherwise give. The whole set is, of course, ♯vi (where ♯ indicates the distance of a major interval from the tonic), V, IV, and ♯iii in the forward direction, with V and IV in both directions, and ♭vi and ♭iii in the converse direction.

But the possibilities are not yet exhausted. Both modes may be changed, and this will give two more distant keys, ♭iii and ♭vi from a major tonic, and ♯VI and ♯III from a minor tonic.

Here is the whole series so far, reckoned from C and giving the intermediate steps:

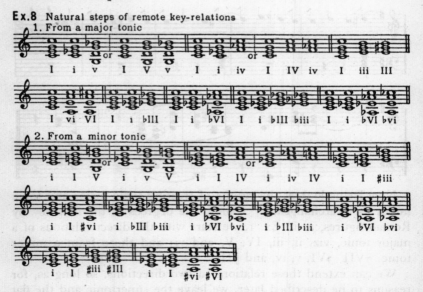

Ex.8 Natural steps of remote key-relations

1. From a major tonic

2. From a minor tonic

Now the relation of such pairs of keys is evident only when they are either brought into immediate contact or put into such prominent positions in a design that the memory holds them together.

Not only do the great masters of tonality not expect us to recognize, without collateral evidence, keys that return after intervening modulations, but they rely upon our not doing so. For example, the modulation to C from A major in the middle of Ex. 4 is the right thing in the right place; but our clever young (or old enough to know better) contrapuntists who Godowskify[1] the classics by combining everything with everything else could easily make it disastrous by introducing the theme of the scherzo in the bass, for it is not a return to the tonic of the scherzo but a beautiful dark purple in the A major trio. I remember an excellent treatise of the seventies that laid down the rule, 'Modulation should not be made twice to the same key in the course of a movement'. The book was laudably observant of the real classics; but this rule showed how admirably the classics escaped being found out in this matter, for the rule is wholly impossible to obey on a large scale.

Probably the most fundamental rule for operations in large-scale tonality is that key-relation is a function of form. It is no use citing passages from the course of a wandering development to prove that a composer regards a key as related to his tonic: the function of development is contrast, not tonic relation. The choice of a key for the slow movement of a sonata, or for the trio of a scherzo, or for the second group (miscalled 'second subject') of a first movement, implies key-relation; but episodes and purple patches in these divisions must be referred to the key of the division, not to that of the whole.

If it be asked how, besides this choice of definite function, the great composers express the fact that remote keys are related, the answer is, 'exactly as in Example 8'. Or else by plain juxtaposition without the intermediate steps. Or even by breaking down the tonic chord into a single note and then building that note up into another chord; though this is a process that lends itself to mystification as well as schematic clearness. But I wish we might be allowed to use the term 'natural' for modulations which show the nature of the case.

Plain juxtaposition may be hardly thought worthy of inclusion among these natural modulations, but it is in many ways the most important of all. Philipp Emanuel Bach and Dvořák (slow movement of 'New World' Symphony) are afraid of it and must interpolate explanatory chords. Not so Haydn, Beethoven, Schubert,

[1] Nevertheless, I get up and snort when anybody else says a word against that great player.

L

and Brahms. When Beethoven wants to put the slow movement of his C minor Concerto in the relation i to ♯III he simply begins on the dazzling new tonic chord; and when Schubert (following the example of Beethoven's op. 106, which has the relation I to ♭vi) puts the slow movement of his last Sonata (B flat) into the relation I to ♭iii (C sharp minor = D flat minor in a convenient notation), he does likewise. The whole point is that the new key comes as a shock, but not as an inexplicable one.

Here are two modulations literally on the scheme of Ex. 8:

Ex.9　Natural modulation from I to ♭VI *(Abschied)*

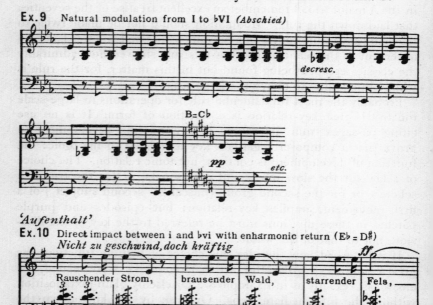

'*Aufenthalt*'

Ex.10　Direct impact between i and ♭vi with enharmonic return (E♭ = D♯)

Modulations that enter the new key through its dominant chord are often hardly less immediate in their effect; and it is hardly necessary to quote the drastic method, conspicuous in Schubert's marches, of hammering on a bass note and suddenly raising it a semitone.

Before going further, there is one other class of key-relations that remains to be described. The best name for it is Neapolitan, for it arises out of a chord known as the Neapolitan 6th, and that chord was developed by the Neapolitan masters (Alessandro Scarlatti and company) who founded this whole system of classical tonality. It comes from making the lower tetrachord of a minor scale conform with the upper, thus:

Ex.11

As the minor scale is artificial and unstable in any case, this modification would be all in its day's work but for the fact that this superlatively minor supertonic actually goes with a major third, just as the flat 6th converges upon the usual major dominant chord. Here is the Neapolitan cadence in its full form (*a*) and its compressed form (*b*), avoiding the major third of the tonic.

Ex.12

If the major third of the tonic is used we may just as well reckon the whole key as major.

Our first definition of key-relation holds good, with one slight change, for all the range of relations established in music from Haydn to Wagner. Two keys are related when *some form of* the tonic chord of one is identical with *some form of* one of the common chords of the other; with the exception of keys a whole tone apart, which are related only when their common chords are unaltered. In other words, a change of mode on either or both sides leaves the key-relation still traceable, so long as the keys are not a tone apart. In no case does a key-relation drag in a third tonic.

The first basis, then, of wider key-relation is that major and minor keys on the same tonic are identical. The fact that the so-called 'relative major' is a convenient point of backward reference, as in Ex. 1, has nothing to do with this matter; it is an accident that has misled the tonic-sol-fa-ists, but has misled nobody else. Not A minor, but C minor is the minor mode of C.

Now the character of the minor mode arises from the artificiality of the minor triad. It would carry us too far to go into this; and I will beg the reader who wishes to dispute it kindly to bear with this doubtless imperfect statement, and to admit that the whole history of classical music shows that from the sixteenth-century *tierce de Picardie* to the present day the minor tonic triad can be replaced by the major with the effect of only adding to the finality of the tonic sense. The major mode is the more resonant: the minor is overcast and struggling with dissonant elements. Consequently a change from minor to major in any direction is an increase of comfort, and a change to tonic major is, normally, a change to happiness. Of course, other factors may intervene; Brahms's kittenish *Die Schwestern* gets along playfully in the minor until the twins fall in love with the same man, and then the major mode shows its higher plangency (I think that is the proper word to-day). Also, happiness too easily won is very near to tragic irony.

Now one of the easiest and lightest forms of pathos in music is the starting in a minor key and, before any action has happened, changing to its tonic major. This, of course, forestalls any further dramatic use of the change unless the work is on so large a scale that it can afford to begin with an almost complete lyric statement. And Schubert's large instrumental forms are notoriously prone to spend in lyric ecstasy the time required *ex hypothesi* for dramatic action. Rossini, whose music is never in a hurry, and least of all when Figaro is exhibiting his patter-singing, had already made this change his chief means of pathos; and Schubert, who was thoroughly seasoned by the Rossini fever which devastated musical Vienna in the twenties, took this over with many other Italian expressions. The beautiful melody with which the A minor Quartet begins owes nothing to Italy until the moment when it quietly goes into A major. Some fifty years later this gift from Italy returned to its native country when Verdi wrote the beginning of his *Requiem*.

This flat supertonic produces four key-relations between keys a semitone apart. From a major tonic there is the flat supertonic and both modes of the sharp 7th to which the tonic is flat supertonic. There is also the indirect relation of the *minor* flat supertonic, a key that would never convey an impression of relation unless in immediate juxtaposition and with schematically demonstrative harmony. But this, as we shall see, really occurs. From a minor tonic there is the direct flat supertonic, but no direct converse relations, since the Neapolitan chord is always major. But there are three indirect Neapolitan relations, viz. the minor flat supertonic, and the sharp 7th in both major and minor modes.

This account, like all verbal explanations of tonality, is dry work; but the treatment of the facts by Haydn, Beethoven, and Schubert is not.

Ex.13 Neapolitan Relations

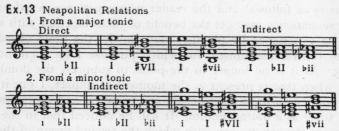

Haydn's last Pianoforte Sonata, in E flat, has its slow movement in E♮ = F♭ = ♭II. This Haydn carefully abstains from explaining; unlike Philipp Emanuel Bach, who, when he put an E flat movement into a D major symphony, annihilated the effect by dramatic bridge-passages in recitative. Beethoven, after using the flat supertonic very impressively at the beginning of the *Sonata Appassionata*, the E minor Quartet, and the F minor Quartet, wrote one of his very greatest works, the C sharp minor Quartet, within the range (but for two small purple patches) between the flat supertonic and the other directly related keys, putting the flat supertonic first and last.

Ex.14 Minor Neapolitan chord, from Quartet in D minor

Schubert was greatly excited by Beethoven's C sharp minor Quartet; but, having written *Gretchen am Spinnrade* at seventeen, he needed no prompting, and the end of the first movement of the D minor Quartet turns the Neapolitan chord into the minor (Ex. 14, p. 149).

The C major String Quintet is one of the greatest of all essays in tonality, and especially in the Neapolitan relations. The whole scheme is as follows: and the reader whose patience is exhausted by these statistics may get the benefit of them together with some aesthetic experience by playing, very slowly, the tonic chords of the key-centres mentioned, for which purpose I set them out in Ex. 15. As it is no longer to the point to suppress the dominant chord when that is present at the moment of impact, I put it and other connexion links as crotchets and quavers, and represent the initial tonic as a dotted minim. It will be noticed that in the first movement the remote key with which the second group of themes begins lasts only during one theme, and then yields place to the orthodox dominant. This is always the case where Schubert's first modulation in a sonata-form movement is unorthodox. The first movement of the 'Unfinished' Symphony is the only example where Schubert's second group is not in the so-called relative major (♭III), as the movement is in a minor key; and he makes no exception to the rule that in a major first movement the second group, however wide a cast it may first make, eventually settles in the orthodox dominant.

Ex. 15 Cardinal key relations in the 1st three movements of Schubert's String Quintet

And here is the very end of the slow movement, showing the relation I ii as exactly as in Ex. 14, besides summing up the whole movement in four bars:

Ex. 16

The finale is half minor and half major and does not, except in the wanderings of a short development, go farther than the dominant major and minor. But the very last bars emphasize the flat supertonic in the boldest way conceivable:

Ex. 17

If this stood by itself we should certainly take it for the dominant of F; but so grand is the tonal poise of the whole movement that in its full context it is more forcible an assertion of C major than any normal cadence. It may truly be said to have been prepared for by the whole course of the Quintet. This is not to say that the first movement had not its diffuseness and redundancies, like every large instrumental work of Schubert; though the other three movements are accurate to a bar in their timing. But defects may co-exist with qualities; and Schubert's defects are often half-way towards the qualities of new art-forms. Upon Brahms the influence of Schubert is far greater than the combined influences of Bach and Beethoven; and this quintet concentrates most of the points which Brahms took up. If the original version of Brahms's Pianoforte Quintet as a string quintet with two 'cellos had not been destroyed, its scoring would have given us a still more vivid reminder of the Schubert Quintet. As it is, the end of Brahms's scherzo owes much to Ex. 15, and is, in fact, the only classical parallel to it.

One more excursus into theory and I will leave the patient reader to enjoy his Schubert in peace with the aid of whatever light this essay may have given.

If the scheme here given includes such a wide range of key, why does it exclude any keys at all? To begin with, why does it refuse to change the mode of the supertonic and the flat 7th?

Obviously, any theory that tries to 'forbid' these modulations condemns itself. The only permissible question about them is: what do they mean? And when we ask that question, we get a sensible answer. To begin with, take Ex. 5. We noticed that this key of the flat 7th persisted in sounding like the dominant of ♭III, and that Gretchen's despair is vividly expressed by the failure to lead to any such key. That is the point: you may go to a key, but you may find it impossible to prove that you have reached it. The normal way to establish a key is to knock at its dominant door: and the best way to make sure that it is the front door that you are knocking at, is to get at it through its own leading note. Consequently, if your tonic is C major, you may say:

Ex.18

till you are black in the face; but not even a military bandmaster will believe that you are in D major and not merely knocking at the door of G. If your tonic had been minor, then Ex. 18 would not become D minor, but would either remain exactly as it is, or, as an utmost concession, put a flat to E in the second bar.

What is true of one key-relation is true of its converse; and if nobody will believe that II is a real key when approached from I, then a modulation from I to ♭VII will cast some doubt on the reality of I when we return to it. Besides, ever since Beethoven's 'Waldstein' Sonata and his earlier G major, op. 31, no. 1, ♭VII has become a stalking-horse for the subdominant. When the second key, or both keys, are minor, the ambiguity no longer exists, for dominant chord can only be major. But by this time no feeling of relation is left, for there have been no circumstances that can naturally give rise to it. So poor Gretchen's despair wanders, after Ex. 5, through the dominant into the desolate region of E minor (ii), 'die ganze Welt ist mir vergällt'. Thence she does retrace her harmonic steps back to the dominant and from there rises a semitone to harmonies on the dominant of ♭vi. Again the accompaniment swings back and she returns to the tonic and the burden 'Meine Ruh' ist hin'. She recapitulates the modulation of Ex. 5 and its sequel, but does not go further than the dominant; and then comes the wonderful repose in the long-delayed ♭III, at 'Sein hoher Gang'.

If the composer, starting from a major tonic, can persuade the listener that II is a key and not a mere dominant, the effect is one of strange exaltation; unless, of course, the composer is a mere stringer of borrowed tunes whose key-contrasts mean nothing. That is why this is either the most vulgar of modulations or the most sublime. A miracle was worked in this manner by Beethoven at the long-delayed return of the main theme in the first movement of the 'Eroica' Symphony. Schubert in the slow movement of the Quintet produces a mysterious brightness by going from E to F♯ (II) and refusing to explain it away as the dominant of V.

Ex.19 *Adagio espressio*

1st Violin & 2nd Violoncello continue their design

And thence in the opposite direction through ♭VII as Dominant of ♭III

What of the key-distances a tritone 4th or imperfect 5th apart—
the only ones now left, except enharmonic synonyms of the others?

Here again, the real question has nothing to do with the Unity
of the Chromatic Scale or the Blueness of the Soul or the Wicked-
ness of Hide-bound Academicism, but simply with the problem of
establishing the second key as having a tonic relation to the first.
And this cannot be done with I and ♯IV, major or minor, direct or
converse. Whichever is tonic, the other will be a dominant and not
a key; and, as a dominant, it will turn the first key into a flat
supertonic. In short, Ex. 19 (p. 153) means a Neapolitan close
into B, major or minor,

Ex. 20

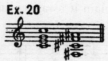

and cannot be made to mean anything else. Moreover, the second
chord is very close in pitch (in fact, identical on the pianoforte) to
its diametrical opposite, ♭V. The two could overlap (with perfect
comfort on the pianoforte and with merely momentary discomfort
in just intonation) and carry the progression right round the harmonic world in three chords.

Ex. 21

Harmonic space is curved like the surface of the earth, and this
tritone is its date-line. We must not ascribe this curvature to any
form of tempered scale. Ex. 20 represents the particular case of
the whole curvature known as the circle of 5ths (C, G, D, A, E,
B, F sharp = G flat, D flat, A flat, E flat, B flat, F, C), which
temperaments, equal or unequal, make join by distributing their
defective intonations to the best of their ability; but the actual
curvature of harmonic space is local, and depends on musical forms
as the curvature of Einstein's time-space depends on the presence
of gravitating matter. Editorial time-space and the occasion compel
me to hurl this dogmatically at the reader. I will only point out
that there are several other enharmonic circles between the short-
circuit of Ex. 21 and the whole circle of 5ths; and will again remind
the reader that no master of tonality expects a key to be recognized

merely by pitch when it returns after intervening modulations. So that if Schubert (or Brahms) goes round an enharmonic circle of thirds in this fashion,

Ex. 22

the reason why we know that Schubert has returned to G and not arrived at A double flat is not because the pianoforte expresses no difference, but because this passage did originally remain in G with no modulations at all, and because it here also returns to the opening theme as usual. If it could be heard in just intonation, the most delicate ear would hardly detect the minute difference in pitch between the G major of the original theme and the A double flat of its return here; and if the ear did note the difference, the inference would not be, 'we are now in the vastly remote key of A♭♭', but 'the pitch is beginning to shift'.

So far we have been dealing with keys treated as related. This field is a wider one than that of merely 'extraneous' modulation, as the Victorian theorists used to call everything outside Ex. 1. Not only do extraneous modulations exist, but they are not confined to the distances of ♯IV and ♭V. Any key may be reached in an extraneous way; and I doubt whether anything but a general retrospect of the whole movement would enable us in the first movement of the last pianoforte sonata to identify F as the dominant of B flat when it has been reached via F sharp minor (= G♭ minor = ♭vi), and so would be equivalent to G double flat, but for the fact that there is an unobtrusive enharmonic modulation before the F sharp minor has come round in the required direction. For a really enharmonic modulation, not a mere change of notation, does make a mystery in which everything becomes possible. It is sometimes supposed that Bach's range of modulation has never been surpassed, and that it was inconceivable until *Das Wohltemperirtes Klavier* made it possible by means of equal temperament. The one supposition is pious and the other merely nonsensical. You cannot enlarge the range of modulation that Bach covered in 'Et exspecto resurrectionem mortuorum', the Chromatic Fantasia, and the Organ Fantasia in G minor, nor Handel's range in 'Thy rebuke hath broken his heart'. But when Bach and Handel go beyond Ex. 1 they intend and achieve miracles; while Schubert and Beethoven, who also work miracles, can cover the whole range with patently normal facts. What our grammarians have completely failed to show, as far as I can see, is just what the purpose of modulations can be. One thing is quite evident, that it is no use quoting harmonic facts without referring to the time-scale in which they are manifested. For want of such measurements our study of modulation becomes as style-destroying as exercises designed to introduce all the known figures of speech into a single paragraph.

For this reason I give no further analysis to the following three illustrations of Schubert's harmonic miracles:

Ex. 23 Begining of *Incarnatus* of Mass in A flat

Ex. 24 Enharmonic changes (slow movement of G major Quartet)

Andante un poco moto

Into A♯ minor = B♭ and so round to G again

Ex. 25 From Trio of the Minuet in Unfinished Sonata (Tonic G♯ mi.)

N.B. Bar 6 is a compression of: so that the key returned to is A♭, not G♯

But I have only touched the fringe of the subject, and I prefer to end with an illustration that shows how all these resources depend on the time-scale.

The first feature in large forms that Schubert handled with supreme mastery was the return of a main theme. This requires a highly developed sense of the degrees in which a key may be established. For instance, if a composer, after having modulated in zigzags over the circle of 5ths, drops into his tonic and his main theme as if this event were merely resuming an interrupted conversation; well, either this is a good joke or it is not. It has to be very good if it will do at all. Haydn, Mozart, and Beethoven may be trusted with it; but you will not find it in early works, and Schubert did not live to produce late ones. Now, as has been said before, the normal way to establish a key, new or old, is to harp on its dominant. In the modulation to the first new key, that of the second group in a sonata movement, the reaching of this point and the proportioning of this 'dominant preparation' is a very difficult piece of draughtsmanship. Mozart mastered it grandly; but Beethoven in his most characteristic early works often preferred to do something cleverer, and make a cast round some other key. Not until op. 29 did his Beethovenish power add the sublime proportions and simplicity of Mozart's dominant preparation to his own new resources. Schubert, whose adolescent works are stiffly imitative of Mozart, never attempted in his maturest works to tackle Mozart's way of moving to his second group, except in the first two movements of the A minor Quartet; and the slow movement seems rather shy and tired by the effort. Elsewhere Schubert's first transition is a more or less violent *coup de théâtre*, moving (except in the 'Unfinished' Symphony) in some direction other than the eventual destiny of the section. This makes it the more signifi-

Ex.26

cant that his returns to his main theme should be among the most wonderful feats of draughtsmanship in all music. Here is his way of returning to his long-lost first theme and tonic after an exposition that has proceeded from I through ♭vi via x y z to what must be taken as V, and then a development beginning in ♭iii and proceeding in a round of keys, returning to D flat (now thus correctly written instead of C sharp), and proceeding thence to a point which would be E double flat if the enharmonic circle were straightened out (and also if any sensible person cared what it was called). But whatever its name may be, its effect becomes that of iii to the long-lost main theme which quietly appears above it, first in a new relation to this minor key, and then in its own position in a key very near in pitch to the original tonic. The distant thunder of the shakes in the bass confirms the impression that we are returning to our opening. Not one artist in a thousand, and that thousand chosen from the ranks of the competent, could be trusted to recognize that it would be facile and inadequate to treat bars 9–13 of Ex. 26 as a real return to the tonic. Beethoven (who had been dead for eighteen months) would have been proud to have written Schubert's quiet swing back to iii and the subsequent thirteen bars of suspense on the dominant. The whole passage should really be begun twelve bars before Ex. 26, for the Dorian character of this particular D minor is a material factor in its relation to the dominant. Schubert's tonality is as wonderful as star clusters, and a verbal description of it is as dull as a volume of astronomical tables. But I have often been grateful to a dull description that faithfully guides me to the places where great artistic experiences await me; and with this hope I leave the reader poised on Schubert's dominant of B flat.

MUSICAL FORM AND MATTER[1]

NOT moral courage, but stark insensibility, is what the plain musician needs if he is to address without trepidation the audience of a lectureship in which he is preceded by four of the greatest living philosophers giving of their best. Stark insensibility, though useful, does not imply a talent for aesthetics; and I brace myself up against my trepidation by asserting in the most confident tones of auto-suggestion that it is as well that, not too late in the history of the Philip Maurice Deneke Lecture, a craftsman should set the example of discoursing from the craftsman's point of view, before the great philosophers have permanently established in this lectureship a tradition of philosophic heights and depths in which we mere artists can only bombinate vacuously.

Of all arts music would seem *a priori* to be the most fruitful field of study for aesthetic philosophy; and I see old friends here who may remember that it was one of my naïve undergraduate ambitions to make a contribution to aesthetic philosophy by a systematic review of music. Forty years on, I come to you with empty hands. Such philosophic rudiments as I might have developed died of examination in the year 1898, and I have since studied nothing but music. And so, with appalling effrontery, I regurgitate here certain platitudes which, with no pretensions to originality, I was already maintaining in the year of the Diamond Jubilee. My excuse is that these platitudes, however obvious to other people, are still neglected by musicians, and that their neglect always leads to confusion.

My first axiom is that the main difference between Science and art is that there is no such thing as Art with a capital A. There is such a thing as Science with a capital S; and the duty of every man of science is to contribute all his discoveries to the endless task of building up the edifice so entitled. Philosophers may argue the mere man of science out of all hope of proving that the universe, in any implicit sense of the term, exists; yet the universe is what he is investigating, and he ultimately believes in no lesser unity. He differs from the artist in that he limits his field of investigation mainly by abstraction, and does this only for the temporary purpose of controlling his observations and experiments. When these have

[1] The Philip Maurice Deneke Lecture, delivered 4 June 1934, at Lady Margaret Hall, Oxford.

led him to some fruitful generalization, it is his duty to let the rest of the universe in upon them; and where the rest of the universe does not agree with him he regards his work as incomplete. It always will be incomplete, and nothing will make him more uneasy than too artistic a completeness in it. Hence, philosophers and men of science will generally repudiate the notion that the Cosmos resembles a work of art. Nevertheless, you will find it hard to convince a musician that a work of art is not a microcosm.

But the duty of the artist is not to contribute to an edifice entitled Art with a capital A. There is no such edifice. There are individual works of art, and it is the business of each individual work to be a whole. The history of every art shows that at all periods there is a tendency, very obvious at the present day, of artists and schools of art to erect some small quasi-scientific abstraction as the basis of a new artistic heaven and earth. The theories of such abstractions ought not to detain a trained philosopher or man of science for ten minutes. They do little harm to art as long as they impel the artist to get on with his work and do not inhibit the efforts of artists who can work on a broader basis.

The question on which music should throw a specially clear light is that of the nature of an artistic whole. The records of classical music encourage the view, which I was delighted to find strongly held by Robert Bridges, that a perfect work of art is by no means a humanly impossible achievement. Human beings select the whole material and conditions of each art-problem, and they can arrange that human imperfections remain outside. I believe that the art of music contains a very large number of perfect examples. We cannot even begin to select these until we have a clear understanding of what constitutes the whole, or wholeness, of a work of art; and we shall soon find that wholeness is incompatible with pedantry. The hypothesis that the composer who achieves wholeness is right will prove enormously more fruitful than the hypothesis that he is humanly certain to be wrong. The most perfect works and styles are often fiercely attacked by critics on grounds which vary according to the taste of the times. A common form of criticism, very much in vogue at present, consists in discovering the fundamental hypothesis of a whole art-form or style, and attacking it as a fatal defect. This would be a not unpromising sign of powers of independent observation in an undergraduate who does not intend to master the art in question. When it is put forward as a contribution to responsible criticism and aesthetic philosophy it is a nuisance.

M

On the other hand, we cannot be satisfied with views so broad and vague as to induce in us a reverence for the fundamental hypotheses of rubbish.

How can we discover and estimate the fundamental hypotheses of a work of art? They are not, as Cardinal Newman suggested in a famous passage, like the rules of a game, to be learnt beforehand, but they are self-explanatory results of the contents of the work. We shall invariably fail to ascertain them if we fall into a confusion between what a work of art is and the way in which it is, or can be, produced. Such confusions are dangers inseparable from some of the disciplines most necessary to artists and critics. The historian cannot see the absolute values of a masterpiece while he is pre-occupied with its position in the progress of that pseudo-scientific abstraction, Art with a capital A. The teacher fails to realize that his criterion of a good model for students is merely his experience of what students can imitate; and the critic, magnificently aloof from such base professional concerns, finds it easy enough to say that technique is only a means to an end, but seldom troubles to find out whether a technical term may not be the shortest definition of an artistic end. Meanwhile the artist is liable to confusions from the opposite point of view; he is naïvely ready to expect from the aesthetic philosophers some guidance as to the practice of his art; and disappointment may make him despise aesthetic theory. But the theory of art, as understood by aesthetic philosophers and ordinary mortals, is concerned with results and not with processes. We may doubt whether any artist ever has produced, or ever could produce, a work of art by means of a correct aesthetic theory. Take, for example, the dogma I have just put forward—that each work of art is an individual whole. Can the artist achieve such wholeness by aiming at it?

On this point the great composers have made spoiled children of us musicians. Music has no temptation to be anything but an art pure and simple; and many works of its great masters are amazingly perfect in conception and usually perfectly preserved. Most other artists regard perfection as rare, and will learn reverently from works not perfect as wholes, not perfectly preserved, and not purely artistic in purpose. Musicians have much to learn from that great and voluminous sculptor who so habitually left his works lamentably incomplete; from that profound classical author whose hidden meaning is so much more important than that which appears on the surface; and from the architect of what Sir Max Beerbohm has so beautifully described as the 'grey eternal walls' that 'yet whisper to the tourist the last enchantments of the Middle Age'. It is obvious that I refer to Torso, Palimpsestos, and the architect of the Oxford Great Western Railway Station. Architects do not consider that the base utility of a railway station compels them to take that Oxford classic as the ultimate aesthetic standard for such buildings; and we musicians must learn to recognize wholeness as mathematicians can recognize infinity, as a quality manifest in any representative fragment, apart from the otiose evidence of the presence or absence of a beginning, a middle, and an end. In all probability, artistic wholeness is a type of infinity; but this is a matter beyond my present scope.

A work that excites admiration for its classical symmetry and balance of form obviously has an important wholeness and unity. Sir Walter Scott himself felt that he had achieved something of the kind in *The Bride of Lammermoor*; and on the other hand, he was very apologetic for the way in which a character like Dugald Dalgetty would run away with him and frustrate his most conscientious efforts to achieve such qualities in *The Legend of Montrose*. We musicians tend rather to set up the criteria with which Scott's conscience bullied him, than to estimate fairly the probability that there may be more wholeness, in the deepest aesthetic sense, in the kind of work in which one or more of the characters runs away with the author. Even in the obviously disciplined models of classic symmetry, the symmetry is only one function of the far higher individuality and coherence that constitute the real whole of a work of art.

Thus the external perfection of many musical classics has its dangers for facile aesthetic theorists, as well as its advantages for those who have the patience for deeper investigation. Similar dangers and advantages are inherent in music as an art unencumbered with external purposes and external relations. Against some of the dangers I was most timely warned, at the beginning of the century, by Professor Andrew Bradley's inaugural lecture in the Chair of Poetry, on *Poetry for Poetry's Sake*; a lecture which I heard him deliver, and which thrilled me by its firm refutation of the heresy that the sound of poetry could be separated from the sense. This lecture accomplished for me something more than its author's immediate purpose of emancipating the notion of 'pure poetry' from the limitations of a Persian rug. It awakened me to the folly of setting *a priori* limits to the powers of this or that art-form to digest material that can exist in a more or less raw state outside. As Bradley puts it, the antithesis lies not between the subject and its poetic treatment, but between the subject and the whole poem. The subject inside the poem is no longer the same as the subject outside.

Neither the humble lover nor the master of pure musical form need entertain any tolerance for theories that deny the supremacy of absolute music. But all history and experience go to prove that the absoluteness of music is a result; that this result remains independent of circumstances that may happen to make music illustrative; and, moreover, that it is a result very imperfectly attained, if at all attainable, by methods that have not early familiarized the musician with the musical treatment of words. It is no mere accident that three of the four greatest masters of absolute music, Bach, Mozart, and Brahms, spent more than half their time in setting words to music, and that the fourth, Beethoven, took enormous pains in the later part of his career to recover the art which he had almost neglected since he wrote exercises in Italian musical declamation for Salieri. On the other hand, the loudest propagandists of 'programme-music', such as Berlioz, are often almost angrily inattentive to what they call the subjects of their works. The titles of Berlioz's 'King Lear' Overture and 'Harold' Symphony are mere instances of shameless mendacity; and if these compositions have obscurities as absolute music the titles do nothing to illuminate them. A quartet of Beethoven is obviously absolute music, and all attempts to illustrate it by Beethoven's biography or the French Revolution are merely sentimental excuses for inattention. On the other hand, the 'Pastoral' Symphony is just as absolute music; and the superior person who thinks it the worse for the fact that Beethoven not only enjoyed thunderstorms and cuckoos and nightingales, but made them recognizable in this music, is just as liable to the charge of petulantly ruminating on second-hand theories of art as the opposite type of listener is liable to the charge of extemporizing sentimental romances instead of listening to the music.

Another obstacle to discovering the fundamental hypotheses of works of art is that special form of confusion between methods and results which is inherent in the technique of the art. The line between the technical and the aesthetic is by no means easy to draw, and is often, even by musicians themselves, drawn far too high, so as to exclude as merely technicalities many things which are of purely aesthetic importance. The greatest musicians, whether composers or performers, have often not cared to draw the line at all. They prefer modestly to regard everything as technique; and the player who devotes his life to the interpretation of such composers as Beethoven will be tempted to commit himself to the dangerous argument that more technique is needed for this purpose than for the most difficult fireworks that have ever been written to show the skill of the player. Four volumes, comprising almost half of Bach's complete works for clavier, were published by him under the modest title of *Clavierübung*, and in the use of such a title he was following the custom of his time. The fact is that every technical problem connected with a work of art has its aesthetic result. The process miscalled by Horace the concealment of art is the sublimation of technique into aesthetic results. There are, for instance, two aspects of the art of instrumentation; first, the art of producing euphony, and secondly, the art of writing for each instrument in such a way that the player enjoys his task. These two arts are inseparable, and the art which shows knowledge of the instrumental technique is not less aesthetic than that which selects and blends the tones. The composer ought to know more about it than the listener, and so he can single out those beauties of sound which are more directly traceable to knowledge of the player's problems. But I do not find in my own experience that this special knowledge attracts much of my attention when I am listening either to new music or to old.

The case is not greatly different from those branches of musical technique that are learnt as disciplines in order to acquire certain general abilities. Such discipline is of the nature of drill, and normally ceases when the general mastery which is its object has been attained; yet some of its technical terms remain the best and shortest descriptions of aesthetic facts. I was once severely rebuked by a friend when I pointed out a specially beautiful example of 'double counterpoint in the twelfth' in an orchestral work. My friend dryly said that there was no beauty in such a merely scholastic device. My memory cannot testify whether I was too polite, or merely lacking in the presence of mind, to point out to him that there unquestionably was great beauty in this piece of double counterpoint in the twelfth, and that it could have been attained by no other device. My friend's prejudice against technical pedantries undoubtedly made him conscientiously blind to a real aesthetic value in this case. No doubt he felt like Tennyson who, catching sight of the word 'anapaest' in a criticism, 'saw that the writer was a fool and a brute'. But perhaps Tennyson was not quite fair. And my friend would probably have been insulted if I had treated him as a child in these matters, by pointing out the passage as one in which a beautiful combination of themes was made to produce a beautifully new set of harmonies by means of transposing the upper one a twelfth lower and keeping the other in its place. He would probably have snorted 'Thanks, I know double counterpoint in the twelfth when I see it'; but at least he would not have missed the beauty of the passage.

Of course there are plenty of vitally necessary technicalities that will never emerge into the kind of importance that can be discussed aesthetically. If an aesthetic philosopher is going to analyse the emotional values of a Greek tragedy, we do not want him to inflict upon us a number of statistics about the use of the nominative and the accusative. But if we should find out that his ignorance of these is such that he cannot tell who killed whom, we had better not put much confidence in his judgement of the emotional values of the tragedy. Even Alice was able to see, without Humpty Dumpty's aid, that in the ballad of *Jabberwocky* somebody killed something, and not vice versa.

I confess that until quite recently I have been much perturbed by the impossibility of producing a non-professional definition of one of the most important categories in music—the category of tonality. The musical treatises are in a tangle of abstruse confusion over it; and the old-fashioned doctrines show such mal-observation of the classics that hardly any but bad composers can always be trusted to handle key-relations in ways which were accepted in my young days as orthodox. It is essential to my argument that no aesthetic aspect of a piece of music should be beyond the reach of an experienced listener without the intervention of some merely professional technical information. The finest master-play and the most artistic construction in games and problems will not bring the rules of chess within the category of self-explanatory fundamental hypotheses of works of art. Now all attempts to define tonality in terms more self-explanatory than a game to the non-musician seem doomed to failure. The best I can do is to assert that it has much the same place in the classics of music that perspective has in the classics of art; with this dangerous difference—that, whereas perspective is an optical science which exists whether painters choose to recognize it or not, tonality is wholly the work of musicians, and, in the classics from the time of Alessandro Scarlatti to that of our modern atonalists, has been intimately associated with certain clearly defined art-forms and rhythmic schemes. Recently, however, my difficulties have disappeared. A musician who, like most of my colleagues, denied the non-musician's capacity to appreciate tonality at all, remarked to me that to describe it to the non-musician was as hopeless as trying to describe red to the colour-blind man; whereupon it suddenly dawned upon me that the difficulty is precisely that of describing red, or the taste of a peach, or any such sensation, to anybody whatever. I have now not the slightest doubt that the non-technical lover of music has much the same sense of tonality that I have myself, and needs only time and experience to supply his lack of the facilities that come from being able to give precise names to key-relations and to remember parallel cases. Furthermore, I have recently come to realize the enormous amount of collateral evidence that composers with a fine sense of tonality bring to bear upon the listener before they expect him to recognize that a piece of music has returned to its home tonic from a distance. Far be it from me to inflict upon any audience the pure aesthetics of tonality; but, according to the principles to which Professor Bradley has helped me, a musical illustration of words can be just as absolutely musical as a passage from a Beethoven string quartet. So I will refer you to my favourite illustration of one of the very subtlest of key-relations. In Wagner's *Rheingold* Fricka expresses in a delightful melody her fond hope that Wotan would settle down quietly when he had a Walhalla to live in, and Wotan soon afterwards answers her with the same theme in a key which gently but firmly contradicts the whole harmonic basis of her hopes. It is possible to sing the part of Wotan magnificently without having the slightest idea that this key-relation serves any purpose but the convenience of the voice; and Wagner would have been as thoroughly bored by my theoretical explanation of it as the prophet Tiresias would have been bored by the schoolboy's complimenting him on his knowledge of the present, the future, and the future-perfect. But every singer finds himself expressing Wotan's gentle irony with a subtlety which he could never have learnt from a life-long study of the words apart from the music; and every listener feels the irony.

By this time you will be impatiently waiting for examples of music in which the notion of an external subject-matter is manifestly impertinent. But before we reach this stage, if we can reach it at all, I must ask you to bear with me while I give some account of my own experience as a composer. The objections to my doing so are not more obvious than the answers to them. In the first place, it is desirable that one should talk about things one really knows. In the second place, the experience of a composer has nothing to do with the merits or demerits of his work. No doubt mine is a bad case; for I compose in a classical language, which nowadays is one of those things which simply are not done. Composers of the future and critics of the present often tell me in the strongest terms what they think of such conduct. Good manners forbid me to express my candid opinion of *them*. Let us first clear the ground by two classical instances of the value of a creative artist's own experience as a thing independent of the value of his work for others.

Perhaps the most crushing of many crushing things that Brahms is recorded to have said was the question he asked in tones of friendly solicitude when a composer (let us hope a young one) showed him a voluminous and laborious work. Brahms turned the leaves of the score with simmering patience, and then asked, 'Tell me, do you find it fun writing all this?' History, at least that important artistic branch of it which deals in anecdote, proverbially refrains from relating what happened after the point of the anecdote is reached. But it is material to our inquiry to consider the possible answers to Brahms's question. If the composer had the spirit to answer 'Yes', it is Brahms who would have been crushed—unless he really thought the composer worth helping. In that case the next question would be 'Do you find that writing all this helps you to understand music better?' Or, as a powerful and saintly Oriental asked Florence Nightingale, 'Do you find yourself improving?' By which he meant 'believing more in God'. The possible answers to such questions ramify in many directions, some of them profitable, others hopeless. Gluck could say nothing that would encourage Handel to try to teach him counterpoint; and Miss Nightingale saw that it was hopeless to teach sanitation to the Oriental saint.

Let us turn to another *locus classicus*—one of Arnold Bennett's smaller works, entitled *A Great Man*. This little novel I regard as a fundamentally important contribution to the theory of artistic creation. The Great Man is an amiable youth with a weak digestion who, while recovering from a belated attack of measles, writes a sentimental novelette which proves a best seller. Arnold Bennett's account of Mr. Henry Shakespeare Knight's phases of inspiration coincides remarkably with Wagner's account, in letters to Mathilde Wesendonck, of the terrible force with which the inspiration of *Tristan und Isolde* gripped him; and it demonstrates that artistic inspiration is independent of the value of the work. Henry Shakespeare Knight's inspiration could obviously no more have survived even a moderate dose of self-criticism and experience of life than his digestion could tolerate his mischievous cousin's overdose of *marrons glacés*. He manages his affairs much better than Wagner, and has many interesting adventures; but, if these be experience, then experience runs off him like water off a duck's back. We are not told whether his publisher was ever haunted by the nightmare that Mr. Henry Shakespeare Knight's growing experience might so educate him as to deprive the author of his main source of income and the publisher of a still larger margin of profit. Such fears were fortunately groundless; and, while Shakespeare Knight (who soon gained confidence and dropped the Henry) could certainly have answered Brahms that he wrote entirely for fun, the further question as to whether it helped him to understand literature better would leave him blankly wondering what more there was in literature to understand. The fundamental hypothesis of Shakespeare Knight's art is that millions of readers will themselves bring precisely the Shakespeare-Knightly mind to the contemplation of Shakespeare Knight's works. And this complex condition is so far from self-explanatory that it can be realized only in an ephemeral and local phase of an extremely artificial civilization, which in a few years will have so changed that to recover the Shakespeare-Knightly postulates will become a task beyond the most Miltonic powers of scholarship.

Now, the truth must be faced that Arnold Bennett has here given an account of artistic inspiration which is valid for all convincing art, whether it convinces the readers of Shakespeare Knight merely of what they already bring to him, or the interpreters of works like *Tristan* and the last quartets of Beethoven, who can only grow into the experience of these works day by day to the end of their lives. Nor does it make any difference whether the artist works, or describes himself as working, easily, like Mozart, Anthony Trollope, and the ready writer of business letters, or is working like Joseph Conrad in agonized strain at the limit of his endurance. Conrad's case is met by Ferdinand's dictum:

> There be some sports are painful, and their labour
> Delight in them sets off.

The most agonized expressions ever found on a human countenance are recorded in photographs of athletes at the moment of breasting the tape. What else but 'contest' does the word 'agony' mean? The agonists find it fun; and our argument has nothing to lose from substituting for all deeper doctrines of artistic inspiration the simple assumption that inspiration consists in being at the top of one's form, whether mental or athletic. One thing is certain: that your agonist must be in training. Even Shakespeare Knight inherited his talent from a father who had endless practice in writing letters to the paper which were always readable enough to print, though their main exercise for author and reader was complete mental relaxation.

Protected by these great examples of inspiration, or of mental athletic form, I now descend to an account of my own experiences in writing an opera. In spite of a fairly large and long experience as an absolute musician, I was convinced not only of the absolute musical values of the great classics of opera, including Wagner, but of the necessity of attaining all musical values through every detail and every aspect of the libretto. Yet the literary value of the libretto does not matter, as long as certain qualities are present. The composer who can rise to the height of Miltonic or Biblical argument will miss no subtlety in the meaning of the greatest poetry; but his inspiration may easily outrun his literary criticism, so that he may express a true sentiment in setting the words of a poetaster who has expressed only a false one. Fortunately, my poet friend who wrote my libretto, if so fine a poem deserves to be called by so humble a name, was able to bring to his poetry at least as formidable a critical apparatus as I could bring to my music. Moreover, he had the first quality of an opera librettist—that of being bullyable by the composer—a quality in which Wagner, who was his own librettist, was now and then lacking.

When the libretto was approximately ready to be set to music, I tried my first experiment and, with nothing in my head, proceeded to extemporize upon paper a sketch of the music of the first scene. Had I embarked upon a piece of absolute music with so little forethought the result would not have been plausible enough to write down. But I now made the appalling discovery that this irresponsible draft read surprisingly well. It simply does not matter what sort of thickness of musical butter you spread over your libretto, so long as you do not interfere with the pace of the action. The irremediably false step would now have been to go on happily spreading over the play whatever musical condiments I chose, and then scoring the whole thing with increasing elaboration until the result was modern enough to amuse me. (Mr. Belloc's Dr. Caliban expounds a similar method for poets, as the Principle of the Mutation of Adjectives.) That, however, resembled neither the spirit nor the method in which my poet had done his work; and fortunately I already knew that his play was full of possibilities for musical design on a large scale and of high musical organization. I do not mean for a moment that it would fall into the old classical forms any more than the later music-dramas of Wagner; but I began to appreciate a fact, already known to me, but insufficiently valued, that there is at least as much of recapitulation and balance of form in the later Wagner operas as there is in any classical symphony, though on the one hand it takes place on quite different lines, and on the other hand could never be discovered from the words. As a glaring illustration, Isolde's *Liebestod* consists mainly of an exact recapitulation of the last movement of the love duet in the second act. I then said to myself 'Go to; I will mark down the opportunities for such symmetries, and I will block out my first scene by getting these into place and adjusting the niceties of declamation afterwards'. The kind of mental rheumatism which thereupon racked all my musical joints is a thing I had never experienced before and shall never be such a fool as to risk again. The symmetries were all very well, but by the time I had adjusted the words to them the effect was that at every clause somebody was waiting for the orchestra and that the prompter seemed to have deserted his box. All the vocal rhythms were extremely laboured and syncopated. And evidently the style of declamation was one of the most learned achievements of modern music. As for the formal symmetries, I could have proved their existence by a powerful analysis addressed to professional musicians and claiming indefinite latitude on the plea that a conventional exactness is no longer admissible in modern art.

It was quite clear that, whatever method might be right, this must be wrong, and that my original facile spreading of musical condiments over the text had at all events the merit of attending to parts of the problem that were already in existence, and were, in fact, the first that would present themselves to the naïve listener. Fortunately neither the facile sketch nor the rheumatic sketch had wasted more of my time than two hours each. So I was not too tired to proceed on what proved to be the right method. I declaimed my text attentively from point to point, taking for granted the possibilities of symmetry and other absolute musical resources, but not concentrating upon them. The result again took me by surprise. The declamation, being already approximately right, not only fitted itself with little difficulty into the larger formal schemes, but constantly gave rise to other formal possibilities. The correspondence between passages and recapitulations was from the outset more exact than when I had thought of the recapitulation as the basis of my work, and every deviation from exactitude explained itself as a rhetorical enhancement. There was not the slightest reason for resting content with anything that did not satisfy me as music. On these conditions, it was quite possible to work at the top of one's athletic form; or, as the popular but more boastful expression has it, to work with inspiration.

In a voluminous composition there is naturally an immense amount of laborious work, such as the scoring of *tuttis*, which common sense forbids the composer to tackle while the flow of the composition needs his attention. The state of inspiration can nevertheless be maintained throughout these more mechanical tasks if they are undertaken while waiting for light on other problems, or deferred until the rest of the work has been digested. The process of *tutti*-scoring, like that of making a fair copy, will then be as refreshing as we may hope that chewing the cud is to the recumbent cow.

I could certainly answer in the affirmative Brahms's question whether I found all this fun. As to whether it has helped me to understand music, I should consider the labour already amply worth while on account of the way in which it revealed to me the paramount greatness of Wagner as a musical composer, an aspect in which Wagner has seldom, if ever, been regarded, even by devout Wagnerians. But, besides this, it awakened me to the fact that purely instrumental music is not less, but enormously more, dramatic than any music for which situations can be found on the stage. Sir Henry Hadow has remarked that Beethoven's *Fidelio* is dramatic in the sense that his D minor Sonata is dramatic. This is illuminating, but I find myself compelled respectfully to join issue if and when it is held to imply that *Fidelio* is on that account less dramatic than an opera should be. Mozart could not have made the music of *Fidelio* more dramatic or more operatic. But he would have made the poor librettist feel like his own villain Pizarro held at bay by Leonora's pistol. If it were possible to put upon the stage anything so dramatic as the first movement of Beethoven's D minor Sonata, the result would make not only every existing opera, but every existing drama, seem cold. It would not be great drama, for its temperature would be simply insupportable. Once I was haunted by a certain crescendo leading to a climax, and I could not remember where this crescendo and climax came. It was not in *Tristan*, and it was nowhere else in Wagner, but it was of Wagnerian intensity, and was in too rich a language to come from the later works of Verdi, which were the only other possible sources of sufficient emotional force. Suddenly it dawned upon me that it was the passage leading to the quiet coda of one of Brahms's most statuesque and Olympic movements, the first movement of the A major Pianoforte Quartet, a piece which it would be utterly impertinent to connect with any non-musical ideas. From this it was an easy step to the discovery that in the fight between Don Giovanni and the Commendatore, Mozart uses with complete adequacy formulas and musical gestures which are far too cold to find a place in the development of any symphony he wrote at a later age than seventeen.

Doubtless there are some people to whom the use of music for illustrating other things is as abhorrent as the worship of the golden calf was to the law-giver of Israel; but if you wish to break all the commandments of aesthetic philosophy at once you will infer that, because stage music is of a lighter texture than purely instrumental music, therefore opera is a lower order of art. It is indeed an art in which a music can succeed that would have no chance of achieving distinction as absolute music, but it is no more essentially lower than the string quartet, than drama is essentially lower than other forms of poetry.

Another important result of my experiment in opera-writing was that, without causing any change in my methods of musical analysis, the whole façade of classical instrumental art-forms reduced itself to a mere screen-work of co-ordinates, across which the real lines of classical composition display themselves with no more interruption than the forms of a map suffer from parallels of latitude and longitude. When we come to the relation between matter and form in absolute music, you can hardly expect a pupil of Edward Caird to avoid the conclusion that these are different aspects of the same thing. But those who best know the teaching of Edward Caird will know that, however frequent this conclusion, he would not allow his pupils to use it as a *cliché* unsupported by solid and special work. The present argument has still some way to travel before it can deal truthfully with music from which we can rule out all external subject-matter.

Every work of art, from the most absolute of music to the most pantomimic of operas, selects its material in much the same way as the amoeba selects its food; by simply coming into contact with it and extending itself around it. The amoeba has, I understand, also some capacity, mechanical or chemical (why not say artistic?), for attracting suitable food before committing itself to indiscriminate contacts. Without going into inelegant detail, let us frankly use the word 'digestion' as a technical term for the way in which the work of art treats its material. If the amoeba, or the work of art, has begun to put itself outside an indigestible object, it can, so long as the object does not destroy it first, rearrange its contractions so as to put the object outside again. In works of art, this may be done by the listener or spectator, for it always takes at least two people to produce a work of art—the artist and the person who is to enjoy the completed work. We need not discuss the rules of equity between these two. Here again Professor Andrew Bradley has cleared all such barbed-wire entanglements from our field by placing the existence of a poem or work of art in the sum-total of the recipient's experience of it, so that, in short, 'a poem exists in innumerable degrees'. We know, then, that a piece of music exists in innumerable degrees; and we know that in the experience of Wagner, to say nothing of lesser men, its powers of digestion enable it to absorb almost all the other arts. Rude critics may accuse Wagner of biting off more than he can chew; and the listener's digestion may be weaker than the composer's. But there is often no harm in absorbing material without altering it by digestion. For some purposes the presence of undigested material, such as the contents of an ostrich's or even a hen's gizzard, may be an important aid to digestion. The hen swallows tiny stones which enable its gizzard to grind its food. Some works of art have very powerful gizzards. Do not ask me to locate these organs. But, for example, the *Divina Commedia* provides, in the 32nd Canto of the *Purgatorio*, one of the toughest gizzards to be found in any work of art.

We may begin our illustrations of artistic digestion a little lower than the biological level. Crystallization has not yet been found to be in itself a vital process, but it presents a phenomenon highly characteristic of early forms of art. If you drop a piece of string into a saturated solution of certain chemicals, crystals will immediately precipitate themselves upon the string, and will add their own symmetry to whatever symmetrical shape you choose to impart to your string. Whether you can or cannot devise means of withdrawing the string afterwards makes no essential difference to the result. The string is not the art-form, but the crystals could not form without it. Nobody supposes that an acrostic on the Hebrew alphabet causes the poetic merit of the *Lamentations of Jeremiah*; and nobody supposes that this poetry has lost anything in our Authorized Version by the fact that the names of the Hebrew letters have disappeared except as marginal notes, in themselves unintelligible. A large proportion of the music that culminated in the Golden Age of Palestrina was at first crystallized in much the same way around a voice singing a piece of plain-chant or, what answers the purpose quite as well, a secular song, in notes of such enormous length that no human attention will recognize the tune. It is a tautology to say that, as the art develops, its organization becomes of a higher order. And we may assume as an axiom that the organization of any individual work of art is incomparably higher than we could guess from its professional or historical labels. Perhaps there is no period of art whereof the official technicalities are more irrelevant and misrepresentative than in the case of the Golden Age of music. In Palestrina's mature style the original string round which the crystals have grown has long disappeared; and the rest of the officially recognized rules of his art give us no reason why any piece of his music should begin where it does, or come to an end at all. One of the most demoralizing experiences of my youth was the moment when the Shakespeare Knight of Victorian church-music told me that it was folly to publish in thirty-four volumes the complete works of the *Princeps musicae* of the Golden Age, inasmuch as it makes no difference to Palestrina if you turn over two pages at once. This honest man deserves rather to be remembered for his innumerable acts of unobtrusive kindness and his steady devotion to duty, than to be laughed at for successfully representing tastes which he inherited and never pretended either to originate or to transcend.

Did the English Palestrina scholars of the nineties show much more enlightenment in their piety? It is quite true that you might often turn over two pages of Palestrina without noticing it; and it is equally true that the most beautiful lace shawl may condescend to be folded. In the nineties the scholars of Golden-Age music effervesced with information as to the Church mode of a motet, its various points of imitation, and precise harmonic details as to which of its cadences display the Regular Modulations—namely, the

Dominant (which has several meanings quite different from the modern dominant), the Mediant, and the Participant; and which of them display the perhaps still more august Conceded Modulations whose existence is proved by their use by the Great Masters, perhaps in the very masterpiece under discussion. As one who has taken some trouble to follow these high matters, I feel entitled to tell those of you who have not that you need take no such trouble. They have contributed much to my understanding of the proverbial mendacity of statistics, something perhaps to the higher technique of institutional bluff, but nothing to my understanding of Palestrina, nor to my ability to read his scores with reasonable confidence that my pleasure in the imagination of their sound is well grounded.

A correct description of a masterpiece of the Golden Age would again have to deal in the first place with the words. When sceptical research has whittled away all that it can from the pious legend of Palestrina's commission from the Council of Trent, the fact remains that the ecclesiastical authorities did demand that settings of the Mass should be of reasonable length and should make the liturgical words, and no other words, audible; and that Palestrina was able to satisfy these demands by masses composed in a style which he had already been bringing to perfection throughout his life. The proper analysis of a motet would begin by identifying the themes with the words; and by the time it reached the statistics of Regular and Conceded Modulations it would have analysed not only the music but the prose by much the same methods as those of R. L. Stevenson's or Vernon Lee's discussions on the use of words.

With a few more illustrations we shall be able to reach, not the level (on which this argument has really been moving all the time), but the self-evident and uncontradictable condition, of absolute music. One of the greatest masters of absolute music whom I have ever known, Julius Roentgen, introduced me to a glorious Psalm by Sweelinck, *Or sus, serviteurs du Seigneur*. We both of us knew it by heart before we noticed that it was a figured chorale on the tune known as the 'Old Hundredth'. Its 'figures' are almost unrecognizable as those of the tune, not because of anything abstruse in their transformation, but, on the contrary, because Sweelinck's treatment has given the words their natural quantities, whereas the plain tune strained them considerably. The art of transforming musical themes is omnipresent in music that does not conscientiously object to it. It constitutes most of the art of Wagnerian leitmotive; and sad nonsense is often preached about it by theorists and teachers who imagine it to be the basis of logical development in music. Some thematic transformations are good, such as those of the first theme in Brahms's Pianoforte Quintet, and of the motive of world-power as variously conceived by the innocent Rhine-daughters, the malignant Nibelung, and Wotan in his Walhalla; others are mechanical and clumsy, as when Wagner tries to sophisticate the tune of the boy Siegfried's horn into a grown-up heroic theme. Apart from the art of paragraph building, such thematic connexions can give us no guarantee that the music has any more logic than a series of puns.

Here is the text of that Sweelinck Psalm, which I will take the liberty of singing to its proper tune of the 'Old Hundredth':

> Or sus, serviteurs du Seigneur,
> Qui nuict et jour en son honneur
> Dedans sa maison le servez,
> Louez-l'et son Nom eslevez.

Now, as I have already said, Roentgen and I enjoyed Sweelinck's setting as a piece of absolute music long before we discovered its structure as a setting of the 'Old Hundredth'. That discovery increased our admiration only by a mild amusement: first that Sweelinck himself and his contemporaries, such as Michael Praetorius, might have been mere organ-grinders as far as their habit of composition on these lines could guarantee an inspired result; and secondly that if Sweelinck had set the 'Old Hundredth' in any language but French he would have produced a totally different set of derived figures. Here is the whole origin of his figures. Notice that no translation will produce the figures arising out of the last line; unless you can find a language which will give the elision at *Louez-l'et son Nom*, and so obtain a third note for *louez-le*. (Sing a note to each syllable.)

Or sus
> *serviteurs*
>> *du Seigneur* (also augmented in the bass)

Qui nuict et jour
> *en son honneur*

Dedans sa maison le servez
> *le servez*

Louez-le (also augmented throughout the mass of harmony, so as to ring like all the bells in Flanders)
> *et son Nom*
>> *et son Nom eslevez.*

N

Let us return to that incontrovertible dictum that form and matter are different aspects of the same thing. Illustrations of this are ridiculously obvious. The artist and the public often have converse ideas as to what is form and what is matter. To the portrait-painter the sitter is, perhaps in a regrettable number of cases, the given form; and what matters to the artist is his art of painting. To the Philistine relations of the sitter, all high artistic interests are mere form. What matters is the likeness. If the result is an immortal work, posterity will find that its form and matter will be different aspects of the same thing.

Would it be possible to find in music a case where form and matter were interchangeable note for note? There are strict canonic forms which approach this condition very closely. In these one or more voices follow a leader note for note, either at the unison, or with some rigid condition of difference. If the leader itself should be a preordained melody, and if, as is unlikely, we could prove it to have made itself without any liturgical or secular non-musical origin, we should then have an absolute identity between matter and form. Unfortunately, or fortunately, though it is possible for quite elaborate canons to be very beautiful, the strict canonic forms are peculiarly liable to be forced on music from outside. And if there is anything which music certainly cannot digest, it is the imposition of *a priori* abstract musical forms from outside. I have already described how the experience of writing an opera removed from my mind all trace of the illusion that the forms of masterpieces, such as the sonatas of great composers, exist *a priori*. Thus we may for ever cast into limbo everything that we mean when we condescend to use the word 'academic' as a term of vulgar abuse. And let us first of all cast into limbo that dreadful exercise which some of the greatest teachers of composition have, in quixotic loyalty to their own masters, ordained for their pupils; the exercise of making, on themes of one's own, a paraphrase of some particular classic, in the perverse hope that the finer adjustments of a masterpiece can be learned from what are *ex hypothesi* the maladjustments of one's miserable parody. Not such were the exercises of the great composers. Beethoven solved a genuine problem if, as is alleged, he scored Mozart's G minor Symphony from a four-hand arrangement; and one of the great moments in musical history is that in which Schubert at the age of thirteen, writing his first song, *Hagar's Klage*, and, starting with the intention of humbly paraphrasing Zumsteeg's declamation of that interminable poem, discovered, three-quarters of the way through, that Zumsteeg could not compose and that he could.

Now let us take one of Bach's exercises from the *Clavierübung*. It is one of two purely instrumental settings of the chorale, *Aus tiefer Noth*, and is much more restricted by its hypothesis than Sweelinck's setting of the 'Old Hundredth'. The composition is written as if for four voices with the chorale tune in long notes line by line in the treble, each line being accompanied by the other voices in fugue-texture in quicker notes on each current phrase treated by inversion—that is to say, the fugues treat each line upside down as well as the right way up. Musical inversion is popularly supposed to be not only a learned, but an ingenious, device. There is no more ingenuity in it than in holding a page of music upside down before a looking-glass. Everything will invert; the question is, what will the inversion be like? In the case of *Aus tiefer Noth* it so happens that the inversions of the phrases are beautiful, a fact which I have no reason to suppose occurred to Martin Luther when he invented or adapted the tune. We may therefore give to Bach's imagination the credit of perceiving their beauty. 'Canto fermo' in the treble; harmony in three-part fugue by inversion and diminution on each current phrase in the lower parts. Here you have a definition which describes the behaviour of at least 75 per cent. of the notes of the whole work, leaving grammatical necessities to account for the rest. This is a solution of a problem in severe musical discipline, such as could suitably be given to a candidate for a musical degree. Oxford candidates for the degree of Bachelor of Music were given a very similar problem, without specification of any complexity, here in 1896, the 'canto fermo' being a tune of rollicking quality that did great credit to the humanity of the examiner. What is the difference between such an academic exercise and these Bach chorales? The obvious and pious answer is correct. The academic exercise will be thought meritorious if it achieves impeccable grammar, whereas the Bach chorales are consummate examples of musical rhetoric.

Let us accept this pious opinion and proceed to ask whether we could conceive that the rhetoric was Bach's guiding principle, and that this crystalline quasi-mathematical form was a by-product of the rhetoric. Practically the idea is absurd. Though it is ultimately true that every genuine work of art grows, like every living form, from within, we cannot help being conscious of genera and species before we are aware of protoplasm and cells. The form of the figured chorale has been known to composers ever since the medieval descanters evolved the rudiments of counterpoint round tunes whose notes were stretched to the limits of human breath. But it is so far from being a theoretical absurdity that, in the case of the by no means raw material of Luther's own tune, it is the actual fact that the musical rhetoric existed first and last and practically all the time. Even the choice of the Phrygian mode—itself a matter of considerable harmonic organization—was entirely appropriate to the Psalmist's cry from the deep. The Sweelinck Psalm is looser in form; for in it no one voice has the 'canto fermo' *seriatim*. But it is in some ways an even stronger case of interchangeability between form and matter; for Roentgen and I, two musicians whose training and outlook produced a strong recalcitrance to the idea of outside interference with form, had enjoyed its absolute musical rhetoric without suspecting that it had any pre-established form. Both for Sweelinck and for Bach the rhetoric takes its origin in the emotions of the Psalmist and the metres of the German or French versifier. But for Bach's organ-music this step outside the realms of music is as negligible as the step implied in Beethoven's title to a movement which rightly figures as the loftiest summit of absolute music in a delightful book (*A Musical Pilgrim's Progress*, by J. D. M. Rorke), the *Heiliger Dankgesang eines Genesenen an die Gottheit, in der lydischen Tonart*. We do not want to know or to think of the details of Beethoven's illness when we listen to the A minor Quartet. The Sacred Song of Thanks tells of thanksgiving, not of illness, and the section entitled *Neue Kraft fühlend* expresses the feeling of new-found strength as the contrast not of health after sickness but of activity after contemplation. In form the *Dankgesang* is a figured chorale, of which the tune and interludes are entirely Beethoven's own.

The figured chorale is the simplest and most nearly mechanical of art-forms, but time, to say nothing of your patience, fails for more illustrations of indisputably absolute music; and, after all, it is hardly reasonable to expect an absolute musician to describe in words, and without the aid of at least a pianoforte, a music which is not only *ex hypothesi* inexpressible in words but is, as Mendelssohn once explained in a remarkably close piece of reasoning, most definite where words are most at the mercy of the personal equation.

In an article in the Beethoven Centenary Number of *Music and Letters* in 1927[1] I compared the most conventional of Beethoven's

[1] Reprinted in this volume, p. 271.

sonatas, that in B flat, op. 22, with what is popularly supposed to be the most 'formless' of all his works, the Quartet in C sharp minor, op. 131; and I had no difficulty in showing that the improvisatorial C sharp minor Quartet has at least as much predestination as the conventional B flat Sonata, and that the Sonata has, for its own simpler needs, quite as much free-will as the Quartet. And it is doubtful whether in the whole course of some two hundred essays in the analysis of purely instrumental music I have ever made plain to myself and the reader, or interesting to either of us, the question whether, apart from a few unavoidable technical terms, I am dealing with form or with matter. Most readers will probably think I am talking of nothing but form. But how many plays or stories could you describe clearly if you conscientiously omitted the plot? So I will conclude with reference to two pieces of music which continue to give rise to endless disputes as to their musical integrity.

Beethoven is recorded to have said in a moment of depression that his choral finale to the Ninth Symphony was a mistake, and that he wished he had written (or perhaps wished eventually to write) an instrumental finale. At one time the finale of the A minor Quartet was intended for the Ninth Symphony, but this was before either the choral finale or the A minor Quartet was beginning to take shape. It would certainly never have served the purpose. I am a fervent upholder of the choral finale, which is a perfect set of variations presenting to me no more difficulties of musical form than any Bach fugue; and wisdom after the actual event, together with utter lack of prophetic insight into what did not take place, makes it impossible for me to conceive any other finale. Still, apart from the view that the choral finale is a failure, we have to reckon with the less destructive view, promulgated by Wagner, that Beethoven here felt an imperative need to break into words. Sir Walter Parratt was inclined to believe this; but I shall never forget his vivid description of an incident which shows that the Bacchic frenzy of that choral finale is far beyond the power of anything less than music. He saw a man haranguing a crowd and becoming more and more passionate until it seemed as if no human frame could stand such a stress. Suddenly the man broke into a dance, very rhythmic and not ungraceful, and danced his passion away in perfect silence.

Now, let us take a piece of choral music that ends by breaking away from words; the much-discussed case of Brahms's *Schicksalslied*. The text of this Song of Destiny is a poem by Hölderlin in which the first part describes the remote and calm bliss of Elysian spirits; while the rest, which Brahms develops on a larger scale, complains of the blind fugitive lot of mankind, doomed at last to fall into the unknown. Hereupon Brahms transcends the whole poem by an orchestral postlude which recapitulates in a brighter key the orchestral prelude to the Elysian movement. Sentimental persons are apt to see in this the expression of an optimistic contradiction of the poet. Sterner critics accuse Brahms of sentimentality. Both are finding in the music the blunders they themselves have brought to it. They fail to notice that the theme of the prelude and postlude have no actual connexion with those describing the Elysian spirits. Moreover, there is no reason why the effect of the postlude should not be akin to that of poor Francesca's *Nessun maggior dolore*. These things are ruthlessly bigger than the emotions we can bring to them. Sir Frederick Pollock points out that Dante has already quite explicitly transcended the popular view of immortality as 'an existence indefinitely prolonged under improved conditions in Greenwich time'. On this transcendent note, then, let me end, with an appeal to philosophers better qualified than I am to work out the theory that the wholeness of a work of art is a type of infinity.

NORMALITY AND FREEDOM IN MUSIC [1]

'NORMALITY' and 'freedom' are terms which need precise definition and which do not deserve to be used vaguely. Mr. Bernard Shaw has helped to fix the proper meaning of the word 'normal' in the public mind by telling us that his oculist congratulated him on having normal sight and told him that that condition was exceedingly rare. We must not confuse the normal with the usual. Only under specially happy conditions is it usual to reach and to maintain the standard which a doctor regards as normal; but this normality is a real and practical standard, not an unattainable theoretical ideal. At this time of day it ought hardly to be necessary to point out that our criterion must not be that of the criminologists who at the end of the nineteenth century demonstrated to their own satisfaction that they could not distinguish genius from insanity. I have it on the infallible (or at all events indisputable) authority of my own intuition that such writers are condemned to spend many thousand years in Purgatory collecting statistics of the wild-oat crops sown by ten dull persons for every genius into whose private affairs they have intruded.

For the purposes of art the doctor's criterion is not adequate, unless it is applied to every phase of an activity. Art is an activity, and our ideas of what is normal to it must not be confused by notions appropriate only to fixed points. At the moment of breaking a record an athlete's heart is in a condition which would be very alarming to a doctor who should suppose that it was habitual; but the doctor may be expected to know the normal proportions of strain and relaxation for a normal young athlete with a normal capacity for breaking records.

The normal in art is not merely an activity. All art includes conflict, and the vulgarities of bad art and the futilities of doctrinaire fashions all consist essentially in suppressing healthy elements of conflict. Some causes of conflict in art are nuisances, such as imperfections which are not inherent in the character of an instrument, but which merely burden the composer's memory with unconnected details of trivial difficulties, the list of which becomes out of date whenever the instrument is improved. But even here

[1] The Romanes Lecture, delivered in the Sheldonian Theatre, Oxford, on 20 May 1936 (Clarendon Press).

the wise artist is careful lest a too facile use of the improvement
should destroy the character of the instrument. No instrument has
been so completely changed by mechanical improvements as the
horn has been changed since the time of Beethoven by the invention
of ventils: no composer has so thoroughly developed the new
character of the instrument as Wagner has developed the ventil-
horn in *Tristan und Isolde*: and no critic has spoken more severely
of the degeneration of horn technique caused by the ventils than
Wagner in his preface to the score of that work. Improvements in
instruments can remove causes of conflict on one ground, only to
create fresh conflict on higher ground. Mr. Wells in one of his
most fascinating Utopias, *Men Like Gods*, regards the element of
conflict as a defect in our territorial art, and degrades to the level of
wit the devices which overcome the resistance of material. But even
in a world where every man can be a gardener, every gardener a
Luther Burbank, and every chemist a creator of materials with all
conceivable desirable qualities, architecture will still use the force
of gravity paradoxically in the keystone of the arch, and the most
desirable materials will have properties that must be reconciled
with their equally desirable opposites. The normal solution of all
conflicts will be mutual service, and here alone shall we find perfect
freedom.

This will suffice for a definition of freedom in art. Freedom is
not opposed to normality. It is in every sense of the term a function
of it, and I doubt whether my discourse would suffer any material
change of sense if 'freedom' were substituted for 'normality'
throughout the remainder of it.

My present purpose is to urge that we should use this sense of
the word 'normal' as our main criterion for music and for all works
of art. Nothing is more sterilizing than the critical conventions
which demand originality as a *sine qua non* for all artists, and regard
it as the primary condition for the survival of present-day work to
a posterity whose judgement no critic can foresee. Posterity often
preoccupies the critic almost to the exclusion of all knowable affairs.
The criticism of contemporary art should not attempt the impossible. Such of it as reaches posterity will invariably be received with
derision, and some of the derision will be unfair.

From the eighteenth century to the third quarter of the nineteenth century the accepted criterion was correctness. It lent itself
to infinities of pedantry, and its principal irrelevancies were exposed
and immortalized by Wagner in his character of Beckmesser. Far

be it from me to hold a brief for poor Beckmesser: it would be anti-social to whitewash a bogyman so useful for the terrorizing of infant critics. But his criterion of correctness can at the worst only irritate. It does not sterilize or inhibit the activities of any self-respecting artist. It demands some positive knowledge from the critic, and may give the artist some useful information even when the critic is mistaken. The reason why it breaks down as a criterion is that, like Wagner's Fricka, it knows only what is usual and cannot even see what is essentially correct in things that have never happened before. As Fricka forbade the mating of Siegmund and Sieglinde, it would cut off the whole human race by forbidding the marriage of the children of Adam and Eve. But even Fricka did Wotan the service of proving to him that Siegmund was merely his long-suffering cat's-paw and not the free hero whom he needed.

Correctness will not prevent the current criticism of any period from manifestly bristling with abnormalities when we look back on it in the light of later knowledge. But critics do not always fail to recognize the important artists of their day. The neglect and poverty in which Mozart died so young would have been an affair of a few lean years if he had survived it. In fact, poor Salieri's reputation has been terribly blasted by his remark that 'Mozart's death was a good thing for us other musicians, because if he had lived much longer we should all have starved'. If he had lived longer he would have ranked as an elder contemporary of Beethoven. Salieri might have starved, but Beethoven would still have been abused by critics largely because of his enormous reputation, which earned him the freedom of the City of Vienna and a funeral quite as prominent as any burial in Westminster Abbey or St. Paul's. The critics were at fault in judging his works by criteria which they had tardily learnt from Mozart, but this very mistake paid him the compliment of comparing his music with the greatest that they fancied they could understand. What makes them contemptible to us is their failure to see that Beethoven was more distinguished than dozens of other composers now known only to researchers in early nineteenth-century pianoforte music. But even here they were the better for having a notion of correctness according to the traditions of a good school; and Beethoven himself would not have applauded the superior wisdom of a criticism that despised those traditions. If his critics could have praised him for his originality and for creating a new language and establishing a new scientific theory of his art, they would still have been apt to think Dussek and Steibelt far more original.

The doctor's conception of the normal includes everything that is valuable in the criterion of correctness, and allows, or even demands, full scope for originality. It enables us to put our criticism on a basis that saves us from worrying about posterity. It saves us no other trouble, for the doctor himself must admit that it demands more knowledge than he will ever possess and provides no royal road thereto; but this does not make him accept any less lofty criterion. If we trust to more popular criteria we are sure to talk a great deal of nonsense and to deserve little credit for any luck that enables us to talk sense. The very difficulties of using normality as a criterion are profitable. They enable us to learn from our mistakes, and do not prevent us from sometimes doing justice to permanent artistic values.

But we must beware of spurious imitations of common sense. One of the most preciously vulgar of spurious normalities is a certain view of the pianoforte which threatens to become orthodox to-day. A facile common sense insists upon the blow of the hammer upon the string as the essential feature of the pianoforte. Such easy thinking is far from attaining the normal intelligence of a normally acute listener who enjoys good pianoforte music properly played. The ear is not concerned with an X-ray view or an indecent exposition of the inside of the pianoforte. It is concerned with sounds which, whatever their initial impact, die away when they are sustained. There is nothing abnormal or inartistic in a pianoforte touch which reduces or eliminates the element of percussion, any more than there is in flute-playing which is good enough to make the omnipresent consonant F imperceptible in the musical note. Kingsley pointed out in *Madam How and Lady Why* that no amount of chemical analysis of a plum-pudding could disclose the fact that the cook had boiled it in a cloth. The normal idea of a plum-pudding is that of a person who enjoys eating it and digests it without pain. The aesthete who concentrates upon the element of percussion in the pianoforte might as well think it his duty to eat boiled cloth and throw the pudding away.

The pianoforte is an excellent subject for illustrating the elements of conflict in musical art, and a chopsticks pianoforte technique is a characteristic symptom of the usual tendency to annihilate all conflicting elements and to erect the main cause of the trouble into a dictatorship. The percussion, which is the least musical aspect of the instrument, is undoubtedly the cause of many valuable features of pianoforte style; but current theories of the styles of all instruments are infested by crude inferences from the notion that music is made for the instrument instead of the instrument being made for music. It is often seriously urged that nothing should be written for any instrument which would be equally appropriate to another instrument: that clarinet phrases should be appropriate only to the clarinet, oboe phrases to the oboe, and so on. This, as I have often been provoked to remark, is as much as to argue that no gentleman should say anything that could possibly be said by a lady and no lady should say anything that could possibly be said by a gentleman. For the normal treatment of an instrument it is not enough to find out what is good for that instrument. The question is: what is the instrument good for? In the case of the pianoforte, its immense range of expression is largely due to the fact that its evanescent tone is, more than that of any other instrument, suggestive. By common consent the greatest master of pianoforte style, and the one whose music is least translatable on to other instruments, is Chopin, who demands and implies immense power without any *martellato* devices; and who puts a greater strain than any other composer upon the suggestive capacities of a *sostenuto* touch. The power of suggestion is a factor in normal life and normal art.

Let us consider some more general examples of what is normal for such music as Western civilization has learnt to understand and enjoy during the last five or six centuries. First we have to consider from what centre or foci this whole art of music has radiated. Primitive origins and primitive music are beyond the scope of my inquiry, which concerns only what is, or should be, normal for music-lovers in our Western civilization. The centre of our musical aesthetic system is unaccompanied vocal harmony. And here at the outset of this inquiry we encounter a typical instance of the dangers of popular prejudice as to what is normal. The man in the street will ask 'why harmony rather than melody?' But unaccompanied melody is a much more complex matter, for the development of harmony has destroyed for us the Oriental view of melody as consisting merely of a single line of sounds. The most unsophisticated Western listener hears an unaccompanied melody as the surface of some implied harmony; and the experienced musician will in many cases hear it as a bass. Bach, not only in his magnificent unaccompanied solos for violin and violoncello, but in many long passages in his toccatas and preludes, writes pages and pages of melody to which no good bass can be supplied, for the simple reason that they are their own bass. This is like a line-drawing which, unaided by any shading, contrives to convey illimitable effects of perspective. The manner and execution may appear as primitive as Edward Lear's picture of the Co-operative Cauliflower walking towards the Setting Sun, his steps supported by Two Confidential Cucumbers: but this is a drawing which no one can suppose to be more prehistoric than the story which it illustrates.

The conditions of Bach's unaccompanied violin and violoncello music make such remarkable exercise in suggestion quite normal. We may profitably compare them with Max Reger's unaccompanied works for the violin, which, though ostensibly modelled upon Bach, are full of passages that are merely unsupported melodies. Reger has simply failed to grasp the nature of the problem. It was quite clear to Bach's earliest biographer, Forkel, who describes it as the art of writing in one part so that it is impossible to add another. Nevertheless, in the first half of the nineteenth century, when Bach's art was being rediscovered, musicians of the calibre of Mendelssohn and Schumann were so unaccustomed to prolonged stretches of unaccompanied melody that they made incredibly naïve attempts to supply accompaniments to these works. They were quite right in regarding long stretches of unaccompanied melody as abnormal in keyboard and ensemble music. What they failed to realize was: first, that there is nothing abnormal in the wish to hear a violin or a violoncello without accompaniment; and secondly, that in the nature of the case these single melodic lines are more normal than the polyphony which an unaccompanied violin can be forced to achieve. In the service of music Bach did coerce it to extraordinary exertions in polyphony: exertions which have recently been found to be far more normal in relation to the primitive violin-bow of Bach than to the otherwise more resourceful modern bow.

From this digression, then, we have learnt something about melody which Mendelssohn and Schumann have evidently forgotten, but which is essential for the understanding of polyphony. Melody is analogous to line-drawing, and the modern musician is accustomed to a melody that implies harmony as the modern draughtsman is accustomed to a line-drawing that implies perspective; but melody and line-drawing may have powers of their own which are independent of these implications. The ancient Egyptians showed great powers of line in figures where both eyes were visible in profile while the body was viewed from the front and the legs again in profile. The scale of a genuine folk-song often coincides with our major mode, but also often refuses to conform to our harmonic ideas. What it never does is to behave in a way which needs our harmonic explanation. 'Annie Laurie' is quite a pretty tune, but its first seven notes are obviously the work of a lady or gentleman picking out sweet appoggiaturas on the pianoforte. Such melodic lines are recent products of harmony. They are no such firm basis as the Gregorian tones and folk-melodies on which polyphony was founded.

Our whole musical culture suffers, as it already suffered in Bach's time, from neglect of what has been very rightly called the Golden Age of music, a period culminating in Palestrina (d. 1594) when all highly organized music was conceived for the harmony of unaccompanied voices. Nowadays the works of this period are best known to specialists who know too little of other music, and whose view of the period itself is often exclusively liturgical. The centre of Palestrina's art was liturgical; but to be at the centre of the musical universe is not enough if our view is confined to our own position. Still less will it suffice to be at the circumference of a small circle near the centre. Some enthusiasts tell us that the virginal and viol music of the sixteenth century is at least as fine as the choral music. They are not wrong in being enthusiastic about it for its own sake, but if they see no more in the choral music than they see in the special objects of their enthusiasm we need not worry them by trying to enlarge their view.

The choral music of the sixteenth century, both sacred and secular, represents indeed a golden age of all that is normal to choral harmony. Musical education itself was then in perfect tune with the free practice of the art. It began at the right mental age with the training of choir-boys in real music. The rules of strict counterpoint were the result of at least two centuries of experience with a constantly growing refinement of perception. They were not, as the late W. S. Rockstro maintained, 'the precepts to which the Great Masters gave their loving obedience'; on the contrary, they were generalizations by shrewd observers of the practice of the great masters. And it is only in later times that the subject of strict counterpoint has been wrought, by clumsy attempts to bring it up to date, into a shocking tangle of mendacity and special pleading inflicted upon excusably sceptical undergraduates. In the sixteenth century the path of progress was the path of purity. And there was no motive for revolution so long as the interests of the unaccompanied chorus were all that mattered. Can we conceive a more normal and more purely musical centre for the aesthetics of music than the perfection of the unaccompanied chorus?

That perfection was not attained by excluding all other influences on music. The spoken word is the normal purpose of the human voice, and the masters of choral music never contemplated the notion of eliminating the elements of conflict between speech and song. On the contrary, Palestrina was acclaimed and encouraged by the Church as the greatest master in the art of reconciling highly organized polyphony with clear declamation. This problem was not as difficult for Palestrina as it is for modern musicians. His musical rhythms differed from ordinary speech-rhythms hardly more than the rhythms of quantitative verse. The rhythms of later music correspond to those of vigorous bodily exercise, and conversation is not more difficult to reconcile with the control of the paces of a horse. Dance-rhythms and speech-rhythms are at opposite poles of the musical sphere. As the unaccompanied chorus stimulates the highest human activities,

> Blest Pair of Sirens, Pledges of Heaven's first Joy,
> Sphere-born harmonious Sisters, Voice and Verse,

so the dance-rhythms are best served by less musical means gravitating towards the drum. The naïve person who tells you that what he likes in music is rhythm will listen to the strains of a military march with undiminished, if not increasing, enjoyment as they recede into the distance until the sound of the big drum alone survives. But we need not accept this solution of his mental conflicts as normal.

In musical history nothing is more impressive than the catastrophic revolution which seems to have obliterated the school of Palestrina immediately after his death. The symptoms of this revolution are commonly described in text-books as consisting in grammatical licences, such as the unprepared dominant seventh and other harmonic details, which are supposed to have wrecked the whole of Palestrina's aesthetic system. Composers and teachers who are weak enough to yield to pressure from journalists have actually been persuaded to imagine that the way to progress is always through a revolutionary theory of harmony. We might as well ascribe the origins of great revolutions in literature to the earliest author who can be found to have split the infinitive. No great change in art has ever owed its origin to anything less than some all-pervading and urgent necessity. The urgency has never consisted in the mere need to 'get away from' this or that established order. Boredom may be as terrible an infliction as Samuel Butler implies when he tells us that it is the ultimate and most drastic remedy of the hospitals of Erewhon; but great artists are too busy for it and do not stop to inquire whether their material is new or old. The urgency of the monodists at the beginning of the seventeenth century derived none of its force from such mean motives as jealousy or weariness of the perfection of Palestrina; and Monteverdi's unorthodox use of discords came from no *a priori* theory, though he was an excellent master of urbane controversy who could prove both to his critics and to his followers that his style had not grown by accident. His works on the lines of the classical polyphony were, indeed, aggressively rough. He was evidently already thinking of other things when he wrote them, though much of their harshness is within the letter of the classical laws. Nothing could be more futile than to suppose that his harmonic licences could in themselves have any more power than stylistic affectation or ordinary bad grammar to effect an artistic revolution.

Every schoolboy knows that Mantua is dangerously near to Cremona. Now Monteverdi was under the patronage of the Duke of Mantua at the time when the first Cremona violins were being made. The monodic revolution does not mean the downfall of polyphony. It means the rise of the whole art of instrumental music, both as an accompaniment to the voice and as an independent aesthetic sphere. Even the narrower issues of the revolution are vast enough. There is the very existence of the solo voice, which had hitherto distinguished itself from the chorus mainly by extremely decadent fashions in ornamenting the top parts of madrigals; and there is the natural discovery that the most interesting and profitable field for experiment was that of musical drama. The great artist will not miss his opportunities. At the beginning of the century those who had mastered the art of Palestrina could continue for one more generation to write pure polyphony if they lived, like Orlando Gibbons, far enough away from the centre of the great experiments. In Italy itself the first quarter of the seventeenth century was distinguished by the publication of magnificent editions of Palestrina's works; and the actual decadence of choral polyphony showed itself in the vogue of music for vast piles of multiple chorus, facile as the decadence of some happily obsolescent kinds of modern orchestration. But for a young man to be indifferent to the rise of instrumental music in the early seventeenth century was to be no artist at all.

And the path of progress was no more, as in Palestrina's time, the path of purity. In fact, there was no path. Immense areas of ground needed clearing, and the task of laying foundations had to be accomplished with very little guidance as to what was to be built upon them. Most of the music of the seventeenth century suffers too much from the privations of pioneer work to be attractive to any but historians; and our modern revivals of it awaken fashionable interest mainly through the accessories of stage decoration, though we are now too conscientious to believe in the kind of collection, called Gems of Antiquity, in which the pearls of Caccini and Monteverdi are served up in rich salad-dressings of nineteenth-century harmony. The supreme merit of the early monodists has nothing to do with their impatience with older art, an impatience which was a source only of weakness. Nor does it lie in their very rare and occasional achievement of a well-balanced artistic result. It lies in their grasp of the normal facts concerning instruments in themselves and in relation to voices. Compared with this, their equally firm grasp of essential principles of musical drama is a side-issue. All their problems were far beyond the reach of conscious logic, and to produce mature works of art was as hopeless a task for the monodists as to arrive at Wagner and Brahms at once; but the logical sense of the Italians, while it sometimes inhibited them from available sources of beauty, did help them to formulate important fundamental principles.

When we cross the Alps and study the works of Monteverdi's contemporary, Bach's mighty predecessor, Schütz, we find ourselves in a much less disciplined world. Schütz sometimes produces, by a mixture of luck and inspiration, deeper and more perfect things than we shall ever find in Monteverdi; but he also falls into traps which would never have deluded an Italian master. For instance, he does not know that, while most instruments can support voices, no voice can support an instrument; that if you sing in a bass voice, a violoncello will provide a bass for you even if it is playing higher notes than you are singing, but that you may growl your loudest till doomsday and fail to supply a bass for the violoncello. This is an elementary illustration of one of the normal paradoxes in musical technique. It is a matter which is settled by experience and not by convention. Schütz was too normal an artist to base theories upon his mistakes, and in any case art succeeds not by theory but by trial, with or without error. Even Monteverdi experimented first, and theorized afterwards in self-defence.

Bach and Handel were born in 1685, and so grew up into a musical world which had already evolved a mature aesthetic system from the work of the seventeenth-century pioneers. The harmonic language and the principal art-forms of eighteenth-century music had already become classical in the work of Alessandro Scarlatti, whose son Domenico is much more familiar to us by reason of his fantastic anticipations of a later art. Dr. Schweitzer has remarked that of all arts music is that in which perfection is a *sine qua non*, and that the predecessors of Bach were foredoomed to comparative oblivion because their works were not mature. This view is a useful corrective to the prevalent habits of musical historians, who find inexhaustible interest in the progress and tendencies of seventeenth-century music, but who become tongue-tied and perfunctorily pious when they have to deal with Bach and Handel. Their difficulty lies in the fact that the historical position of a work of art is not a matter of aesthetic importance. Speaking loosely, we may call any knowledge historical that saves us from misinterpretations, or that enables us to distinguish the synthetic products of a syndicate of nineteenth-century ballad-concert accompanists from a genuine 'gem of antiquity'; but the relevant part of this knowledge is concerned, not with history, but with the contents of the genuine antique objects. A work of art normally exists for its own sake, and not for its position in history. Art-forms themselves do not exist in the abstract, however habitual they may have become to those who use them. They are the forms which normally arise from the artist's proper use of his materials; and the wise artist will have no *a priori* objection to composing on the lines of their general types. Their rules are not trammels, but means of securing liberty. Their conventions are devices which have been found convenient. Why waste your powers of invention on rediscovering ordinary trade methods? The great artist will not discard conventions until he finds them inconvenient, or unless he invents something better. It is stupid to use a convention in a way which shows that you have missed its point, but it is no cleverer to violate a convention because you do not understand it.

When we speak of the age of Bach and Handel, we use an expression that would have puzzled their contemporaries; and when we

o

study any music of that age we encounter the flattest contradiction
of any criteria of originality and progress. In the first place, not
even Bach's most pious pupils could have hoped that posterity
would regard except with an indulgent smile their personal conviction that he was more than a scholastic musician of local fame; and
in the second place, nobody suspected even the opportunist Handel
of being in advance of his time. Bach, to the few critics who knew
of him otherwise than as a brilliant organist, was always hopelessly
out of date. When he was nineteen he played figured chorales to
Reinken, a man ninety years of age, who exclaimed: 'My son, I
thought this art would die with me, but it lives again in you'; and
Bach's last composition, dictated on his death-bed, was a figured
chorale. The age of Bach and Handel is an age in which those two
composers stood alone. Handel's contemporary fame rested on
works which we have forgotten, and on aspects of his best work
which do not appeal to us.

Burney lived to welcome the symphonies of Haydn, and wrote
his *History of Music* after the aesthetic system which comprehends
the two very different worlds of Bach and Handel had in our
modern estimation been completely swept away by the dramatic
impulses which inspired Gluck and led through Mozart and Haydn
to Beethoven. Yet Burney could give us a delightful account of
days spent with Gluck in Vienna, and then proceed to write the
later chapters of his *History of Music* without showing any suspicion
that Handel's operas were less important than his oratorios, or that
the chief revolution in recent music did not consist in 'new ways
of taking appoggiaturas and notes of taste'. Nor, with the exception of Gluck himself, were the masters who followed Bach clearly
conscious of any revolution. Instrumental polyphony had struggled
into precarious life by the time of Bach and Handel; they were the
only composers who brought it to maturity, and their contemporaries thought them pedantic for doing so. Their music survives
for us because it is normal in a completeness which no other music
of the time attained.

The customs of a period have no power to establish works of
art as classics. Handel's profession was primarily that of an opera-
writer, and recent efforts have done much, both by criticism and by
performance, to rehabilitate him in that capacity. Moreover, the
comparatively perishable part of those many oratorios which use
dramatic forms gains a new life when we abrogate the veto of
Handel's Bishop of London, who nipped biblical opera in the bud

by forbidding the use of stage costume and scenery for the performance of *Esther* in its original shape as a masque set to an adaptation from Racine. A distinguished colleague of mine, who has recently tried the experiment in Glasgow, finds that Handel's *Saul* 'simply walks on to the stage'; and, indeed, when its production becomes thus normal, the naïve elegancies of Saul's daughters become only too characteristic when the infallible rhetoric of Handel's music is reinforced by costume and action. Revivals of Handel's operas, like revivals of Monteverdi's, will always owe much of their interest to costumes and scenery, as, indeed, they did in Handel's own time; but they also owe more than their promoters are willing to admit to the alteration, or cutting out, of elements which to Handel and his audience were essential. There is no question that coloratura singing was carried to decadent extremes; and the very existence of the male soprano voices that executed the roles of Richard Cœur-de-Lion, Julius Caesar, and Alexander was an abomination which society at that time was already feebly trying to explain away, and which became simply illegal in the next century.

The conditions under which poor Bach worked were neither metropolitan nor otherwise opulent. He furnished his church cantatas week by week, as the parson furnished his Sunday sermon; and a trustworthy tradition tells us that the performances were generally atrocious and that a subsequent flogging for the ringleaders of the choir was almost part of the ritual. I have already cited Bach's unaccompanied violin and violoncello solos as an example of normality under paradoxical conditions; and we need not be surprised that the practical hugger-mugger of his poor resources at Leipzig should have left unimpaired his infinite capacity for producing normal choral and instrumental music. So long as his works were out of fashion their chief reputation was that of enormous difficulty. Practical experience reveals that their difficulty is soon overcome. His vocal writing is too profoundly influenced by instruments to be comparable with the classical normality of Handel's; but such an influence is not essentially more abnormal than the coloratura singing of which it is indeed a particular case. As a whole his aesthetic system remains intelligible to-day in spite of the fact that many of his instruments have become obsolete and that his treatment of the orchestra has been replaced by totally different methods. It is the privilege of a completely normal art to carry with it into later ages the essentials of its environment. We do not need the modern critic to tell us that Antigone's view of the importance of decent burial is Victorian. Sophocles has not left the matter as a ready-made convention, Victorian or Hellenic, but has convinced us that it was a matter of eternal importance to Antigone. To perform Bach properly, we must understand the capacity and character of his instruments, and must not read irrelevant elements into his aesthetic system; but some contemporary elements were irrelevant, and need not be reproduced. For instance, the choir need neither receive nor deserve a flogging.

The musical revolutionaries who followed the age of Bach and Handel were blandly unconscious of those masters, and aware of themselves as revolutionaries only in the person of Gluck. Fashion merely cultivated a sentimental and romantic rhetoric; but what really happened between the death of Bach and the death of Beethoven was, as Gluck alone explicitly demonstrated, the dramatization of the whole art of music. Here again we may profitably compare the immense and popular importance of this with the trivial abstruseness of so much internecine propaganda of the present day. What the later eighteenth and early nineteenth century needed was neither iconoclasts nor pioneers, but conscientious artists, who were rebuked much more often for pedantry than for boldness. As a matter of fact, both Haydn and Mozart enjoyed a conspicuous popularity. It is difficult to compare their popularity with any phenomenon of recent times, for nowadays mass production has an incalculable effect in disguising from the keenest investigator what the public really wants; or, indeed, what sections of humanity can be described as the public in any sense. It is normal for all persons, even artists, to react to their environment; but this does not mean that great men will accept their environment uncritically. On the contrary, the great man will pay his environment the compliment of hoping that it will react sanely towards him, though he may be unable to conceal his disappointment. Nobody who is deceived by the modern phenomena of mass-production can be in a position to arbitrate when artists and the public get on each other's nerves. I venture to express my personal feeling that an extravagant vogue for my pet aversions would disquiet me less than the present lack of wide popularity for most contemporary music. But I see no grounds for pessimism about the music itself. Our boldest as well as our most conservative musicians show a far firmer grasp of normality than is shown in many of our fashionable methods of criticism.

We have not outgrown the habit of regarding Beethoven as a

revolutionary artist, and we cannot deny the fact that his lifetime coincided with many highly unmusical political events radiating from France and ending in the Congress of Vienna: a sequence which to some minds may seem an anticlimax not unlike Beethoven's descent from the 'Eroica' Symphony for his fallen idol Bonaparte to his pot-boiler the 'Battle' Symphony in honour of Wellington. But, enormously as the power of his art increased with its range, his development maintains a perfect continuity with the art of Mozart and Haydn. He is often supposed to have contributed little to the expansion of harmony except a harshness of style imputed to his lack of talent for counterpoint. But the main fact about Beethoven's harmony is that its phenomena are manifested on a much larger time-scale than any known to earlier music, and that neither orthodox nor advanced theories of harmony have yet attempted to see farther than the next chord but three.

Beethoven's harmonic details show many personal features of style, but he is only rarely and experimentally a writer of lyric music on a small scale; and it is in the lyric art-forms of the romantic Schumann and Chopin that we must look for the kind of harmonic detail that exists mainly for its own sake. In spite of the constantly increasing pregnancy of Beethoven's style, the occasions are rare when it suits his purpose to call attention to harmonic novelties. When he does so, the result is baffling to theories of harmony that are confined to the grammar of single sentences, and is sometimes a direct appeal to our pre-harmonic instincts. The mysterious unaccompanied D sharp near the beginning of the Violin Concerto is unharmonized, and flagrantly avoids explanation until a later harmonized passage explains it as a perfect example of sweet reasonableness.

The most dramatic moment in the first movement of the 'Eroica' Symphony is marked by a harmonic collision which theorists are to this day unable to explain as a chord, though some of them are still foolish enough to try. You might as well ask an anatomist to explain the 'blind mouths' about which Milton is so angry in Lycidas. This famous collision in the 'Eroica' Symphony was probably one of the earliest ideas which occurred to Beethoven while he was planning the first movement, though in the nature of the case it does not appear in his very copious sketches until he has reached the point at which it happens. It is then sketched with extreme care in repeated efforts to determine the exact moment of the collision and to reduce its acoustic harshness to the faintest sound that can express the dramatic meaning. At the rehearsal Beethoven boxed the ears of a favourite pupil who accused the horn-player of making a wrong entry; and, indeed, the musical sense of the naïve listener must become corrupted by an intolerable deal of harmonic theory before the acoustic harshness of the passage can offend it. The futility of such theory betrays itself by the fact that it can take no account of Beethoven's pains to reduce the discord to a thin veil of sound. To the orthodox harmonic theorist the light tremolo of Beethoven's finished version is no better than the chopping quavers of his first sketch.

Beethoven was not naturally endowed with the enormous contrapuntal facility of Mozart; but polyphony was vitally necessary to him, and the rugged style in which he developed it was intensely personal without being either an affectation or a mere makeshift. The most penetrating thing ever said about Mozart was the utterance not of a musician, but of Edward Fitzgerald, who said that 'Mozart is so beautiful that people cannot recognize that he is powerful'. Those who not only realize Mozart's power, but can understand his style in detail, are struck by the fact that his smoothness is adamantine, and that if it suits his purpose to be harsh he can be as ruthless as Beethoven. He is then, in fact, more ruthless, precisely because he is as logical as Dante, whereas Beethoven is as untidy as Shakespeare.

What is hopelessly beyond the range of harmonic theorists, whether orthodox or revolutionary, is precisely the principle that most widely extends the scope of harmony—that is, the relation of harmonic resources to the time-scale of the whole music. There is no traditional theory of classical tonality that has clearly distinguished the key systems of Beethoven's works as wholes from a chaos in which anything might happen. Of course, if you merely draw up a list of key-relations and lay it down that those which Cherubini did not happen to use are forbidden regardless of contexts, you will soon find that Beethoven left no forbidden regions unexplored, but you need not conclude from this that outside Cherubini's legitimate area Beethoven's tonality is either chaos or equivalent to staying at home. Domenico Scarlatti could visit the remotest tonal regions as a prince or a barber in the *Arabian Nights* could travel by magic carpet. Some of Beethoven's contemporaries would claim to ascend Mount Everest in a Bath chair.

To people who understand harmony as something wider than can be explained in the grammar of three successive chords, Beethoven's extension of the range of harmony is as epoch-making as Wagner's; and, like Wagner's, is a function of the time-dimension of his music. Current ideas as to the peculiarity of Wagner's harmonic style are unduly influenced by the fact that these peculiarities are most strongly concentrated in the prelude to *Tristan und Isolde*, the most single-mindedly impassioned of all his works. Beginnings and endings always remain in the mind longer than any other parts of a work of art, and so we impute to Wagner an all-pervading harmonic abstruseness which in fact occupies only a few special regions even of *Tristan*, whereas he often enjoys making music by the half-hour on a harmonic vocabulary that would not have puzzled Alessandro Scarlatti. In any case, an essential point in his boldest harmonies consists in some long-distance purpose which, as he is dealing with words and dramatic events, fortunately lends itself to popular explanation. Thus, the opening of *Tristan*, which the grammarians explain as a plus-quam-Thucydidean anacoluthon with several contradictory roots, is a theme which in the course of the music-drama represents overpowering love, and is designed to combine with another harmonically abstruse theme representing predestined death. But no peculiarities of Wagner's style are more than details in his enormous achievement of so recasting the whole fabric of music that it became capable of moving step by step continuously with his drama instead of breaking into fragments limited by the older classical forms. Here again we have a matter of popular and general urgency infinitely beyond the scope of the grammarian.

We need not go as far as Wagner for examples of the long-range meaning of interesting harmony. In Mendelssohn's time one of the greatest English musicians fell into the clutches of a harmonic theorist who, happening to be a homoeopathic doctor, invented a homoeopathic theory by which to classify every chord that could be found in print. Our great musical educator, who should be remembered for better things, introduced this theorist to Mendelssohn. A pious legend reports that the theorist asked Mendelssohn the name of the first chord in his Wedding March; to which Mendelssohn replied that he neither knew nor cared. The theorist then proceeded to expound to Mendelssohn the roots of this and all other chords. And we are told that after a few minutes of this exposition Mendelssohn abruptly left the room with signs of acute physical distress. The first chord of the Wedding March confuses the key of E minor with that of C major in order that the courtly splendours of those typical Elizabethan squires, Theseus and Hippolyta, may fade with the torchlight of their departing procession into the twilight of the re-entering fairies.

We are told that of late years the harmonic vocabulary of music has been incalculably increased. I confess to feeling sceptical as to the importance of all changes of vocabulary in all languages. In my youth the English vocabulary gravitated round two words, 'rotten' and 'rippin''. I am credibly informed that these have now been replaced by 'septic' and 'wizard'. The consequences of such an extension of the English language are doubtless incalculable, but I question whether they are equivalent to anything more important than 'new ways of taking appoggiaturas and notes of taste'. A terrible amount of *a priori* theory is put forward, often by artists themselves, as an explanation of the principles of their art; but, as in the time of Monteverdi, much of this has been forced upon musicians as a measure of self-defence. And to suppose that a correct theory of art is an essential, or even a normal, condition for creative activity is like supposing that a doctor must be a quack who inculcates in his patients a belief in the magic power of the word 'ninety-nine'. The serious objection to the quasi-scientific theories on which many of our artistic revolutions nowadays base themselves is that they are for the most part far too laborious to admit of any normal activity at all.

A recent example of a theory harmless to those employed in the manufacture is shown in the music of Debussy, who was supposed to have discovered a new heaven and a new earth in the whole-tone scale. But, though he sometimes reduced it to a formula and always polished his work meticulously, he did not begin with it, and he was obviously outgrowing it before he died. Orthodox theorists can expose the fallacy of the whole-tone scale with ridiculous ease, and Sir Walford Davies has pointed out that the scale is merely the projection of a peculiarly luscious and classically intelligible chord into one octave. It is no more dependent on equal temperament for its existence than the long over-familiar chord of the diminished seventh which Browning intended when he praised the mild Galuppi for the super-Wagnerian miracle of 'sixths diminished, sigh on sigh': and it is quite easily absorbable into the classical scheme of harmony as a chord that is capable of six unexpected enharmonic alternatives as against the four possible meanings of the diminished seventh. Debussy would under no circumstances have been a prolific writer, but his whole-tone scale, in spite of the

volumes of laborious theorizing that have been devoted to it, was
no inhibition to him. I doubt if there were many talented young
musicians in the latter half of the nineteenth century who had not
stumbled upon it as an amusing effect in extemporization on the
pianoforte. It has been forced upon organ-tuners throughout all
the centuries since organs became big enough to necessitate the
arranging of their pipes in symmetrical opposition in order to dis-
tribute the wind pressure evenly.

Narrow, artificial, and pedantic as was the aesthetic system that
based itself on the whole-tone scale, it was, while it lasted, a stimulus rather than an inhibition to the highly sensitive artist in whose
works it is most prominent. But nothing more infuriates an artist
who devotes himself to such a system than the discovery that it
can be absorbed into the main stream of classical thought. This
discovery does, indeed, annihilate all the special theories of the
system. But there are very few special theories of art which do not
accomplish their best work by being annihilated. Sound hygiene is
extremely irksome to the hypochondriac, but freedom returns
with normality; being, in fact, the Nature which Horace tells us
you may vainly hope to keep out with a pitchfork.

WORDS AND MUSIC: SOME *OBITER DICTA*[1]

THE principles which govern the musical setting of words, whether prose or poetry, are dangerously easy to formulate on an *a priori* basis of common sense; and in recent times musicians have sinned more deeply than men of letters in laying down facile generalizations that not only ignore the nature of music, but reduce poetry to prose. It is interesting to see Parry, one of the greatest recent masters of English music, deliberately setting forth an unmusical view of poetic declamation, and being corrected by the author of the ode which he set for the bicentenary of Purcell. Robert Bridges wrote several essays on musical declamation, which are no less authoritative on music than they are on prosody; but whether he would agree better with my heresies than with Parry's is a question which it is now too late to settle.

In the history of music the sixteenth century has been called the Golden Age; and the tendency of modern criticism is to extend that period backwards into the fifteenth century, so as to include a wider and wider range of the noble art that falls short of the consummate purity of Palestrina and Victoria. Morley's *Plaine and Easie Introduction to Practicall Musicke* (1597) sets forth the theory and practice of the Golden Age, and refers to John Dunstable (d. 1453) as if to a classic whose name everyone ought to know, though perhaps only as a legend. Now Dunstable was as remote from Morley and Palestrina as Bach is from us. In spite of the intensive labours of Roman Catholic choirs, secular madrigal societies, and such eminent artists of vocal ensemble as the 'English Singers', the Golden Age itself is to most concert-goers almost as legendary as its name implies. As its product consists essentially of unaccompanied vocal music, there are no material difficulties whatever in the revival of its culture. Without such a revival our standards of musical culture are like those of a Renaissance which knows no Greek.

In one aspect unaccompanied choral music ought to be the most absolute of all arts, inasmuch as it needs no apparatus but the human voice, the most perfect of all instruments if it is not corrupted by imitating cruder mechanisms. On the other hand, there

[1] First printed, 1938, in *Seventeenth Century Studies, presented to Sir Herbert Grierson* (Clarendon Press).

is a manifest artificiality and, as Plato strongly felt, a degradation in using the human voice without human speech. Hence, the music of the Golden Age presents us at once with the extremes of musical abstraction and of dependence upon words.

One of the first elements of conflict between speech and song is the natural tendency of the singing voice to refrain from articulation. The voice prefers to prolong a vowel indefinitely, and through most consonants, except those which hum and buzz, cannot sing at all. This kind of opposition is more fundamental than that between speech and song, for it is an opposition between the voice and music itself. It is even less natural for the singing voice to achieve a definite scale than to articulate syllables. But through the reconciling of fundamental oppositions the highest art achieves a nature of its own. In no way is this more astonishingly manifest than in the ascertainable fact that an unaccompanied chorus, trained in the art of Palestrina, achieves, without any theoretical knowledge whatever, a mathematically 'just intonation' that is beyond the possibility of any instruments with a fixed number of notes.

The theory of just intonation is beyond the scope of this essay; but the classical practices in the treatment of words are fortunately easy to ascertain, and not difficult to describe. One of the few things that we know about ancient Greek music is that it maintained a one-to-one correspondence between musical time-values and metrical quantities. We also know that the strophe and antistrophe of a Greek chorus were set to the same music. This enables us to learn from Aeschylus that the flow of music, like the flow of quantities, was expected sometimes to ignore pauses which grammatical sense would require, and that the same music might be used to describe indifferently the kittenish charms of a lion-cub and the tragic fate of the shepherd's flocks when the adult animal developed according to the course of nature.

In the rondels and rotas of the thirteenth century the correspondence between poetic and musical rhythm is still fairly close. Long and short syllables alternate in lilting iambic and trochaic feet, which the music reproduces in a prevalent triple time sung at a pace hardly slower than that of speech. With the development of polyphony this correspondence disappeared; and though the musicians were often poets and the poets musicians (as was Machault), early polyphony is an art in which the connexion between the verbal and the musical rhythm is definable only in abstruse and involved technical terms. We cannot always be certain how far such technicalities represent truths, and how far they degenerate into evasions subconsciously designed to conceal the fact that responsibility for the matter has long ago ceased to exist. Responsibility certainly had ceased to exist by the time of Palestrina (c. 1525–94), though there were then many useful conventions governing the setting of words, and many habits, some good and some bad, by which certain words were selected as standard subjects for musical illustration. In an elaborate polyphony each voice, with one generic exception, would have far more notes than syllables, but every singer knew certain rules by which a run of notes would be assigned to a good vowel; and the composer collected his text at the beginning of each phrase without troubling to range the syllables under the notes. The generic exception was the part that sang a *canto fermo*, or theme round which the whole polyphony was woven. This theme was often given in notes of such enormous length that all rhythmic value was lost, and the singer distributed the syllables more or less evenly throughout the whole *canto fermo*, breaking the long notes into breathable ones as he chose.

After everything that modern research has achieved in whittling away the plausible story of the part played by Palestrina and the Council of Trent in the reform of Church music, the demonstrable fact remains that Palestrina's most famous works are models of musical declamation and were accepted as such by the authorities of the Church. It has been shown statistically that the *Missa Papae Marcelli* stands out among Palestrina's works by the systematic plan that the voices shall begin every clause exactly together before they diverge and break up in repetitions. The listener hears the sense of each phrase once for all in the highest voice, so that subsequent repetitions will not confuse him.

Not many even of Palestrina's earliest works show much trace of the abuses in Church music to which the Council of Trent undoubtedly objected. But early in the sixteenth century Obrecht and other Flemish masters habitually produced Masses which made it impossible for the officiating celebrant to find his place. Two parts out of six might be singing, with many repetitions, the text of the Gloria or the Credo; but the tenor might be singing the *canto fermo*, not only in notes of unbreathable length, but to words celebrating the miracles of Saint Martin, while another voice would be singing a Latin Christmas carol, and a third not less conspicuous voice would be singing in a lively rhythm a French song to its original and not always decorous words. There are no such improprieties in Palestrina's Masses, but his first published volume begins with a *Missa Ecce Sacerdos Magnus*, throughout which a *canto fermo* is sung to the text: 'Ecce sacerdos magnus qui in diebus suis placuit Deo et inventus est justus'. Before the Council of Trent intervened, such a feature probably passed as a graceful compliment to the Cardinal or Pope to whom the volume was dedicated, but the Mass cannot have been convenient to the celebrant who had to time his actions according to its unusual length, while the compliment to the 'great priest' was persistently more conspicuous than the liturgical text.

It is beyond my purpose to discuss in detail the art of setting the text of a Mass; but I may raise certain points of general interest. To a sixteenth-century master with a gift for extended composition, the Mass is the occasion for a musical art-form representing the summit of his purely musical aspirations, much as the symphony and the string quartet give scope to the highest ambitions of the nineteenth-century composer of music for music's sake. Whatever may be the current conventions in the treatment of certain words, the Mass transcends the details of musical illustration as the subjects of the Madonna and the Crucifixion transcend the merely illustrative scope of the painter. But the point that is of immediate interest to us is that in the sixteenth century the proportions of the liturgical text were favourable to the development of a music that was most free at the climax of the service, and most restricted where there was danger of prolixity and anticlimax.

At a later date the orchestral and harmonic resources of Bach and Beethoven were such that it was impossible to treat topics like the Crucifixion, the Resurrection, and the Life of the world to come, on less than the largest possible musical scale. The Gloria and the Credo thus became the most voluminous and dramatic parts of the composition, and inevitably tended to dwarf the Sanctus, which should be the culminating point of the Mass. But in Palestrina's art the scope of illustration is merely decorative; and the effect of the large bulk of words in the Gloria and Credo is to make the composer devise a kind of music which delivers the words tersely and with few repetitions. On the other hand, the few words of the Kyrie, the Sanctus, the Benedictus, and the Agnus Dei give the sixteenth-century composer a welcome opportunity to broaden his designs by repeating the words with cumulative effect. Thus, in spite of what Dr. Schweitzer rightly calls the appalling difficulty of setting the theological metaphysics of the Nicene Creed to music, the text of the Mass gave the sixteenth-century composer excellent opportunities for music that could both fit the highly specialized occasion and develop its own abstract musical consistency. Moreover, there was plenty of opportunity for well-defined differences between one Mass and another. Between the Credo and the Sanctus of a Mass there was sung a setting of a text appropriate to the day. If the text possessed a traditional plain-chant setting, the composer might derive the themes of his motet from that plainchant; and if he wrote a Mass for that particular day the themes of his Mass would develop those of his motet. Thus, one of Palestrina's greatest Masses is written for the Assumption of the Virgin, and is based on the themes of his great motet, *Assumpta est Maria*, the opening of which is derived from the plain-chant of its text. Similarly, his Mass for Whit-Sunday is the *Missa dum Complerentur*, which is expanded from his highly dramatic motet describing the events of the Day of Pentecost.

Luther was musician enough to leave room for a hardly less consistent musical scheme in the services of his Reformed Church; and the researches of the late Professor C. Sanford Terry enable us to follow the coherent musical structure of the services of the Thomaskirche in Leipzig during every day of Bach's long tenure as cantor. English music has had no such luck. King Henry VI was a good musician; but that royal saint lived only during the dawn of polyphony, and his music is archaic beyond our comprehension. Henry VIII's musicianship was probably not equal to his classical scholarship, but it was certainly better than Cranmer's, for there is no evidence that Cranmer was musical at all, and he left the Book of Common Prayer in such a shape that no coherent scheme of Anglican Church music is possible.

When we call the sixteenth century the Golden Age of music, we think in the first place of Palestrina, and of a Church music purified from archaic corruptions and innocent of the instrumental, secular, and dramatic elements that fermented throughout the music of the seventeenth century. But the Church can claim not more than half the bulk, and perhaps not more than half the aesthetic value, of Golden-Age music. The other half consists of madrigal and similar secular music. Now there is a sense in which perfect works of art, like infinities, cannot be compared with one another. In any case, what is right for one is uniquely right for it, and wrong for any other. But, when we have weighed the results of a long experience of different kinds of art, we may allow ourselves to conclude that one kind of experience outweighs another, without implying any depreciation of the lighter experience. On the whole, I feel entitled to say that the greatest motet will probably be greater than the greatest madrigal; and I do not expect a composer who has written nothing but madrigals to be of the same calibre as a great composer of motets and Masses. On the other hand, we may point to Masses which are based on madrigals. Long after the Council of Trent had condemned secular elements in Church music, Palestrina's *Missa Vestiva i colli* remained in high esteem; and another Mass, *Già fu chi m'hebbe cara*, is on one of those madrigals to a mildly improper text for which Palestrina expresses penitence in the preface to his setting of the Song of Solomon, a late *magnum opus* in which he atones for his early wild oats by illustrating the love of Christ for His Church in music of a *genius alacrior*.

At this point we are confronted with one of the chief sources of confusion in the evidence of musical treatment of words. Even in art-forms and periods most involved in convention, there is always a difference between music that has been originally conceived for its words and music that has been adapted from other settings. Well-meaning choral societies will produce a Mass of Palestrina without producing the motet on which it is based—an absurd procedure when the motet is by the same composer, for the motet is the quintessence of the Mass, and it is only by a *tour de force* that the Mass achieves anything better than a dilution of the motet. All its themes belong by rights in every detail of declamation to the motet, and their various adaptations to the text of the Mass are all more or less ingenious and artificial.

Now the great motets are not less sensitive in their treatment of words than the great madrigals; and the art by which the music of madrigals illustrates the words is always intimate, and often astonishingly subtle. Some of the illustrative devices are merely punning or cryptographic; but such quaint devices, though amusing enough to describe, form no part of the composer's inspiration, but are harmless customs for which conformity is easy and protest not worth while. The real madrigalian art is inveterately illustrative. It is subtle in ways more intelligible to the singers than manifest to the listener, though there is nothing to prevent the result from being musically convincing. For the critic this illustrative aspect has the danger that it may distract his attention from pure musical values.

But in the first and last resort the composer is more interested

in music than in words. He will find that the way to produce the
best music is to base it faithfully upon the words to which it is
first composed; and we are entitled to guess *a priori* that a composer
who is not deeply sensitive to the words he is setting will not have
much purely musical depth in him. But we shall meet with many
disappointments if we expect classical composers to retain their
pristine literary sensibility after their music has taken solid shape.

The occasion of the first appearance of the word 'madrigal' in
the English language is a glaring illustration of this. We are informed that it is not found as an English word before Yonge's
Musica Transalpina (1588). Yonge's avowed purpose is to render
the music of Italian madrigals available to singers in an English
translation which does not consider the original sense of the words,
but only 'the affections of the note'. In other words, Italian madrigals are to be sung to English words that are not translations at all,
but independent poems composed with no respect for anything but
the musical rhythm. We need not consult the originals of Yonge's
madrigals to guess how impossible it is that the finer points of the
Italian composer should be reproduced.

Similarly the slightest carelessness in editing an English madrigal
can ruin a delightful point, self-evident to the singers, and not
beyond the possibility of reaching listeners who have become
familiar with the work. Listen to Dr. Fellowes in his preface to
his complete series of English madrigals:

> Any re-arrangement of the original position of the words is indefensible,
> and may often involve the destruction of an effect purposely designed by
> the madrigal composers. In this matter their dramatic treatment of the
> words was often very subtle; but as an illustration of thoughtless editing
> we may quote the penultimate bar of 'I follow, lo, the footing' (No. 17 of
> Morley's five- and six-voice Canzonets), in which the composer has
> designed that, after many bars of breathless racing, the word 'caught'
> shall occur in a different vocal part on each of the four beats of the bar,
> and be sustained until all the voices sing the final word 'her' together in
> the final bar. Yet in one published version of this Canzonet the point
> has been entirely destroyed by a gratuitous and unnecessary repetition of
> the words in the Cantus part.

A device of the same kind, but Greek in its simplicity and accuracy, is shown in Weelkes's *Three Virgin Nymphs*. Three voices
represent the virgin nymphs in the plain rhythm of the words with
a triad high enough to sound bright without being unpleasantly
shrill. The nymphs 'were walking all alone', and the voices accord-

ingly walk up and down in closely overlapping scales, leaving the
third voice all alone for a few notes after the others, 'till rude
Sylvanus chanced to meet them'. Sylvanus is a rude bass voice
whose themes and rhythms throw the trebles into confusion, though
all join in the tale of how he 'leap't and snatch't at one'. In the
outcome the composer evidently does not wish us to be clear as to
who it was who said 'Come back and bliss me' (rhyming with
'kiss me').

Our English composers of the early seventeenth century were
by no means provincially minded; but though our own troubles
ruined our Church music, we were far enough from the Continental
centres of musical revolution to continue for the first quarter of
the century in undisturbed development of our madrigal style.
Our sense of key had always tended to become more rigid than the
subtleties of Palestrina's harmonic compromise with the Church
modes. And we retained from archaic times a robust taste in discord, more especially in collisions between major and minor thirds,
which are even more shocking to nineteenth-century, if not to
modern, ears than they had become to Palestrina. It will doubtless
pass for correct to say that the modulations of *O care, thou wilt
dispatch me* are 'remarkable for the time at which they were written'. Of all faint praises, this is the most damnable and futile.
These modulations are remarkable for all time. There was no technical hindrance to Weelkes's writing them at the beginning of the
seventeenth century. And there was no technical reason why he
should not have written utter nonsense. What is remarkable is that
he means by them exactly what Schubert or Brahms would have
meant, and is able to express that meaning by the supreme luck of
genius that has preserved him from discovering that he has none
of the apparatus of instruments and art-forms on which Schubert
and Brahms rely.

That condition of creative art which we call inspiration, and
which transcends self-conscious reasoning, is manifest in whole
schools and forms of art, almost as clearly as in the masterpieces
of individual men of genius. In the Golden Age it seems as if the
madrigalists, great and small, cannot go wrong. Before the seventeenth century has accomplished its first quarter, its most thoughtful
composers seem unable to go right, though they theorize with
great intelligence. But the theoretic propagandists of a new art
seldom show a fine intelligence as to the principles of the old art
which they would supersede. Milton's praise of Henry Lawes shows

P

that, like Lawes, he thought clearly and obviously about contemporary music; but, when he claims that the 'tuneful and well-measured song' of Lawes

> First taught our English music how to span
> Words with just note and accent, not to scan
> With Midas' ears, committing short and long,

he reveals that he has completely forgotten, if he ever understood, the principles of that madrigalian art of which his own father had a respectable mastery. There is no conflict between notes and accents in the madrigalian style; for the musical rhythms have a freedom which, to begin with, eliminates all possibility of conflict between accent and quantity.

Early in the seventeenth century Thomas Campion (1567–1620) blasphemed, like Milton, against his own charming talent for rhyme, and became sadly entangled in efforts to reconcile the conflict between accent and quantity in his theories of English verse. He was technically an accomplished musician, with a pretty gift for melody on a small scale; and he wrote a compendious treatise on what purported to be counterpoint, though it amounted to little more than a collection of rules-of-thumb by which tunes could be harmonized in the narrow circle of major and minor keys into which the subtle harmonic compromises of modal counterpoint had declined.

Neither Milton nor Campion was conscious that the new musical developments of the seventeenth century were in many ways at least as effective in strangling musical composition as in liberating it. The 'tuneful and well-measured song' of Henry Lawes anticipates the tune and measure of eighteenth-century music; and the composer's preoccupation with the scansion of 'just note and accent' leads him to over-punctuate the words and interrupt the flow of his music.

The fact is that the whole basis of musical rhythm has, by the time of which I am speaking, become muscular in a much grosser sense than any speech rhythm. In sixteenth-century music there is no conflict between speech rhythm and musical rhythm. The singers distinguish between *arsis* and *thesis*, the up-beat and the down-beat; and this normal distinction may sometimes correspond to accent, and sometimes to quantity, and may be at all times easily overridden so long as the voices come together at full closes. This is a very different state of things from that in which rhythm is as

strong as the paces of a horse. It was already becoming coarsened
in that direction by the time of Milton and Henry Lawes; just as
the harmony was becoming coarsened in the direction of modern
tonality, and the subtleties of modal harmony were disappearing.
Milton stands almost alone among poets in the accuracy of his
allusions to music, which are not less scholarly than the rest of his
art; but his vision of music is almost as prophetic as that of Adam
with his eyes opened by Michael. Bach might have been the
organist whose

> volant touch
> Instinct through all proportions low and high
> Fled and pursued transverse the resonant fugue.

But Bach was not born until nine years after the second edition of
Paradise Lost; and though his predecessors developed a 'volant
touch' and the mastery of all rhythmic proportions and devices of
fugue, they seldom achieved coherent works of art.

The relation between words and music does not become a subject of first-rate aesthetic importance except where the art of
musical composition is on the same plane as that of poetry. The
music of Campion and of Dowland does not pretend to achieve
anything higher than pleasant little tunes, which have for us a mild
exotic charm because of certain archaic elements in their harmony
and rhythm. The archaism of the harmony consists mainly in
decadent survivals of modal tonality. The archaism of the rhythm
consists in the fact that the stiffness of modern musical rhythm
has not yet entirely overborne the free speech rhythm of older
music. In Dowland's best-known song, *Awake, sweet love*, the prevailing rhythm is modern triple-time, which persists through the
first eight lines without the slightest ambiguity; but the music of
the ninth and tenth and the thirteenth and fourteenth lines falls
much more naturally into groups of four beats, though, as there are
three of these, the triple-time may still be allowed to persist. Now
Dowland ranks with Campion and Lawes as a musician who, in
setting either his own or other poetry, meticulously fits his music
to his words; but a modern composer, regarding musical accent
from the standpoint of Wagner and Hugo Wolf, would be apt to
accuse Dowland of scanning 'with Midas' ears, committing short
and long'. Our notion of triple-time commits us to a hard accent
on the first of every bar, and is shocked when Dowland begins:
'*A*-wake, sweet love', and still more shocked when Dowland not

only makes his tune repeat itself symmetrically, but repeats the whole song note for note to another stanza. Brahms has been severely blamed for the 'faulty declamation' of his setting of '*Wie* bist du, *meine* König*in* / *Durch* sanfte Güte wonne*voll*'. But his declamation is remarkably like Dowland's. Now here the self-conscious literary musicians, including both Wagner and Hugo Wolf, are wrong, and the Elizabethan and Jacobean poet-musicians are on the side of the poets and of Brahms. No modern musical criterion is shallower than that which regards as lazy and primitive the setting of different stanzas of a poem to the same melody. Brahms regarded such strophic melody as a far higher achievement than *durchcomponirtes* declamation.

It is not Dowland, but we, who accentuate falsely when we put hard, muscular accents into his triple-time; but, apart from details of scansion, every poet will also set high aesthetic value on the persistence of a tune that transcends the particular emotional details of different stanzas. Some of the most successful alliances between music and poetry have been those in which Scott and Burns have written or completed poems to pre-existing folk-tunes. If you write modern music to Scott's *Jock of Hazeldean*, you will find at the outset some difficulty with the cross-accent on 'ladie' in the first line, 'Why weep ye by the tide, ladie?' And you will get into serious difficulties with the line: 'And you the fairest o' them a'', where your tune cannot avoid an impossible stress on the weak antepenultimate syllable. But the folk-melody has an upward turn that facilitates the cross-accent on 'ladie', and enables Scott to compose his poetry freely to the tune throughout. Such masters of lyric melody as Schubert and Brahms avail themselves constantly of the fact that even with the full muscular strength of modern musical rhythms, the strong beats of the bar constitute only one form of accent, which may be easily counteracted by the length of a note, by its height, by its harmonic colour, and by incidents in the accompaniment. Only a flat-footed kind of melody or dance-rhythm habitually brings all these elements on to the beat.

The Wagnerians certainly formulated a quite inadequate theory of musical declamation, based on a nineteenth-century stiffness of musical rhythm, and cognizant of no language except German, which is perhaps of all languages the one in which accent is most rigidly dominant over quantity. The French language is at the other extreme; and the most impeccable French composer is not afraid to bring the first beat of a bar on to an *e muet*. The Italian language has strong accents, but gains enormous musical flexibility by the custom of treating any number of successive vowels as if they were a single syllable, neither eliding them nor marking the rhythmic point at which one changes into another, even as between different words.

We have never learnt to treat our English vowel-syllables thus; nor can such Italian privileges become a precedent for us. On the other hand, it would be a pity that the enormous musical possibilities of our language, with its varied texture of Teutonic, Romance, and classical threads, should be inhibited by a German theory of musical and poetic rhythm which is too provincial even for the classics of German poetry and German music. Our own provinciality is of a different and less patriotic kind. And we have been saved from its worst possibilities by the fact that Handel did us the honour of becoming a naturalized Englishman and setting his greatest music to English words. But, apart from Handel, we have learnt most of the classics of vocal music in translations; and the translations have, until quite recently, been the work of persons who achieved a highly specialized technique that strikes a balance between three evils: ignorance of the original language, ignorance of English, and ignorance of music. These now obsolescent, if not obsolete, translators also made a profession of writing specially for music; and when they added to their responsibilities the profession of musical critic, woe betide such composers as Stanford and Parry, who declined their services and turned to such unprofessional persons as Milton and Shelley and Bridges.

The chief effect of a long tradition of musical translations was that English composers had no reason to suppose that nonsense was inadmissible in classical vocal music. The study of original musical classics will show that, as a rule, music, even in the most conventional art-forms, has a basis of common sense in such matters as the repetition of words. The British sailor's idea of 'a hanthem' is, unfortunately, true of many unintelligent imitations of the classics; but a first-rate composer, composing in his own language, will certainly manage to find a single appropriate theme covering the sentence, 'Bill, fetch me that there 'andspike', before the chorus develops the fugue which breaks up the words and piles them into *stretto*.

It would be tedious to search out and enumerate cases where mistranslation has violated the composer's common sense. Sometimes with biblical texts grievous conflicts of loyalty may arise be-

tween the rhythms of our Authorized Version and those of Luther's
Bible. Thus Mendelssohn, at the first performance of *Elijah* at
Birmingham, had to submit to the destruction of a most important
point in his overture because it would have been considered blasphemous to alter the text, 'But according to My word', so as to
fit the phrase, '*Ich sage es denn*', which looms ominously in the
wind-instruments throughout the orchestral fugue that follows.
The music loses a fine point without becoming unintelligible; but
our Victorian composers piously renounced the presumption of
understanding either classical music or theological dogma. Thus
generations of schoolboys and choir-boys have been brought up to
believe without question in a 40th Article of Religion which no
theologian has ever explained, but which Barnby, in E, stren-
uously proclaims; the doctrine that 'As it was, it was in the
beginning'.

The classical tradition of musical declamation lies elsewhere.
Artists have a right to be judged by their strokes of genius, and
not by their lapses. Handel's musical rhetoric is so superb that
we may safely guess that, wherever a beautiful phrase misfits the
words, Handel is adapting it from something else, sometimes quite
unscrupulously, but more often sacrificing fitness of detail to the
fitness of general impression. Thus, in *Messiah*, the chorus
'For unto us a Child is born' presents us with a rather disconcerting stress on the word 'For'. On the other hand, the theme of
'And the government shall be upon His shoulder' is magnificently
suggestive of taking up a burden with zest; and the descent on the
word 'shoulder' is musically pictorial and fitting to the metaphor,
without being comic. But both phrases originally meant something
quite different and much simpler. The chorus is developed from
an Italian duet, and the first phrase was *No, da voi non più fidarmi*,
and the other theme is a scolding accusation of falsehood, with a
glide on the word *lusinghieri*. And I shall never cease to hope that
some day an original version will be found of 'He shall feed His
flock'. Most people object much more strongly than I to the accent
'He *shall*', but I am far more grieved by the evident loss of meaning
in the rise and fall of the notes set to the word 'shepherd', and later
to the word 'weary'. There must have been a time when that very
remarkable musical phrase had words which it expressed with the
same astounding rightness that is famous in Handel's declamation
of 'He turned their waters into blood', and the falling seventh at
'sheds delicious death'.

Let this suffice for a hint as to the problem of musical declamation in detail. But the larger and more important question is that
of musical composition on a large scale in relation to the treatment
of words and of dramatic situations. Here we come to the tragedy
of English musical history. The faculty of composition on a large
scale is gloriously manifest in our literature. On the other hand,
our artistic habits are not tidy, and our tidy artists are highly
specialized and limited. Yet we may truthfully claim, not only
that no problem of composition in literature has been too great for
our courage, but also that no problem has been left unsolved with
as high a perfection as art has ever attained. It is not discreet to
claim that *Paradise Lost* is a faultless poem, or that it propounds a
possible enterprise; but it is folly to deny it the qualities of faultless
poetry and perfect form. Music is of all arts the least tolerant of
accidents that warp its essential perfection; and most musicians
would be the better for a training in the criticism of arts in which
perfection is seldom originally possible in whole works, and in
which we are accustomed to recognize it in things grievously mutilated by time. But, after making due allowance for the special
opportunities and responsibilities of music, we may fairly conclude
that the records of English literature show qualities of composition
not less extensive and profound than those of German music from
Bach to Wagner. We cannot conceive that such powers could remain long inhibited by any external causes, though every period
has its own special forms of art and its own limitations. Yet in
music our talent for composition has undoubtedly failed to stand
the strain of adverse influences, until recent times, when perhaps
we may flatter ourselves that we have overcome most of our
obstacles and inhibitions.

In the music of the Golden Age it is not easy to be sure whether
a musician has or has not the gift of composition. Motets and the
higher types of madrigal demand a flowing style; but the composer
seldom has to occupy as much as five minutes with his largest single
design. Still, much grandeur of design can be expressed in three
minutes. On such a scale Tallis and Byrd can prove themselves to
be great architects, whose powers of composition cannot be exhibited in short quotations, and whose omnipresent merit far transcends that of epigrammatic wit. In the early seventeenth century
no large musical art-forms had been devised; and until the time of
Bach and Handel most composers, even of vocal music, clung, as
drowning men to a straw, to such devices as the ground-bass, a

pregnant theme repeating itself many times as a bass to a varying superstructure.

Even a haphazard set of quotations from Henry Purcell gives us the impression of the work of a composer quite as great as Bach or Handel, and more different from either of them than they are from each other. His treatment of words is always interesting, and at its quaintest not merely quaint, even when he commemorates the king's narrow escape in a storm by making the chief bass singer of the Royal Chapel sing 'They that go down to the sea in ships' in a descending scale of two octaves from top D to bottom D. His sturdy British independence of the Italian art of recitative was already commented upon by his countrymen when that art was still a novelty. The fact is that the art of recitative is that of the rise and fall of spoken language stylized in musical notes, and that every language ought to develop its own type of recitative. Parry comments shrewdly on the wisdom of Charles II in sending his most talented choristers to France to learn from Lully, the great master of French ballet, how to write English Church music. But in this matter of recitative Purcell anticipated the dramatic resources of a later epoch, and, 'in spite of all temptations to belong to other nations', remained an Englishman.

But the musical privileges of remaining an Englishman are few; and neither politics nor the traditions of other English arts have been kind to music. Our docility in obeying foreign fashions fails to be educative because we have not the presumption to obey with intelligence. Charles II showed excellent taste and common sense in sending Purcell and Pelham Humfrey to study under Lully; but he disconcerted our English musicians by appointing the inept Monsieur Grabu over their heads as court musician. And, though Dryden was gullible enough at first to praise Grabu above all English masters, he also mistrusted music so profoundly that he firmly established the miserable tradition that an opera, as understood in England, was a play in which all occasions for music lay outside the plot. In *Dido and Aeneas*, to a libretto by Nahum Tate of the firm of Tate and Brady, Purcell achieved a music-drama which anticipates by some eighty years the full fruition of Gluck's operatic reforms; but the work does not seem to have been appreciated in Purcell's lifetime, except at Mr. Josias Priest's boarding-school, for which it was written, and where it was performed between 1688 and 1690. By the time Dryden had learnt to think better of Purcell, the musical disjointedness of English opera was an established fact. Dryden's *King Arthur* is a voluminous work; and Purcell's music to it is important, but has nothing whatever to do with the play. His masques in *Timon of Athens* and *The Tempest* are musical fragments that contribute nothing to Shakespeare. This Jew-and-Samaritan relation between music and the stage persisted until the second quarter of the nineteenth century, and ruined the last work of Weber, who wrote in his best English to Planché, the librettist of *Oberon*, in these words:

I must repeat that the cut of the whole is very foreign to all my ideas and maxims. The intermixing of so many principal actors who do not sing, the omission of the music in the most important moments—all deprive our Oberon of the title of an opera, and will make him unfit for all other theatres in Europe.

It is impossible to suppose that the English talent for musical composition on a large scale could have been crushed by any adverse influences or foreign dominations if it had been comparable to our talent for composition in literature. The popular theory for our failure is that English music was 'crushed beneath the ponderous genius of Handel'. But for most of his life Handel dominated England as a writer of Italian operas; and the ultimate effect of his oratorios was by no means to crush our native talent, but to inflate it. He was far more dangerous to our composers than Milton was to Keats. In the first place, Keats had the sense to recognize the danger; and, in the second place, Milton is a very elaborate artist. Beethoven revered Handel as the master of all masters, and declared that no one else produced such stupendous effects by the simplest means. But Handel's means are so simple that some portion of Beethoven's acumen is needed to see in Handel the art that conceals art, and to distinguish it from the effrontery that avoids art. At the present time most musicians are terrorized out of writing anything that does not profess to be a new language on some abstruse or subversive theory that contradicts all classical tradition; but many of us can vividly remember the prevalent tendency of the advice given to young composers in later Victorian days. It could all be summed up in two principles. Be sublime. At the age of twenty-one follow exclusively the practice of great masters in the works which they composed at the age of sixty and upwards, avoiding as reprehensible indiscretions all the practices by which these masters developed their style in earlier works.

And so it has come to pass that we have neither made our own

musical traditions, nor learnt solid lessons from the foreign music
to which we are so laudably hospitable. We do not know from
first-hand experience where and why the conventional repetition
of words is excellent in some classical art-forms; and we are equally
at a loss as to the steps by which Wagnerian music-drama developed the kind of musical composition that forbids unrealistic
repetition of words as unnecessary and, therefore, disturbing. It
is not very difficult to spread some kind of musical continuum over
a play, as one might spread butter over bread. Nor is it difficult to
make short musical themes serve as labels to the nameable ideas
and incidents of a drama. If this were all that Wagner achieved,
his works would probably have made no permanent impression,
and many composers would not have wasted their lives in producing
enormous numbers of operas which attempt this and nothing more.

A mature Wagner opera is organized as highly, and almost as
purely musically, as a Beethoven symphony. Its organization is on
totally different lines; and any analysis that attempts to apply symphonic terms to Wagner is doomed to fantastic abstruseness. But
the analysis of Wagner's music into hundreds of short themes
associated with dramatic incidents and thoughts carries us no farther into his principles of composition than the compiling of a
dictionary of his words. The music is no more built from these
details than the drama is built from its words. Behind and above
this apparatus, the music is architectural on a scale actually from
ten to twenty times larger than anything contemplated in earlier
music; and it is true to the architectural nature of music; its symmetries are expressed in recapitulations as vast and as exact as
those of any symphonic music. Words are not thus recapitulated,
nor is the singer often conscious of taking part in a recapitulation,
since the musical declamation fits the words at every moment, and
the voice-part itself, therefore, does not recapitulate. The music of
the death of Isolde recapitulates the whole peroration of her love-
duet with Tristan in the second act; and in *Götterdämmerung* Siegfried, guilelessly telling his sworn enemies the story of his youth,
not only takes the inevitable course of recapitulating the music of
the forest-scene, but, after the brief interruption of his death-wound,
completes the musical recapitulation by dying to the strains of
Brünnhilde's awakening.

These recapitulations are only a few obvious cases forced upon
the listener by the externals of the drama; but the whole tissue of
Wagner's mature music is similarly architectural, without being in

the slightest way warped by any survival of earlier classical forms. Wagner thus presents us with the extreme case of the reconciling of oppositions between verbal and musical principles. The modern composer has no excuse, even in lyric music, for giving even a classical poet grounds for Tennyson's complaint that 'these song-writers make me say twice what I have only said once'; and if the modern composer of vocal music has the sense and the skill to set lyric poetry to a lyric music instead of to a prose declamation, the world may yet become the richer for songs as unscrupulously musical and perfectly metrical as the music of those ignorant and absolute musicians Mozart, Schubert, and Brahms.

BRAHMS'S CHAMBER MUSIC[1]

THE chamber music of Brahms is comprised in twenty-four works, which probably represent scarcely a quarter of the bulk of composition which he devoted to that branch of his art. Works of art are like icebergs; what is allowed to see daylight is but a fifth of the whole. Great artists differ externally in their way of disposing of the underlying bulk; but its proportion probably remains much the same. Some, like Handel, combine an enormous physical industry with a Johnsonian indolence, and, writing as easily as Johnson talked, give it all to the public in the forms occasion demands. Others, like Bach and Mozart, are not less adroit in using the daily occasion, but are always exploring in organization and technique; so that, as Brahms said of Schubert's six hundred songs, there is something special to be learnt from each work. Inspiration is a wind which 'bloweth where it listeth'; but it prefers to visit artists who are constantly practising their art. 'Genius', said Beethoven, 'is always prolific'; and Beethoven, of all men of genius, practised his art with a technique that changed with the nature of each work. This made it impossible for his art to thrive on methodical mass-production; his innumerable sketches for each individual work are the substitute for the enormous productivity of those masters whose technique was more reducible to routine. The habit of sketching saved him at all events from the necessity of writing half a dozen completely scored symphonies in order that one might survive. It is not known how far Brahms sketched in Beethoven's way; that is to say, by dashing down, on one stave to a line, the whole course of a composition, leaving harmony, texture, and instrumentation for consideration at final stages, and committing oneself to nothing that cannot be as easily altered as improvised, if need be, in a dozen such sketches, all of which will then retain the spontaneity of improvisation enhanced by every gain of insight. The method is admirably convenient for a style in which the texture does not determine any important features, and it is a necessary method in all branches of vocal music where words are to be declaimed with dramatic continuity. But where the texture determines the course of the music, outline-sketching becomes less efficient, and the composer

[1] An article published in Cobbett's *Cyclopedic Survey of Chamber Music* (Oxford University Press), 1929.

must rely on carrying the flow of the music in his head through all the labour of detail. A fugue is composed from the texture outwards; and in the many bad fugues that have been published, the failure is more often in the general composition, which has never been successfully taught, than in the counterpoint, where decent craftsmanship is not unusual. A set of variations cannot be sketched at all, for it presents nothing to write but full detail.

Hence Brahms, whose style was from the outset almost evenly balanced between the most dramatic sonata form and the highest polyphony, can have effected comparatively little by the practice of outline-sketching. As he took extraordinary pains throughout his life, and especially during his last illness, to destroy all unfinished and unpublished manuscripts, we are almost reduced to guess-work as to his methods of composition. A few sketches are preserved in the library of the Gesellschaft der Musikfreunde in Vienna; these comprise some beginnings of small pianoforte pieces and sketches of a projected orchestral overture in E flat minor, but no sketches of extant works are known. On the other hand, it appears from Brahms's correspondence that many important finished works were suppressed; and it is by no means certain that the art of music has not lost more than it has gained through Brahms's exceptionally scrupulous judgement as to what was fit to represent him. For instance, there were two pianoforte trios, in D and E flat, written about the time of that in C major, op. 87; and at least one of these was preferred to the C major by Clara Schumann, a most candid friend and fastidious critic. Again, Professor Jenner of Marburg, in an account of his experiences as a student of composition under Brahms, tells us that what we know as the First Violin Sonata, op. 78, was really the fifth. The actual first violin sonata was in D minor and was written in the period comprised between the Pianoforte Sonata, op. 1, and the original version of the B major Trio, op. 8. Brahms had arranged for its publication, but the manuscript went astray. The loss is undoubtedly to be regretted; if only as a document in the history of the art, the work must have been as important as the B major Trio. But had the manuscript been found some ten years later, it is extremely unlikely that Brahms would then have published it. His recomposition of the B major Trio after twenty-odd years will show us, as will nothing else in the history of music, how ruthlessly he treated anything that seemed defective to his mature sense of movement. Of the other three unpublished violin sonatas there is no individual record.

We may, then, assume that Brahms attained the mastery shown in all his published work by means of a much larger bulk, not of sketches, not even of exercises (though these he also carried on in a correspondence of exchange and mutual criticism with Joachim), but of actually completed works, most of which would have passed as masterpieces to anybody but their composer. The fact that the extant works have by no means passed without dispute as master-pieces, and that controversy is maintained about them to the present day, may indicate that opinions can differ as to what constitutes good technique in music; but if the critic lives who has thought more deeply than Brahms on the matter, that critic's opinions will meet with even more opposition than Brahms's work, in proportion as they are more above the comprehension of the aesthetic official mind.

The most convenient way to enter into Brahms's aesthetic sys-tem is to begin with his first extant piece of chamber music, the B major Trio, op. 8, and to compare it with the new version pub-lished between twenty and thirty years later. To call the later ver-sion a revision is absurd; and to talk of passages in the original as being excised in the later version is like saying that incidents in Schiller's *Jungfrau von Orleans* have been excised in Shaw's *Saint Joan*. What Brahms has done in his later version is to take the broad openings of the first movement and finale (about sixty-four bars each, down to the transition passage to a contrasted key) and to use them as the openings of movements otherwise entirely new; different in sentiment, in theme, in form, and, above all, in sense of movement.

In music, as in life, this sense may be either active or passive; there is the movement of the athlete and the movement of the passenger in the motor-car. In neither case does the measurement in miles an hour determine the aesthetic value of the motion. Even in the most passive movement it is only by jolts, vibrations, and the apparent contrary movement of the surroundings that the motion is realized; and when the roads are good, the car well made, and the driver capable, the faint and rhythmic remaining traces of motion suffice to lull the passenger to sleep. Such is the much-praised Rossinian 'sense of pace', in virtue of which Figaro stands singing *Largo al factotum* at ten syllables a second, pointing sym-metrically to right and left as the music swings from tonic to dominant; and thus the Rossinians gibe at Mozart's slowness with the solemn insolence of a *nouveau riche* giving the dust of his limousine to the riders who brought the good news from Ghent to Aix.

Now it is one of the first principles of sonata style that it is dominated by an active rather than by a passive sense of movement. All kinds of movement may, indeed must, be there, but sonata style is neither architectural nor cosmically epic, but thoroughly dramatic. The sublime motion by which the dead and living are 'roll'd round in earth's diurnal course with stocks, and stones, and trees' is present in the form of a tempo which, in spite of the violence often done to it by sentimental and arbitrary virtuoso players, does not undergo abrupt or capricious change any more than the paces of a horse; a quick tempo, or changes in tempo, can, merely as such, produce no sense of active movement unless the composer exerts his invention by varying the proportions of his phrases.

Mozart, in the finale of his *Musikalischer Spass*, held up the mirror to the nature of all road-hog composers in the following cadence-theme:

Ex.1 *Presto*

It must be heard in its context for the full fun to be revealed; but, *a priori*, a movement in which that is the nearest approach to a terse procedure will be a slow business however fast it is played; indeed, the quicker the tempo the more open the confession that actual progress is disappointing.

Now the period of Brahms's early works was singularly disturbing to the cultivation of a sonata-like sense of movement. The music-drama of Wagner, though only just about to ripen to the undreamt-of technique and scale of *The Ring*, had already fired the imagination of young composers (not, at first, excluding Brahms and Joachim) with the possibilities of a kind of movement which, instead of exhausting itself within each of the four usual divisions of a sonata (say, in ten minutes), should be capable of carrying on dramatic action for hours *pari passu* with a poetic stage-drama. Had

the Wagnerian propaganda ever been precisely formulated as concerned with a generalized and positive problem of movement, it is
conceivable that controversy might have taken less mutually repress-
ive lines; and certainly the issues would have been far less confused
had it been possible for Wagner to produce *The Ring* before asserting his aims, instead of using for their illustration works like *Tannhäuser* and *Lohengrin*, which every honest musician has now long
since admitted to be almost evenly balanced between the true but
immature Wagner and a composer more of the order of the pompous Spontini, if not rather of the pariah Meyerbeer.

Even if Mendelssohn, then so obviously the great master for
whom nothing seemed difficult or obscure, had not died most in-
opportunely in 1847, before he had time to realize that the new
tendencies in music were more important in their essence than in
any crudeness of their first expression, the controversy would still
have wasted much energy as between 'classicists' who reduced all
instrumental art-forms to pre-established jelly-moulds, and 'roman-
ticists' to whom all music existed for purposes of illustration. As
a matter of fact few composers have written more 'programme
music' than those 'classicists' Mendelssohn and Spohr; and the
real issues of musical development have never been divided into
such obvious oppositions. But it was true that Mendelssohn's
musical forms, though immediately effective, were too loose to
serve as a foundation for the art of any future master who had
attained enough insight to admire them intelligently; while Spohr's
forms, to say nothing of his mannerisms, had in his ripe old age
settled down to a mastery like that of the 'spot stroke' in billiards,
which became a nuisance calling for the institution of 'spot-barred'
matches. Meanwhile Schumann had raised an attractive side-issue,
not at first recognized as such, by his symphonies and chamber
music, in which everything is started in rigidly square antithetic
epigrams, and a distant effect of development is produced by long
slabs of cumulative sequence; in short, a kind of musical mosaic
which has its own merit and the merits of its precious material just
so long as it does not pretend to be a painting. Nothing shows more
glaringly how the musical propagandists of all parties in the
eighteen-fifties failed to grasp the essentials of their art than the
fact that Brahms was from the outset criticized, admired, and perse-
cuted as a follower of Schumann. It was natural to assume that
the subject of Schumann's famous article entitled *Neue Bahnen*
would be an artist in sympathy with Schumann's art; but it showed

scanty appreciation of Schumann to suppose that, while he had health and strength to write that article, he would have devoted it to an imitator of his own style, to say nothing of entitling it 'New Paths'.

Brahms's art was from the outset so manifestly beyond the scope of all parties that partisans of opposite tenets eagerly proved their intelligence by claiming him as among their leaders. The genuine freedom of his art-forms made his pianoforte sonatas acceptable to the romantic extremists grouped around Liszt; while it was evident to anyone whose interest in the classics was not merely conventional that, with inequalities conspicuous by their rarity, this music showed a mastery of classical technique unknown since Beethoven. Brahms never accepted the position of leader of a party, and neither journalists nor friends could have forced that position upon him but for two things: his own horror of artistic bureaucracy and *claques*, and the catastrophic revulsion which took place in Joachim's feelings towards Liszt when, after his friendship had ripened to intimacy, he made the acquaintance of Liszt's more serious compositions and found in them every quality of style and emotion that most repelled him. This and the indisputable fact that Liszt, if not himself responsible for the position, was the centre of a press-bureau almost as well organized as Meyerbeer's, brought about an explicit declaration of estrangement between the masters of the two main musical forces of nineteenth-century music—forces that perhaps might never have been sundered if German and Hungarian musical party-politics could have been as separable from aesthetic-moral judgements as English parliamentarianism. Both these forces lost incalculably by the separation, for Joachim's own profoundly original fountain of composition finally dried up, Liszt was deprived of all the interchange of ideas by which Joachim exercised so stimulating an influence upon Brahms, and Brahms himself did not escape from a somewhat ascetic attitude towards artistic resources which he would have had no difficulty in developing to legitimate purpose had not the word *lisztisch* become current in his correspondence with Joachim as a synonym for 'damnable'.

As to Wagner, in whom the real issues of the *Zukunfts-Musik* were finding their goal, Brahms's attitude was never satisfactory to his partisan friends; and in his later years persons who tried to curry favour with him by talking against Wagner met with fierce rebukes for their pains.

Let us now see what light is shed upon the problems of musical

Q

movement in the eighteen-fifties by comparing certain themes in the two versions of Brahms's B major Trio, showing his views of the problem before and after he had formed his style.

The first theme, extended for over sixty bars, is common to both.

These twelve bars, the mere first phrase of a long lyric melody, already suffice to raise a problem in sonata style. Such melodies are rare as opening themes of sonatas, and from such an opening it is a *tour de force* to swing naturally into dramatic action.

Brahms was from the outset quite aware of the difficulty; and two solutions were possible to an artist of his calibre. Either this melody must be a normal item in a scheme that is breaking away from sonata style, or it must be an exceptionally big item in a normal sonata scheme. There is, of course, a *via media*, the cheerful ambling along in the king-can-do-no-wrong convention that pervades all bourgeois music from Mendelssohn's D minor Trio, onwards through Rubinstein, till a highly experimental government intervenes and, innocently enacting that composers shall be paid by the crotchet, causes a temporary return to a sixteenth-century notation in which the standard note is worth four times as much. Brahms's instinct went to the root of the matter no less in the first version of his B major Trio than in the last. I place, one below the other, the first phrase of the main 'second subject' in each.

2nd Version

The early theme, as far as quoted, is only half the sentence, and it cannot be followed up except by shorter phrases. Its movement is, intentionally and effectively, slower than that of the opening theme, which will contrast with it as sunshine after gloom, but which will never again sound so big as it did at the outset. The young Brahms's instincts were right when he broke away from the ideas of a formal recapitulation of such material when it is due to return after the development. The fugato digression which he is inaccurately said to have 'excised' in his later version is no fault in the earlier scheme, which does not break down until the ambitious young composer is confronted with the impossible task of ending with a grand climax on his main theme; whereupon he anticipates the recent policy of the composers whose government paid them by the crotchet, and winds up with an imitation of a chorus and organ, in semibreves and minims presto.

To get thus excited over a naïvely beautiful melody is what inexperienced composers might call taking it seriously, and what conventional critics would call taking it too seriously. The first time Brahms really took this theme seriously was when in the light of full experience he became inspired with the possibilities of a scheme in which it should be the largest item instead of a mere indication of the average flow. From that moment the first movement and finale became new compositions having literally nothing in common with the old but their first sixty bars. Some years ago an eminent violoncellist had a misadventure in a public performance of this work. He knew only the final version, and knew it as nearly by heart as first-rate chamber-music players are in the habit of knowing well-rehearsed works. But he had not even realized the existence of the old version, a copy of which had been mistakenly put on his desk, and it was only on turning the page that he found himself confronted, in full career of performance *coram publico*, with

a totally unknown continuation. This nightmare shock could happen
with no other printed piece of chamber music, and even here could
not have happened to the violinist. For Joachim, who had a strong
dislike of a long rest for the violin at the beginning of a chamber
work, complained that it made the opening sound as if the violin
was to enter after the tutti of a concerto, and made Brahms interpolate a little arpeggio figure three times during the first twenty
bars of the early version. A violinist would therefore notice at once
if he had the wrong version, for Brahms afterwards overruled
Joachim's objection, and decided that if that opening was to inspire
him to a new composition it needed no such tinkering.

The 'second subject' themes of the two versions of the finale
show up still more obviously against each other.

It will be seen that the young Brahms has good reason to write
'più presto' over his pretty F-sharp-major melody, and that the
quickest possible tempo will never make these twelve bars anything
more lively than four bars of a leisurely 9/4 rhythm covering only
half of his first sentence. Then this twenty-four-bar sentence, having closed in the tonic, must be followed by a second part with
wider range of key and higher lyric pathos, culminating in a return
to the first strain more fully scored. After lyric inaction on such a
scale, whatever else might be right, orthodox sonata procedures
must be at least partially wrong, and it is not surprising that of the
many interesting and some abstruse features of subsequent developments only one, a quiet passage leading to a crescendo at the
beginning of the coda, could be used in the later version, where it

sounds ten times bigger and more romantic than in its original context.

The new work is not an unmixed gain upon the old, especially in the finale, where the experienced Brahms grips the young Brahms so roughly by the shoulder as to make us doubt whether a composer as angry with the sentimentalities of his own youth would not be over-ready to tease and bully or, still worse, to ignore young composers anxious to learn but less sure of their ground. But his attitude to the scherzo shows that his impatience had nothing in common with the timid fretfulness of the Superior Person, who will never get over the climax of the glorious tune of the trio, in which the three instruments, finding themselves able to blaze away in the grandest style of a Viennese waltz-band, do so without the smallest scruple. Brahms, finding that the resulting quality of tone happens to be excellent in spite of its resemblance on paper to the most commonplace failures of its kind, not only retains this passage in his later version but puts its most impertinent final gesture an octave higher. *Pecca fortiter* is his motto. The original end of the first movement fails because the three instruments cannot imitate a chorus and organ; the trio of the scherzo succeeds because if an orchestra can sound like that it will sound very well indeed. From the genteel fear of vulgarity Brahms was as free as the most Norman of duchesses.

With his early treatment of lyric or episodic forms Brahms later found little matter for regret; and it was only at the end of the scherzo that he found his mysterious early coda too clever and, as usual, too slow. With the adagio the case is more complex. In its original form it consists of a mysterious dialogue between the pianoforte and the strings, followed by a lyric episode in the subdominant, after which the dialogue returns, with a wonderful new modulation. Just before the close it breaks into an abstruse discussion of one of its figures, allegro doppio movimento (i.e. at exactly double the pace, so that the change is more in notation than in tempo). This rises to a climax with many abrupt dramatic gestures, after which the last clause of the adagio dialogue closes the movement in its original mysterious calm. In the new version the probability is that, as in the first movement and finale, Brahms was inspired by new material to set the old opening in a more sublime light. Nothing can be less likely than the commonly accepted view that he rejected the E-major episode because of its resemblance to Schubert's *Am Meer*: the resemblance is of the kind which amateurs

discover with infantile ease, but which to persons experienced in
composition is like 'puns partially intelligible with the aid of
italics and a laryngoscope'. Brahms's own views of such 'reminis-
cences' may be conveniently cited here. To a composer friend
who apologized for borrowing a theme from one of his symphonies
he wrote to the effect that 'plagiarism is one of the stupidest topics
of stupid people; you have made into one of your freshest themes
what was only an accessory detail in my work'. And when somebody pointed out a resemblance between certain points in the finale
of his C minor Pianoforte Quartet and Mendelssohn's C minor
Trio, his now famous comment was, 'Any fool can see that'. The
main objections to the original E-major episode are that the pizzicato accompaniment, which looks picturesque on paper, is disappointing in sound, even with the finest playing, and that Brahms
has failed to make its irregular phrasing and broken conclusion
express that freedom of form which is already so conspicuous in his
earliest work, e.g. in the wonderfully placed extra half-bars, expressed by 3/2 time at the beginning of the first movement in both
versions. In the new version of the adagio we are confronted with
a totally new middle part, a passionate stream of subtle melody in
G sharp minor (the same key as that of the second subject in the
first movement) worked out on a very large scale. The concentrated
gloom of this contrasts with the mysterious brightness of the opening, which returns with all the greater mystery and simplicity. The
strange allegro doppio movimento coda is no longer needed and
disappears without leaving a scar. One extra bar in the penultimate
cadence is all that is required to bring in the last line.

Between these two different works with the same openings and
the same opus number lie most of Brahms's remaining chamber
music and the development of nearly his whole range of style.
After thus sketching the nature of the changes Brahms made in the
B major Trio, we shall find it easy to follow the course of the other
extant works.

The next published piece of chamber music is the first sextet,
in B flat, op. 18. Here we find in a mature form the expression of
a deliberate reaction towards classical sonata style and procedure—
a reaction which Brahms had achieved wittily and violently in his
first orchestral Serenade, op. 11, originally written as a divertimento
for solo instruments. In the B flat Sextet Brahms is no longer con-
strained to unite new and old elements under the cover of jokes to
justify his masquerading, like Beethoven in his Sonata, op. 31,

no. 1, and other transitional works. Humour the sextet displays in Haydnesque measure and Beethovenish breadth at the end of the luxurious rondo-finale, and the tiny scherzo is circumscribed within limits that might have sufficed for the earliest Beethoven. But these points are not irreconcilable with a pervading Olympian calm, asserted in the opening and maintained throughout at a height which annihilates the distinction between 'classical' and 'romantic', and which is as far above formality as it is above more tempting foolishnesses. Joachim, to whom Brahms at this time sent all his compositions to be criticized movement by movement, found that the opening theme moved in its twelfth bar too abruptly to the rather remote key of D flat, and suggested to Brahms that instead of beginning at once with all six instruments it would be better to announce the first nine bars (already a significantly irregular phrase) in the violoncellos and viola, letting the violins sail in with the connecting tenth bar so as to take up the theme in their own octave by way of repetition; after which the modulation to D flat would sound as welcome as it is rich. This is the scheme followed in the opening of the B flat Sextet, as we know it, and the effort of imagining it otherwise shows us the difference between Joachim's suggestions and the question-begging generalities of critics to whom everything is a matter of taste and inspiration, an indefinable and incommunicable essence of just what the critics happen to like at the moment. The finale likewise opens with a statement of its theme by the violoncello, repeated in the upper octave by the violin; and Brahms pointed this out to Joachim as a further result of his advice: a statement, however, to be taken playfully, as such treatment of a strophic rondo-theme is a matter of no technical subtlety.

The slow movement is a magnificent set of variations of which Brahms made a pianoforte version that he used to play many years afterwards. Though this was only a case of unwritten score-playing, we may be glad that the arrangement has been published; for every contribution of Brahms to the aesthetics of the pianoforte as a vehicle for the expression of general musical ideas is a contribution valuable to the special character of the instrument in proportion as the ideas are remote from what would occur to the hand of an extempore player. As the next three works we have now to consider, besides thirteen of the remaining nineteen, are works with pianoforte, this is a convenient opportunity for dealing with his general treatment of such combinations. The statement that the piano does not blend with other instruments either indicates a fact of positive aesthetic importance, or, in its more common question-begging form, 'does not blend satisfactorily', is a testimony to a type of professional incapacity manifested by pianists who have no experience of chamber music. Nothing blends with anything unless you know the measure of the contrasts involved. The bass-tuba does not blend imperceptibly with the trombones: hence Wagner invented a special family of tubas and developed for them a characteristic life of their own in his *Ring*, also inventing a double-bass trombone in order that the trombones might have their own deep bass. But in *Tristan, Meistersinger*, and *Parsifal*, that is to say, in two works written after the first two *Ring* operas, and in a final work written exclusively for Bayreuth and with the fullest experience of Bayreuth conditions, Wagner was as satisfied as Brahms with the earlier use of the tuba as a bass to the trombones, leaving it to correction at rehearsals if the player fails to blend where contrast is not intended. Orchestral players expect to be instructed by conductors, and it is, if anything, more usual for great conductors to understand something of composition than for great composers to know how to conduct.

From this it may be inferred that, after every allowance has been made for superior opportunities and education, chamber-music players, especially pianists, would have much better current ideas as to their business if it were their habit to perform under the baton of composers or conductors versed in chamber music—an important qualification, for no amount of purely orchestral experience will give either composer or conductor the remotest idea of the totally different values which single instruments assume when the orchestral environment is removed. As to the pianoforte in chamber music, it is nowadays high time frankly to admit that the Schumann tradition itself is not faultless even in regard to Brahms. It naturally accepts Schumann's Pianoforte Quartet and Quintet as normal, if simple, solutions of the problem; and this is as hopeless a basis for tackling Brahms's trios and quartets as to use Haydn's trios as a basis for the study of Beethoven's, or even of Mozart's. Chamber music, in the sense understood by Mozart, Beethoven, Brahms, and the Haydn of the string quartets, begins to exist when every note essential to euphony is assigned to the instrument which is in a position to play it, when no instrument is so constructed that in playing one written note it produces artificial overtones by combinations of organ-stops or harpsichord octave-strings, and, lastly, when the whole organization rejects unnecessary or colourless doublings in the unison. When the pianoforte is combined with groups of other instruments, this last criterion has to be reconciled with another, known to all the classics since the days when Palestrina wrote double and triple choruses; namely, that when voices or instruments are divided into antiphonal groups, the harmony of each group must be complete in itself, even when the groups are sounding together. Schumann satisfies the antiphonal criterion, but, like Haydn in his trios, at the ruinous cost of making it constantly impossible to decide which of two players in unison is the more unnecessary.

One of Brahms's most often quoted maxims was, 'If we cannot write as beautifully as Mozart and Haydn, let us at least write as purely'. The notion of purity was primarily applied by him to part-writing in the generalized grammatical sense of harmony and counterpoint; but the matters usually classed under the head of instrumentation are the more extensive consequences and cases of the same grammatical laws, even where they seem to work out in opposite ways, like a balloon rising 'in defiance of the law of gravitation'. On purity, in the sense of economy in instrumentation, Brahms acquired the severest views, stimulated by the criticism and advice of Joachim, whose ear in such matters was probably the most sensitive since Mozart's time.

The questions here involved must not be confused with matters of what is commonly called 'colour' in music. Brahms is supposed to be an indifferent 'colourist', and many official Brahmsians defend him as 'more concerned with what he has to say than how he says it'. Our notions of pure instrumental colour, however, will never do justice to Brahms—or indeed to any symphonic or chamber music—so long as we think that Wagnerian instrumentation sets the normal standard. Wagner writes habitually for the stage, and his instrumentation stands, with all its marvellous refinements, to the general problems of sonata style as the language of a drama stands to the question of what styles are good in novels and narrative poems. Yet, in spite of the incredible naïvetés which Wagner-bred critics and conductors (or even composers) commit when they discover chamber music late in life, it would be an excellent thing for pianists who think Brahms's chamber music incorrectly balanced in tone to learn the trumpet or tuba and experience the rough side of the tongue of a respectable conductor when they show a deficient sense of the weight of their instrument. Two quotations from one

of the tersest works in Brahms's ripest and most powerful style
(the Trio in C minor, op. 101) will define the issue completely. The
'second subject' of the first movement is scored thus:

and, after ten more bars, is taken up by the pianoforte with the
following scoring:

The crudest of pianists cannot make a mistake as to the effortless
sonority and transparency of the few notes in which the piano richly
harmonizes the powerful melody of the low strings in octaves; but
even a good pianist whose classical experience of his instrument is
based mainly on Chopin and Liszt, with an occasional condescen-
sion to the Schumann Quintet, is apt to feel insulted and ridiculed
in every professional fibre when he has to learn that beyond a ringing cantabile in the little finger of his right hand he must use no
more energy in his counterstatement than in his accompaniment
of the strings, and that, instead of getting excited by the enormous
'pianistic' possibilities of his part conceived as a Chopin Ballade,
he must put all his pianistic inspiration into blending his left hand
with the pizzicato of the strings, which then becomes one of the

most exciting sounds ever imagined in chamber music. At least it
will if the string-players have not been so permanently discouraged
by the theory of pianistic incompatibility as to have forgotten that,
like harpists, and unlike pianists, they can produce twice as much
tone by spreading their chords instead of cutting them short.
Brahms took this for granted, and accordingly does not give the
violin the arpeggio signs which are necessary for the left hand of
the pianoforte. Not until Reger discovered that string players had
forgotten their own instincts and required an arpeggio sign to every
three-part and four-part chord to prevent them from choking it,
did it ever occur to an experienced composer to provide such
signs.

The violoncello part of these pizzicato chords reveals another
point, inasmuch as there is not one composer in a hundred, especially among 'great colourists', who could be trusted not to make
chords of them instead of single notes. But the bass of such chords
vanishes before the top, unless the player puts all his accent below,
a precaution which is impossible in any tone above mezzo-forte.
Single notes, which look so humble on paper, provide the only
sonorous bass, and, blended with the playing of a pianist who has
a Bayreuth contrabass-tubist's knowledge of the weight of his instrument, give all their weight to the chords of the violin.

Another pizzicato passage that has caused much disappointment
and censure is the quiet beginning of the development of the
Violin Sonata in G major, op. 78:

Brahms must have suffered much from the conventions of
'pianistic' pianists (their average standard of intelligence has, in
fact, greatly improved since mechanical and phonographic records
have enabled them to hear themselves as others hear them); but
he did not anticipate a time when violinists, who would harp this

passage like angels if they thought it part of a popular piece of musical cookery, could think that classical chastity compelled them to tighten these chords into dry clicks while the pianist, in a burst of 'noble manliness without sentiment', uses six times the tone that Brahms requires for his ethereal melody over its distant bass.

But the most crucial case of a pizzicato passage is in the third movement (or scherzo) of the last violin sonata (in D minor, op. 108). This, in the light of the published correspondence between Brahms and Frau von Herzogenberg, proves that he was always willing to act upon good advice that condescended to concrete facts instead of moving in an aristocratic atmosphere of the *je-ne-sais-quoi*; and in its own light it exemplifies one of the most important relations between form and instrumentation, namely, that a version of a theme that would seem impossibly crude or artificial for a first statement may be the one acceptable and admirable thing by way of counterstatement. Thus, the passage just quoted from the G major Sonata is a return, not a first statement. Again, no reasonable person has ever objected to the orchestral version of the theme of the rondo of Beethoven's E flat Concerto, first announced in magnificent solo style by the pianoforte; and in the finale of the G major Concerto everybody is delighted with the variation in which the pianoforte repeats the theme which would have been unplayable in a literal transcription of the original orchestral announcement. But both these counterstatements would be out of the question as original themes. In stage music, where everything has to fit the action of the movement, and musical form as such has no power to pick up lost threads, this relation between form and texture is either almost undeveloped, or developed in ways which would require another special essay to identify. But in all the opposition to Brahms nothing has been commoner than the two tricks, first, of criticizing his counterstatements as if they were initial statements, and, secondly, when a pianoforte statement and a string statement prove to be equally brilliant, of saying that Brahms is a follower of Schumann and never gets away from the pianoforte.

The pizzicato passage in the D minor Sonata is the recapitulation of the main theme of the scherzo (Ex. 8 opposite).

In the opening statement the pianoforte gives the theme in cold octaves instead of two-part contrary motion, and the violin chords are half-sustained with the bow. But Brahms originally made them pizzicato, and changed them into *arco* chords when Frau von

Herzogenberg persuaded him that it was otherwise impossible to get a convincing colour into the opening. The pizzicato becomes rich and delightful as a new colour in the recapitulation when added to the contrary-motion two-part harmony. That two-part harmony itself would have wasted its opportunity if it had been used at the opening instead of cold octaves.

We are now in a position to resume and conclude the chronological survey of Brahms's extant chamber music in the light of the principles here illustrated.

The two huge Pianoforte Quartets in G minor, op. 25, and A major, op. 26, were for Hanslick (the first journalist to support Brahms since Schumann) the centre of Brahms's art from which he was to deviate at his peril. Useful as Hanslick's support was to Brahms, it came from an unfortunate quarter as regards its effect on musical history; for Hanslick was the original of Wagner's Beckmesser—in the first draft of the *Meistersinger* text that character's name is actually Hans Lich. He found in these quartets the direct result of the last works of Beethoven; an appreciation based mainly on the correct conviction that such abstruse works were the sort of thing a high-minded young composer would study. Brahms, who made and kept friendship with Hanslick as a gentleman of culture and benevolent intentions, cannot be supposed to have had much respect for the judgement of a critic to whom Beethoven was acceptable only in his middle works, as being puerile in his first period and decadent in his third; to whom Haydn and Mozart were court composers, an aria of Bach a piece of running clockwork, and Palestrina as incomprehensible a hocus-pocus as Newman was to Kingsley. If this is not a fair account of the light Hanslick was able to shed upon the classics, it is a quite adequate statement of what the general reader will get from a perusal of his writings in so far as they are not devoted, much more amusingly, to violent abuse of

Wagner, Berlioz, and Liszt. The loneliness of Brahms was intensified by the accession of such a partisan.

In these two piano quartets the forms are peculiar to Brahms, and
in some respects to the works themselves. The themes, especially
in the A major Quartet, have a way of grouping themselves in pairs,
the members of each pair alternating in an actual binary form which
narrowly escapes self-completion by breaking out at the last moment
into the wider field of dramatic action. This is quite a different
state of things from the problem raised by the opening of the B
major Trio; Brahms has already in the B flat Sextet thoroughly acquired the swing of classical sonata-movement and is now enlarging
his scale. To deal successfully with the enormous spaces which these
pairs of themes and counterstatements fill to repletion, Brahms, for
all the resulting length, summons up an energy which is really identical with terseness. For obviously, as regards the use of materials, a
monument made of twenty Stonehenge blocks is a terser product
than one of the same size made of a million bricks. The difference
between such masonry as that of these quartets and that of the proverbially *lapidarisch* Bruckner is that Brahms takes his risk in forms
of lyric melody, whereas Bruckner's materials are huge Wagnerian
Nibelungen-Ring processes. On the very rare occasions when
Brahms writes an introduction, he shows as much mastery of such
processes as Wagner himself; see the introduction to the finale of
the very next work, the Quintet, op. 34. But it is one of the points
on which, perhaps, he felt himself driven into opposition to the
tendencies of the day, and he nearly always begins plumb on the
tonic with his main theme. The exceptions show that he had plenty
of invention in other directions, and that his view of fine imaginative
introductory flights was rather that they were too easy to be often
true.

The connexion between form and instrumentation becomes more
and more intimate as the composer's mastery grows. Brahms had
already shown an astonishing maturity in the scoring of the first
version of his B major Trio, which becomes crude only where the
composer's material has made the task of a climax impossible.
From the outset Brahms showed an immense talent for counterpoint, and Joachim, whose delicate ear could not tolerate the
slightest harshness, saw to it that Brahms should never allow a
contrapuntal device to attract attention by even a Beethovenish
collision. Hence, from first to last, Brahms had unlimited means
of making his themes do duty as humble but not lifeless accompani-

ments; and this is one of the resources which make the forms of
these two quartets possible. For pages together Brahms's texture
at all periods invites analysis as close as that of a Bach fugue, while
the form is as dramatic as instrumental music can be without
attenuating itself to the drastic simplicities of the operatic stage.
An error, very mischievous in the teaching of composition, is that
which, fascinated by this thematic analysis, mistakes its 'logic' for
that of the composition as a whole. An example from the Quintet,
op. 34, will show where the logic really lies.

Ex.9

The fact that the semiquaver figure is a diminution of the previous theme is an item of high aesthetic value, but does not constitute the 'logic' of Brahms's exposition. Any other semiquavers
that fitted the harmony and kept within the rhythm might be substituted without destruction to the real scheme. But close up those
gaps in the rhythm (e.g. by fitting the semiquavers of bar 6 into the
last crotchet of bar 5) and mishandle the process to the close on the
dominant, or drift in some other direction, and all the thematic
connexions in the world will not put sense or life into the drama
you have stultified. Later on, when the semiquaver figure has
become a quiet accompaniment to long lyric stretches in the 'second
subject', Brahms makes the pianoforte preserve it accurately, but
simplifies it into—

Ex.10

because an exact version would be a little more difficult, and therefore a little heavier in a pianissimo for the strings.

Before returning to finish the account of the first two pianoforte
quartets, it will be convenient to quote another transformation of
this theme, in order to deal with the general topic of metamorphosis
of themes as practised by Brahms. His anti-Wagnerian friends got

into difficulties when they tried to distinguish his classical ways of
development from the damnable heresies of Wagner and Liszt, for
their analysis never got beyond the identification of themes, and
was not up to ordinary police methods at that. But when Brahms
turns the first eight notes of his opening theme by a simple rhythmic displacement into the lilt of an ancient ballad, thus:

Ex.11

the stroke of genius is of the same order as those by which Wagner
develops the thought of world-power from the Rhine-maidens'
golden toy through the darkness of the Nibelung's mind to the
foredoomed splendours of Walhalla. In point of form it differs
from this and similar miracles in Beethoven's B flat Trio, op. 97,
in that Brahms's transformation is immediate. But, immediate or
gradual, such transformations are governed by a very different law
from that which permits or even encourages the counterstatement
of a whole theme to take a form that would be unconvincing as a
first statement. A metamorphosis or a fusion of two originally
separate figures into a new unity has either the value of an independent inspiration or it has none. It cannot be accomplished mechanically. Brahms would have jumped at the sprightly combination of
the boy Siegfried's horn-theme with that of his sword; but the
attempt, in *Götterdämmerung*, to turn that horn-tune into an expression of matured virility by sophisticating its rhythm would no more
have satisfied him than the text of *Götterdämmerung* satisfies that
perfect Wagnerite, Bernard Shaw.

This art of thematic metamorphosis was completely mastered by
Brahms with inexhaustible fullness and no vestige of artificiality in
his very first works, and pervades every opus, vocal and instrumental, from the Sonata, op. 1, to the *Vier Ernste Gesänge*, op. 121,
and the small posthumous collection of figured chorales, op. 122.
It is the musical essence of Wagnerian leitmotive, and as such its
function is not architectural, but illustrative and decorative. It
cannot create noble proportions in composition, but it can and
must enhance them or condemn itself. Thematic organization can
no more build Wagnerian music-drama or Brahmsian symphonies
than tracery, mouldings, and stained glass can build cathedrals.

We may now return to opp. 25 and 26 and finish with a brief
history of each remaining work.

THE G MINOR PIANOFORTE QUARTET, op. 25. The first movement
is one of the most original and impressive tragic compositions since
the first movement of Beethoven's Ninth Symphony. The association of two themes (characteristic of these quartets), one in G minor,
the other in B flat, produces an astonishing dramatic result when,
after the development section, the recapitulation begins, not with
the first of the pair, but with the second in the sunniest G major.
Still more astonishing is the transformation of the whole latter half
of the enormous procession of triumphant and tender 'second
subject' themes in D major into tragic pathos in G minor; an
operation on a scale unprecedented in classical music, and surpassed
only by Liszt's transformation of the bulk of the first movement of
his 'Faust' Symphony into the Mephistophelian scherzo; a comparison by which perhaps Brahms would not feel flattered. How
much the work owes to Joachim is not known, but the austerely
diatonic transition to the 'second subject' must, as we know it, be
very different from the passage which Joachim found 'positively
painful'. The second movement, entitled 'Intermezzo', is, in outline, a gigantic scherzo and trio, each highly organized and independent in the details of their form. In style it is a mysteriously tender
and pathetic romance, and, with its strange 9/8 rhythms and its
muted violin, is one of Brahms's most typical movements. The following andante is another enormous design in dramatic A-B-A
form, the broad main theme (a lyric melody in E flat) leading in
a spaciously developed transition-passage to an exciting military
episode in C major. At the climax of this, where Brahms has no
more scruple in writing orchestrally than he had in the scherzo of
the B major Trio, the solo pianist who incautiously lets himself go
will find himself playing wrong notes; and, if asked to correct these,
will complain that the passage is badly written for accurate playing
with full tone. This is true, but it seems a roundabout approach to
the discovery that Brahms knows how to balance the pianoforte
against the strings in his most violent climax. The main theme
resurrects itself out of a ruinous crash in C major, and swings round
to its original E flat by a change of harmony which delays its course
for only a few bars.

The finale, a Hungarian rondo inspired to terrific energy by that
in Haydn's 'Gipsy' Trio, came as a great shock to the Superior
Person. Its sectional, dance-like structure is a bold addition to the
high organic resources of the whole work, and is brought into complete harmony with them by the wonderful cadenza, in which all its

R

themes are combined in a polyphony as accurate as Bach's and a rhythm as fantastic as Liszt's. The fact that this movement is, from beginning to end, without precedent or parallel in Brahms's other works is in itself a fact with plenty of precedents and parallels in Brahms and the classics.

THE A MAJOR PIANOFORTE QUARTET, op. 26, gave those who could understand it at all much less trouble to digest than the G minor. Its serenity is Olympian and the high spirits of its finale are, in spite of Hungarian traits, athletic rather than Bacchanalian. Indeed, the C major theme in the 'second subject' region of the finale stretches to the utmost limit the possibility of arching a slow theme over a quick tempo without collapsing from sonata style into Wagnerian operatic obliteration of tempo. Brahms, however, knows what he is doing in thus testing the matter. Terser and more aphoristic methods are for older men; an unaffected young composer is wise in learning to tell his story in full before his experience has enabled him to judge which half to omit in order that the half may be greater than the whole. Critics who have no respect for youthfulness of this calibre are preparing for an old age that will be merely unpleasant for themselves and others. There are abundant economy and halves greater than wholes in other musical dimensions and categories throughout Brahms's early works; and the all-pervading problem of movement is eminently one where the broadest solutions must precede the terser ones.

The first movement is of statuesque beauty, but anyone who imagines on that ground that it is cold will be lucky if he has the experience of happening to hear or recall the climax where its recapitulation breaks into the coda, and to mistake it for a crescendo in a Wagner opera. The mistake is quite possible, and the effort to place the passage will be amusingly confined to the highest climaxes of *Tristan* or *Die Walküre*. No insight into the emotional values of the purely instrumental is possible until we abandon the popular delusion that because good stage-music is, in its own surroundings, more exciting, it is made of more passionate stuff. With the exception of Mozart the great masters of sonata form are inhibited from operatic writing not by lack of passion but by excess of concentration in their passion.

The slow movement of the A major Quartet, another masterpiece of romantic colour with use of mutes, is in a fully developed rondo form, a fact that, with the size of its themes, involves a length which it is a triumph of economy to keep within bounds. The first theme may be usefully quoted as an example of the kind of phrase that can occur to no composer who is not constantly in the practice of setting words to music.

Ex.12

We have no evidence that this ever was associated with words; but, besides its five-bar rhythm, those triplets with their manifold drift of connexion are unmistakably the invention of a composer to whom all the shapes that verbal sentences can take are objects of musical interest, to be interpreted, not by Wagnerian declamation fitted into an orchestral scheme, but by musical sentences equally intelligible in themselves. We must learn to understand Brahms's mastery of absolute musical form in the light of the fact that fully two-thirds of his work, from first to last, was vocal, and that this prince of absolute musicians was the most circumstantial of verbal illustrators where words were involved. That is why there is no composer with whom it is more futile to impute unauthorized 'programmes' to his instrumental works.

The scherzo and trio of the A major Quartet are a pair of binary movements developed far beyond the limits of mere melodic form, and constitute in their alternation a movement fully on the scale of the others.

A hundred and twenty years earlier Bach had impudently plagiarized Brahms's main theme in the overture to his Fourth Partita in the *Clavierübung*; no doubt with Brahms's full pardon.

QUINTET IN F MINOR FOR PIANOFORTE AND STRINGS, op. 34 a. Here we come to the climax of Brahms's first maturity. The work was originally written as a string quintet with two violoncellos (like Schubert's) instead of the more usual two violas. To us, who are accustomed to its terrific power as a pianoforte quintet, it is not surprising that Joachim, after thorough practical proof with his colleagues, persuaded Brahms that no mortal strings could cope with its climaxes. Brahms then arranged it as a sonata for two pianofortes, published as op. 34 b. The result was magnificent as to power and clearness, but the total loss of string tone is regrettable in the quiet passage at the beginning of the coda of the first movement, and a real difficulty to the understanding of the mysterious introduction to the finale. Finally, the work took its shape as a pianoforte quintet, the most sonorous of all extant works for piano-

forte and strings, and yet the most lightly scored. The first movement has already been quoted; it is powerfully tragic. The slow
movement is a broad lyric in A-B-A form. The thunderous
scherzo in its main body follows the form and modulations of that
in Beethoven's C minor Symphony more closely than Brahms ever
elsewhere followed a single example. The resemblance disturbs
nobody, and the trio, a big, triumphant binary melody in the major,
goes its own Brahmsian way. The finale is, like that of the A major
Quartet, a big binary movement with the development section
omitted, or rather replaced by a considerable discussion between
the recapitulation of the 'first subject' and that of the second. This
form was amplified from Mozart by Schubert, whose spirit pervades
this quintet more than any other work of Brahms, though from first
to last it is by far the most conspicuous influence in the origins of
his style. Beethoven is the founder of his art-forms, and Bach the
founder of his polyphony; but their influence on his style is as
impersonally general as the influence of the sum of classical literature upon Milton. Brahms was bound to Schumann by every tie
of personal affection, sympathy, gratitude (with him no irksome
feeling), and sorrow, but Schumann's music had no more influence
on his style than Spohr's, for whose *Jessonda* he confessed to an
auld-lang-syne affection of the kind which he personally could
never lose. Schubert, however, is always looking over his shoulder,
and in this quintet might have been guiding his pen for pages, in
the second subject of the first movement, the main theme of the
slow movement, and the whole body of the finale. The savage flat
supertonic acciaccatura (D flat C) at the end of the scherzo comes
straight from the end of Schubert's Quintet, and from nowhere else
in the whole history of final chords. And the art-forms of this
quintet are the nearest conceivable approach to what Schubert would
have achieved had he lived to bring his instrumental unorthodoxies
to mature consistency, not through those amputations by which a cock-
sure teacher can so easily implant in his pupil a profound scepticism
as to any part of a work being more necessary than any other part,
but by accumulated experience of what his ideas really imply.

From the opening onwards, the F minor Quintet abandons the
device of alternating couples of themes, and thus sets itself free to
expand its material more rapidly. This freedom henceforth extends
over every type of Brahms's forms.

Brahms would have acted more kindly to posterity, and not less
prudently for his own reputation, if, instead of destroying all his

unpublished works and sketches, he had made legal provision that ghouls should not be allowed access to his grave until fifty years after his death. No doubt the best string-players of 1947 would come to the same conclusion as Joachim and Brahms himself about the original version of the F minor Quintet, if it could be called up from the flames; but they would learn incalculably more than that conclusion from the experience which led to it. As things are, however, the only four notes which indicate that the Pianoforte Quintet is not an intact original are at the beginning of the introduction to the finale, where the pianoforte has to do duty for the original second violoncello. This, however, need cause no distress if the pianist can be shaken out of his professional etiquette to the extent of realizing that the lack of pianistic character in his faintest audible touch is here a merit instead of a defect. The violoncello is here equally deficient in 'cellistic tone. It is the character of all whispers to have no character.

SECOND SEXTET IN G MAJOR, op. 36. From the symphonic massiveness which annihilated op. 34 as a string quintet, this sextet shows a delightful reaction. The first sextet was sonorous like an organ, or better, like Mozart's Serenade for thirteen wind instruments. The G major Sextet is the most ethereal of all Brahms's larger works, and is penetrated by sunshine which the shadow of the earthly pathos of the slow movement eclipses only to reveal the corona and the stars. The first movement swings along in rhythms which are now subtle as well as broad; its development, like that of the A major Quartet and many of Brahms's later first movements, concentrates itself around a single remote new key instead of rapidly modulating. Here it does not go to this distant key (C sharp minor) until it has opened in D minor with one of the most brilliant contrapuntal *tours de force* extant, which, like all the counterpoint Brahms admitted into his mature works, presents not a note that does not strike the ear as the best possible melodic step in the best possible harmony. The *marche-ou-je-t'assomme* ingenuity of similar canonic devices in, e.g. the tenth of the Variations, op. 9, on a theme of Schumann, was in after years marked by Brahms with a huge ' ? ' in the copy of a friend.

The scherzo of this sextet is of a new kind and tempo, its main poco allegretto (2/4 time) portion being a highly organized binary movement with two well-defined themes and considerable development, aerial in scoring (like the whole work) and quietly plaintive in an elfin way. The key is G minor. The trio is a rousing dance

(presto, 3/4), returning to the main movement in a picturesque
diminuendo. Brahms's scherzos generally have a simple da capo
with no coda, and, unlike Beethoven, he does not usually alter the
dynamics or scoring of his da capo so as to necessitate writing it
out in full. But here he does so because the original quiet end,
without change of a bar in the plan, breaks away in a lively rush of
triplets. Altogether a study of childhood worthy of Haydn, Wordsworth, or even of life itself. Still more profound is the slow movement, a set of variations in E minor on a theme more subtle than
has ever been so treated elsewhere. The theme is binary, but its
sections are not repeated until after two quiet variations; it arises
in wrath in the third and fourth variation, where the repeats reveal
its firm solidity. The fifth variation is separated from the others by
a few bars of quiet introduction, upon which it unfolds itself in
the major, in a tempo half as fast and therefore twice as big (the
semiquavers continuing the original quaver motion, so that no
change of pace is felt). And so, sustained by an adequate coda, this
last variation arches itself over the whole like a sky in which all
clouds are resting on the horizon and dazzlingly white. This movement is the quintessence of Brahms, in a form which neither
puzzled his admirers nor offered to his opponents a region of art
in which they could imagine that their writs were current. Not so
the finale, which presented far too wide a range of style for the
growing band of 'Brahmins' to feel comfortable. The movement
is not less brilliant than subtle, one of the very few which Brahms
opens by preluding in harmonies that lie obliquely across the key,
and misleading rather from the fearless simplicity of its first cantabile theme (another sublime study in childhood) than from the
abstruse intellectuality that was imputed to it by Deiters and other
friends of Brahms.

FIRST SONATA FOR PIANOFORTE AND VIOLONCELLO IN E MINOR,
op. 38. This first extant duet of Brahms is a work of dark colour, in
which full advantage is taken of the superb bass that a violoncello
can give to the pianoforte, even in massive pianoforte chords, provided that all meaningless doubling is avoided. In this work the
violoncello hardly rises beyond its tenor region. The first movement marches like 'gorgeous tragedy in sceptred pall' until the
quiet major end of its indignant 'second subject' is, in the recapitulation, expanded into a pathetic coda in which the movement
expires in peace.

The development is very broad, and is remarkable in form for

using very large unbroken passages of the exposition, instead of
following the orthodox habit of breaking the material up. There is
no slow movement; the middle movement is a graceful minuet in
A minor, with an exquisitely coloured trio in F sharp minor, requiring a rather slower tempo for its proper expression (though
Brahms gives no indication). The finale is unique in chamber
music in being a strict fugue with a free middle section and a da
capo. The most official of 'Brahmins' used to call this 'the crabbed
and canonic finale'. It would have done their souls good to have it
proved by experiment that their musical schooling had made them
really hate all fugues as Byron hated Horace, and that they would
have automatically talked of the 'sublime poetry in which the
severest art is used but to conceal art' if this fugue had been introduced to them as by Bach. With later composers the noses of such
critics are in the air and their fingers in their ears the moment the
composer answers a one-part melody by another part a fifth higher;
no further evidence is required that he is guilty of writing a crabbed
fugue. With performers (not excluding some orchestral conductors), a more particular obstacle to the enjoyment of this finale is
the widespread doctrine that the only element of a fugue which
is fit for publication is its subject. This is a mistake, for the virtue
of classical countersubjects is that, even when there are two or
three of them in combination, they are so contrasted in rhythm,
type of melodic movement and phrasing (e.g. staccato leaps against
smooth conjunct runs), and harmonic function (as, for instance, a
chain of suspended discords), that they are all transparent to each
other. And as most of the middle section of this finale consists of
a most graceful dialogue in which the countersubjects are turned
into melodic schemes in binary form, it is folly to ignore them in
the exposition. Further trouble is caused by the fact that the look
of the page is exciting enough to tempt the pianist to far too quick
a tempo. Players who have reverently treated the fugue in Beethoven's D major Violoncello Sonata as a proposition by no means
unnegotiable, come to this fugue-finale of Brahms with something
like the feelings of the pianist whose fingers sink into the cushions
of Chopin's most powerful Polonaise after he has been struggling
with the end of Schubert's *Wanderer-Phantasie*, or the still more
wild-cat score-playing of Brahms's first pianoforte works.

TRIO FOR PIANOFORTE, VIOLIN, AND NATURAL HORN, IN E FLAT,
op. 40. The invention of the ventil horn had by the middle of the
nineteenth century turned one of the most primitive of instruments,

which possessed no scale but the harmonic series (ratios $\frac{1}{2}$, $\frac{1}{3}$, $\frac{1}{4}$, &c.) as 'open' notes, with the addition of such muffled adjacent lower semitones or (with extreme muffling) such tones as could be obtained by partially closing the bell with the hand, into an instrument with a complete chromatic scale and a capacity for blending imperceptibly with all other orchestral tones throughout its compass, except if forced to extreme height, when it becomes nervous. This capacity for blending depends, however, upon the horn-player's retaining one of the classical methods in use with the primitive instrument, by which the tone of the 'open' notes was softened so as to allow the 'closed' notes to be used, where melody required them, without obvious patchiness. In 'the first fine careless rapture' of the ventil horn this habit was abolished, like aristocratic manners in a reign of terror, and the ventil horn threatened to become no better than that 'chromatic bullock', the ophicleide. Stronger language could not be used than that of Wagner in the preface to *Tristan*, the very work which first fully explored the possibilities of the ventil horns, and not a page of which could be re-scored without them. Yet Wagner says that he would have made up his mind to do without the new instrument, had he not found that by careful practice under proper instruction the player could acquire *nearly* the qualities of the old horn style.

Brahms was doing nothing more reactionary than illustrating Wagner's preface to *Tristan* when he laid special stress upon using a valveless horn with an E flat crook for this trio. He explained to his friends that if the player were not compelled to blend his open notes with his closed ones, he would never learn to blend his tone in chamber music at all. Nowadays, when every horn-player accepts the demands of *Tristan* as classical, it is not necessary to risk a public performance of Brahms's Horn Trio on the natural instrument, on which many unavoidable difficulties are merely vexatious. But every horn-player should, before resting satisfied with his easy mastery of this work on the modern instrument, find out, by practising it on the E flat crook without using the valves, what a wonderful variety of tone-colours it presents when he is compelled to blend closed notes with open ones. On the modern instrument he is in no danger of playing brassily as in the days of Wagner's preface to *Tristan*; the trouble nowadays is that the soft legato technique is distributed uniformly, one may not unfairly say artlessly, over the whole scale, and that the player has no longer the slightest idea of what his instrument could do if he played Brahms, to say nothing

of Mozart and Beethoven, on the intended *Waldhorn* method.
When he has explored that possibility to its limits, then let him use
the ventils to remove merely vexatious difficulties and minimize the
risks of aesthetically expressive difficulties. But the attitude of a
chauffeur to an obsolete make of motor-car does not lead to distinction in the fine arts. All wind-instrument players must live by
orchestral work in default of scope in chamber music, and many
orchestral wind-players must imperil even their orchestral technique by scavenger-work in revues and cinemas. In these conditions, financial endowment is required if a horn-player is to have
leisure to discover what Brahms's trio really means.

The first movement is in a form which Brahms may have remembered to have seen in a little-known violin sonata of Mozart in C,
where an andante theme alternates with a lively allegro in the complementary key, the two sections then recurring (both in the tonic)
so as to balance in a binary form without development. Brahms's
balance of keys is new and delicate (andante 2/4 in E flat; 'più
mosso' 9/8 in C minor and G minor; andante again in E flat; 'più
mosso' in E flat minor and B flat minor, so as to lead to andante
in G flat, with a dramatic crescendo leading to a climax in the tonic
followed by a solemn dying away).

The scherzo is exceedingly lively, and gives the horn plenty of
scope for energy. A personal reminiscence may be pardoned here
and may serve to indicate that many statements in this article have
been left in the form of unsupported dogma merely from lack of
space. When I played this trio with Joachim and Rüdel in Berlin
in 1902, I was ferociously attacked by a critic for 'not feeling the
impertinence of bolting like that in the presence of Joachim'. But
during rehearsal Joachim had found neither my first nor my second
starting of the scherzo fast enough, and he was exactly satisfied with
my tempo at the concert. In the quiet B major passage where the violin
and horn pull the theme out by holding every third note for an extra
bar while the pianoforte interpolates pianissimo arpeggios, a custom
has long arisen of taking a slower tempo. This I can testify,
from the above experience, to be a mistake. Though this way of
'augmenting' a theme (here devised for the first time) became a
characteristic of Brahms's later style, he had not yet come to the point
when his action was so rapid and his texture so concentrated as to
compel him to slacken his tempo. The time when marks like 'più
sostenuto' are required for stormy and exciting developments is
not reached until the G major Violin Sonata, op. 78; in the Horn

Trio Brahms is still solving his problems on the broadest lines. This B major episode is no ruminating profundity or concentrated development, but the lightest and most playful episode in the work.

The dramatic mystery and gloom of the powerful slow movement are lightened by one gleam of grey dawn before it closes in darkness. This gleam foreshadows the theme of the finale, which, in full sonata form, closes the work in a glorious hunting-scene; appropriately, for to what other purpose is the natural horn called *Waldhorn* and *cor-de-chasse*?

TWO STRING QUARTETS, IN C MINOR AND A MINOR, op. 51. The history of Brahms's Pianoforte Quintet, and the fact that up till now his two other works for strings alone were sextets, may incline us to believe that Brahms had extraordinary difficulty in reducing his massive harmony and polyphony to the limits of four solo strings. We know that he destroyed an unascertainable number of string quartets before the appearance of op. 51, and it is very unlikely that this pair of works was fashioned with ease. Their criterion is of impeccable economy and purity of quartet style, if we do not inculcate a disciplinarian idea that it is a crime to *succeed* in making four solo strings sound like an orchestra. On that disciplinarian view we shall, without any need to use our ears, not only condemn the agitated middle episode of the andante of the A minor Quartet, with its tremolo accompaniment to a canonic recitative between violin and violoncello, but shall deliver to the common hangman the development of the first movement and the main bulk of the scherzo of the very quartet of Beethoven from which the author of the article 'Quartet' in Grove's *Dictionary* cited, as the criterion of quartet style, a passage 'for which the most perfect earthly orchestra would be intolerably coarse'. Brahms's string quartets, especially the A minor, have plenty of such ethereal passages, and to expect a big string quartet to consist of nothing else is like expecting a cosmic epic, which provides the only environment in which the lines Matthew Arnold cites as 'touchstones of poetry' can grow, to provide lines of no other type.

Another difference between Brahms's string quartets and those of Beethoven and Mozart is that there is far more double-stopping. This might be expected in any case from the fullness of harmony necessary for even the most ascetic statement of Brahms's ideas; but his double-stopping has no tendency to destroy his quartet style; the four instruments retain their individuality even though, as at the end of the romanze in the C minor Quartet, the viola sounds like a pair of deep-sea horns and the violoncello like all the harps of the sirens. How the purity of chamber-music style may be affected by double stops will appear from a glance at the opening of Schumann's Pianoforte Quartet, which shows pressing practical reasons why it should have been a quintet; while, perversely enough, the Schumann Quintet might, from first to last, be arranged as a quartet, or even as a trio, such loss as might exist being compensated by the disappearance of characterless doublings. Double-stopping will spoil a quartet style in two ways, first by succeeding in making it into quintet or sextet style, and, contrariwise, by interpolating casual notes needed for the harmony but coming from nowhere. The following detail from the unscrupulously brilliant wind-up of Brahms's F major Quintet, op. 88, neatly defines the issue:

Ex.13 Viola

It is amusing to hear a good player practising this nasty corner and swearing at it for its 'ineffectiveness'. Its business is to supply necessary notes which would, even if accessible, be a nuisance to the instruments who have to make themselves 'effective'. At the cost of a trivial difficulty Brahms gets these notes into an intelligible pattern. The necessities of the case might have led to the following arrangement—

Ex.14

which would have been easier to play, but which Brahms would have certainly rejected as a clumsy and unrhythmic makeshift.

The first movement of the C minor Quartet is a dark and stormy tragedy, the 'second subject' being not less agitated than the first. The lines of the exposition are broad and flowing, while the development is, as in the following A minor, compressed.

The romanze is the first slow movement in which Brahms puts his full resources into a simple A-B-A form, both sections being regular binary melodies, and all necessary development being supplied by the subtlety of the few bars which contrive the return to the main theme. So original are the rhythms and so gorgeous the scoring and the variation of the main theme on its return, that the movement has often been supposed to be far more complex than it really is.

The scherzo is in its main body like a querulous brother or sister of that of the G major Sextet, in darker colour throughout. The trio (also analogous to that in the sextet as regards major mode and the contrast between duple and triple time) is highly picturesque in scoring.

From the F minor key of the scherzo the opening figure of the short finale arises in wrath. Brahms never indicates that two independent movements are to follow on without break; but not only does he in all cases calculate the effect of the last chord of one movement on the first of the next (Haydn and Beethoven are very particular in this matter), but he here for the first time contrives to make a short finale gain in weight by its effect as a kind of epilogue to the previous movement and to the whole work. Such is the sense of the finales of the C major Trio, op. 87, the Violoncello Sonata, op. 99, and the Clarinet Trio, op. 114. Their wonderful completeness of form and climax is disguised by their extreme terseness, but produces an effect of the noblest proportions and final emotional aptness if the listener regards these movements as codas to the preceding scherzos.

This impression of finality is enforced in the C minor Quartet by the fact that the opening figure of the finale is a compound of those of the romanze and the first movement. This might have happened without intention, but the allusion is made quite explicit in the last bars. As a single movement this finale is not one to flatter the 'Brahmins', but players who have outgrown mad-bull methods of attack find it excitingly sonorous, and listeners find it a convincing and impressive end to a work full of tragic passion.

The A minor Quartet, though also full of tragedy and often dark in colour, has abundance of relief, the 'second subject' of the first movement being one of the most attractive and graceful passages Brahms ever wrote. Polyphony of Bach-like thoroughness and Mozart-like euphony is the normal texture except for the tremolos above described, and these occur in passages of close canon. In the first movement the pathetic first theme (placed obliquely across the key) is foredoomed to a tragic end. The slow movement is a broad and elaborate A-B-A design with considerable expansion in development and coda; its ruminating first theme is of a kind that many 'Brahmins' have eagerly imitated under the mistaken impression that such things can be achieved by 'logical development'.

In the place of scherzo the third movement is a slow minuet with pathetically drooping cadences, alternating with a polyphonic trio in duple time and running rhythm, twice interrupted by the minuet-tempo with a combination of the two themes, wonderfully transforming that of the trio.

The finale is a lively rondo, not tragic, but master of its fate and in high spirits of a kind which exhilarate the listeners without suggesting that their temper is to be trifled with.

THIRD PIANOFORTE QUARTET, op. 60, in C minor. This work had been drafted, how far finished we do not know, at the same time as the other two pianoforte quartets. It was then in C sharp minor, but we do not know whether the key relation of the other movements was the same as now, nor indeed whether the draft proceeded beyond the first movement. The scherzo was long believed to be of a still earlier period and to have been expanded from that of a violin sonata written on the musical letters of the name of Joachim's friend Gisela von Arnim (Gis, e, la) by Schumann, Brahms, and Dietrich, each writing a movement. Joachim himself was under this impression until he saw this sonata again some years after Brahms's death, and found that the scherzo (which it was then decided to publish as a posthumous work) had no resemblance to that of op. 60 beyond being in 6/8 time, free in form, and of a fiery temper.

The first movement of op. 60 seems in its original form to have got into difficulties, the nature of which it is useless to guess. All we know is that at the time of the first draft Brahms told a friend to think of the opening as of a man resigned to utter despair; a description which still holds good in its present form. For the rest, it has been a misfortune to critics, especially to the 'Brahmins' themselves, that the work was ever known to have had a history. Hanslick dropped expressions about 'the technique of a beginner', which showed how unlikely it is that Beckmesser ever will attain the status of a beginner even in the knowledge of the art which he most sincerely admires. The only passage in the whole work which might have been achieved with an earlier technique than that of the B flat Sextet is the grandiose transformation of the first theme in the development, with its Schubert-like twofold appearance in B major and G major. If, as is likely, this belonged to the first draft, its retention with its drastically simple scoring only shows that a great artist's view of the range of styles that can be united in one work of art is that of a 'spectator of all time and existence'. It gives rise to a far more drastically simple passage by which the recapitulation (which is in an unexpected new key) leads to the abrupt tragic coda. From beginning to end the first movement is written

with a technique as far beyond that of the two other piano quartets
as Beethoven's Fifth Symphony is beyond the possibilities of his
Second. We have no record of the changes Brahms had to make
in this work, but they must have been enormous; for Joachim told
me in private conversation that in its first version this C minor (then
C sharp minor) quartet was 'very diffuse'. And, as we have seen,
its two predecessors, though not diffuse for their own purposes,
strain to the utmost permissible limits the length of their themes
and the completeness of their statements and counterstatements.
A work that can have seemed to Joachim diffuse in comparison with
the G minor and A major Quartets cannot have proceeded for more
than two or three successive staves upon the lines of op. 60 as we
now know it. Diffuseness is the last quality to impute to a work in
which the Schubertian process already cited and the leisurely handling of the 'second subject' of the slow movement give an effect of
exceptional breadth. A comparison of that Schubertian process
with typical examples by Schubert himself will show that Brahms
has made and repeated his point in the time it takes Schubert to
show the pattern of his sequence. No other works of Brahms, not
even the First and Fourth Symphonies, show so wide a range of
forms. The most astonishing novelty is the casting of the 'second
subject' of the first movement into the form of an eight-bar melody
ending on a half-close and followed by a set of five variations. In
the recapitulation, which is very unexpectedly in the bright dominant key of G major, Brahms begins with two new variations
marking the return to the old ones by an expansion, the original
third and fourth variation being expanded into the tragic coda.
The key of G major had been arrived at as a revelation of the predestined result of a mysterious incident in the opening of the movement, when over the first pause on the dominant a pizzicato E
natural asked an unexpected question, to which an immediate fortissimo replied with what was evidently an angry refusal to consider
it. Thus Brahms is now developing his forms entirely from their
dramatic import outwards, as in the maturest works of Beethoven.
He was always too great an artist to set up forms *a priori* and shovel
his music into them; but he has now reached a level of organization
at which *a priori* notions of form not only fail to illustrate his work,
but often simply mislead.

The short and powerful scherzo is best understood as both a
reaction from and a coda to the audaciously abrupt tragic end of
the first movement. Some of its themes are near enough to the

style of the Sonata, op. 1, to have deceived Joachim (as we have seen) into a mistaken 'recollection' of it as a draft of that early period, but the form and technique is of Brahms's ripest. Bull-headed attacks will get nothing out of this movement, which demands (and rewards) perfect tone-production and the most articulate phrasing, especially the Schubert-like but compact G minor theme, with its solemn ritardando cadence in the major.

The slow movement begins with what has always been acknowledged to be one of Brahms's greatest and most original melodies. It is in the remote key of E major; this key-relation first occurred in Beethoven's C minor Concerto, and soon afterwards Brahms used it again in his First Symphony.

This andante comes as near to full sonata form as Brahms permits in his extant slow movements, the only exception being that in his classical exercise-work, the Serenade in D, where it is significant that the tempo-mark adagio is almost impracticable for the long, trailing lines of its form. In the C minor Quartet nothing can be grander and more natural than the flow of the whole. The development is represented by two steps of a glorious modulating sequence, and the recapitulation of the very leisurely 'second subject' is represented by a coda-like summary.

In the finale certain obvious but superficial resemblances to features in the first movement and finale of Mendelssohn's C minor Trio caused comments which provoked Brahms to his oft-quoted remark about the habit of 'mutton-heads' who notice such things. Apart from this, no movement of Brahms has been more misunderstood; it is usually taken far too fast, and the tranquillo directions in the mysterious development (the first and most elaborate development of a kind peculiar to the composer) seem often to escape notice. Little help can be given to uncomprehending players and listeners by pointing out the incredible molecular combinations of its thematic organization; it is easy to dismiss such things as pedantries, though it is demonstrable that in great music they are worked out to atomic accuracy without attracting attention, whereas in pedantic music they are a bluff which breaks down if you 'call' it. The only clue to this finale, with its childlike pathos and power, is in a clear understanding of the nature of tragedy, as distinguished from the merely pathetic or melodramatic. Those to whom Brahms's Third Pianoforte Quartet is not one of the greatest pieces of all purely tragic music may go and keep company with Hanslick in a heaven consisting of the A major Quartet and such passages from the middle works of Beethoven as can be seen to be in good taste without any reference to such tiresome things as contexts.

THIRD STRING QUARTET IN B FLAT, op. 67. The tragic work that proved indigestible to the orthodox 'Brahmins' was promptly followed by a Haydnesque comedy that gave far more offence. Solemn people do not like being teased, and in real life Brahms never quite got over the teasing habit. But he did not take the trouble to tease people whom he disliked; and that is where the humour of the alternately teasing and coaxing first movement of this quartet resembles Haydn's and differs radically from that of Wagner, who certainly did not like either Beckmesser or the original Hans Lich.

The slow movement is, in form, like a popular version of that in the A minor Quartet. It does not deserve disparagement, but it does suggest the probability that Brahms had among his rejected works written many like it, on the border-lines of easy conception and laboured execution, and that here we have the only example that did not overstep those lines. Undoubtedly he would have become far more popular if most of his slow movements had been replicas of this.

The third movement, a scherzo in form and a passionate lyric in style, has always made a profound impression. It is, both in its freely expansive main section and in its trio, a viola solo, the other strings being muted. It requires a moderate tempo and great natural freedom of rhythm in the viola part.

Throughout the first movement, scherzo, and finale of this quartet the prominence of the viola has rather scandalized the orthodox, but there is nothing in it antagonistic to quartet style. The criterion of absolute equality of the four parts is impracticable and allows for nothing but the most complex styles. The effect of giving special prominence to the viola, or (as in Mozart's last three quartets) to the violoncello, is, as here, a special effect of colour; and obviously to give special prominence to the second violin would be either to produce an accompanied violin duet or, in excess, to exchange the terms 'first' and 'second'.

The finale is a set of variations on one of the most kittenish themes since Haydn. Brahms nowhere shows a profounder insight into sonata style than in his clear preservation of the melody throughout a set of variations when it is a movement in a sonata. In the sonata style we feel our way by identifying the themes as melodies; hence a set of variations as part of a sonata should not, in Brahms's opinion, treat the mere harmonic and rhythmic scheme

as equivalent to the melody in the ways which are so interesting
and desirable in independent variations.

Nothing could have been easier than to drag in the ghost of
previous movements in free variations towards the end of the
finale; in this way a popular idea of musical evolution is readily
jerry-built when invention fails. But Brahms does something very
different. Towards the end of these Mozart-Haydn melodic variations the main themes of the first and second subjects of the first
movement are combined not contrapuntally but with the melodic
lines of the variation theme. And so the work expands in grand
proportions and childlike happiness to its close.

FIRST SONATA FOR PIANOFORTE AND VIOLIN, IN G MAJOR, op. 78.
This fifth of Brahms's efforts in the most difficult of all problems in
chamber music solves its problem in terms of an extraordinary
predominance of cantabile, in which the violin is leading almost the
whole time. In the first movement the development is the only
stormy passage in the whole work, and room is made for its crowded
incidents by slackening the tempo ('più sostenuto')—so that the
'poco a poco tempo 1mo' which leads to the return is a slight
accelerando, a point not always understood by good players without
special experience in Brahms.

The adagio is a solemn, dramatic, and highly developed A-B-A
movement with themes of great rhythmic freedom and a coda in
which those of the agitated middle section are 'augmented' in a
passage of tremendous depth. The influence of the adagio of
Beethoven's G major Sonata, op. 96, may be suspected here.
Disaster awaits performers who attack the middle section without
understanding that Brahms uses the words 'più andante' in their
correct Italian sense of 'going on', i.e. faster.

There is no scherzo, and the finale is a gently flowing rondo in
G minor, ending in the major only in the coda. The theme, though
its rhythmic initial figure suggests that of the first movement,
comes from a couple of songs (*Regenlied* and *Nachklang*) written
some years earlier; but a flood of light is thrown on the nature of
musical form and rhetoric by carrying the comparison beyond the
first two bars. It will be found that not only is the continuation
different in each of the songs, but that within the sonata there are
several fresh continuations, rising in proper order to their climax.
An equally significant point is the use of the theme of the slow
movement for the second episode and coda of this rondo. It is no
mere ghost, such as can be easily evoked by writing out the old

S

theme in the notation of the new tempo in disregard of the resulting stagnation of movement; but it consists of the first six notes of the adagio with a new continuation that makes it not only the warmest but the most urgent theme in the finale. In the coda its new iambic rhythmic figure gives rise to a series of modulations anticipating on a small scale the solemn end of the Third Symphony.

TRIO IN C MAJOR, FOR PIANOFORTE, VIOLIN, AND VIOLONCELLO, op. 87. Three movements of this work are on the largest possible scale, while the short finale is, as has been suggested above, best understood as if the scherzo had led to it. The first movement is as broad as those of the first two pianoforte quartets, with the difference that its numerous themes, instead of being immediately of the utmost permissible breadth, are terse statements with unlimited powers of expansion. The style is grandly energetic with deep shadows of mystery, the mystery of nature rather than romance. The development is remarkably Schubertian and transforms the first theme into an 'augmentation' for which Brahms requires a quicker tempo, an unexpected phenomenon for him, especially in so late a work.

The slow movement is a glorious set of variations on a theme of heroic pathos, akin to that of the first sextet, but on a higher plane. At first one might think that the quiet fourth variation in the major mode was an exception to Brahms's rule that in sonata works variations should preserve the melody, but in this movement there are two simultaneous melodies, one for the strings and the other for the pianoforte; and here the pianoforte theme is carried straight through with ornamentation which combines the harmonic luxuriousness of Brahms with the schematic accuracy of Mozart.

The dark pianissimo scherzo, with its huge white cloud-bank trio, is extremely difficult for the pianist to execute with the necessary lightness of touch, but never fails to make an impression. The finale, on the other hand, is usually ruined by being played far too fast, when nothing results but an admirably terse exercise in form. In real life it is full of humour and mystery, and leads to a magnificently sonorous end. Brahms's notation goes too far in prescribing common instead of alla-breve time, but at all events it conveys a hint.

STRING QUINTET IN F MAJOR, op. 88. This comparatively neglected work is one of Brahms's most unconventional compositions. It has all the sonorousness of the first sextet, and one is tempted to think that Brahms enjoyed in it a feeling of relief after the restraint which string-quartet writing imposed on his love of full harmony. The first movement begins with a melody so tuneful and square that only by comparison with earlier works can we realize how terse Brahms's form has now become. The slow movement is one of Brahms's very greatest inspirations. A tragically impassioned declamatory theme in C sharp minor (3/4 time, *grave*)[1] is worked out into a movement that might almost stand alone as a complete cavatina. Then a quiet little binary scherzo in A major 6/8 appears and completes itself. The *grave* returns, quickly at first, but rising later to more than its former passion. When it has died away again, the A major scherzo appears in an alla-breve presto variation. Then the *grave* returns for the last time, beginning now in A major, but working round to its utterly tragic conclusion in C sharp minor. But now comes the miracle, predestined from the outset. The final chords hover between C sharp, as a resigned major chord, and A major as a dark submediant, the more despairing from its having been the tonic chord of the scherzo interludes. At last the A major chord gives way to an unexpected D minor chord, which, as subdominant, brings about a final plagal close to the whole movement in A major. Nothing else like this is to be found in music; and it shows what Brahms could achieve by his abstention from all such chromatic resources as could distract attention from the function of simple tonality in sonata form. It is as certain as any 'if' outside the world of winged pigs, that if Brahms had thought fit to develop a modulating style like Reger's, he would have abandoned sonata forms altogether.

The finale of op. 88 is not a movement whereby to convert the Anti-Brahmins; and least of all Brahms's movements does it yield up any secrets to wild-cat attacks in performance. It is in the highest of spirits which one cannot but imagine enhanced by the hilarious reaction which high-spirited creatures often experience at the sight of shocked solemn faces whom their levity has surprised. Yet it is not humorous, and has no more leisure for jokes than an athlete in mid-play. In form and texture it combines the tersest sonata form with the closest fugal polyphony; and it hardly takes six minutes in performance.

SECOND VIOLONCELLO SONATA IN F MAJOR, op. 99; SECOND VIOLIN SONATA IN A MAJOR, op. 100; TRIO IN C MINOR, op. 101. These three works were all produced in the same year, and (like Mozart's last three symphonies produced within six weeks) make an

[1] It first occurred to Brahms in 1855 as a sarabande for pianoforte.

excellent concert programme, their contrasts being, in the nature of the case, exactly what represented the happiest reactions of the composer himself.

They are the tersest of all Brahms's works, the only passage which takes up any room on paper being the 'cloud-capped tower' opening of the coda of the first movement of the A major Violin Sonata. Their forms, though presenting few abnormalities, show all the more clearly in their extraordinary compression that Brahms never constructed on an *a priori* scheme and never exactly repeated a form.

The F major 'Cello Sonata gives this instrument far more range than it had in op. 38. This is splendidly illustrated by the transition from first subject to second.

Ex.15

The broken rhythm of the main theme and the ways in which it is transformed into sustained figures in the course of development constitute a notable addition to the resources of sonata style. The whispering chromatic episode in F sharp minor at the beginning of the development is another peculiar feature, and in its choice of key prepares the ear for the remote key of the slow movement. The tremolos for the pianoforte and (legato across the strings) for the 'cello shocked the orthodox at the time this work appeared, but Brahms knows no aesthetic criteria but those of the ear and of the individual work as a whole, and does not hesitate to add two magnificent new colours to the resources of chamber music. The 'cellist should keep the bow evenly on the two strings involved, with a movement hardly distinguishable from a sustained double note; and the pianist should observe that Brahms follows Beethoven (in the D major Trio) and Liszt *passim* in regarding the best tremolo as not indefinitely fast but consisting of an exact even number of notes. The marks of damping down the sound (*sf p; f >mp;* &c.) should be carefully acted upon. Brahms, however, once found himself playing this sonata with a 'cellist of no great promise or accomplishment, and accordingly opened the throttle of the pianoforte and let her rip and roar. The 'cellist's voice penetrated the din with the complaint, 'Master, I can't hear myself at all'—and Brahms barked back at him, 'Lucky for you'. But this is not the way classical traditions should be formed.

The slow movement in F sharp major, the key a semitone above the tonic, might have been written in G flat, had not its important modulation (after the return of the main theme) to D major been a troublesome affair to read in E double-flat. The unusual key-relationship is thought out with the profoundest thoroughness and accuracy. There are three important earlier classical examples which neatly show the stages of progress in the handling of such ideas. First there is Carl Philipp Emanuel Bach, who in a symphony in D major has a short middle movement in E flat. To justify this he introduces it by a dramatic passage tacked on to the end of the first. Translated into English prose this means, 'grotesque and foolish as it may seem to the sober listener, it is absolutely true that the slow movement is in E flat'. Very different is the procedure of Haydn, to whom such a key-relation is a paradox true enough to be worth stating violently. In his last pianoforte sonata, which is in E flat, the slow movement is in E natural (= F flat). Haydn begins the slow movement straightforwardly on its tonic, and pointedly begins his finale with the one note which, unharmonized, most flatly contradicts the key of the slow movement without re-asserting the key of E flat until the bass explains it. The third stage is represented by Beethoven in his C sharp minor Quartet and (in a more extreme form) by Brahms here. To Beethoven and Brahms this remote key is simply that of the flat supertonic, as used ever since mid-classical tonality of major and minor modes in scales of all pitches communicating with each other by chords in common. The founder of classical tonality, Alessandro Scarlatti, already used this flat supertonic so constantly in ultra-minor cadences that the form of chord in which it conveniently occurs is called, after his *scuola*, the 'Neapolitan sixth'.

This F sharp major slow movement compresses a great amount of design into a small space, which nevertheless seems able to expand without limit. The pizzicato of the 'cello here makes a splendid and novel bass to the full harmony of the pianoforte and is worked to a tremendous climax when the strain is brought back after the dark remote depths of the F minor middle episode. Hausmann, with Brahms's approval, made a great accelerando at this crescendo, thus providing a natural means of carrying the resonance of the pizzicato over the notes before they dry up.

The impassioned and highly developed movement which takes the form and place of scherzo and trio requires free rhythm and more legato and cantabile in both instruments than the look of the page suggests. The opening pianoforte theme, though difficult, should not be conceived as a brilliant *tour de force*. Other contrasted themes must press forward, but as a whole the movement is not to be hustled. The great melody of the trio is also in no hurry, and in the B major passage beginning seventeen bars after the double bar, the pianist must realize that his light figures are no mere accompaniment but are outlining the continuation of the melody. The rondo which ends the sonata with the smallest and most childlike of Brahms's finales is one of those cases where the small finale has the effect of an epilogue to the previous movement. Brahms liked a lively tempo for it. In any tempo it is difficult to achieve the necessary lightness of touch and accent in both instruments.

The A major Violin Sonata, op. 100, is throughout one of Brahms's most melodious works. It is sometimes known by the 'mutton-head' title of '*Meistersinger*' sonata, because of its first three notes, but Wagner's own text tells us that the *Meistersinger* rules enact that a song counts as original when it does not trespass upon 'more than four syllables' of another master-song.

The first movement, with its impressive coda, does not strike one as very terse until its proportions are actually measured against those of, say, the A major Quartet, op. 26. The slow movement is an alternation of andante and scherzo, a counterpart in pastoral comedy to the sublime mystery of the slow movement of the F major String Quintet. Here, if ever, we must judge by ear and not by eye; the dangerous little learning in form leads to a state of mind which refuses to be convinced that two lines and a half of andante can be correctly balanced against two pages and a half of vivace; yet in point of time such is the result, and not one master in a hundred (on the plane in which there are hundreds) could have guessed it. As in the rondo of the G major Sonata, the andante theme here has a different continuation every time it recurs. It is more often played too slow than too fast; for, though broad, it should not be adagio. The direction 'vivace di più', on the second appearance of the scherzo theme, does not, as it might, mean only 'vivace again', but 'faster than before'. In any convincing tempo it is very difficult to play with a sufficiently light and accurate pianoforte touch, and, in the second version, the pianoforte should be light enough for the violinist to risk playing his pizzicatos without effort. At the juncture of the two tempi there should be no perceptible ritardando or pause, and where the last 3/4 cadences are 'augmented', the rhythm should be felt not as a syncopation but as a change to 3/2 time, thus:

1 2 3—1 2 3—1 2 3 4 5 6—

The finale is a rondo, deeply thoughtful in tone, and so terse that a description of its form would convey the impression of a movement three times as long. It is often played too fast, but suffers still more from being played with too small a tone and too timid a style in its opening theme, which should be taken as one of the outstanding cantabiles for the fourth string. The tempo should be measured by reconciling the alla-breve time-signature with the compression of four bars of this cantabile into two bars in double-stopping towards the end of the movement.

The C minor Trio concludes this group of works with one of Brahms's most powerful creations. The first movement is tragic in the heroic manner of Coriolanus, not of Hamlet, Othello, or King Lear. For all its pride, however, it has its tender moments, especially in the beginning of the C sharp minor passage in the development. After the passionate close of the first movement, the 'presto non assai', which takes the place of a scherzo, hurries by like a frightened child. It is one of Brahms's most impressive pieces of tone-colour, and has something in common with the intermezzo in the G minor Quartet, op. 25, though with its shuddering trio and its coda on an entirely new theme combined with the opening phrase in a strange augmentation, it is all over in about the time the earlier work takes for a couple of statements and counterstatements.

Another child of the gods, free from terror, greets us in the exquisite andante with its mixture of 3/4 and 2/4 bars (which do not always make the same 7-beat or 5-beat phrases) and its quite simple A-B-A form with eight regular bars of playful coda. Then, in full sonata form, comes the grimly energetic finale, which in the latter part of the 'second subject' requires a slower tempo for its crowding, tempestuous incidents. Everything is in dark minor keys until the moment arrives for the coda, which transfigures the main themes in solemn triumph in the major.

SONATA IN D MINOR, op. 108. Here Brahms achieves a violin sonata on a symphonic scale, and obviously as full of effortless power as any conceivable quartet or sextet. The first movement is unique in that its entire development portion is on a dominant pedal, which is reproduced as a tonic pedal in the coda. From Joachim I learnt that at the first *forte* Brahms made a decided animato which he might as well have marked in the score; this, of course, implies that the tempo of the outset must be broad, though, of course, flowing. The cross accents of the impassioned 'second subject' require not less emphasis and tone in the single notes of the violin than in the big chords of the pianoforte. The most difficult passage is, of course, the intensely quiet development on the long dominant pedal. The violin, which begins it by distributing the opening melody with its counterpoint across two strings, must keep the bow over both strings in the manner of double-stopping instead of letting the passage sound dry; the pianist must let all his melodic figures quietly penetrate the whole texture, and the moment where the violin holds a high E for a bar, before climbing down the scale of D major, must assert itself like a long sun-ray through the clouds.

The slow movement is a cavatina, that is to say, a single melody achieving the spaciousness of an entire movement by expanding without allowing a middle section to partition itself off. This idea was first achieved by Haydn in his wonderful little D minor Quartet, op. 42; and even the cavatina of Beethoven's Quartet, op. 130, has more of a separate middle episode. Such simplicity comes of the concentration of a life's experience; it cannot be imitated by merely writing a tune and refusing to develop it. The third movement puts far more than the contents of a scherzo into four minutes of plaintively elvish music in a design which, without an enclosed middle section, ranges from F sharp minor to the immense distance of F major. The history of its scoring has already been described.

With the finale we return to symphonic dimensions in a powerful sonata rondo with a grandly tragic climax. The only passage which is liable to be misunderstood is that in its middle development where the violin, after stating a cantabile transformation of the opening figure (in G minor), accompanies the answers of the pianoforte with a syncopated countersubject. Here it is important not to let the tone of the violin become dry or husky against too full a pianoforte; the well-meant practice of letting the violin murmur indistinctly against a leading pianoforte passage is (*pace* César Franck in the second movement of his violin sonata) always thoroughly unsatisfactory in its result. With an even balance of tone we appreciate the depth of the harmony and the dramatic force of its modulations.

STRING QUINTET IN G MAJOR, op. 111. At its first London performance, before printed parts were available, I distinctly remember that there was no difficulty in hearing the violoncello with its theme in the lowest bass under the Niagara of sound in the other four high-lying instruments, who seemed to me to be 'letting themselves go' without scruple. This shows the importance of properly balanced marks of expression to the composer, and of exact observance of them, for we know that at first there was great difficulty in getting the opening theme through; and Brahms went so far as to draft a scoring (the draft has been preserved) in which the upper strings divided their movement with alternating rests, so as to halve the mass of tone while still keeping the movement going. This, however, was abandoned as patchy in colour, and, as the experience of a listener with no score to guide him shows, by the time Joachim brought the work to London, the difficulty was triumphantly settled by damping the violins and violas to a mezzo-forte as soon as the violoncello enters. If nowadays the opening still fails, that is because the players get too excited to act according to directions. The whole work is an immensely powerful outburst of high spirits. The first movement seems unlimited in its capacity for expansion, and actually has a leisurely tonic-and-dominant peroration in its coda such as had not been heard since Beethoven's 'Eroica' and Ninth symphonies; yet the movement is by no means long. The adagio is another cavatina, if its form admits of codification at all, and is one of the most impressive of all Brahms's tragic utterances. Its proper tempo is slower than that of any other movement in classical music since the largo of Beethoven's C minor Concerto.

Then comes an exquisite, plaintive little scherzo and trio, with a simplicity of effect which conceals a microscopic complexity of polyphonic detail; no figured chorale of Bach is more closely knit.

The finale, beginning in a foreign key, is a sonata movement of such range and vigour that the listener will never realize how short it really is. At the end its coda breaks away into a completely new dance-tune, the phrases of which reel down in bacchanalian irregularity to explain themselves with impudent assurance as connected with the main theme by ties as intimate as a borrowed visiting-card.

Brahms was beginning to talk of regarding this work as representing the end of his career, when the wonderful clarinet-playing of Mühlfeld inspired him to four more works which made another definite extension to the range of his own style, and restored wind instruments to the place in chamber music appointed for them by Mozart.

The Trio for pianoforte, clarinet, and violoncello, in A minor, op. 114, is overshadowed by its great neighbour, the Clarinet Quintet; but it is by no means the small and unimportant work it is often supposed to be. From Steinbach I learnt that Brahms at first intended its opening theme for that of a fifth symphony; and if the first movement and slow movement had been followed up on a larger instead of a smaller scale, or had the finale been pathetic instead of alternately defiant, reflective, and humorous, the work would not have been easily eclipsed. The first movement is broad and full of romance, with a development which, as usual in Brahms's later works, is compressed and thoughtful, and must not be dryly delivered. The colour of the coda, especially the last line, is very romantic, and in the slow movement, which is in a broad arioso-sonata form, no more gorgeous colouring has been achieved in chamber music. Not less charming in colour is the following andantino, which is in the form of a minuet in A major with two trios (F sharp minor and D major). Its themes have been severely censured, but are inseparable from their ingenious scoring.

The finale is over in five minutes, and contains everything that a full-sized sonata movement has room for. Its development, like some in Beethoven's last works, is a single process of a sequence of falling thirds, and should, if properly interpreted, be as full of a sense of the silent workings of gods, fates, and nature as any similar monumental simplicities in Greek tragedy.

THE QUINTET IN B MINOR FOR CLARINET AND STRINGS, op. 115, made an immediate impression which eclipsed the Trio, and would have eclipsed the Clarinet Sonatas had they not appeared after another year's interval, and been from the outset regarded as smaller works. The Quintet is one of the most original and also one of the most pathetic of all Brahms's works. Its ambiguous opening in a key that seems to be D major instead of B minor is another interesting development of an idea suggested by Philipp Emanuel Bach in a sonata beginning

Ex.16

and carried out by Haydn in two of his most subtle quartets, that in B minor, op. 33, no. 1,

Ex.17

and the later work, also in B minor, op. 64, no. 2, where there is no explanatory harmony until the decision is made (Ex. 18). Haydn

Ex.18

is thinking of the effect of these openings on repetition after the close of his exposition. His idea, though of far-reaching truth, does not pretend to take a higher form than wit. With Brahms it becomes a moment of sublime pathos and beauty when the end of the exposition leads back, not to the first bars (though these have the necessary ambiguity for Haydn's point) but to the entry of the clarinet on the full chord of D.

Ex.19

The abrupt catastrophe of the first movement, leaving barely time to re-establish B minor after having recapitulated the 'second subject' in another key, is, like the similar case in the first movement of the C minor Pianoforte Quartet, op. 60, balanced by the effect of the next movement following on with the same tonic. Here, however, it is the slow movement that follows, in a seraphic B major melody with muted strings. A wildly romantic middle section in the minor, with extraordinary arabesques for the clarinet, works itself out on still broader lines of melodic binary form. In spite of its strict form, it is unlike anything else in classical music; but if one has the good fortune to hear a genuine Hungarian band whose leader happens to be a clarinettist, one will be thrilled on recognizing exactly Brahms's treatment of the instrument here. The passage leading back to the main section is exceptionally dramatic, and no subtler stroke has ever been achieved than that by which the last bar of the common time does duty for the first bar of the 3/4 opening theme,

Ex.20

The third movement is unique in form. It begins with a pair of themes in D major, common time, andantino, which, after a climax, come to a quiet close. Then a transformation of these themes in contrapuntal combination, 2/4 time, 'presto non assai' (the beats hardly faster than those of the andantino), is worked out in B minor into a terse binary movement with a contrasted 'second subject' in syncopated rhythm in F sharp minor. The whole exposition of this is pianissimo. After some development a complete recapitulation follows, with a coda that bursts out vigorously and leads without change of tempo to the theme which appeared at the climax of the andantino, and so, in a few lines, to its quiet close in D. The abruptness is not more astonishing than the fact that the effect is more and more convincing on every hearing.

The finale is a set of variations, Mozartean in their strictly melodic principles, with all Brahms's Bach-like logic of polyphony, and unique in the subtlety of their theme, which, for all its apparent simplicity, cannot be expressed by a single voice. After the fifth variation, which is in 3/8 time in contrast with the previous 2/4, the 3/8 bars are merged into the 6/8 bars of the first movement, the opening theme of which appears and combines with the cadence of the 3/8 variation. And so the work closes in sorrow.

The two CLARINET SONATAS, op. 120, no. 1, in F minor, and no. 2, in E flat, end Brahms's chamber music. It is noteworthy that they are described as for clarinet and piano, not vice versa as with all classical violin and violoncello sonatas from Mozart onwards. Yet the piano is, if anything, less subordinate to the other instrument than in the G major Violin Sonata. As the forms are extremely terse the range they cover is very large. In the F minor

Sonata the first movement is full of passionate melancholy, the coda, with its strange canonic development of an ornamental figure arising out of the main themes, being specially impressive. The two middle movements are both in the same key, A flat major, a thing unprecedented in four-movement sonatas, and of delicious effect here where both are so short, the slow movement being an A-B-A design highly organized in detail, and the scherzo the most deliciously Viennese of all Brahms's works. The finale, in rondo form with very whimsical themes, is high comedy of the wittiest kind.

The E flat Clarinet Sonata begins with a quiet first movement in a mood not unlike that of the first movement of the A major Violin Sonata (also headed allegro amabile). The mysterious triplet episode in the development is one of those profundities which players inexperienced in Brahms are apt to reduce to the aesthetic level of the multiplication table. Players who cannot make of this movement one of the most mellow products of all chamber music should leave Brahms alone.

There are only three movements, the second being an impassioned scherzo in E flat minor with a sonorous trio in B major (= C flat). The finale is a set of variations on an andante theme in 6/8 time. The fifth variation breaks into vivace 2/4 time in E flat minor, and then settles down in a peaceful coda which finally arouses itself to a spirited end.

Students of chamber music should not neglect Brahms's two arrangements of these clarinet sonatas for violin and for viola. These are on quite a different plane from the use of a viola as substitute for the clarinet in the Quintet and Trio, though Brahms authorized the issue of parts so transcribed. But in the Trio and Quintet the relation of the clarinet to the string parts makes it impossible to alter the position of anything, and transcription accordingly reveals all the points where the viola fails to represent a clarinet. But with these sonatas Brahms could use a free hand. In the violin version he sometimes alters the piano part. Joachim, who would have nothing to do with transcriptions as a rule, took great pleasure in playing the violin version of both sonatas. The viola version is better, besides being a welcome opportunity for viola players. In it the piano part is unaltered, but the viola part is a fine demonstration of the different characters of the instruments. The viola is querulous and strained just where the cantabile of the clarinet is warmest. The lowest octave of the clarinet is of a dramatic blue-grotto hollowness and coldness, where the fourth string of the viola is of a rich and pungent warmth. A comparison of Brahms's viola part with his original clarinet part makes every difference of this kind vividly real, and these viola versions deserve frequent performance in public.

If every one of Brahms's works in sonata form rewards the effort of a reasoned defence on all points on which attack has been directed, this is not because Brahms is either himself infallible or acceptable only to those who are ready to take him as gospel. It is, on the contrary, because Brahms was so far from thinking himself infallible that he consented to the publication of nothing to which he had not devoted more severe criticism, long after the work was finished, than could be collected from all the sensible remarks that have ever been made on his works since they appeared. In his early days, what his own criticism might have let slip was subjected to the sensitive ear and practical experience of Joachim, and Brahms's docility was strictly reasonable, never revolting against the authority of proved fact, and therefore never imputing unsympathetic motives to so disinterested a friend. The result is that the defence of his works is an infinitely more fruitful line of criticism than that of attack; for attacks are easy on superficial grounds, while the defence rests on bedrock.

SOME ASPECTS OF BEETHOVEN'S ART FORMS [1]

Music, which often combines the symmetry of architecture with the emotional range of drama, has the misfortune to be accurately describable only in technical terms peculiar to itself. Chiaroscuro, values, perspective, are experiences in the ordinary use of human eyes, apart from the art of painting which turns them to its own artistic purposes. Architectural concepts are deeply rooted in the minds of persons innocent of technical knowledge: the human being knows his own size, and the intellect of Macaulay is not severely taxed by the discovery that nothing could be more vile than a pyramid only thirty feet high. But with music a conception so elementary and vital to the art of Beethoven as classical tonality is utterly unidentifiable by anybody without some practice in actually reading music: so much so that in the time of Mozart the boy Samuel Wesley was thought to give a proof of prodigious genius when at the end of a concert he remarked that 'the programme was badly arranged, for all the pieces were in the same key'. The facts of key relationship can be quite clearly illustrated to young and inexperienced music lovers, but the illustrations must consist of the music itself. After a series of good musical illustrations has been digested, verbal analogies from perspective, colour, values, and any other visual facts may become useful. But this is because the naïve listener already possesses the right musical sensations. These are as direct as the colours of a sunset or the tastes of a dinner. Connoisseurship comes from experience, not from verbal explanations.

Since, then, the accurate description of any piece of music is inevitably technical, it follows that a great length of such description goes but a short way. I am not, of course, speaking of the unlimited opportunity the music of Beethoven gives the tone-deaf essayist for talking about the French Revolution; that merely leads to the inference that the proper way to enjoy the Fifth Symphony is to read Carlyle and *The Scarlet Pimpernel*. I refer to honest attempts to find out where the second subject of the Seventh Symphony begins, and how the first movement of the Fifth is all 'built up' from a single figure of four notes. These expressions are

[1] From *Music and Letters* (Beethoven number), Vol. III, No. 2, April 1927.

typical of the unsound analysis which prevents many lovers of music from continuing to appreciate what the naïve listener has no difficulty in enjoying. The term 'second subject' is, for reasons which will soon appear, the most misleading in the whole range of our British musical provincialisms: it is unknown in Germany, where the term used in its place is *Seitensatz*, a term conveying no false ideas, since the word *Satz* can mean anything from a single phrase to a long paragraph, while the epithet *Seiten* means no more than that this is secondary to the *Hauptsatz*. The result of the unfortunate English terminology is that you cannot, even if you try (and many teachers do not know that they ought to try), eradicate from the young mind all traces of the notion that in the sonata forms the word 'subject' means 'theme', as it does when we are talking of fugues. Now there is a large but by no means overwhelming number of sonata works in which there are two conspicuous themes contrasted in key and texture. It is perhaps easier to construct an effective movement with such a pair of themes than with material less easy to analyse. Two composers who lived through and survived the time of Beethoven wrote all their sonata works on such pairs of themes, eked out with 'brilliant passages', and were firmly convinced that they were carrying on the tradition of Mozart. Hummel was Mozart's pupil, and Spohr actually told Joachim that he hoped some day to write six quartets in 'really strict form with shakes at the end of the passages'. Now there is nothing inherently wrong in having running passages between two contrasted themes; and a shake is the natural way of ending a run by turning its movement into a faster but stationary vibration, instead of merely ending with a bump or an interruption. Similarly there is no reason why a brown tree should not be a feature in a landscape. These things are often conveniences, and it saves trouble to make a convenience into a convention. But we need not put up with a convention that is no longer convenient.

It was not Beethoven's forms but his dramatic power that gave him the reputation of a musical revolutionary. Neither in fact nor in contemporary opinion could his art forms be regarded as subversive of the principles on which Mozart and Haydn worked; for those principles were themselves thought modern, and the mature works of Mozart and Haydn were in point of time less remote from the middle works of Beethoven than the symphonic poems of Strauss are from the compositions produced in this present year. Interest in the history of musical theory is not strong enough for me to be in a position to say what the orthodox opinions as to sonata form were in Beethoven's time. We know, however, that musical theory has never had the advantages of Alexandrine criticism, though it has had more than its share of Alexandrine pedantries. But the Alexandrine critics had to deal with languages already remote and with masterpieces already selected as classics. Musical theory has had to struggle with material hardly ever more than a generation older than the theorist; and the generic inferiority of the theorist to the creative artist shows itself in the choice of authorities for 'classical' procedure. If these authorities were avowed, the mischief would not be serious: students would know that 'normal' form is 'normally' exemplified only by Spohr and Hummel; and an extravagant fancy for Spohr's style is easily outgrown and as harmless as a child's appetite for toffee.

But the names which orthodoxy associates with this 'normal' form are those of Haydn, Mozart, and Beethoven, three composers who differ from each other in their treatment of form as profoundly as they differ in other aspects of style and matter. They resemble each other not less profoundly. But I search even Mozart, the most symmetrical of composers since Bach, and the exemplar chosen by Spohr, for any work that can be said to be a model for Spohr's procedure. The first difficulty is to find two movements by Mozart that are sufficiently alike to produce any such uniformity of procedure as can have served Spohr's purpose. Of course, the general resemblances of Mozart's hundreds of examples of any form are as striking, on a superficial acquaintance, as the general resemblances of Chinamen. But people who know the Chinese well do not find them much more alike than Europeans. Musical forms need intimate knowledge before we can pretend to tell one specimen from another. Strange to say, the first movement of Beethoven's *Sonata Appassionata*, one of the most violently dramatic of all his works, approximates unusually closely to Spohr's scheme, while the first movement of the 'Waldstein' Sonata even has shakes at the end of the passages. Yet a mid-Victorian Oxford Professor of Music, who is the authority quoted by the great *Oxford English Dictionary* for the word 'contrapuntal' (Beethoven had 'not enough contrapuntal resource' for the purposes of his Mass in D), laid down that the 'Waldstein' Sonata was not in true sonata form because its second subject was not in the dominant.

I propose to base a survey of Beethoven's art forms on two specimens, the one chosen as the closest approximation, by Beethoven

. T

or any composer, to 'normal' sonata form; the other chosen as outwardly the most abnormal of all his larger works.

The 'normal' example is the first movement of the Pianoforte Sonata in B flat, op. 22. This sonata is neglected by pianists and despised by the Superior Person. But Beethoven set great store by it, though he had already written such impressive and original works as the Sonatas, op. 2, no. 2, op. 7, op. 10, no. 3, the wonderful String Trios, op. 9, and was at the time occupied with the String Quartets, op. 18. 'Die Sonate hat sich gewaschen', he wrote to his publisher; an expression fairly equivalent to R. L. Stevenson's claim that '*The Master of Ballantrae* is a howling cheese'. Beethoven felt that while dramatic force and surprising originality were all very well, it was a fine thing to achieve smoothness also and to show that he was no longer inferior to Mozart in Mozart's own line. Hitherto his works were never less Mozartean than when they resembled Mozart externally. You have but to compare Beethoven's Quintet for pianoforte and wind instruments, op. 16, with the Mozart work which it emulates, to see that point for point Beethoven is doing something slight, diffuse, and yet rigid, where Mozart's quintet is important, concentrated, and supple. Beethoven could not master Mozart's technique by imitating Mozart or by restricting his own ambition; and in op. 22 he first achieved an entire work in which mastery of Mozart's forms is attained without either the timidity of the works with wind instruments or the self-assertive boldness and abruptness which in many of Beethoven's other early works are the characteristic mask of that timidity when he has something unusual to say.

Before analysing the Sonata, op. 22, it will save trouble to dispose of the main false issues that have misled students and music lovers as to the nature of musical forms in general.

1. Not only do the terms 'first' and 'second' subject have no reference to a couple of themes, but there are no rules whatever as to the number or distribution of themes in any sonata movement, except in the case of rondos. In rondos it is, of course, improbable that a square-cut melody whose function is to return several times after contrasted episodes should itself furnish all the material for those episodes. But when musical theorists wonder at the 'bad proportion' of the first movement of Beethoven's Sonata, op. 111, because the second subject consists of a single declamatory two-bar phrase, repeated with ornamentation and, after an echo of its last

notes, plunging into a stormy new version of the first theme, their idea of musical proportion corresponds to no fact in the genuine sonata style. So long as they entertain this idea Haydn is as much a sealed book to them as the most oracular styles of Beethoven. Themes have no closer connexion with larger musical proportions than the colours of animals have with their skeletons. In the sonata style three things are fundamental, and can abide the question as to balance and proportion. These fundamental things are key system and phrase system, both of which can be reduced to technical analysis; and dramatic fitness, which can be discussed only descriptively and analogically, but which constitutes the all-pervading distinction between the sonata style and the earlier non-dramatic, architectural, and decorative styles which culminated in Bach and Handel. (I am well aware that the denial of dramatic style to Bach and Handel will provoke a not ungenerous resentment where the word 'dramatic' is understood loosely; but 'drama' is too valuable as a precise term implying action for us to use it for every conceivable exercise of rhetorical or pictorial power, from sunsets to cathedrals.)

2. As the balance of sonata forms (or any forms) depends on principles other than grouping of themes, so does the much-talked-of 'logical coherence' in great sonata styles also lie elsewhere. The notion that music can be logically connected by mere thematic links has done almost as much harm to composers as to theorists and teachers. Many superb compositions have a wonderful scheme of thematic connexions, but these connexions can of themselves give no security that the logic is any better than if it consisted of a chain of puns. If a composer is using a polyphonic style, then his very language is based on thematic connexions; but for that very reason they provide no guiding principle for form as a whole. Fugue, for example, is not a form, in the sense in which we speak of sonata form: it is a texture, not a shape. Compositions may be written in fugue, as poems may be written in blank verse. A composer whose music is dramatic, as all true sonata style is, will probably tend to use a richer and more evidently intellectual style as his experience and practice grow; and so he will tend to get a larger number of different ideas out of one theme, instead of having several different themes and a smaller range of contrast. But you cannot confine a composer of Beethoven's calibre to this single obvious line of development. The power to make the most of all possible derivatives of one theme grows with the power to use a totally new theme in an

unexpected position. Perhaps the most advanced of all Beethoven's works is the Quartet in A minor, op. 132. Here, where the whole main section of the second movement consists of 120 bars ringing the changes on the following combination:

Ex. 1

its trio contains four fantastically contrasted themes, two of which happen to have been scribbled down years before as a little Alle-mande for pianoforte. Moreover, in the first movement there occurs in the development section (i.e. just where orthodoxy expects logic to be most evident) a theme which it is futile to try to derive from anything heard before or to connect with anything heard later.

Ex. 2

In the works of Beethoven's middle period you will not find 'logic' any more infallibly in the connexions of themes than in his earliest and latest works. The Sonata in D minor, op. 31, no. 2, is a highly finished composition, marking emphatically the change from his first manner to his second, and distinguished by the advanced logical cogency of its treatment of themes. Yet palmistry is not more debilitating to the mind than the attempt to derive the last six bars of the slow movement from any theme that has been heard before.[1]

It will save trouble to investigate this case here, though it antici-pates my main argument. Even if analysis were to derive the theme of these six bars from anything heard before, the ear of the listener would get no benefit from the analysis. The theme sounds new, and no argument will make it sound less new. No doubt things as new have been derived from old material, but then the composer shows us every step of the process. For instance, in the B flat

---

[1] I give no quotations from Beethoven's sonatas, for it is unlikely that anybody will attempt to read this article without having at least Beethoven's pianoforte works at hand.

Trio, op. 97, Beethoven takes the third, fourth, and fifth bars of his main theme

and turns them into this:

Put these two ideas side by side, and it would be an idle fancy to build an argument on any discoverable resemblance. But Beethoven does not put these two ideas side by side. He transforms the one by a long and slow process, every step of which is clear, until he reaches the final transformation. Without this process we might hazard, as a far-fetched guess, that the quavers of the second quotation could be derived by diminution from (*a*) of the first quotation, but no mortal ingenuity could guess that there was any connexion between the trills and figure (*b*); and there is none, until Beethoven works out his long process of development.

No such process is present at the end of the slow movement of op. 31, no. 2, and therefore the 'logic' of that epilogue must be compatible with the fact that the theme is new. As soon as we dismiss thematic connexions from our minds, we fall back upon the very first thing the naïve listener would notice—the enormous slowness of the main theme. In true music, a slow theme is not the same thing as a quick theme played slowly. Slowness is bigness; how big in the case of this movement you can very conveniently measure as follows. The main theme occupies sixteen bars, closing into a seventeenth, and forms one symmetrical sentence, during which nothing can happen. The naïve listener is duly impressed by this; but the student who can read a certain amount takes the whole sentence in at a glance, and, while making no positive mistake about its slow tempo, does not exercise his imagination to the purport of realizing any difference between it and a similar proposition in minuet time. Now let us measure the actual dimensions of this theme. Crotchets at 48 to the minute is a very fair metronome tempo for the whole movement, and it makes the first theme fill precisely one minute. Whole bars (dotted crotchets) at 72 is a good moderate tempo for the finale, which should not sound hurried; and now see where bar 72 brings you! Nearly to the end of the exposition. Consider the end of the Adagio in the light of the dimensions thus revealed. The enormous first theme (or its latter half) has returned for the last time and has for ever closed on the tonic. Over the tonic pedal a new theme sails in, and tells its whole tale in two bars. Another voice repeats it, and its last notes (occupying a third of a bar) are reiterated throughout another bar, until the last bar of all brings the movement to an end actually on its sixth and last quaver. A human figure placed in front of the sphinx, so as to show the colossal scale.

3. If themes cannot determine the logic of music, neither can a single figure really form the 'idea' of a whole movement or section. In the second movement of the A minor Quartet the 120 bars of its main section are, indeed, built up from the two bars of double counterpoint quoted above; but those two bars are not the 'idea' of the movement, nor is

Ex.5

the 'idea' of the Fifth Symphony. These figures, these smallest recognizable portions, these molecules of music, are like single words. A single word must have accumulated a long history before it can become so much as a political slogan: even as an established slogan it must first be led up to in a stump oration. Musical figures represent ideas only when the figures have been incorporated in musical paragraphs. The abrupt statement, interrupted by pauses, of the first four bars of the C minor Symphony misled Spohr into taking the single word for a whole idea, and he accordingly thought the opening inadequate for a serious work. As a matter of fact the first sentence does not come to a stop until the twenty-first bar, and then it is evidently only the first half of the statement. Spohr's mistake was exactly that of the Wagnerian leitmotive labeller who, whether as an enthusiast or as an anti-Wagnerite, analyses Isolde's *Liebestod* into a dozen one-bar themes, giving a psychological name to each, not noticing the psychologically and musically vastly more important fact that the dying Isolde (or rather the orchestra) is singing the whole last 100 bars of the great duet in the second act.

4. Closely akin to the error of identifying the 'idea' with any single figure that happens to persist, is the error of running away with the first apparently completed sentence before you have made sure that the issues raised by its context are not essential to your understanding of it. Some time ago I issued, in connexion with my orchestral concerts, an analysis of Beethoven's Ninth Symphony, in which I described the form of the slow movement as subtle and skilfully handled. A capable critic, in the course of a very generous review, fell foul of Beethoven for his form and of me for imputing skill to his handling of it. The critic asked 'where is the skill in abandoning your idea as soon as you have stated it?' But the first question is, what is the idea? I take this opportunity of clearing up a point which my analysis, by taking it for granted, really failed to put on its proper basis, though I think the truth could be read between my lines. The naïve listener does not suppose that the 'idea' of *Hamlet* is contained in Hamlet's soliloquies and requires no plot for its expression. And when he listens to this music his *naïveté* will have to amount to tone-deafness if he can fail to notice that the great melody, with its tender echoes and its dying fall, marks that repeated fall with a sudden bright chord—

Ex. 6

upon which, in the key of that chord, a new melody enters in a new swinging rhythm. The first theme returns in an ornamental variation. The naïve listener recognizes the bright chord in its place; the second theme follows in another key naturally connected with that chord. As, however, it is not the same key as before, the first theme cannot return in its old position, and an interlude is necessary before the second variation can enter. It enters with all the more effect, and the naïve listener will expect the bright chord in due course. Instead comes a solemn modulation to what musicians call the subdominant, and what naïve listeners feel to be a point of repose towards the end of a big piece of music.

Ex. 7

And so the 'idea' is now at last completely stated and Beethoven does not 'abandon' it, inasmuch as it has covered three-quarters of the movement and has left nothing to be said except by way of the subtlest and profoundest of epilogues. No doubt there is the logical possibility of objecting *a priori* to the spreading of an 'idea' over ten minutes in this manner. But you must not maintain this objection and claim at the same time to understand Wagner's music dramas. The fact is that nobody would have thought that there was anything wrong with the slow movement of Beethoven's Ninth Symphony if they could not read musical notation and so be struck by the unusual appearance of the changes of time-signature.

THE B FLAT MAJOR SONATA, op. 22. Let us now go through the first movement of the Pianoforte Sonata, op. 22, mentioning other works as they serve for illustration. The first movement begins abruptly with three bars all on the tonic chord of B flat, containing a figure in a pregnant rhythm, of which the semiquaver group will be constantly used. (Mark this semiquaver group *a*.) The continuation is a cantabile which in four bars closes into a passage in which *a* is worked up on the tonic and dominant, ending in a half-close on the dominant (bar 11). Thus far we have a statement which, by ending on the dominant and by its energetic businesslike manner, strongly suggests that it will be followed by a counterstatement, that is to say, by a restatement of the same material with a different outlook. A single bar (plus preliminary beat) with an uprush of *a* from the bass is all that does duty for this counterstatement. It leads to three bars of sustained harmony in quite a different style, drifting down to the dominant of F. On this dominant, C, six bars of a tremolando figure follow, with the sole purpose of impressing upon us that we have left the key of B flat and are intending to settle in F, not as by way of going from one part of a decorative design to another, nor as a necessary variety of key in an argumentative work such as a fugue, but as a dramatic event, the first turning-point in the action. Students are far too often allowed to think that these passages of dominant preparation owe their existence to an unsophisticated style of harmony, and that with greater harmonic wisdom they disappear. With greater harmonic wisdom they may be very much modified; and indeed nobody has ever gone further to modify them than Beethoven in earlier works than op. 22 (e.g. op. 10, no. 3); but, modified or plain, they are as necessary to Brahms as they are to

Mozart. Indeed, we must recognize their function in Wagner and Strauss before we can fully appreciate Mozart's and Beethoven's power in the handling of them.

At bar 22 the section misnamed 'second subject' begins. First, there is an eight-bar phrase closing into another theme. The running bass which supports these eight bars arises out of a scale at the end of the preceding 'dominant preparation'. This fact is a mere ornament of style, and if the sonata were to swarm with such facts, the 'logic' of the music would still depend on principles deeper and radically different. The next theme, beginning at bar 29, is a new melody of great distinction, built on rising sequences and closing, after eight bars, into itself, with the obvious purpose of being repeated. We have, then, reached a point where the action of the music is at leisure for melodies to behave like lyrics with a regular stanza-form. But we shall always find that in masterpieces of sonata style this behaviour is not allowed to interfere with the dramatic action. A phrase of this length will repeat itself, perhaps (as here) with ornamental variation, as far as half or three-quarters of its length, but then it will take a new turn and will expand into something unpredictable. In the rare cases where a broad theme is repeated entirely (as in the E major theme of the first movement of the 'Waldstein' Sonata) the theme will be austerely simple and the passage which follows its repetition will be enormously expanded. At all events the composer deals warily with the repeating of a theme that ends on its tonic. When it ends with a half-close the matter is different; for when it begins to repeat itself the listener is unable to guess whether the repetition is going to be exact and so leave the theme unfinished, or to substitute a full close and so complete the matter by answering instead of repeating a question. The principle the composer acts on is that at all events dramatic continuity must be maintained and that these passages of repose must not relapse into mere strophic songs. Here, in op. 22, the repetition of the melody diverges at the seventh bar, with an unexpected modulation and an outpouring of rapid motion on the surface (bar 44). Below the surface the harmony moves slowly, veering back to F in the course of four bars. With this a climax is reached, and the rapid semiquaver movement forms itself in a brilliant four-bar phrase on chords expressive of a full close in F. This closes into another four bars which repeat the same cadential matter in another position. Then (bar 56), on a tonic pedal, we have a quiet two-bar phrase closing into its repetition in a higher position.[1] In this repetition the supertonic is flattened (G flat) which gives a special point to the device of repeating the last bar twice, first with the natural, then with the flattened note. The device of breaking off and reiterating the last bar of a cadential phrase clearly means that a stage of the action is coming to an end. You will not find this device in Bach or Handel, for they have no dramatic interest in thus marking the sections of their designs. Their contemporary, Domenico Scarlatti, uses it constantly, 'hammering in his points', as Parry says, 'like a mob orator'. Bach's son, Johann Christian, the London Bach of the Bach and Abel concerts, uses it typically, and Mozart caught it from him, though he would have undoubtedly arrived at it in any case. Here again, we are not masters of its meaning until we can trace the principle in Brahms and in the music dramas of Wagner and Strauss. In op. 22 this quiet cadence-theme is, however, not the end of the exposition of the first movement. A new theme, going straight up the scale and down again in a strong rhythm, enters with drastic force, and closes into three bars of tonic-and-dominant cadence which allude to figure *a*, the only piece of thematic 'logic' since the detail of the bass in bar 22.

Before discussing the development section let us review this exposition in the light of general principles and classical precedents. No one who has analysed the movement of a drama, or of a great piece of prose, can fail to recognize that our analysis has depended on two things: first, the assertion of key and key relation, which is, so to speak, the topography of music, and secondly, the lengths of the phrases. What themes these phrases contain, and whether one phrase alludes to another not in immediate juxtaposition, whether, in short, the whole composition is written on one theme or on a dozen, are questions entirely secondary to the proportions and contrasted movements of the phrases. In the present case, even if we ignore the semiquaver digression from bar 44 to bar 55 (a digression which has no discoverable connexion in theme with what has gone before), we cannot account for the second subject with less than four totally distinct themes. The quiet penultimate theme on a tonic pedal has, indeed, a quaver figure which might be regarded as an augmentation of figure *a*, but Beethoven gives no evidence that he so regards it or expects it to be recognized. By a sufficiently elaborate and imaginative process you can derive any theme from

---

[1] With the music before him the reader will understand that I speak of one phrase as 'closing into' the next when the closing chord is not within the rhythmic period but at the beginning of the next period.

the figures of any other theme; indeed, if your analysis is so fine as to recognize a figure in a single note, you can derive the whole records of the art of music from that figure. But the ear of the listener to whom the music gives pleasure does not appreciate so fine an analysis. What reaches the ear in the first movement of op. 22 is a pair of distinct themes, figure *a*, and a cantabile before the key of B flat is left, and four other distinct themes in F, besides an independent passage of preparation on the dominant of F, and a spacious digression before the cadence-themes. The result is obviously very different from the scheme of two subjects or themes, of which the second is to be a cantabile, while the intervening spaces are to be filled up with 'Hi diddle diddle, the cat and the fiddle' by way of 'brilliant passages' which, according to Spohr, must end with a shake. It so happens that in the present instance both the cantabile and the brilliant passages are there; but their place among the other ideas gives no support to the theory that they come there by rule. To ask which of the four themes in F is the 'real' second subject is as futile as to ask who are the hero and heroine of *A Midsummer Night's Dream*.

We come now to the development of this movement. The function of the exposition has been to assert two keys, the tonic and (in this case, as usual) the dominant. Other keys occur, if at all, only as purple patches, and here the only suggestion of the kind is the modulation at bar 44 which started the brilliant digression from the cantabile theme.

The function of the development is to travel through a wider harmonic range and to make the known themes of the exposition break up into new combinations. Actually new themes will give a development a lighter and more episodic character, unless, as in the 'Eroica' Symphony, the design is on an enormous scale which leaves room for highly organized use of the old material as well. Any passage that stays long in one key will almost certainly be in a key not heard in the exposition (the exceptions are extremely interesting and do not produce the impression that the key is already familiar), and will probably be on the dominant of that key, thus arousing expectation and in no way reproducing the manner of an exposition, except in so far as concerns the bridge between first and second subject.

The development of op. 22 begins with two bars of dialogue on figure *a* in F, which is just as likely to be a dominant as a tonic. The strong scale-theme breaks in, treating it as a dominant and

leading in four bars to the note D, on which bass we have the whole
six bars of the quiet tonic-pedal theme of bars 56–61, with its
doubts as to whether the supertonic should be flat or natural. Now
here we have a typical instance of the subtlety of classical tonality,
for though this is an exact transposition (except in position of parts)
of the passage which we accepted as on the tonic of F, half-major
and half-minor, nobody can possibly mistake it for D major in
its present context. It is unquestionably the dominant of G, and
it arouses anticipation of some event in that key. But the scale-
figure, now in three-part and four-part polyphony, angrily drives
us from dominant to dominant, two bars of scale-figure alternating
with two of figure *a* as a continuous run. Three of these four-bar
steps, then, drive us from the dominant of G minor to that of C
minor and thence to that of F minor. Figure *a* with an arpeggio
pendant then moves alone in no less than seven two-bar steps, the
bass moving still more slowly by tones and semitones so that from
bar 90 (where, ignoring differences of octave, its progression really
begins) it descends from C to the E flat reached in bar 104. The
whole fourteen bars thus constitute a dramatic decrescendo, not
less unmistakable in its effect though the actual drop of tone is confined to the single bar 105, which Beethoven requires to fall from
fortissimo to piano. We are now on the dominant of A flat, of all
keys the most unlikely to lead to our tonic. The scale-theme stirs
in the bass in four-bar phrases. The harmony changes to a dominant of F with a minor ninth which even in pianissimo presses
severely on the D natural of the scale-theme below. Thence it
drops to the dominant of B flat (our tonic), also with its harsh minor
ninth, which does not yield until the latter half of the fourth bar.
The tension of expectation is great and is kept up for fifteen bars,
ending with a pause (bar 128).

And so we are at home again and the recapitulation begins. The
whole phenomenon of recapitulation is one of the most subtle
things in music, and is usually dismissed by critics, and by some
composers, as merely the part of a design which may be mechanically copied from a previous part. And it would be idle to deny
that in the physical process of writing a large composition the recapitulatory portions are a more mechanical task than the rest, and
may well be deferred until matters of greater difficulty are settled.
But we must not confuse the practical technique of writing and the
function of the imagination. No great composer making full use of
his mature powers ever thought of a recapitulation merely as a part

which is the transposition or copy of another part. It is his profoundest instinct to think of recapitulations as things coloured by
the first statements and all that has happened between. (Of course,
a recapitulation is not an immediate repetition, exact or varied, of
a section with nothing intervening; such immediate repetitions,
when exact and on a large scale, merely treat music as if it were
spatial, like a picture or a building, and give the listener an opportunity to take another look before passing on to a new aspect or
place.) One of the first conditions of musical invention is the
capacity to conceive the effect of a statement not only in its first
context but in the possible ways in which it may return. Students
would obtain a far sounder grasp of the forms of pure instrumental
music if they were made to read Wagner's later operas with a strict
injunction never to label the short leitmotives until they had mapped
out all the long passages which are recapitulated as wholes. To take
an instance already cited, Isolde's *Liebestod*, which recapitulates
the entire last movement of the love duet in the second act, is as
long as the longest stretch of recapitulation to be found in any
classical symphony, being almost exactly the length of the whole
second subject in Beethoven's 'Eroica' Symphony. And it is by no
means alone in Wagner's designs. Of course the circumstances of
Wagnerian music drama enormously emphasize the psychological
and dramatic value of the principle that a recapitulation depends
for its effect on the new light thrown by its immediate antecedents
in relation to the original statement. We should do well to see in
Wagner's mature art of composition a magnified and popular illustration of the principles of pure music, instead of contenting ourselves with the old view shared by his earliest partisans with his
most violent enemies, the view that he is formless and a mere
illustrator of words from point to point.

In the recapitulation of a classical sonata-movement the first
thing to notice is, obviously, any point which differs from the
original statement. In well-conceived works you will not find that
such points are mere digressions introduced for the sake of variety.
If there is to be a recapitulation at all (and Haydn was far from
thinking this necessary, nor did Beethoven disagree with him), the
composer will not be afraid to make it exact. Yet there will always
be some difference, possibly very slight, but of the kind that makes
'all the difference'. It will be as if the original matter were something you had seen with one eye, and the recapitulation were something you saw with both. One point where there must be some

change is at the moment of transition to the key of the second subject. As the second subject is to be recapitulated in the tonic, the passage which changed the key cannot remain unaltered, unless the change has been effected (as in Beethoven's First Symphony) by the old Italian practical joke of treating a mere half-close on the dominant as if that dominant were a key instead of a chord. Beethoven's treatment of this joke is amusing in his *Namensfeier* Overture, op. 115, written about the same time as the Seventh Symphony. For the dominant chords of the exposition he substitutes tonic chords, with the gesture of a debater taking a metaphorical argument literally and turning it to his own advantage. But even at this juncture a change in the recapitulation is not to be ascribed to mere practical necessity: and in the Sonata, op. 22, we have a beautifully typical case of a great master's procedure. The opening had been perfunctory to the verge of insolence; and as we have seen, its counterstatement had been reduced to a single bar and a quarter. Now turn to bar 140 and see how the two new bars of vigorous dialogue on *a* make the whole retrospect stand out in relief. Then comes the uprush corresponding to bar 12. It reaches a higher note, and five bars are required instead of three for the drift down to the dominant, which is now our own dominant of B flat, not that of F. From this point the passage of dominant preparation and the whole of the second subject are recapitulated in the tonic with no alteration except occasional shifts of octave, not always necessitated by the limited compass of Beethoven's pianoforte at that date. There is no coda; the movement ends in the tonic exactly as its exposition ended in the dominant.

Perhaps we are wise after the event; but the perfunctory first subject is almost a sufficient indication that the weight of the movement is so poised upon a luxurious second subject that the recapitulation of the second subject is the inevitable and sufficient end of the story. Such is the case with most of the sonatas of Domenico Scarlatti that were known to Beethoven. The openings are drastically bald assertions of a tonic from which the elvish Domenico bounces off into a dominant or some remoter key, there to pour out a number of ideas, some sentimental, but most of them rattling away with a fantastic keyboard technique, and always ending with a cadence phrase broken up into smaller and smaller fragments. It is a mistake to read into Scarlatti any anticipation of Beethoven's uses of remote modulations or powers of development; these things he anticipated only as *The Arabian Nights* anticipates modern travel and wireless telephony; but the root of the sonata style is in him.

Certainly Beethoven had no feeling that he had done an easy thing in shaping this movement and the slow movement without codas—rather he felt like a sculler who has got his boat to a difficult landing-place without changing his stroke. *Die Sonate hat sich gewaschen.* Codas and other grand and clever features he had already often achieved. His triumph here is to achieve noble proportions without any startling features. The perfunctoriness of the first subject is, as we have seen, essential to the scheme. This 'normal' movement is in the paradoxical position of being quite unlike any other movement in Beethoven, Mozart, or Haydn. So are all the other mature movements of these composers. An analysis that does not detect this is no nearer to the truth than a child's scrawl that represents the human face by a circle containing two dots for eyes, a line for the mouth (curved upward for joy and downward for grief), and a nose in profile. Shorter first subjects Beethoven had written before, and was to write later. But the early ones, like those in the Sonatas, op. 2, no. 1, and op. 10, no. 2, were in works on as small a scale as the opening indicates, and, by the way, the same absence of coda is to be noticed. And the later ones are associated with much more rapid and powerful dramatic action.

It would detain us too long to analyse the other movements of op. 22 in detail. The slow movement is in fully developed sonata-form, like the first movement, but with a main theme so cut off from the rest that Beethoven actually draws a double bar between it and the transition theme that is to lead to the second subject. The sections are as follows: First subject, bars 1–12; transition, bars 13–17; second subject, bars 18–30; development, bars 31–46; recapitulation of first subject, bars 47–57. At this point comes the characteristic touch which makes the recapitulation more solid (or stereoscopic) than the exposition. Instead of the formal close in bars 11 and 12, a single bar (57) leads without break to the transition theme. This theme goes at its third bar through the tonic minor and takes another four bars (instead of two) to reach the second subject, which is recapitulated in the tonic without change. No coda is required.

Beethoven was probably quite as proud of the minuet and trio as of the more elaborate parts of this sonata. Space and opportunity fail here for the discussion of such fine detail as goes to these lyric interludes in the sonata forms. The topic of Beethoven's (or Mozart's) rondo forms is second only to that of his first-movement forms. The rondos of Mozart's concertos are as large and rich as rondos can possibly be; and Beethoven took a special delight in working out luxurious rondos on Mozart's lines. His usual tendency is to make his rondo theme as primitive and self-repetitive as possible (see the rondos of the Sonatas, op. 28, op. 53, and op. 90), so that the listener may be thoroughly impressed with the sense of rondo style from the outset. In the same way, when he expanded and quickened the minuet into the scherzo, he did not abandon the dance style but emphasized it more vigorously than anybody could have conceived possible. In op. 22, however, the fitting conclusion is a rondo of Mozartean suavity, and accordingly Beethoven writes one of his most graceful themes and admits no suspicion of caricature. Here are the sections: rondo theme, bars 1–18; transition theme, bar 18½ modulating to dominant at bar 21, and settling there for the first episode, about bar 22. Like many such episodes and second subjects of Beethoven's finales, the material of this dominant section avoids standing out very plastically and soon (about bar 36) shows a disposition to return to the tonic. This is in accordance with the principle that all the dramatic interest of a rondo centres round the returns to the rondo theme in the tonic. Here this is not reached until bar 49. The second episode begins at bar 67 and is in and around the tonic minor. Its material consists of the transition theme treated with argumentative polyphony, and alternating with a new theme in bustling demisemiquavers which actually makes up a kind of binary form, appearing first in F minor from bars 72 to 80, and then again in B flat minor from bars 95 to 103. The rondo theme returns (after some anxious inquiries) at bar 112. Then the transition theme is so handled as to bring about a recapitulation of the whole first episode in the tonic, thus making it behave just like a second subject. This brings about a drift to the subdominant, in which key the rondo theme puts in a prompt appearance (bar 153), soon veering round to the tonic where it has its final entry as a whole (bar 165). The last eighteen bars (from bar 183) are a coda, very subtle in phrasing and detail.

THE C SHARP MINOR QUARTET, op. 131, no. 14. Now that we have seen the uniqueness of this most normal of Beethoven's sonatas we shall be in a better position to appreciate the fundamental normality of his most unique work, the Quartet in C sharp minor. The idea that Beethoven, in such works as this, 'broke the mould' of the classical forms is fatally well-expressed in that metaphor.

There was no mould to break. The art forms of Haydn, Mozart, and Beethoven were not moulds in which music could be cast, but inner principles by which the music grew. The great family likeness between hundreds of Mozart's movements does not prove that they are not alive. Their differences are as vital as those which distinguish one Chinaman from another; and with study the differences soon become vital to us. But with Beethoven's later works the differences are more conspicuous than the resemblances. If form means conformity to a mould, then indeed Beethoven's last works require a separate mould for each. Does this, then, mean that there is more form in these works, or less form, than in works that will all fit one mould? Evidently the mould metaphor is unprofitable: when we come down to anything more detailed than the most childish generalization, Mozart is no more comfortable in a mould than Richard Strauss. Let us take the C sharp minor Quartet from point to point and see what it tells us when we are unencumbered by *a priori* notions.

It begins with a fugue, of which I quote the subject for convenience.

Ex. 8

The method of a fugue is argumentative; and while its argument is proceeding dramatic action is in abeyance. This fugue is clearly bent on its own business and shows no sign of being an introduction to anything else. Space forbids a detailed analysis, and only a detailed analysis can throw any light on a fugue. Three points, however, can be made here. First, a fugue, inasmuch as it is not a dramatic form, has no tendency to emphasize its changes of key, or even to single out a return to its tonic as an important event. Hence there is something unusually formal in the eight bars of clearly cadential tonic-and-dominant at the return to C sharp minor (marked by a double bar and four sharps in this score, bars 83–90); and the preceding ethereal passage in A for the two violins, answered by D for the viola and violoncello, is also considerably more like a distinct event than one would expect in a mere fugue. In short, this fugue has subtle signs that it is part of a work in sonata style, though the hard dramatic facts of that style are not allowed to disturb its quiet flow. Secondly, the range of key is very small,

U

being practically confined to directly related keys; that is to say, keys in which the chord of our tonic (C sharp minor) can be found. (The reader must not be misled by the change to six flats at bar 45. Beethoven had a great dislike to writing double sharps and would change his notation on the slightest hint of such trouble. A few accidental double sharps would have kept the whole passage visibly around D sharp and F sharp.) Thirdly, both the beginning and the end of this fugue throw strong emphasis on the flat supertonic (D natural). In the subject the minor sixth (A), with its sforzando, is reflected by D natural in the answer, which has been put into the subdominant (instead of the orthodox dominant) for this very purpose. The counterpoint of this answer even emphasizes G natural, the flat supertonic of this subdominant. At the end of the movement the flat supertonic is so strong that the major tonic chord is almost in danger of sounding like a dominant. This danger is averted by a D sharp five bars before the end. As the final chord dies away, the violoncello rises an octave; the harmony vanishes into unison as the other instruments echo the rising octave.

The rising octave, a semitone higher, begins a lively, self-repeating eight-bar tune, pianissimo, in a quick 6/8 ('allegro molto vivace'). So the key is D major, flat supertonic to C sharp minor, and, in spite of all the emphasis that prepared it, utterly unexpected. The viola repeats the tune, which the violin resumes at the fifth bar and continues with another eight bars that overlap into a new theme, evidently destined to be a transition theme. We are unquestionably moving in sonata style and have left the fugue behind us. Now what will become of the sonata form in these extraordinary circumstances? From the fact that the movement is in this strange key, we may expect that it will not modulate very widely, for fear of losing its bearings or damaging its special key-colour by reminding us of the C sharp minor which is so firmly established by that great and solemn fugue as the key of the whole work. Again, the development of a sonata-form movement is bound to be argumentative: and here again the fugue has forestalled us. Accordingly this D-major movement, which has started with a rondo-like tune, sets out at bar 24 with a highly organized transition theme which expands until at bar 44, having overshot A major (the dominant), it finds itself poised on a chord of C sharp major, dangerously near the key of the fugue. After a pause the situation is saved by the bold stroke of playing the first theme again actually in E, the dominant of the dominant. This is 'dominant preparation' with a vengeance; and four more bars lead safely into A major, where (at bar 60) a lively second subject begins. But it behaves like the second subjects of Beethoven's rondos and allied types of finale, and soon shows a hankering for the tonic and for a return to the first theme. At bar 84 the theme does return. At bar 100 it moves to the subdominant, and thence takes a new course leading to a passage on the chord of F sharp major, corresponding to that which ended on the chord of C sharp. From here, however, six bars lead easily back to D, where (at bar 133) the second subject is recapitulated. This, of course, leads to the subdominant, just as happened in the rondo of op. 22; and here, as there, the main theme enters in the subdominant before swinging round to the tonic. A spacious coda, greatly developing the transition theme, now ensues and brings this delicate movement to quite a brilliant climax, which, however, dies away abruptly.

Eleven bars of declamatory interlude lead, in a few firm steps of harmony, to A major. A theme in two repeated strains ('andante ma non troppo e molto cantabile') initiates a great slow movement in the form of a set of six absolutely strict variations, with a coda which, as is typical of Beethoven's procedure, begins as if to make another variation but drifts away, after the first phrase, into foreign keys. Most of the variations reflect only the harmony of the theme, and in the second variation ('più mosso', common time) an extra bar at the beginning displaces the rhythm, while in the second part of the mysterious, syncopated fifth variation (allegretto, 2/4) there is an extra bar in a more unexpected place. Otherwise the fact that each variation is in a different tempo and style cannot in any way weaken the strength with which the theme is grasped. It is not the naïve listener who finds this movement 'chopped up' by these changes of tempo. After the sixth variation (in 9/4 time with a most original rhythm and more resemblance to the melody of the theme than has hitherto been shown), the florid triplet passages which the four instruments give out in dialogue are unmistakably beginning a seventh variation, but at its eighth bar a long trill leads slowly to C major, the first change of key in the whole movement, which, of course, has hitherto been confined to the harmonies of its theme. In C major a fragment of the original melody is given in a quicker tempo (allegretto), and it moves excitedly back to A major, where the first eight bars of the theme appear in their original tempo, surrounded by a glory of trills. Again at the eighth bar a trill rises slowly, this time to F major. The fragment of the theme in an increasingly excited allegretto leads back to A, again in the original tempo (Beethoven's intention is certain though his directions are confused); and in a coda of fourteen bars, the details of which cost Beethoven immense pains, this slow movement dies away with broken accents from the cadence of its theme.

Now follows the most childlike of all Beethoven's scherzos. Beyond being in alla breve instead of triple time it does not differ from the form laid down by him in the Fourth and Seventh Symphonies. The key is E major. The trio begins with a tune in E, and contains four distinct ideas, the last two of which are in A. The first da capo of the scherzo has its repeats written out in full in order that (as in the Seventh Symphony) a large portion may be at first kept mysteriously subdued. The whole trio is made to come round again, and so there is a third appearance of the main body of the scherzo. The tunes of the trio then try to prove themselves irrepressible. But repressed they are, and the scherzo dies away in a mischievous whispering passage which suddenly swells out to a fortissimo end. So far this description might apply to half a dozen of Beethoven's other scherzos. What is peculiar to the scherzo of the C sharp minor Quartet (apart from its childlike spirit) is the joints of the form; the humorous treatment of its first four notes, a humour which is heightened at each recurrence when the trio leads back to the main theme; and the strange diminuendo leading to 'poco adagio' in the middle of the second part of that theme. Such things are always typical and yet always unique.

Catastrophe overwhelms the end of the scherzo. Its last three notes are savagely repeated on a G sharp, and then a solemn slow tune ('adagio quasi un poco andante') is given out by the viola in G sharp minor. Its first strain is repeated by the violin, and a second strain, finishing the tune in eight bars, is divided among the instruments and repeated. After this, three more bars move to C sharp minor, and so lead to the finale.

At this point we must survey the keys which have been heard in the course of the work. The fugue may be taken to have established C sharp minor with a firmness beyond the power of any mere introduction. The 'allegro molto vivace' was then able to maintain itself in D major, the flat supertonic, but could not venture far afield, and so had a finale-like second subject that speedily returned to its tonic. The slow movement, in A major, was confined to the key of its theme throughout six and a half variations. It then made the only modulatory purple patch in the whole quartet, by going

outside the circle of directly related keys into C major and F major
(the pair of keys that are so important in the introduction of the
Seventh Symphony). The scherzo was confined to E major and
A major.

Now, at last, in the introduction to the finale we have heard the
dominant of C sharp minor. And now at last it will be, at all events
theoretically, possible to cover a wide range of key and have some
expansive and argumentative development. Let us see what happens. The Finale begins with four bars of a savage tonic-and-
dominant theme in quavers and crotchets. (We will call this the
anapaest theme.) Thereupon follows a wild yet square-cut tune in
dotted rhythm and tragically sardonic mood. It occupies sixteen
bars, of which the last four are a sad echo, emphasizing D natural
(our flat supertonic) in an ominous way. Then follows (over an
undercurrent in the sardonic dotted rhythm) a new theme which
must be quoted. Note that answer in the second violin.

Ex. 9

We will call this the mournful theme. With its rondo-like symmetrical eight-bar shape and its immediate full repetition in the
bass, this theme strengthens the conviction that the Finale is in no
hurry to take action as yet. The anapaest theme reappears below
the dotted rhythm and then pretends that it was part of the sardonic tune which is resumed from its fifth bar. Suddenly, after its
twelfth bar, action is taken. In four bars we reach E major (the
usual relative major) and a theme of extraordinary pathos, in
dialogue between the instruments, occupies twelve bars of tonic
and dominant before it reluctantly moves up first one step, then
another, and then tries hesitatingly to come to a close, which is
frustrated by the drift of the harmony into F sharp minor. Thus
the second subject has occupied only twenty-one bars, and has been
thoroughly typical of Beethoven's ways in a finale of this kind.
The first themes, anapaest and sardonic tunes, burst out in F sharp
minor, the subdominant. Now if this Finale were going to be a
rondo these themes would have entered here in the tonic; and the
fact that they are in another key, however closely related, at once
convinces us that this is no rondo, but a movement of highly organized development. And after the twelfth bar of the sardonic tune

we find the development in full swing. The austere simplicity of its first process may be realized if we take the new counterpoint of rising semibreves which accompanies the figure of the sardonic tune, and put it all into one line, starting the first steps (five bars before the double bar and signature of two sharps) in the extreme bass.

Ex.10

If this line does not stretch to the crack of doom, it at all events lands us in a key which, though not remote from C sharp minor, is quite incompatible with it. In this key of B minor a new development of the anapaest theme arises. Modulating in seven bars to D, it now proceeds in a couple of six-bar periods (thrice two) to land itself on the dominant of C sharp minor. Here, relapsing into four-bar periods (trust your ear, not your eye), it continues for eight bars. Suddenly all trace of any theme vanishes. Beethoven writes *Ritmo di tre battute*, and in this three-bar rhythm the music vibrates grimly on the dominant for twelve bars. Then the recapitulation begins. The vibration still continues above while the anapaest theme is tossed to and fro in the bass. Its four bars are expanded to eight. The sardonic tune, on the other hand, is expanded in another way. It is not allowed to take its original shape, but its first four bars are treated in a tonic and dominant dialogue, with a new counterpoint of semibreves. This occupies sixteen bars, which seem much more spacious than those of the original tune. The mournful theme now enters in the subdominant, and we are surprised to find that after its repetition in the bass it drifts into a quiet passage on the last figure of the sardonic theme with a running accompaniment like that of the later stages of the development. And this passage lasts some time: thirteen bars. What does it mean?

It means that the second subject is going to be recapitulated in the flat supertonic! The wheel has come full circle. The whole quartet is a perfect unity, governed by the results of the initial event of that modified first movement which maintained itself in the flat supertonic after the opening fugue had firmly established the key of C sharp minor. Hence the restraint in the matter of modulation, even in the Finale, where Beethoven was free to expand in argumentative development. His power of modulation is really unsurpassed even by Wagner, but this fact is generally ignored or disbelieved, because the occasions on which Beethoven exercises the power in any obvious way are very rare. Before concluding this brief survey of the C sharp minor Quartet, let us glance for a moment at another quartet in which Beethoven's long-distance feeling for tonality is shown in this same matter of the flat supertonic. The first movement of the F minor Quartet, op. 95, places that harmony prominently at the outset in a form subtilized from the similar but plainer procedures at the openings of the *Sonata Appassionata*, op. 57, and the Quartet in E minor, op. 59, no. 2. The second subject, in D flat major, is a pathetic cantabile twice interrupted by fierce outbursts in its flat supertonic (written as D natural to avoid the awkward notation of E double flat). In the recapitulation, in F major, this would become G flat. Schubert at the white heat of his inspiration and, to judge by his unfailing subtlety in such matters, Brahms are probably the only other composers who could be trusted to see that G flat will have no real power here, having used its power at the opening, and being in any case closely alike to D flat in tone colour; so that the apparently commonplace natural supertonic is the one harmony that can recapture and intensify the ferocity of the original passages. Nobody would have noticed anything wrong if Beethoven had missed this point: G flat would have been formally correct, and perhaps people might have had clever theories as to why Beethoven did not write it as F sharp.

Let us return to the C sharp minor Quartet. We have now reached this wonderful recapitulation in D major. But a more wonderful stroke is pending. The pathetic way in which that second subject wandered into a key a tone higher (originally F sharp minor) leads it here to the dominant of E, and a further similar step leads it to a chord of C sharp major. This, instead of behaving as a dominant, is taken as the tonic major; and the whole subject is recapitulated again. The pathos is enhanced by the fact that the tonic major has never before been heard in the whole work. This beautiful gleam of hope and consolation is a typical example of tragic irony; for the ensuing coda is unsurpassed anywhere in Beethoven for tragic power. A detailed analysis would take up too much space and would raise no issues that have not been dealt with to the best of my ability already. Two points must be mentioned. First, the 'answer' to the mournful theme, quoted above, is taken up and turned into an emphatic and unmistakable allusion to the first four notes of the fugue. For reasons already discussed, I am generally sceptical about such long-distance resemblances, where the composer has no means of enforcing his point; for instance, I shall never believe that Beethoven intended the transition passage to B flat in the first movement of the Ninth Symphony to fore-shadow the choral finale which comes three-quarters of an hour afterwards. If he had meant anything by the resemblance, he could have made his meaning clear in the introduction to his finale, where he calls up the ghosts of the previous movements. But here, in the C sharp minor Quartet, he goes out of his way to accentuate his point; the point refers to the very beginning of the work, and not to some transitional passage heard only twice in its course; and not only is the point thus explicable but it has no other explanation. The other matter is the reappearance of the flat supertonic in a shuddering cadential passage that breaks in upon the height of the passion; having no connexion of theme with its surroundings, and requiring no such connexion.

This essay deals with form, and therefore does not profess to discuss emotional contents. But true form is as inseparable from emotional contents as the plot of a play. What, after all, is the strictest possible notion of form? Are there any pieces of music so constructed that a complete definition of their form will account for every note? Would not such pieces achieve the theoretical ulti-mate possibility in the way of strictness? Strange to say, this is no mere theoretical possibility. When Bach writes a piece in which a known chorale-tune is treated by several parts in close fugue, phrase by phrase, while another part gives out the phrases in their order, in long notes at regular intervals, this form actually does prescribe for most of the notes in the whole piece, and the exigencies of counterpoint seem to determine the remaining notes. Such a form is a not unreasonable exercise for students; and a student's exercise appears to differ from Bach's in no discoverable matter of form. But whereas the student is proud to achieve grammatical correct-ness, Bach's chorale-fugue is a masterpiece of rhetoric. Now if we are correct in our view that an art form grows from within instead of being moulded from without, then it ought to be possible to regard Bach's choral fugue as having reached its strict form by inner rhetorical necessity. And again this is no abstract absurdity. Bach wrote two entirely different strict chorale-fugues on *Aus tiefer Not*. The original tune was undoubtedly moulded by the words to which it was set: and if rhetoric moulded the tune why should it not mould the polyphony? The practical fact that Bach must have known beforehand that his art form was going to be so strict has nothing to do with the principles that guided him to prefer the better rhetoric of two equally strict and correct turns of harmony.

The forms of Beethoven's last works show, the more we study them, a growing approximation to that Bach-like condition in which the place of every note can be deduced from the scheme. The more the forms differ from each other the more strictly do they carry out their own principles. Thus they are stricter than the forms of op. 22; the pianoforte itself having proved far too inexact for Beethoven's latest ideas. As to the 'strictness' of poor Spohr's projected set of quartets with shakes at the end of the passages, it compares with the strictness of Beethoven's C sharp minor Quartet as railway trains in a fog compare with the stars in their courses.

ELGAR, MASTER OF MUSIC[1]

THE Editor's invitation to write a few words about Elgar impels me to utter indiscretions which I believe to be less dangerous now than they would have been twenty years ago. Perhaps cowardice is the only motive that could have prevented me and others from uttering them then, for indiscretions are most valuable where they give most offence. I do not mean personal offence to individuals, but offence to fashions; and Elgar's relation to the fashions of his day is peculiar. On his side, it is quite simple in the all-important respect that he did not care two hoots for fashions, but wrote as a sincere artist, entirely to please himself. On the other hand the relations of fashions to Elgar are very complex, and will have become wholly unintelligible to historians a generation hence. At present, however, these trifles obstruct the view, as the donkey's ears obstructed Mark Twain's camera when he photographed the Matterhorn. Moreover, Elgar suffered from a shyness which revealed itself in unexpected forms, and, in particular, made him avoid talking about music in the presence of anyone of whose capacity to understand him he was not quite assured.

At the present moment, I feel very strongly the need of inculcating a better and wider appreciation of Elgar's art. To certain elements of his style and taste I have always been recalcitrant; and one of the elementary lessons that people must learn if they are to come to terms with anything outside the most habit-ridden contents of their own minds is that greatness in art is not a matter of taste at all. Nobody ought to say that he likes what he does not like; but it is childish to measure great things by one's likes and dislikes. And by continually taking one's temperature in likes and dislikes one develops no fine artistic sensibilities, but merely becomes a chronic aesthetic valetudinarian. I myself don't like a Wagnerian atmosphere, and I like it least of all in *Parsifal*. I prefer Beethoven's atmosphere to Wagner's, because the atmosphere of a man who has a profound sense of responsibilities and whose chief sorrow has come from his failure to live up to it, is more sympathetic to me than the atmosphere of a person whose axiom is that what he wants, it is his duty to have, and that the means he uses to gain it are washed

---

[1] Written at the request of the Editor of *Music and Letters* (the late Mr. A. H. Fox Strangways) for his issue of January 1935 (Vol. XVI, No. 1).

away by a magic potion. Hence, the asceticism of the knight of the
Grail and the sickness of Amfortas do not satisfy me as a reaction
to the sanctified irresponsibility of Tristan and Isolde.

For somewhat different reasons, I am out of sympathy with the
Oxford Movement, and have a strong squirearchic recalcitrance
against Cardinal Newman. There are plenty of other directions in
which my natural dislikes are strong. But I have not the slightest
intention of going through life regarding those reactions as valuable
aesthetic discoveries, and turning myself into the kind of ass who
has discovered a vulgarity in Wagner without the slightest capacity
to discriminate between Wagner and Meyerbeer, or into the more
formidable type of don who combines an anti-priggish reaction in
favour of Sullivan with a righteous indignation against Elgar's
Straussian panache and his Pisgah sights of popularity. It may be
that, apart from the tune of 'Land of Hope and Glory', the most
popular aspects of Elgar's style are not the best. But Heaven be
praised that the British public of to-day is capable of showing a
popular opinion in favour of any ambitious music at all. The vul-
garest and most *nouveau-riche* trait in all connoisseurship is the fear
of vulgarity. I once knew a professor of music who thought the
Finale of Beethoven's Seventh Symphony vulgar. I don't know
whether he thought Cherubini a great composer. Beethoven certainly did, and quite possibly thought Cherubini greater than himself. But there is such a thing as a sense of proportion in life and in
art, and that sense has never been developed by a kind of donnish
connoisseurship which reduces everything to a level far below the
learned profession of catering. Nobody treats wine as frivolously
as our connoisseurs treat their first impressions of a composer of
Elgar's calibre. In the first place, there is nothing that the British
connoisseur hates so much as mastery. He scents it from afar as if
it was something wrong with the drains, and promptly proceeds to
infer that the master has not had a university education. Elgar's
own attitude towards our university musical traditions might justi-
fiably have been one of contempt. As a matter of fact, it was as
generous as Beethoven's attitude towards Cherubini. *The Dream
of Gerontius* was as nearly as possible a failure on its first production at one of our festivals; but when it was adequately produced in
Germany it made a tremendous impression, and Richard Strauss
publicly hailed Elgar as a *Vorwärtsmann*. After this triumph, Elgar
had the sincere and generous humility to ask our English Cherubini
for his candid opinion of the work, to which Cherubini replied that

he liked 'the clothes better than the body'. The autograph of Elgar's *Dream of Gerontius* has a note in words which I have forgotten, but which are a touching expression of the conviction that this was the best that the composer could ever do: words equivalent to Beethoven's note on his Mass in D, 'written from the heart; may it go to the heart'. What conceivable use can there be in answering a genuine appeal for advice by a general condemnation of the work as superficial? It is not as if our British musical academics were an immensely prosperous and popular group like the Victorian painters. There has been no British musical equivalent to Burlington House in any of its aspects. Elgar had a genuine respect for our sincere and idealistic English masters of music, and this was the recognition they gave him.

As to Elgar's mastery, nothing but sheer ignorance can bring it into question. To put the clothes before the body, his orchestration is as wonderful as Strauss's would be if Strauss's harmony were clean and his economy severe. That is to say, for Elgar's purposes it is the most perfect orchestration conceivable. It is astoundingly subtle, uncannily efficient, and utterly original. I am not so sure about his mastery of form; that it is masterly there is no reasonable doubt, but, like the form of the Cherubinis of all artistic periods, it is apt to fill up space with sequences on figures that are not sufficiently pregnant to show well under the amount of repetition forced on them. Yet I do not know any English compositions that are more free from this fault than Elgar's, except some that have definitely abandoned the classical forms and language.

Our Cherubinis do not attempt to say anything about the soul of Elgar's work. That is a mysterious thing that eludes analysis. One's sympathies may be rather with other souls; for not every reaction of taste is like mere connoisseurship of wine. Between souls there is personal reaction on both sides even if one soul encounters the other only as embodied in Elgar's Violin Concerto. If your approach to Elgar's Violin Concerto is donnish and censorious, the concerto will behave to you exactly like a shy person with a vein of irony. It will then suffer acutely, if you are conducting it or playing it. So will you; and serve you right. I am not claiming that it is a faultless work, nor that it represents my idea of a concerto. I prefer it to represent its own ideas. The Violoncello Concerto is a much less important work, and is much more accessible to me though (or perhaps even because) it is not in the great classical forms, and therefore, amongst other liberties, is unencumbered with the necessity, technical or conscientious, for a large acreage of sequential developments. And Elgar's humour is of the highest order.

I have had to interrupt the writing of this little screed in order to rehearse and conduct a performance of what I believe to be Elgar's greatest work, the 'symphonic study' *Falstaff*. It seems to me one of the immeasurably great things in music, and entirely free from anything that can be imputed to Elgar's other works as faults. One of R. L. Stevenson's best fables tells of a touchstone the light of which revealed the truth. Many other touchstones were found before the genuine one was produced. In each other's light they were all dark, but each one showed some glow in the light of the true stone. If I want to understand anything in Elgar's music to which I find myself recalcitrant, I shall in future stand on *Falstaff* as on a mountain (you will see at once that the equator of a recumbent Falstaff provides an excellent place of observation), and shall trust in what the infinite charity of this work can tell me of Elgar's meaning in other things. This charity extends even to Prince Hal's conversion into Henry the Fifth. So, I believe, did Shakespeare's. It sheds a humorous light on the tub-thumping finale of the beloved 'Enigma' Variations. (By the way, I cannot subscribe to the 'Auld Lang Syne' solution of the enigma: the counterpoint is not nearly good enough; the translation into the minor is like adding 'barks like a dog' to the riddle about the hen-pheasant, 'in order to make it harder'; and any composer designing a counterpoint to the melody would be practically certain to make it fit the bass also.)

A report is now current that Elgar originally ended the Variations quietly, and that this Finale was forced upon Elgar by more experienced friends. If this is true, for Heaven's sake let every effort be made to recover the original Finale. There is always the possibility that Elgar himself may have found it inadequate; and in any case the present Finale has enough humour to entrap the humourless. I fell badly into the trap myself when I first heard its solemn organstrains with their facile descent into prestissimo semibreves. But we do want to know how Elgar rounded off the work before he was induced to put a brass hat on to it instead.

Meantime, let us be thankful that popular and official recognition had the sense to recognize in Elgar a master, in spite of our inveterate prejudice against everybody who does not profess and call himself an amateur.

DOHNÁNYI'S CHAMBER MUSIC[1]

DOHNÁNYI showed proclivities for the writing of chamber music in his earliest days (*vide* Grove). In his compositions we have art in which the form arises organically from the matter. We also have mastery, describable in academic terms and traceable beyond anything that academies have codified. Fortunately, there is no need for Dohnányi to justify himself to the critics of the future by writing feeble passages to show his modernity, for he is a musical administrator as well as a composer, and the contemporary composer, whatever his tendencies, has no grievance against either the programmes or the performances of the Philharmonic Orchestra of Budapest as directed by Dohnányi.

Meanwhile, Dohnányi's own work shapes itself without interference or inhibition from external pressures. The things that have influenced it are such as make for the freedom that comes from mastery, though this does not mean that Dohnányi has been influenced only by perfect works of art. Mastery in the sonata forms and style is nowadays attributed automatically to the influence of Brahms, and Dohnányi unquestionably owes much to his intimate knowledge of Brahms's works and also to some considerable acquaintance with Brahms himself. Passages in Dohnányi's ripest works can still be traced to an origin in Brahms. For instance, it is impossible to know the 'augmented' return of the theme in the first movement of Brahms's Fourth Symphony and fail to recognize it in principle and dramatic effect when we meet the device in Dohnányi's Violin Sonata, op. 21. It is the influence of a master on a later master, and such influences operate with complete disregard for common notions as to the nature and obligations of originality.

But the influence of Brahms is neither in form nor in style the dominating feature in Dohnányi's work. The preface to the Philharmonia miniature score of his First String Quartet in A major, op. 7, describes the first movement as of classical perfection in form, and the whole as modelled on Brahms in themes and part-writing. This is an acceptable criticism, but it needs adjusting to the fact that when Brahms's way of moving was anything like as easy-going as that of the first movement of Dohnányi's A major

---

[1] An article contributed to Cobbett's *Cyclopedic Survey of Chamber Music* (Oxford University Press), 1929.

Quartet, it was also more reckless of consequences. Dohnányi's music, even in his early works, shuns boredom absolutely; and the easy fluency of the first movement of the quartet owes more to this instinct than to any classical models. In later works the fluency is developed into a distinct type of movement more akin to the music-drama or symphonic poem than to the older sonata styles, but here, with all its mastery, it is little more than typical youthful ease within limits approved by orthodoxy.

Dohnányi's eight published chamber works may be conveniently discussed in chronological order without classification. The Quintet for piano and strings, op. 1, need not detain us long. Noble though it is in themes, it probably owes much of the impression it early made to the fact of the composer's taking the piano part at the early performances on, or shortly after, his début as one of the greatest of pianists. In itself the work is not much more than a conservatorium prize-winner of its period; and its scoring is less enterprising than its forms. An experienced listener, unbiased by the playing of the composer, might perhaps suspect that there was something unusual in the freedom from bathos in the otherwise youthful style. And so we may be wise after the event, but the detached judgement is more likely to be that the first quintet, op. 1, is what the Germans would call *eine brave Musik*; a well-behaved composition, perhaps not better than the sextet produced at the same time (mentioned in some works of reference but never published).

THE SONATA IN B FLAT MINOR, op. 8, for piano and violoncello, is an important work. The first movement is the most weighty and majestic, and its themes are well able to support their Brahmsian treatment. A lively scherzo in G minor, with a quiet trio in E flat, shows that the intention of the work is not tragic, and in the variation theme of the finale we already encounter the wit which becomes one of the prominent characteristics of Dohnányi's developed style. The notion of using the themes of the other movements, neither as apparitions breaking in upon the finale nor as rhetorical allusions at its climax, but as integral figures in a regular set of variations, is adopted by Dohnányi from Brahms's String Quartet in B flat, and is here enthusiastically developed with more ease and less cogency than similar devices in later works.

THE QUARTET IN A MAJOR, op. 7, the first movement of which has already been mentioned, has many interesting features of form. Its second movement applies the variation form to the purpose of a scherzo (in this case with a well-defined trio) in a way which Dohnányi develops in two later works. Details remind one super-ficially of the second movement of Brahms's C minor Trio, but the form, with its burden in the tonic major, is quite new. The only other external influence on the style is the Haydnesque breaking up of the burden by measured pauses at the end, a joke rather too elementary for the style of the whole work, and certainly not trace-able to Brahms. The sombre slow movement is the ripest, though not perhaps the most attractive, part of the work. No page of the quartet could have been written by anybody but a consummate contrapuntist; in the first movement the inversion of the first theme forms the bass of two of the most striking passages, and the prin-cipal return of the main theme of the slow movement is given to the bass with powerful effect.

The finale is amusing, but is one of those youthful diversions in which no liveliness of tempo can avail to bring the pace above an imperturbable amble. At first this seems humorous and inten-tional, especially when the first episode (C sharp minor, the Finale being in A minor) enters as a quite separate section drawling canonically over drone-chords and frankly rejoicing in its laziness. Apart from the question whether the humour, like the Haydnesque joke at the end of the second movement, is on the same plane as the general style, doubts arise as to the composer's intentions when the main theme (a Hungarian minor scale descending from E to E with an augmented second in both tetrachords) is later on de-veloped in a fugato with a four-bar rhythm as rigid as any dance-music. Interest and surprise are present to the last, but the art of movement is lacking. Much may be learnt by comparing this finale with that of Dohnányi's later chamber works, the Quartet in A minor (written in 1926), where we seem to have the mature and energetic expression of the high spirits which fail to find an outlet in the earlier work.

THE SERENADE IN C MAJOR, for string trio, op. 10, while appar-ently a much slighter work, makes a great advance towards the attainment of Dohnányi's later style. Dvořák's little Terzetto for two violins and viola may or may not have been in Dohnányi's mind, but the comparison between the two works is instructive. In both cases the composer might have sat down to write the first movement with nothing particular in his head, getting inspiration in due course from the pleasure of handling the delicate instru-mental medium. The important movement in Dvořák's Terzetto

is the finale, where inspiration arrives in a set of variations on a
single epigrammatic musical sentence with unsymmetrical rhythm
and recondite harmonies. Here, and nowhere else, we may find a
prototype of Dohnányi's variation themes as exemplified in the
beautiful fourth movement of this serenade. But Dohnányi's wit
and technique are too resourceful to keep him waiting for inspiration until a fourth movement. The opening march soon proves
dramatic as well as witty, and provides the first example of the kind
of short cut which becomes so important a characteristic of Dohnányi's later forms, and which enables him to weld whole sonatas
into a unity like that of a symphonic poem without loss of the
terseness of true sonata style, and without any feeling that material
is lacking for the later movements when they draw upon themes
already employed. Nobody would believe *a priori* that a march
could adequately represent a da capo after a trio by three meditative murmurs of its first bar followed by a figure like a sneeze; but
such is the end of the first movement of this serenade; and the
finale, after a vigorous career as a fully developed rondo, ends by
bursting into the trio of the march. This dies away, and the work
closes with the same figure as the march, without alluding to
the first theme. To the learned musician the humour is accen-
tuated by the fact that Dohnányi is here following the precedent
of the classical serenades and cassations which began and ended
with a march (*vide* Beethoven's String Trio, op. 8). Each movement of this serenade has some point of form or style peculiar to
Dohnányi's mature works. The second movement, entitled 'Ro-
manza', ends on the dominant with an effect akin to that of the
Mixolydian mode and also to the tendencies of much recent Spanish
music (*vide* Granados, the *Goyescas, passim*; Mixolydian for major
keys, and Phrygian for minor). The third movement is a scherzo
in fugue style, in which a trio-like theme is eventually combined
with the first theme in double fugue. The key is D minor, which
follows dramatically upon the Mixolydian close of the F major
Romance and, ending in D major, makes the only deviation in all
Dohnányi's works from the key-system of classical models. This
deviation arises quite naturally and is in artistic harmony with the
ostensibly irresponsible style of the whole. From D major the G
minor of the beautiful theme and variations follows inevitably.
This movement is the most serious and romantic part of the work.
Ending in G major, it is an admirable antecedent to the prosaically
witty rondo-finale, with its theme plunging into C via D minor,

x

its mocking vein, and its indignant end with the trio of the opening march.

A student of the relation between musical form and dramatic expression could hardly fail to see in this serenade clear signs that Dohnányi was not only an inveterate comedian but an artist with a genuine gift for operatic writing; he has, in fact, composed three operas and a pantomime. It is not altogether agreeable to the orthodoxies of criticism to note the dramatic vein in his instrumental works; for the usual way to recognize a composer's ability to write operas is by discovering his inability to do anything else. And Dohnányi's chamber music is without flaw in the purity of its style and the complete freedom from anything dependent on stage conditions for its effect. But, just as the theme of the slow movement of Brahms's A major Quartet shows rhythms that could only have been invented by masters of the musical treatment of words, so the forms and devices of Dohnányi's chamber music, from the Serenade onwards, have a Mozart-like perception of what is and what is not adequate to produce intelligible form with rapid movement, a perception which betokens a composer who can handle stage-drama with a fastidious perfection of musical form. This is not necessarily connected with staginess of style, as Mozart demonstrated once for all. The power to move at any and every pace from point to point of the plot is essential to both drama and pure music. Sonata forms themselves arose from those of music-drama, and a sonata style that is not essentially dramatic is nothing. On the other hand, the sonata has its own rate of movement, which is not that of the drama. Its forms are based on two principles: first, its rate of movement, and secondly, its exposition of key-relations in sharp contrasts on a large scale. Why Bruckner and Reger should have encumbered themselves with these forms is a mystery which must remain unsolved, seeing that they were really suited to neither composer. Dohnányi's rhetorical power, and his mastery of texture on certain schematic but elaborate lines, make it indifferent what forms he uses, so long as he keeps himself and us interested; but the interest is neither dramatic nor formal. Dohnányi, with far greater variety of form, is incomparably nearer to classical foundations. In his mature work there is no stroke of form without its dramatic value, and no stroke of drama that does not serve to complete the form. The question of tonality is intimately connected with that of movement, and from the outset Dohnányi's sense of tonality is classical on other than conventional grounds. A mere list of the key-relations in the First String Quartet shows that his power of modulation is not likely to be frittered away in the facile exercise of musical wit. The first movement, in A major, has F sharp (minor and major) for the complementary key. The second movement has C sharp minor plus major (D flat) for its main theme, and A major plus F sharp minor-major for its trio. After the close in D flat the slow movement follows in F minor, alias E sharp. These three movements transposed a semitone higher would give the series of rising major thirds (B flat, D, F sharp) to be completed in an enharmonic circle by the finale. After the chord of F minor, try the effect of the Hungarian-Phrygian descending scale E, D sharp, C, B, A, G sharp, F, E; and it will be seen how vigorously Dohnányi takes up the line of thought marked by Haydn, Beethoven, and Brahms when they place in juxtaposition movements in widely distant keys. The episodes in C sharp minor (afterwards recapitulated in F sharp minor) and F major complete the symmetry of the whole previous set of key-relations.

THE SECOND STRING QUARTET IN D FLAT, op. 18, reveals the full power of Dohnányi's art, and, amongst other things, the attainment of an artistic fusion of what may be called Wagnerian or symphonic-poem movement with the essentials of sonata style. The first movement combines a slow introductory phrase with a quick tempo. This is not more than has been done by Beethoven (Sonata, op. 31, no. 2, Quartets in E flat, op. 127, and in B flat, op. 130, to say nothing of the first movement of the Sonata, op. 109), but what is new, as well as brilliantly successful, is the organization of vast spaces of development at full speed with the slow theme running through them. Many composers have tried this and have simply failed to notice that the tempo has merely become a matter of notation, and that what is heard is merely the original slow tempo accompanied by vibration, which achieves fussiness without movement; whereas, instead of this nightmare paralysis, Dohnányi achieves Wagnerian movement together with the swift dramatic action of sonata style. As we listen to these mature works we are aware from the outset that large processes are developing at leisure, and it is difficult to believe that the whole scheme is completed in less than half an hour. The Bruckner-Wagner qualities are there, though Bruckner could hardly express himself in less than an hour; the sonata qualities are there also, except for some sacrifice of the old swiftness of movement. The scherzo of the D flat Quartet moves only as does the storm in *Die Walküre*, driving rain beating incessantly on the same spot. Yet the sacrifice of classical movement has positive results and differs widely from the stagnation of our modern Rossinians. The real movement is latent, as in Greek choruses; and it is only necessary to note the effect of the Phrygian end of that scherzo (on the dominant of F minor) followed by the chord of C sharp minor on the beginning of a molto adagio, to see that the action of this music has that intensely and maturely dramatic quality by which a situation prepared for generations explodes in a moment into an inevitable catastrophe.

The finale is the adagio in C sharp minor, which gathers up the themes of the scherzo and first movement, working them first into its own tempo, which finally approaches that of the introduction to the first movement. Thereupon it settles on the chord of D flat major, and builds up a climax and decline for over forty bars all on the opening theme, with which the first violin dies away (on the unresolved sixth).

THE VIOLIN SONATA IN C SHARP MINOR, op. 21, is a work in a similar vein of romantic pathos, with a quiet first movement more nearly on the lines of Brahms, as has already been shown in regard to the 'augmented' return of the main theme. Yet this very detail is worked out in such a connexion with the end of the development as to produce the Bruckner-Wagner movement typical of Dohnányi's maturer works. The second movement, which follows without break, is one of Dohnányi's variation-scherzos, and it works in a longish episode on the 'second subject' of the first movement, which is made to behave partly like a variation and partly like a trio. The finale bursts out as soon as the scherzo has died away. Beginning with the motto-figure of the first movement (C sharp, D sharp, E) in shrill chords, it transforms the rest of that theme into an agitated strain, somewhat as Liszt turned the whole first movement of his 'Faust' Symphony into a Mephistophelian scherzo; but this is not rigorously carried out. On the contrary, this finale develops on its own lines, not unlike a free scherzo with a quiet trio (A major) and a return in a foreign key with modulations. As soon as the tonic (C sharp minor) is reached the music settles on a long dominant pedal and, after a great climax, returns to the tempo and opening of the first movement, bringing the work to a romantically pathetic close.

THE SECOND QUINTET IN E FLAT MINOR. With mature masterpieces a class-list in order of merit is the most futile impertinence, but this is certainly the most immediately impressive of Dohnányi's works, even if we include his orchestral music.

Here we have, even more unmistakably than in the D flat Quartet, the perfect fusion of sonata style with Bruckner-Wagner movement, and a finale that gathers up the threads of the first movement with an effect of normality not before attained. For this normality is quite different from that achievable by a style which is a mosaic of short epigrams, as in Schumann's Fourth Symphony; and an impassable gulf separates it from the worldly wisdom of Saint-Saëns.

Dohnányi's mastery of the severest forms of counterpoint has an intimate connexion with the art which rounds off the whole design in little over twenty minutes, while seeming to go through vast cosmic processes from the outset. The enemy would blaspheme at a list of the contrapuntal devices in this work, and would say *a priori* that such a tissue of inversions and diminutions and augmentations and combinations was as incompatible with poetic inspiration as the construction of a triple acrostic in palindromes. He would also say the same of Bach's B minor Mass. And Metastasio 'expiring in a canzona' is not a greater 'formalist' than Bach, blind and on his death-bed, dictating *Vor deinen Thron tret ich hiemit* in four-part chorale-fugue by inversion.

Elaborate contrapuntal devices are to music as argumentative dialogue is to drama. The writer who still thinks such things clever will dissipate his action in his proud pursuit of them. The writer whose command of them is supreme will find in them a powerful means of concentrating his action, as Beethoven came to do, though his mastery of counterpoint was by no means supreme. He did not, however, think these things clever, but he grasped their purport and found them necessary. Dohnányi, who could at any time have amused himself with the most outrageous contrapuntal talks, produces in his Second Quintet a counterpoint in which every combination is a masterpiece of tone-colour, and every masterpiece of tone-colour is the result of fine counterpoint. This is the relation between form and drama in another category.

The tone of the whole work is very sombre, only the delicious scherzo-variations affording relief to the prevailing solemnity. The finale is almost entirely in fugue, beginning slowly with the strings alone until the piano enters with a chorale-tune which must have brought the spirit of Bruckner from his communings with Wagner in Walhalla to bless Dohnányi for bringing his grandest ideas into relation with human time as well as Wotanesque eternity.

As in all Dohnányi's works, the scoring is rich and yet economical. It conveys the ideas in the fewest notes with the finest sounds and the most practical technique. So long as it conveys ideas, no scoring will be popularly regarded as brilliant. A great Russian composer has classified orchestration as (*a*) that which sounds well with competent sight-reading, and wonderful after proper practice; (*b*) that which does not sound well until it has been adequately practised; and (*c*) that which does not sound well under any circumstances. This classification makes no allowance for ideas, and provides for nothing more than the culinary department of musical art. Certainly Dohnányi's scoring is not fool-proof enough for that Russian first class, unless competent sight-reading is held to include an instantaneous grasp of the composer's idea on the part of every player. Very few great ensemble works will sound well throughout with even the best of sight-reading. The highest type of great instrumentation is that which requires much practice, but which sounds wonderful as soon as it begins to sound well.

THE THIRD STRING QUARTET in three movements, in A minor, is a large work, but less serious than the D flat Quartet. The impassioned first movement has a temper that averts tragedy by letting off steam in a long, runaway coda. The middle movement is a lovely set of variations, and the direction 'andante religioso' is rather a warning not to play too fast than a claim to any such solemnity as that of the E flat minor Quintet. The finale is in high if satiric spirits. In the first movement some notable concessions are made to recent tendencies in harmony, chiefly by way of obstinate clinging to one key by some voices after the others have gone the opposite way.

Three operas and a pantomime are what it is hardly slang to call 'a good alibi' for having produced no more than eight pieces of chamber music. Nothing is more necessary in an age of artistic experiment than that composers should test the objective reality of their ideas by writing operas. Verdi produced *Falstaff* when he was in his eightieth year. If Dohnányi will continue to that age producing chamber music and operas in the present ratio of eight to three, there will be no excuse for complaining of the exhaustion of the higher artistic resources in modern music, 'absolute' or illustrative.

THE 'LEAN ATHLETIC STYLE' OF HINDEMITH[1]

APROPOS of the Violin Concerto and the second Pianoforte Sonata which are about to be broadcast, I have been invited to contribute to *The Listener* something like a general estimate of Hindemith's work. My chief qualifications for the task are two: one, the general qualification that I have no ambition to determine any living composer's place in history, as seen in any future, near or remote; and the other, the personal qualification that I have met Hindemith and played with him both in his own works and in the classics. I cannot guess, and nobody can guess for me, whether this personal privilege has made any essential difference to my attitude towards his music. My own impression is that I had formed my opinion as to its essential healthiness and vitality before I met him, and that our meeting only hastened, though greatly, my readiness to believe in the importance and justification of his compositions. It is not irrelevant here to remark that he worries no more about posterity than I do, nor more about present popularity. He simply wants to get on with his work, and to keep in practice. He plays classical music like an angel and takes for granted the highest possible standard of technical achievement.

A few years ago I conducted a performance of a piece he calls *Kammermusik No. 1*, and wrote programme notes on it which now conclude Volume IV of my collected *Essays in Musical Analysis*. Space is not available here for quoting my statements about Hindemith's special theories, though this would save me much trouble. But for the reader (that is to say for the listener) the best advice is, at most, like that of the steward of the Clyde steamer who said to the passenger who wanted help in descending the saloon stairs, 'Leggo yer han's and yer feet and ye'll come doon by yersel'. To that end let me quote just this from my published essay. 'I know what I like, and I know what bores me; and I am at present quite satisfied to know that I like Hindemith and that he does not bore me. As far as I can judge, his music does not bore many people, though it annoys some. He is never very long, he thumps no tubs, and he makes the best of modern life. Professor Saintsbury retained to his last days a hospitable mind, but among tendencies in modern

[1] From *The Listener* of 30 December 1936.

art he drew the line firmly at two things. One of these he called "bad blood", and the other "rotting". Both are as impossible to Hindemith as to an athlete. His music is at least as serious as a game, and that is something far more serious than anything that can put on solemnity as a garment.'

Most modern pianoforte music is far too unreadable for any player to derive pleasure from it except after many hours of careful technical practice; but for pages together the technique of Hindemith's Sonata No. 2 is, apart from what is paradoxical to the ear and therefore unfamiliar to the fingers, not more difficult than that of sonatinas for young players, and the unprejudiced listener, if his own playing is equal to that, can hardly introduce himself to Hindemith with better prospect of understanding (one might almost say mutual understanding) than by trying to play this sonata first before he listens to an adequate rendering of it. One of the main principles of Hindemith's art is that there shall never be an unnecessary note in the harmony. Every note shall be as directly essential to the idea as in Bach's strictest polyphony. This neo-classicism goes far beyond Bach in its severity, for, except in music for the clavichord and for the unaccompanied violin and violoncello, none of Bach's music consists only in the written notes. The octave-registers of the organ and the harpsichord often multiply the written sounds by three, and the Greek aristocracy of the fully written parts of Bach's orchestral and chamber music relies upon the slave-system of the continuo—the figured bass filled out on a keyboard instrument by a a player who left no empty spaces unless he was told by the director to play only the bass.

It is really with Mozart and Haydn that the 'lean athletic style' begins, and their dummy accompaniments are the devices by which the orchestra and the interior harmony provide their own domestic service. Hindemith does not approve of dummy accompaniments in his own work, and he surprised me by the severity with which he regarded some quite light musical equivalents to an engraver's cross-hatching in one of his early violin sonatas, which he would have preferred to replace by something more like line-drawing. But he is no pedant. Even romanticism, driven out with a polytonal pitchfork, comes back—but not as an 'ism', for the true romance is nature lurking round the corner.

The Second Sonata consists of four movements (or three and an introduction to the Finale), all in classical forms easily traceable if you find (as I do not) that the naming of forms is the shortest way towards the enjoyment of music. The form of the first movement (Moderately fast—why set forth the original German tempo as if it were a technical term?) is quite orthodox as to exposition of two groups of themes, with development, recapitulation, and coda; and perhaps this information may help some listeners to enjoy a work of which the harmonic language does not remain within classical orthodoxy for a single line. But, like Walther's singing in *Die Meistersinger*, it steps firmly and unerringly in its own path. The second movement (Lively) is a very short scherzo. The third movement consists of an introduction (Very slow) to a Rondo (With movement, *bewegt*) which, as its title implies, consists of a recurring theme alternating with episodes. Hindemith is the converse of Dr. Johnson's naïve friend, Edwards, whose efforts at philosophy were frustrated by the irruption of cheerfulness. Nothing frustrates Hindemith's cheerfulness; but romance in its truthful form of beauty may break in at any moment, as for instance when this Rondo, on its last page, indulges in comfortably fat chords, repeating its main theme in several clear and separate keys, slackening back to the tempo of the introduction, and ending quite solemnly. Let me urgently repeat my advice to every listener who can play the pianoforte for his own pleasure to see what he can make of this sonata with his own pair of hands.

For the Violin Concerto no such advice can be given. The violinist is inside the work; and if anyone thinks he can read the score to himself in an arm-chair, he is either deceiving himself or being wise after the event. So my advice is metaphorically that of the steward of the Clyde steamer. I have not yet heard this violin concerto, and my shortest way to know it would be to conduct it. Without that I can, from an examination of the score, assure you that every bar is evidently the work of a master who imagines precisely the sound of every note he writes; though for me the trouble of assembling such unfamiliar sounds outweighs the pleasure of reading them in the score. Listening and performing are other matters, and for very experienced score-readers, but for no others, the pleasure of listening may be enhanced by following from the score.

The listener will gain nothing by thinking of other violin concertos. The prominence of the solo violin is here secured by the fact that there are no violins in the orchestra. The string section consists of four violas, four violoncellos, and four double-basses. The wind band is utterly unlike any classical group. It consists of two piccolos, an E flat clarinet (the squeaky treble of military bands), a B flat clarinet (the classical instrument), a bass clarinet, two bassoons, a contrafagotto, a cornet-à-pistons, a trombone, and a bass tuba. The percussion consists of four tambourines without jingles, of a kind sometimes found in jazz bands. They are of different sizes so as to give sounds of different though not definitely musical pitch.

The movements are numbered I to V, but are in effect three. The first movement is entitled 'Signal' and is a dramatic introduction ('Broad majestic minims') marching with a steadiness which the increasing excitement of the cornet cannot hurry, to the eventual entry of the solo violin, who dominates the second movement (Very lively) throughout a wild atonal career which is lacking neither in romance nor in quotable themes. The third movement is entitled *Nachtstück* (i.e. Serenade). Its tempo is 'Moderately fast quavers', which, as there are twelve in a bar, means a slow movement. In such a tempo, beauty always intrudes upon Hindemith's severity without compromising his atonality or polytonality (or whatever else you may call his language). The fourth movement strides in 'Lively crotchets' at three a bar, setting out with a sturdy theme for the cornet which is developed for several lines before the violin takes it up. Twice the violin has a strange kind of cadenza accompanied only by the jazz-drums and a few groans from the tuba. In the second cadenza the violin is muted and the tuba is silent. Suddenly the violin breaks into perpetual motion in alla breve time, two in a bar, and ends the concerto in what is numbered as a fifth movement (V: 'As fast as possible'). Except for a few momentary explosions this *perpetuum mobile* is pianissimo throughout. The piccolo has an excellent tune which it plays from time to time in rather erratic keys, and at one point the pizzicato strings provide a waltz accompaniment across the duple time. Schumann began two of his finales *So rasch wie möglich* and then twice (in each case) ordained *Noch schneller*. Hindemith is more reasonable; he asks only that the final running out of this humorous and naughtily picturesque work should be *Wenn möglich noch schneller*. And perhaps the passages lie more smoothly and so can be played faster. Anyhow, all reasonable players who are not shocked by a non-classical language delight in the magnificent adequacy, for its purposes, of every note that Hindemith writes.

PREFACES TO CADENZAS FOR CLASSICAL CONCERTOS

[Sir Donald Tovey was a player and composer of cadenzas for classical concertos. In 1937, the Oxford University Press published three such cadenzas, and more were projected. To each he wrote a preface, and the three prefaces printed here give, both generally and particularly, his considered views on the whole subject of extemporization.—EDITOR.]

(a) TO THE CADENZA FOR BEETHOVEN'S FOURTH PIANO CONCERTO
(OP. 58, IN G MAJOR)

MY efforts at written cadenzas to classical concertos may be less productive of misunderstandings if I supply some explanation of the principles on which I have written them. The ideal classical cadenza would be an actual extemporization by a player capable of using the composer's language and above the temptation to display anything so banal as 'a review of the progress of music since the composer's date'. Nowadays organists are the only musicians who have occasion to develop their powers of extemporization; and the average modern composer is far too preoccupied with the invention of abstruse harmonic styles to practise extemporization at all. Even that pioneer harmonist who sought in vain to recover the Lost Chord was, on her own confession, doing no more than let her fingers wander idly over the noisy keys. This is not what Beethoven understood by extemporizing: he said that no artist deserved the title of 'virtuoso' unless his extemporizations could pass for written compositions.

On the other hand, there is much truth in the view that all great art seems as if it were extemporized. And as long as the conditions of performance convince us that music is actually being extemporized, we make more allowances than we are aware of. When we merely hear a record, or a broadcast, we become far less tolerant of pauses and stretches of 'er . . . er . . .'; and we begin to scoff at the camouflage with which the instrumental player translates these into brilliant arpeggios and scales. A natural hesitation may be one of the highest achievements of rhetorical art; but it needs extremely

315

accurate timing. The immense labour shown in Beethoven's innumerable sketches for all manner of works, from the greatest to the slightest, is mainly devoted to giving the written work the rhetorical perfection of an extemporization. For the process of writing music is so slow that it tends, far more than the writing of words, to inhibit the virtues of an extemporaneous style.

The natural defect of extemporized music is that the extemporizer's memory is unequal to the task of achieving the architectural symmetries which great music habitually produces by actual recapitulation on a large scale. A knack of remembering a few pregnant phrases may achieve something astonishingly like recapitulation; and, conversely, few people would guess that when Mozart, in *Die Zauberflöte*, shows us a fairy-tale prince falling in love with the portrait of the fairy-tale princess, Tamino's aria recapitulates nothing whatever except a cliché which differs from other clichés only in being the right thing in the right place. But nothing is more fatally easy than to extemporize large architectural symmetries on paper, with your first statements safely recorded and at hand for copying. The consequences of this and of other material circumstances in the writing of music are that the typical defects of extemporaneously written music are far less tolerable than those of unwritten extemporization. By all accounts, Beethoven's actual extemporizations, which he could extend to as much as an hour, were overwhelmingly impressive, and probably owed but little of their impressiveness to the trivial detail reported in the statement that Beethoven extemporized passages far more difficult than any that he published. A faithful record of his extemporizations would probably seem to us, and to Beethoven himself, both empty and wild, with frequent fine ideas already better expressed elsewhere. But it would certainly be incomparably better than the written cadenzas which Beethoven extemporized on paper. Only one of these is great, the biggest of the three cadenzas to the first movement of the C major Concerto, op. 15, which I have described in my analysis of that work (*Essays in Musical Analysis*, Vol. III, p. 67). This cadenza raises to the level of the *Waldstein* Sonata the whole of a beautiful but loosely built early work, greatly underrated by Beethoven himself. Another cadenza attempted to gather up loose threads, but Beethoven evidently found that this was a hopeless task, which could only introduce mechanical stiffness into what had at all events a natural exuberance and flow. So, for once, he achieved on paper a grandly improvisatorial peroration which by

sheer contrast made the rest of the work seem a close-knit argument. I should never dream of writing another cadenza to Beethoven's C major Concerto.

The Concerto in B flat, op. 19, published as the second pianoforte concerto, is really earlier than op. 15. Though the first movement is full of pretty things, its looseness is past praying for. The
rest of the concerto is excellent early Beethoven, and an attitude
of contempt towards the whole work is no sign of more than
commonplace critical sense. But one of the most amusing minor
details in the growth of Beethoven's style is the downright ill-
tempered fugal cadenza with which, some years later, he kicked its
first movement downstairs. As the great cadenza to op. 15 is too
sublime for my competition, so this cadenza to op. 19 is too good
a joke. No wonder the orchestra seems so frightened by it as to
close with only six mild bars of the long-forgotten ritornello.

The C minor Concerto, which Beethoven valued so highly as to
sacrifice to it the reputation of his first two before publication of
any of the three, is ill-served by the perfunctory and dry cadenza
Beethoven afterwards wrote for it. He can never have extemporized as feebly as that; and even if he ever did, the mere spectacle of
the composer in the act of extemporizing would lull the listener's
critical faculty. Nowadays the listener could recover more easily
from the most absurd anachronisms than from Beethoven's own
authentic failures either to record an extemporization or to construct
a coda in the place of a cadenza.

Of Beethoven's cadenzas to the G major Concerto, one set is
tolerable and, when played by Schnabel, almost convincing. The
other, inscribed by Beethoven with the pun, *Cadenza per non cadere*,
is far sillier than the pun. Early in this century an excellent player
made her début in Berlin with the G major Concerto and played
this cadenza. I have always felt sorry for the critic who had to live
down years of derision because he said her cadenzas were ' downright unmusical'. His judgement was better than his information.

The written cadenza to the E flat Concerto is, of course, an
integral part of the composition. It is not, as often described,
accompanied by the orchestra; for the actual cadenza is only
eleven bars of purely cadential flourish, and the pianoforte has
already settled down to a recapitulation of the last two-thirds of the
orchestral ritornello eight bars before the orchestra begins to take
part in it.

The queerest of all cadenzas is the fantasia for pianoforte and kettledrums which Beethoven wrote for his arrangement of his Violin Concerto for pianoforte. From it I have been unable to learn anything definite. The arrangement of the whole concerto is not without significant points, but these can be appreciated only in private study; and public performances reveal nothing but ineptitudes.

As with other inconvenient survivals in classical art-forms, there are cogent reasons which impelled great composers to tolerate the extemporized cadenza in concertos. There is no more voluminous single design in classical music than the first movement of a concerto. Not even the first movement of the 'Eroica' Symphony is both longer and more close-knit than movements like the first movements of Mozart's longest concertos. Such movements need great symphonic codas. Now, how is a symphonic climax to be achieved by a combination of a solo part which must dominate, with an orchestra which cannot rise to a climax without drowning the solo? Obviously, the orator must perorate, and the orchestra must remain in spell-bound silence because the peroration is or seems to be extempore. In the days of Mozart and Beethoven the concerto was usually played by the composer and the extempore cadenza automatically solved the problem of the coda. With Mozart the codas of the greatest symphonic first movements do not go far afield, and his concertos do not need longer cadenzas than those in the collection he provided for many of them, sometimes with several alternatives.

Brahms's cadenzas have been published posthumously. It is unlikely that he would have consented to their publication, for they are early efforts and not quite mature. But they show that his ruthlessness in destroying every unpublished work of his that he thought immature has deprived us of much that was beautiful, and probably of things that would have enlarged our notions of his range of thought.

Clara Schumann's cadenzas to Beethoven's G major Concerto will always command the affection of every musician who came into contact with her or her pupils, and may well inspire affection in others; none the less for the slightly feverish Schumannesque warmth that pervades the harmonies.

With Beethoven's Third and Fourth Pianoforte Concertos and his Violin Concerto, the written cadenzas to the first movement should cover as nearly as possible the ground of his largest symphonic codas. As has been already pointed out, there is no impassable gulf between the style of such codas and the style of an improvisation. But a written cadenza must bear analysis, and many things that may be forgiven or remain unsuspected in an actual improvisation will be inadmissible in such a fixed record, for precisely the reasons that they would be inadmissible in a symphonic coda. For example, few cadenza-writers and few cadenza-players can resist the temptation to quote exactly and extensively those purple patches that the composer does not want to be quoted again. The dreamy passage in B flat by which Beethoven effects the transition to his second group in the G major Concerto, looms so large in the imagination of most players that it is very apt to become an obsession in the cadenza. But Beethoven's own attitude towards it shows that even when he reproduces its colouring by a corresponding dream in E flat in the recapitulation he carefully forgets its melody. In both contexts its function is active and transitional, and it is quite out of place in a coda. On the other hand, the development section of a classical concerto tends to have the character of an episode, and as such its features are almost predestined to reappear in the coda. The player is in some danger of betraying that he knows only his own part in these quasi-episodic features, if he remembers them at all. There is also the opposite but less serious danger that in combining their orchestral with their solo features the player may violate the style of his instrument. But this is a venial sin; and, generally speaking, there is not the slightest harm in allowing a cadenza to exceed the technical limits of the rest of the concerto; indeed, this was expected in classical times. What is not permissible is such a display as will make the rest of the work sound thin: otherwise there is no harm in things that can be shown to be anachronisms, such as my mildly Thalbergian pedal effects, or the very advanced technique of Joachim's perfect cadenzas to Mozart's Violin Concertos in D (K. 218) and A (K. 219).

There is no limit to the range of key in Beethoven's larger symphonic codas, but there are inexorable conditions for the direction and distribution of the modulations. The wider they are, the more cogently must they converge on to the home tonic. The archetype of bold modulation in a peroration is shown in the coda of the first movement of the 'Eroica' Symphony. In my cadenzas to the G major Concerto and the Violin Concerto I have begun with strokes of genius externally rather like that at the beginning of the 'Eroica' coda. I am justified in calling them 'strokes of genius' because they are actually Beethoven's. Much as they seem to resemble each other, they are, in origin as well as in results, entirely different. I forbear to give a further analysis of my cadenzas. Some thirty-five years ago I confided the plan of my G major cadenza to a great player whose authority, already high in the year of his untimely death, would have become supreme if he had lived to old age. Though an excellent all-round musician, he lacked the experience of a composer, and was somewhat shocked at the 'undigested recapitulations' implied by my scheme. Tact prevented me from assuring him that, without 'information received', he would never suspect any such features in the result. At that time, and until quite recently, I did in fact always extemporize my cadenzas, including violin cadenzas (played on the pianoforte), a practice which I began at the age of thirteen, and which is none the less a first-rate exercise in composition because of the desirability that it should be restricted by some relevance to a classical composer's style. Whatever objection may be urged against my present efforts, the obvious *a priori* cavil against laboured excess of scholarship will not apply. If one cannot achieve a natural fluency on paper after forty-five years' practice of extemporization, why ascribe the failure to excess of scholarship?

Cadenzas to finales need never be long; and in the Finale to the G major Concerto Beethoven expressly says, "La Cadenza sia corta'. It is an incident in one of Beethoven's greatest codas. To modulate widely in it would be a crime, for Beethoven has already provided his highest light of modulation in the F sharp major passage shortly before the cadenza. I believe my cadenza to be the right length; for I do not think that a mere flourish would be adequate; and the middle of the movement provides excellent cadential material for pulling the coda together. The intention of my last two chords is, of course, to provide a question for the horns to answer when the orchestra re-enters. Accordingly, strict time is essential here. Generally speaking, the players of written cadenzas are apt to become unintelligible from excessive rubato. This comes, paradoxically, from lack of practice in extemporization. The experienced *improvisatore* in any art is at special pains to satisfy Beethoven's demand that extemporizations should seem passable as written compositions; and a reasonably strict time is one of the first conditions of such an illusion.

My cadenzas will not have failed in their object if they stimulate players who most dislike them to develop the art of extemporizing.

The possibilities of cadenzas to Beethoven's Violin Concerto are incalculable: and the whole work is, like all violin concertos, less liable to damage from incongruous cadenzas than any pianoforte concerto. Violinists, even if the technique of Paganini were equal to a really extemporized unaccompanied violin music on a symphonic scale, cannot, either in extemporization or in written music, keep themselves afloat very long without the support of the orchestra; and a long violin cadenza detaches itself so obviously from its surroundings that the worst conflicts of style cannot detach it much more.

In practical matters of art, historical scholarship is far more in need of severe restraint by aesthetic sensibility than vice versa; and if we are to worry about it in the matter of cadenzas, we may as well revive the practice of playing the first movement of a concerto in the first part of a four-hour programme, and the other two movements in the second part; taking reverential care, in the case of Beethoven's Violin Concerto, to include among the intervening items the violinist Clement's Sonata on One String with the Violin Reversed. Similarly, as I have remarked elsewhere, scholarly performances of Bach's Church Cantatas should end with the thrashing of the leaders of the choir.

From Beethoven's queer arrangement of his Violin Concerto for pianoforte we can learn a few interesting details as to what he might have written, or did actually sketch, when unrestricted by scruples of violin technique. Even apart from the violin these details are aesthetically not improvements, and the dire necessity of providing something for the left hand drives Beethoven to sheer blasphemy against the sublime calm of the Larghetto. And Clement's one-string sonata can hardly have been more topsy-turvy than the pianoforte cadenza that Beethoven wrote under the stimulus of relief from restrictions of violin technique. From it nothing can be learnt, unless it be the speculative possibility that the intrusive little four-square quick march for drums and pianoforte may be a topical allusion to the march in *Fidelio*. An indigestible topicality is a normal stimulus to the making of cadenzas and a normal reason why they prove perishable. By all means let them exist and perish, if they are genuinely extemporized. The beauty of the perishable extemporization is different from anything that can be readily achieved in the permanent record; and, as I have indicated in the introduction to my cadenzas to Beethoven's Fourth Pianoforte Concerto, the conditions of concerto form give cogent reasons for admitting that beauty as a necessary adjunct.

Nevertheless, I cannot resist the temptation to try and write for Beethoven's Violin Concerto cadenzas which will contain as nearly as possible what ought to happen in symphonic works. Joachim's magnificent cadenzas are on written record at all stages of his career. What he played at his début in London at the age of twelve already shows the nobility of his style in the days of his diamond jubilee. From his cadenzas in their middle and penultimate versions I adopt certain recognizable features. It is foolish to avoid what is exactly right, from fear of falling into the obvious. What is exactly right will in most cases be obviously right; but nothing is less obvious than the proverbially world-wide difference between the obvious and the exact truth. (Not that there can be an exact truth in cadenzas unsupplied by the composer.) Joachim's chromatic end to the final trill was always beautiful—his later habit of ending it very slowly and without turns seems to me an over-refinement acceptable only in quasi-extemporization from him in person. This chromatic shake becomes a necessity to me after my device of interpolating a digression to C sharp minor in order that Beethoven may seem to repeat Handel's remark, 'Welcome home', to the violinist whose cadenza had modulated widely. This digression may perhaps shock some musicians; the facts of classical key-relations have not yet found their way into current musical orthodoxy; and modern harmonic theories are, like old ones, too much preoccupied with chords in detail to inculcate either large or clear views of the classical or Wagnerian handling of keys *in extenso*. I believe my digression to be the most Beethovenish feature that I have contributed to the cadenza, and it is exactly proportioned to the epilogue that Beethoven has provided.

By the way, I am decidedly against the reading which, in that epilogue, makes the violoncello answer the theme in the bassoon. The fact that such an answer is in bad counterpoint with the violin is not decisive against it; Beethoven is notoriously insensitive on that point, and, like Shakespeare, Handel, and other great untidy artists, cannot be corrected without danger of injuring the ultimate subtleties of his thoughts. What is decisive against it is that the violin figures are not a counterpoint at all, but are themselves the answer to the theme, and ought never to be disestablished by combination with a more literal answer. Yet the reading is one which cannot be proved spurious. I should be quite satisfied to learn that it found entrance through Beethoven's pianoforte arrangement; in which case I would cheerfully see it (as the Bastable children said) 'buried in obliquity' beside the other blasphemies of that deplorably authentic document.

The other feature which I am conscious of deriving from Joachim is his attack of three-note chords in repeated semiquavers. Persons whose knowledge of violin music is more exhaustive than mine may have encountered this device elsewhere; but in my experience it is unique, and, in fact, I can imagine no other fitting occasion for it. It is obviously out of place in chamber music, and it has no pretty or brilliant effect that could make it popular in displays of 'virtuosity'. But it is uniquely appropriate and effective as an allusion to the first forte of the tutti, and, since Joachim showed the way, I can no more avoid it than Joachim and I could avoid using Beethoven's themes.

The cadenza to the Larghetto need not be more than a single flourish confined to the dominant of D and ending with Beethoven's mysterious grace-note crotchets. But I cannot resist the temptation of providing a basis for alluding to the Larghetto in my cadenza for the Rondo. Had these features been integral parts of Beethoven's composition, the slow movement and finale might have come to be regarded as a single design. The history of criticism might then have escaped the donnish insensibility of D'Indy's strictures on the poverty of Beethoven's key-system in his over-ornate Larghetto; and the gigantic personality that inspires and controls the child-like high spirits of the Rondo might have been always recognized as arch-Beethoven.

Far be it from me to claim that my present efforts can achieve any such result. I can only repeat that, as with my other cadenzas, if I could imagine anything better than what I here present, I should either wait until I had written it or pray for grace to recognize it when I hear or see it produced by someone else.

I claim to have recognized (independently of others unknown to me) the natural meaning of Beethoven's six grace-note crotchets leading to the Rondo. They were certainly as much a mystery to Joachim as to everybody else, for Joachim provided them with a counterpoint in majestic double-stops. This would, I am sure, have delighted Beethoven. But it is no more likely to have occurred to him than Kreisler's ingenious combination of the second-group

theme with the cadence-theme in the first movement; which probably would have delighted Beethoven still more. Yet I am as certain
of the correctness of my construing of those grace notes as the
Tichborne Claimant was certain that *Laus Deo semper* was Greek
for 'the laws of God for ever'. So let me follow Bach's custom of
giving a pious motto to his MSS., and conclude thus:

The pupils of Joachim are not the only music-lovers who will regard his cadenza to Brahms's Violin Concerto as an integral part of the composition; and those friends who know of Joachim's unbounded generosity and kindness to me throughout the last twenty years of his life will think that I am the last person who ought to come forward with a cadenza of my own. But Joachim's own truthfulness is my best example and excuse. Thirty years after his death, I feel, like many other musicians, that the time is ripe for providing violinists and Brahms's Violin Concerto with something that does not depend on Joachim's unique personality to make itself intelligible as a coda to the first movement of that strenuous and symphonic work. The circumstances that impelled Brahms to entrust his cadenza entirely to Joachim were personal and highly pathetic. More than enough has been published about the causes that estranged the friends for many years. The Violin Concerto was Brahms's first step towards reconcilement with the friend who had so powerfully helped him to ripen his early style, and had throughout the time of estrangement continued in unceasing and efficient propaganda for the recognition of his works. No gesture of gratitude could be nobler than the tribute of leaving to Joachim the task of crowning the Violin Concerto with a cadenza. And yet this gesture narrowly escapes being one of the major disasters in the history of a specially dangerous musical art-form. In the first place, Brahms could not issue a prohibition against the use of other cadenzas than Joachim's. Least of all could he nullify his gesture by writing a cadenza himself. I am not aware of any record of his opinion of Joachim's cadenza, and I doubt whether in the circumstances he would have allowed his judgement free play.

Apart from personal matters, Joachim's cadenza goes far to justify Brahms in shirking a problem which only Brahms could have solved, if any perfect solution were possible. Yet I am convinced that Brahms's own solution would have been simpler, clearer, and more perfect than Joachim's. And I am quite certain that if Joachim had encountered his own cadenza as the work of someone else, he would have strongly objected to its obscurity. He himself spoke to me of one of its passages as 'disagreeable', and explained this as a playful mimicry of Brahms's querulous voice when raised in argument. The explanation is delightful as between private friends, but the passage does not explain itself. Unexplained, such intimacies have no more place in permanent music than the cryptic allusions to trivial events in the love-letters of Robert Browning and Elizabeth Barrett have in literature.

On general principles, Joachim's cadenza has the serious technical defect of presenting without a bass certain themes which cannot stand unsupported. One of these themes, the figure of ninths near the end of the development, gives rise to the 'disagreeable' passage which Joachim explained to me: and I cannot find any means of making it intelligible in unaccompanied violin-writing at all. The other is, of course, the plaintively cajoling episodic counterpoint in the C minor episode of the development. It certainly ought to play a large part in the cadenza, but it ought not to try to exist without its bass.

I cannot expect other musicians to find my cadenza, which they do not know, clearer or easier than Joachim's, which they have always known. And in this very point I am compelled to make a much more difficult affair in presenting the episode-theme with its proper harmonic draughtsmanship than Joachim makes of it by leaving it unsupported. Perhaps my intention, in bars 30–5 of my cadenza, will become more unmistakable with the aid of the following translation. I leave to violinists the option of finding better bowings than mine; but my legato and my continuous semiquaver movement are essential parts of my idea. An evenly flowing tranquillo tempo is indicated. Rubato would mean chaos, as it generally does in unaccompanied violin music, where composer and listener are in any case achieving a *tour de force* in expressing and understanding harmonic sense at all.

For the rest, I must expect my cadenza to seem both slight and difficult to players who are accustomed to the richness of Joachim's. My general principles of cadenza-writing are explained (above) in the preface to my cadenzas to Beethoven's G major Concerto. Here,

as in my other efforts, I aim at producing the features of a symphonic coda. The difficulties of this task are enormously greater with an unaccompanied violin than with the self-sufficient pianoforte; and unaccompanied violin music that conveys a sense of symphonic harmony cannot lie technically within the possibilities of extemporization.[1]

My last bars are almost identical with Joachim's, for the position of Brahms's final trill leaves no other option. In the epilogue the stringendo and animato indicated by Brahms have caused widespread misunderstanding, which will become aggravated as editors gain confidence in altering Brahms's severely economical and accurate directions. The 'stringendo poco a poco' lasts exactly for the four bars over which Brahms has extended it with a dotted line; and the following animato represents practically the steady tempo of the fortissimos in the opening tutti, admissibly (though not, I think, advisedly) a shade faster, but with no hurrying whatever. Thus the stringendo serves merely to restore energy once for all after the tranquillo, which, as always with Brahms, has meant a decidedly slower tempo. On the other hand, Brahms could hardly have represented the animato by 'tempo 1mo', for the quiet opening of the work, though not tranquillo, is conceived as on the slow side of the main tempo. The essential point is that Brahms's tempi are always steady with an elasticity that lies not in hurryings and slackenings, but in prompt response to the mood of each passage.

Among English readers shocking misunderstandings have been broadcast by the English translator of Dr. Altmann's excellent preface to the miniature score. Dr. Altmann tells us that Brahms on two occasions adjured Joachim to be ruthless in suggesting improvements in the violin technique of the concerto, and playfully added, 'You can't impress [me] except by many suggestions and alterations'. This the translator represents as 'fearing that Joachim was not bold and strong enough in interpretation. "Your sole means of impressing the world is by making alterations and suggestions" he wrote in joke.'

But the translator's own boldness and strength of interpretation is no joke.

---

[1] In the original separate issue of this cadenza preface, Sir Donald Tovey made a similar disclaimer to that which appears on p. 323. It is suitably omitted here, but should not be forgotten.

THE MAIN STREAM OF MUSIC[1]

MY title is a metaphor which is useful so long as it is not over-worked. It is obviously so loose an expression that it cannot be misunderstood. Ruskin has somewhere pointed out that accurate writers are much more often misunderstood than those whose in-accuracy coincides with the inaccuracy of the average reader. Far be it from me to insult my audience by suggesting that any such mythical person is present among us. I only wish to make sure that we shall all mean the same thing when we talk of the main stream of music; though you may find food for thought in the fish which I propose to catch in those waters. But you will be disappointed if you expect me to mention other than the most hackneyed musical subjects. The main stream of music is what we all think we know.

The metaphor is obviously useless if it is extended to speculations as to the source of the stream. The source of a river is usually supposed to be that spring which lies farthest from the mouth; but many tributaries must have been united before the waters were worth calling a main stream, and the title is not earned until, as a pious teleologist once preached, it has pleased Providence to bring large rivers into contact with important towns. We need not trouble ourselves about origins, nor about branches of art which are too remote for any but specialists to understand. The Siamese have, I am told, two principal musical scales, so constructed that, if one note is identified with a note in the scales of our classical music, none of the others can be placed in our scheme. There are musicians in Europe and America who tell us that we have no right to talk of the main stream of music until we have incorporated the Siamese and hundreds of other oriental scales into our own system. Ostensibly this attitude represents breadth of mind. Practically, it is quite compatible with views about our own music which are almost absurd enough and narrow enough to deserve the status of fashions. The exquisite urbanity of the oriental musician usually conceals his contempt for our claims to understand his art. There is, doubtless, a main stream of Siamese music for the Siamese.

My present purpose is to sum up the important facts about the main stream of music as I understand it—in other words, as I think

[1] The Annual Lecture on Aspects of Art (Henriette Hertz Trust) of the British Academy, read 29 June 1938.

it ought to be understood. Such an attempt is as provocative and as far-reaching as that which was made late in the nineteenth century by Sir John Lubbock to elicit opinions on what were the hundred best books. The inquiry was very profitable so long as the Bible was reckoned as one book, and so long as Ruskin, after ' drawing his pen lightly through the needless, and heavily and blottesquely through the rubbish and poison' in Sir John Lubbock's list, was free to amend his selection of a few of Sir Walter Scott's novels by the injunction 'Every word'. Early in the present century one of our popular magazines instituted a similar inquiry, limited to the question of what was the greatest musical composition. Clara Butt, with commendable spirit and sincerity, named Elgar's *Dream of Gerontius*. Joachim, thinking the question foolish, wrote down a short catalogue of classical music, covering most of the ground that I propose to cover to-day. The editor of the magazine did not see his joke, but commented on the fact that all this music was German. Now in neither case is it permissible to suppose that the bias of these artists was patriotic. It was a tremendous experience for any artist to take a leading part in the early production of so important and highly organized a masterpiece as *The Dream of Gerontius*; and the experience must have been intensified by the rare circumstance of singing in one's native language with none of the disadvantages of a translation. In Joachim's case patriotism could have had only the effect of tempting him to include Hungarian and Jewish music, neither of which figured in his list at all. He always admitted that the music of the sixteenth century, in which the Germans had not been supreme, was a sealed book to him; and every musician must face the fact that, if our musical culture is to begin with the music of the eighteenth century and we are to refrain from passing judgement on our contemporaries, most of the music of the eighteenth and nineteenth centuries that can pretend to belong to the main stream has been written by persons whose native language was German. As far as classical music is concerned, a German music-lover is in less danger than any other patriot of becoming provincial in his tastes through patriotic prejudice. The patriotic prejudices of other nations are more likely to lead to narrow and eccentric critical standards. In the present irritable state of the world it is dangerous to express one's candid views on these matters. With the exception of our noble selves and our trusted allies, the nations which can enjoy candid criticism of their artistic limitations are few, small, and exceptionally intelligent. Therefore, on this topic, my lecture must be deficient. Resting dog-like on my elbows, I watch from my tower the settings and risings of the stars; but upon my tongue has stepped a mighty Oxford.

And yet, 'in spite of all temptations to belong to other nations', I have to begin with what those who do not know the facts will believe to be an extravagant claim for English music from the earliest beginnings of counterpoint down to almost a generation beyond the Golden Age. It is impossible to maintain a theory that the main stream of music is something that we have never heard of or are never likely to hear of. The actual size of the stream is not in question. Compared with the Mississippi, the Thames is only a creek. Perhaps, according to Mississippi standards, it might have been entitled to be considered part of a river in the prehistoric times when it joined the Rhine and a few other European streams in what is now the bottom of the North Sea; but our artistic metaphor of the main stream is not concerned with prehistoric matters; and the most patriotic American must admit that his own civilization originally grew round the Thames long before it developed round the Mississippi, and that neither Huckleberry Finn nor the more highly educated Tom Sawyer owed to the background of that mighty river the admirable English style of his creator.

I have no intention of tracing the main stream of music any farther back than to a period in which the art was already something without which the experience of all music-lovers to-day is incomplete. And the time has long passed in which any reasonable musician could doubt that the music of the sixteenth century indeed deserved its title of the Music of the Golden Age, and ought as such to be made the foundation of our musical experience and culture. It has not yet attained that position, and until we have permanently freed ourselves from the notion that it is an archaic matter of interest only to specialists, our musical culture is as imperfect as the classical culture of an eighteenth-century gentleman who returned from his Grand Tour with the information that the Apollo di Belvedere and the Venus de' Medici represented the ultimate standards of classical art, in comparison with which the Elgin marbles, with their quaint, thick-necked horses, were objects of historic interest.

No competent musician will nowadays deny that a musical culture that does not include the sixteenth century is like a classical scholarship that does not include Greek. I personally have neither desire nor leisure to explore musical regions which seem to me

archaic; and as a listener I even confess myself bored with most of
what is transitional and interesting mainly for its consequences.
Time is not wall-space, and no multiplication of museums will extend it. For me the main stream of music becomes navigable at
the end of the fifteenth century with such composers as Josquin des
Prés, and remains smoothly navigable throughout the sixteenth
century. At the beginning of the seventeenth century, it enters into
regions partly mountainous and partly desert, and becomes choked
with weeds. In the eighteenth century, it is drastically cleared up
by Bach and Handel, and drained off into various smaller channels
by other composers. In the middle of the century these channels
reunite and carry the main stream in another direction, represented
by Haydn, Mozart, and Beethoven. In the nineteenth century there
emerges the facile, half-literary distinction between the classical and
the romantic which has been used with fatal efficiency in tracing
the obvious and obliterating the essential.

At this point the metaphor of the main stream is becoming a
nuisance, and I shall therefore have little further use for it except
as a term of reference by which to distinguish the kind of art that
has branched away from it or been diverted into a backwater. But
the regrettably large number of musicians who are not widely and
deeply read in sixteenth-century music will now begin to suspect
me of patriotism, for I must roundly declare that, in spite of my
conscientious objection to any such bias, I am convinced that
throughout the sixteenth century, and for nearly a generation of the
seventeenth, English composers contributed largely and adventur-
ously to the main stream of music. Even so, a musician who for
their sake neglects Palestrina is like a classical scholar who knows
no Attic Greek. Palestrina's music, besides being in the main
stream, is also of the centre: another useful metaphor. Palestrina
achieves and represents consummate purity. But scholarship may
be so confined to the centre as to have no settled conviction about
the circumference. There is a dreadful tradition—I wish it were
only a legend—of an eminent Greek scholar who would allow
neither himself nor his pupils to read Homer lest the Homeric dialect
should corrupt the purity of their Attic Greek. It is difficult to see
in what sense such a person's education has not been a total loss.
Such a purist confesses to a very weak faith in the strength of his
own grasp of pure style. For the musician, a firm understanding of
the strictest purity of Palestrina's mature works is as vitally necessary as Attic Greek is to the classical scholar; but that understanding

has not begun to exist if it is in any danger of being weakened by an equally developed capacity to enjoy music throughout the wide range of sixteenth-century styles, both sacred and secular, that lie outside the scope of the Spanish and Roman schools; and in these styles by far the most extensive range is that of the English masters, who not only continued to use, with vital fitness, archaisms which were too harsh for Palestrina and Victoria, but often anticipated the solid tonality of the nineteenth century, and even the romantic modulations of Schubert and Brahms, without any loss of the subtlety and freedom which sixteenth-century harmony owes to its derivation from the ecclesiastical modes.

The chief practical obstacles to our understanding of sixteenth-century music have come from the misuse of its grammatical discipline, in forms shockingly corrupted and mutilated, in our academic training. Modern musical scholarship is making praiseworthy efforts to remedy this, and in England the efforts have all the better chance of success because we have always been notoriously provincial and have allowed many foundations of old traditions to remain, instead of following the explosive methods by which our livelier neighbours extirpate the past. The only serious defect in our efforts at a renascence of musical education is that they are directed to students of the wrong mental age. In the sixteenth century, academic counterpoint was a practical matter for choirboys with unbroken voices. The sceptical undergraduate is definitely too old for it. And we do not solve his difficulties by combining in one process the elementary problems of the inky little schoolboy with the refinements of adult scholarship. Nothing is easier than to make those problems laborious, and music is probably in not much worse case than other subjects of culture in its liability to suffer from educational methods that have from the outset consulted the sole convenience of the teacher, and in the outcome have shown that the teacher's own education has miscarried.

The labours of Canon Fellowes have recently made a sound practical grounding in English sixteenth-century music possible for everybody who can as much as sing in his bath. Hitherto, we have suffered from the tendency of musical scholars to present their results in ways not available for performance. Editions of old music in more practical form have for the most part been the work of Philistine adapters, who have no scruple in substituting what they would have written themselves for every detail which they do not happen to understand. In consequence of this, every experienced musician feels an instinctive lack of confidence in any edition of old music that does not retain obsolete clefs and other inconveniences of notation. It is only in the most recent times that we can trust an editor to make old music legible without thrusting his own entirely opaque personality between us and the composer. But now Canon Fellowes has published in a most practical form a complete corpus of all the secular English vocal polyphony of the Golden Age, and he is advancing with the complete works, sacred and secular, of one of the greatest masters in all music, William Byrd. I do not know a finer achievement in musical scholarship, and I have no patience with the view, sometimes expressed by persons who ought to know better, that it is a narrow special research into matters on the border-line between music and literature. Doubtless there is some patriotic indiscretion in speaking as if Byrd ought to be as important to present-day music-lovers as Bach or Beethoven. But it is high time that musicians should recognize: first, that the music of the sixteenth century is quite as essential to their aesthetic education as any later music; and secondly, that Tallis and Byrd are among its supreme masters. Canon Fellowes's single-handed achievement compares favourably with that of the editors of the *Bachgesellschaft*, who, beginning their labours in 1850, the centenary of Bach's death, produced nearly fifty annual volumes before their labours were roughly complete. Their standard of scholarship varied incalculably from the eminence of Rust and Kroll to the ineptitude of persons whose names I forget; and the edition, though an absolute necessity for every musician's library, was, as Schweitzer points out, planned and executed in the most unpractical way conceivable.

Now, though an enormous amount of Bach's work is producible in the ordinary course of every musician's education, so that its central item, the Forty-eight Preludes and Fugues, should be, as Schumann said, 'the young musician's daily bread', his great choral works need the apparatus of a good, though not necessarily, or even preferably, large, chorus, and an orchestra rather specially constituted and trained. But there is no sixteenth-century music which cannot be perfectly studied and practised by eight singers sitting round a table. That admirable group of artists, 'The English Singers', manage to cover most of its range with six. Exquisite voices and ripe musicianship are obviously necessary for their standard of performance; but there is no reason why ordinary human beings should not return to the Elizabethan practice of sitting round a table at home and producing their music out of their part-books. Thanks to Canon Fellowes's labours, any English masterpiece of the Golden Age can be obtained for a few pence in a score perfectly legible to everyone who can read ordinary staff-notation, and edited with the highest scholarship and the sanest common sense. Dr. Johnson's *Dictionary* was rightly held by himself and all right-thinking English connoisseurs to show that a single Englishman could surpass the labours of any number of French Academicians. The Johnsonian common sense was transcendental in some ways, and limited in others. I have not yet discovered the limitations of the practical common sense of Canon Fellowes.

Early in the seventeenth century the violins ousted the flat-backed nasal-toned family of viols, and instrumental music began to assert itself. The harpsichord was already, in its early form of spinet and virginals, a resourceful instrument that amused William Byrd and other great Tudor composers. Queen Elizabeth herself condescended to be a great virtuoso in keyboard music; and English patriotism does not outrun discretion if we claim that this interesting backwater—the instrumental music of the sixteenth century—was thoroughly explored by English composers. The healthiness of a backwater depends upon its access to the main stream and its immunity from the encroachments of the Corporation dump. Unfortunately, the subsequent history of English music up to recent times has been a deplorable story of frustration, stagnation, and drifting into silted-up channels. There are periods in which it may be fairly said that English music has itself consisted of the Corporation dump. Our greatest musical genius, Henry Purcell, was born either fifty years too soon or fifty years too late: too late to be a master of the Golden Age, now that instrumental music had flooded out every landmark of Palestrina's art: too early to gain command of the future resources of Bach and Handel. His opera *Dido and Aeneas*, written for the pupils of Mr. Josiah Priest's boarding-school, with a libretto by Nahum Tate, of the firm of Tate and Brady, achieves musical coherence and anticipates every quality of the operas in which Gluck reformed dramatic music nearly a century later. If Purcell had been allowed to write more operas on such lines he would have carried a recognizable main stream of music through all the tangle of mountain-torrents and parched arroyos which the musical historian finds so interesting in the eighteenth century, but which is so distressing to the searcher for mature masterpieces who is not deceived by the nineteenth-century cookery which makes the *disjecta membra* of seventeenth-century music palatable to the concert singer. To anyone who realizes what might have been achieved for and by Purcell, the honoured name of glorious John Dryden deserves always to be accompanied by a heartfelt recitation of the 109th Psalm. That completely unmusical time-server began by insulting Purcell and other gifted English musicians in a panegyric of an obviously incompetent Monsieur Grabu, whom King Charles II had foolishly set at the head of his court musicians, and whose work proved more perishable than waste paper. A few years later Dryden mended his manners towards Purcell in his public utterances, but proceeded to dam the whole future current of English dramatic music by ordaining that the music of his operas should be confined to characters outside the real action of his plays. Thus, even when Dryden condescends to adapt Shakespeare's *Tempest*, he contrives that Purcell's music for it shall have nothing to do with Shakespeare. And what should have been Purcell's most important work, *King Arthur*, has not the smallest chance of taking shape as a coherent musical scheme. We not only accepted the consequences of Dryden's Philistinism throughout the next century, but imposed them with murderous results upon one of the greatest dramatic composers of the early nineteenth century, Weber, who found, when he had already committed himself to writing an opera for the English stage, that the librettist, Planché, neither knew nor cared to learn that a composer of dramatic music was concerned with the coherence of a music-drama as a whole. Planché cheerfully said, 'And now we will show them what we can do next time'; but it was already obvious that Weber's time was fully occupied in dying of rapid consumption.

We can hardly doubt that, if the musical resources of Bach and Handel had been at Purcell's command, his genius would have had the power to break through the bonds of the Philistines, and in fact I know no other case where musical genius has come into the world so manifestly at the wrong time and place, without having found the opportunity to develop some other art or science more ready for the work of a great mind. For we cannot doubt that a talent for music, in spite of its highly special nature, is part of a very much larger general ability which has become concentrated upon music by circumstances less normal than we are apt to suppose. In more recent times we have noticed that great Russian musicians have been army generals, admirals, chemists, and other useful people before they were recognized as musicians; yet so professional is the prestige of music that a presentable musicianship will always take precedence over whatever the musician has achieved in other ways. Berlioz was discovered by W. E. Henley to be a fellow-craftsman in literature, and is, in fact, far more impeccable in the handling of words than in his musical technique. Yet we shall never think of him, or of that other excellent prose-writer, Schumann, except as a musician.

And now a few steps of argument, which I need not work out, may lead to some notion of the way in which the main stream of music passes from one country to another. Each nation has its own forms of musical talent, and will be ready to take leadership when its special talent is what is needed. The argument is facile, but not, as far as I can see, dangerous. Before the Golden Age became golden, the difficulties of polyphony were best surmounted by a certain kind of ingenuity which the Flemish races possessed in an eminent degree. They did not possess in a primary degree the sense of physical beauty. When ingenuity had accomplished its task, the Latin races found in music an art ready for the development of their sense of beauty; and the Hispano-Roman school represented by Victoria and Palestrina was the result. Latin logic and Latin euphony supplied some order in the chaos which ensued when the principles of instrumental music began to subvert the pure vocal aesthetics of the Golden Age. And in later times it has generally been the Latin musicians, especially the French, who have cleared up the issues when music has lost its way.

Nobody who is capable of measuring the gulf that separates the art of Palestrina from that of Bach and Handel will be surprised at the fact that the whole of the seventeenth century was spent in pioneer efforts and small sporadic achievements before such masters could emerge. What emerged with them was the stupendous phenomenon of absolute music, which, in spite of every practical and historical argument against it, has dominated all the central musical thoughts and instincts of later composers, even when they most explicitly oppose it. It is very doubtful whether Bach and Handel were conscious of it. On the one hand, it is quite certain, and has been demonstrated in detail by Schweitzer and Pirro, that Bach's whole musical vocabulary is dominated by a musical symbolism, partly ancient and partly original, which associates definite turns of melody and rhythm with definite words; so that, to take a grotesque instance, it costs him less trouble to use a high note in referring to the High Priest than to avoid that harmless absurdity. The symbolism is often profound, and has been said by some musicians to explain features of Bach's style which they otherwise had felt to be obscure. But it is equally certain that most of us have enjoyed at all events Bach's instrumental music without feeling any need for such explanations. Indeed, so powerfully does Bach convince absolute musicians by the absolute musical perfection of his art that the demonstration of his musical-verbal symbolism has been known to provoke fierce resentment and violent denial of obvious facts.

Such difficulties are not confined to music; and every musician should fortify himself with their complete solution in a document which never once refers to music, Andrew Bradley's lecture on *Poetry for Poetry's Sake*. Bradley deals with the heresy of those who say that the essence of poetry consists in the sound quite apart from the sense; and he repudiates that doctrine by pointing out that when a poem has come into existence, what is commonly called its subject is no longer outside the poem, and that the true antithesis lies not between subject and treatment but between the subject and the whole poem. With Bach and Handel, the absoluteness of music is forced upon us by its overwhelming intrinsic power, which utterly transcends all words except those Biblical words and notions which have become either so universal that only absolute musical beauty can symbolize them or so meaningless to us that any formula will do for them. Thus, there is nothing really new in Bach's absoluteness; nothing, indeed, that could force a doctrine of absoluteness upon his consciousness. In spite of the ostensibly abject dependence of Golden-Age music on the details of its verbal text, composers had from early times used their musical symbolism merely as the Hebrew poet might use the form of an alphabetical acrostic for the *Lamentations of Jeremiah*. Such customs helped and hindered the composer no more than the faint rulings on manuscript paper when our handwriting has a tendency to sprawl. We simply disregard them. As to verbal texts, it is notorious that the singing voice early insisted on stretching single syllables beyond all recognition where the vowel was favourable, and that musical forms demanded the repetition of parts of sentences, often regardless of sense, until eventually our own English musical Corporation dump emitted a strange theological dogma, that of the Chorister's Fortieth Article of Religion:

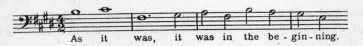

As it was, it was in the be-gin-ning.

which perhaps we may take as a symbol of the Eternal Verity of Absolute Music.

And yet absolute music is not absolute nonsense. All difficulties in reconciling its existence with historical facts and practical common sense come of our habit of confusing processes with results. The notion of the main stream is a better metaphor for my subject than the term 'classical', and it is also better than the not less important notion that the greatest art is of the centre. Certainly the greatest art is truly central, but we have no right to set *a priori* limits to the size of its circle; and its circumference is so large that great minds may spend their lives in exploration and small minds may live in the belief that the only centre is that of their own parish pump. For Bach and Handel, the aesthetic centre of music, the point from which all musical grammar and all art-forms radiated, was still the aesthetics of the unaccompanied polyphonic chorus, yet neither Bach nor Handel wrote any choral music which did not presuppose the accompaniment of the organ or the orchestra. The great motets of Bach, which are printed as unaccompanied choruses, show in almost every line that Bach is thinking of his basses as doubled by instruments in a lower octave. This does not mean that he has deserted the centre of his art. It means that for him instruments are voices.

Purely instrumental music is, of course, from the outset free from the complications which are produced by association with a verbal text. The chief limitations imposed upon it from without arose from its early association with dance. The symmetries of dance-forms have much in common with the symmetries of lyric poetry; and from them arose the tuneful forms of the suite, which were naturally restricted to a small scale. Yet even in the suites of Bach few of us feel any curiosity as to how his more elaborate allemandes and sarabandes could ever have been danced; and the great suite-preludes, with their forms derived from the overture, the concerto, and the toccata, are still less likely to let our historical curiosity interfere with our enjoyment of their spacious music.

The toccata is an interesting and amusing case of an art-form arising out of human trial and error in the construction and playing of an instrument. The touch of the old organs was unequal and unpunctual. You must run your fingers over all parts of the key-board and walk all over the pedal-board to find out the holes in the road. This done, you could then draw out your full diapasons and see if the instrument had, as Bach put it, 'good lungs'; after which you could settle down to music in its most solid and brilliant form: a fugue imitating the behaviour of a four-part or five-part chorus discussing a subject in dialogue, but usually taking advantage of your instrument to propound a florid proposition beyond the range of the most athletic singer. Here we already have an art-form of which the origins, though grotesquely practical, are entirely musical. If Bach and his contemporaries were not as yet conscious of the absoluteness of music, they were already healthily aware that certain art-forms had a technical usefulness that had nothing to do with words; and throughout the first half of the eighteenth century the absoluteness of music was modestly proclaimed by the laudable custom of publishing great works under the title of 'Lessons'. Bach's Forty-eight Preludes and Fugues, doled out by him to his pupils for keyboard practice, were made to serve a still more practical purpose when he collected them into two books, so grouped as to represent each of the twelve major and twelve minor keys within the tempered chromatic scale, in order to inculcate a system of tuning by which all keys would be equally in tune on keyboard instruments with twelve equal semitones to the octave, instead of tuning a narrow range of the most-used keys as perfectly as possible and leaving other keys painfully out of tune. Two of his most imaginative compositions, the Chromatic Fantasia and the Organ Prelude in G minor, purport to display their most fantastic modulations to the extent of laying stress on chords that would be impermissibly out of tune unless equal temperament were used. It is absurd to suppose that Bach's inspiration lay in this practical purpose. The practical purpose must be fulfilled if the works are to be played; and if the works had not been of transcendental beauty the musical world might not have troubled to fulfil the practical purpose. At all events, nothing could be more ridiculous than to suppose that Bach needed the stimulus of a theory of tuning to enable him to conceive his stupendous modulations; though he evidently had the common sense to understand the theory.

With the advent of Bach, music became an art so congenial to all that is best in the Teutonic intellect that for the next two centuries there is no musical art-form in which German musicians have not produced the supreme masterpieces. There can be no supreme musical art without the qualities of absolute music, whether the art be as compounded with other arts as Wagnerian opera or as exclusively musical as the string quartets of Beethoven. So much attention has been aroused by recent efforts to assign literary meanings to Beethoven's purest music that I must mention the fact; but only to say that I think urbanity towards such silliness is a mistake. Music is (as Mendelssohn courteously pointed out to a troublesome inquirer) not less definite, but more definite, for being untranslatable. The problem of absoluteness in music is not essentially different from that of abstractness in science. Geometry doubtless came into existence in Egypt under the practical persuasion of the Nile floods, which enforced its principles empirically upon the land-surveyors; but it needed the Greek philosophic power of abstraction to make it a science. But in science, and perhaps in philosophy, the faculty of abstraction may become abused, or starved, by prolonged dissociation from the practice of observing facts. Plato obviously went too far when he suggested that the true astronomer should regard it as vulgar to observe the actual stars, but should rather think out how they ought ideally to behave; and Tyndall and Huxley still had reason to warn us of the pitfalls of the 'high-priori' road. Bach, at all events, had both feet firmly planted on the ground, though he breathed the upper ether of absolute music, and in his last work, *Die Kunst der Fuge*, produced a masterpiece so abstract that musicians who might have been expected to know better have denied that it was music at all. In art, absoluteness and purity are not working hypotheses, but final results.

My own practical experience is this: that, though I am by temperament and training the most abstract-minded of musicians and have from childhood practised composition by preference in polyphonic and pure sonata-forms, I find it quite impracticable to teach composition except as musical rhetoric, and I never realized the intense depth, power, and essential meaning of absolute music until I went through the experience of composing an opera. That experience taught me two things: first, that no music could illustrate a situation expressible in drama or lyrical poetry unless it was satisfactory as music; and secondly, that no music written merely to express words has ever achieved one-tenth of the intensity and power of absolute music. Theatre-music is like theatre-scenery: it is a medium in which simple resources and methods produce immediate and vivid effects. This is in itself a severe limitation—too severe for artists who feel the need of more evidently intellectual resources to inspire them. But the supreme operatic masterpieces of Mozart and the later music-dramas of Wagner abundantly prove the soundness of Dean Church's dictum that a scientific criticism refuses to class art-forms into degrees of higher and lower.

To the lover of literature there are difficulties in opera which only a whole-hearted appreciation of music can surmount. To him, if the literary values of the drama are not contemptible, the drama is either a blasphemously distorted epitome of Shakespeare, or at best, as with Wagner, an amateur effort by the composer, whose poetry becomes admirable only in the light of his music. Theoretically, this difficulty is so formidable as to deter many persons sensitive to music and literature from attempting to enjoy opera. Practically, most of us go through life enjoying all manner of mixed experiences by their sum-total effects, without troubling ourselves as to what was incongruous in the elements before they were compounded. Again, there is no false sentiment that does not mimic a true one; and so a great composer may be inspired to write music that expresses a true sentiment before he has time to discover the falseness of the words that he is setting. By the time his music is written the true sentiment is irrevocably there. This insensibility to the exact meaning of the words need not prevent him from setting great poetry to music which reveals the deepest insight into the poet's thought. In the final resort, it will always be the music that tells; and, in spite of all apparent lack of critical taste, the greatest masters of absolute music will always be those who show the profoundest attention to whatever true meaning can be imputed to the words and subjects which they illustrate.

While Bach and Handel were excavating the profoundest depths of the main channel of music, many tributaries were flowing into it from various directions; and, as a matter of history, the subsequent development of music is traceable mainly to the confluence of these side-streams, while the influence of Bach becomes almost untraceable before the nineteenth century. The fourth volume of *The Oxford History of Music* was devoted to the first half of the eighteenth century. The volume is entitled *The Age of Bach and Handel*, and nobody doubts the fitness of the title. It would already have been acceptable in 1840, when Spohr wrote what he called an 'Historical' Symphony, of which the first movement was in the style of Bach and Handel, the second in that of Mozart, the third in that of Beethoven, and the finale in his own style as representing the latest period a few years after Beethoven had died at the height of his power. Spohr evidently conceived musical progress as something almost as rapid as we conceive it nowadays. But even the most intelligent contemporaries of Bach and Handel would never have guessed that these masters would give their names to their period. If our estimate of Handel were based as it was in contemporary London upon his forty-two Italian operas, instead of upon *Messiah* and *Israel in Egypt*, we should see nothing but common sense in the contemporary judgement as to the rivalry between Handel and Bononcini: 'Strange that such difference should be 'Twixt Tweedledum and Tweedledee.' Most of us know little of Handel except *Messiah* and *Israel in Egypt*. Both of those works were failures in their own day. To his contemporaries Handel was the great man if (and only if) you happened to live in London, where the rivalry with Bononcini took place. If you lived in Germany you would probably know far more of Graun and Hasse. If you lived in Paris your great master would have been Rameau. Nowhere in the world would you find John Sebastian Bach regarded as more than an astonishing player on the organ, a writer of extremely complicated music in obsolete styles, the third choice for the post of Cantor in St. Thomas's in Leipzig, and the idol only of a small group of pupils who found it wise to keep to themselves their personal conviction of his greatness. Even his first biographer, Forkel, dared to say no more of his choral works than that 'They too have their admirers'. Only one of some two hundred Church cantatas was published in his lifetime and before the centenary of his death.

We of the twentieth century are in no better position than our ancestors to identify the main stream of contemporary music. We learn from history at least this: that contemporaries are often preoccupied with trivial matters. In the glorious days of Beethoven the early development of the pianoforte, and especially the extension of its compass to higher octaves, diverted the talent of quite eminent masters, such as Hummel, into one of the most weedy backwaters in musical history. It seems to us incredible that a musician who as a child had been brought up in Mozart's house as a favourite pupil, and who was regarded by most contemporaries as the equal of Beethoven, should have maintained his reputation by works that are the musical counterpart of spacious palaces in which the dignified interior architecture has become invisible in the glare of innumerable glass chandeliers. We can all see through poor Hummel nowadays. Our power of seeing through things has the uses and some of the dangers of X-ray photography: if X-rays are too hard or their exposure too long we see right through everything and into nothing. Life is not long enough for us to try and investigate the bones of Hummel's pinguid organism. But on the whole his contemporaries who regarded him as indisputably representing the main stream of music were more in the right than his adverse critics. We have no evidence that the people who did not admire Hummel could appreciate anything better. Mastery is not enough. But it is a quality of the main stream. When academic criteria become lazily mechanical we may come to regard as part of the main stream some kinds of correct art that have no importance at all. But perhaps plain dullness is less dull than mere ignorance or precious caprice.

The tributaries which were drifting towards a confluence beside and above the deep current of Bach's art united in a new stream which seems at first to be almost as incompatible with Bach as the music before Bach was incompatible with Palestrina. The result was indeed akin to what Kant would have called a Copernican revolution in the whole orientation of music; yet until quite late in the eighteenth century most musicians probably regarded the progress of music as an uninterrupted development ever since the time when Alessandro Scarlatti, a generation before Bach, founded the whole musical language that comprises the art-forms of music throughout the eighteenth and half the nineteenth century. Alessandro Scarlatti was eminently capable of forming a classical language; but he is not nearly so well known to us as his son Domenico, who wrote hundreds of eccentric and crassly unacademic sonatas for the harpsichord, for which he apologized in his prefaces as works merely meant to amuse and not on any account to be regarded as learned. Such work, taken by itself, seems as isolated as a dew-pond; but Mozart, Clementi, and Beethoven assiduously pumped the whole contents of that dew-pond into their own main stream. Similarly, in a later age, Liszt drained off the chromatic iridescence from the dew-pond of Chopin, and presented it to Wagner, with stupendous results.

What was happening during the lifetime of Bach, unknown to himself and unknown to the small and fashionable masters who were innocently promoting it as a form of decadence, was the transformation of the whole of music from an architectural, decorative, and rhetorical art to an art inveterately dramatic in its movement and power. Handel was a consummate rhetorician, and his contemporary fame rested mainly on his operas. Recently some of them have been revived with a *succés d'estime* attained by the reckless expenditure on stage-production of a tenth of the money and ten times the attention that were devoted to these externals by Handel and his supporters; yet the preface to the fourth volume of

The Oxford History of Music is quite correct in saying that as to opera Handel's period represents the darkness before dawn. The fact is that Bach had no disposition to deal with opera and Handel no disposition to reform it, for the simple reason that music itself was no more dramatic than architecture. Handel lived to see the early failures of Gluck, who produced one or two operas in London and who, as Handel remarked, 'knows no more counterpoint than my cook'. But Handel did not live to see or to foretell that this crassly non-contrapuntal composer was soon to reveal to the world a music so dramatic that opera became henceforth the most emotional kind of stage-play, whether its action was as drastically simple as that of *Orfeo* and *Alceste* or as inextricably complicated as *Figaro*. Gluck could have done nothing of the kind if there had not been a radical change in the whole nature of music. In the works of Bach's most famous son, Carl Philipp Emanuel, and his more fashionable son, Johann Christian, who settled in London, this radical change in the nature of music is manifest, though they themselves were conscious of no more positive fact than that their father's style was old-fashioned and his preoccupation with contrapuntal forms pedantic. The change is so radical that we are apt to imagine some such chronological gulf as the century which separates John Sebastian Bach from Palestrina; but as a matter of fact Philipp Emanuel Bach was producing quite mature works in the year in which his father wrote the B minor Mass, and his last set of sonatas was published in the year in which Mozart produced *Don Giovanni*.

It is doubtful whether even Mozart and Haydn were much more aware of the stupendous changes that they were bringing about in the art of music. Certainly none of their contemporaries suspected a great revolution, and our own text-books on formal analysis are so preoccupied with the merest externals of musical forms that, while they take the change for granted, they completely fail to show its essential features. Within the lifetime of Mozart and Haydn the language of music covered a range akin to that of the comedy of manners. Hence, as Edward Fitzgerald profoundly remarked, most people failed, and still fail, to recognize that Mozart is powerful because he is so beautiful. With Beethoven, the language of music enormously increased its range, and Beethoven was able to become the most tragic as well as the most humorous of composers. The technical resources by which he extended his art amount to little more than a combination of the habits of Mozart and Haydn, stimulated in later years by an intensive study of Handel and of the little that was then available of Bach. But in art, as in chemistry and mathematics, such combinations are no mere arithmetical additions. They are integrations that produce results often incalculable and sometimes explosive. Hence the idea arose, and still survives, that Beethoven's position in art is that of a revolutionary, and that his revolutionary tendencies made his later music formless. It is an unfortunate coincidence that during Beethoven's lifetime the French Revolution was going through what a philosophical historian has ironically described as the formula of actually taking place. In his treatment of art-forms, early and late, Beethoven was no more revolutionary than Mozart, and far more regular than Haydn. Neither of those masters had established any formal orthodoxy. They each had widely different habits of their own. Beethoven's forms grew organically from the nature of his matter, and thus grew with stricter and stricter accuracy as long as he lived. Their increasing variety is a mathematical function of that accuracy. If there is any other kind of classical form contemporary with Haydn, Mozart, and Beethoven, perhaps I could name the authors of it; but I do not feel sure, and I prefer to follow the discreet example of Herodotus, who, whenever he has anything scandalous to report, says: 'I know the man's name, but forbear to mention it.'

It is doubtless paradoxical to deny that Beethoven was in an obvious sense a child of the French Revolution; but musical history is full of warnings against facile attempts to trace the qualities of music to the non-musical history of the times. The musical composer is the most detached of all artists. For him the time is either out of joint or irrelevant. Nothing is more self-evident than the Lutheran spirit in Bach, and we know for a biographical fact that his library, apart from music, was mainly theological. We also know that he was highly appreciated by Frederick the Great, who invited him to Potsdam in 1747; but the spirit of Luther had flamed forth a hundred and fifty years earlier, when Palestrina was producing consummate masterpieces of Roman Catholic music; and the spirit of Frederick the Great was much more characteristically displayed in his repeated invitations to Voltaire, which brought that eminently untheological person to Berlin in the year after Bach's death and led eventually to most unedifying and simian squabbles. In any case, art has an unlimited capacity for minding its own business, and history has so much business that not even the art of Thomas Hardy's *Dynasts* can wholly convince the mere musician that history has a mind at all.

The term 'romantic' has a definite and useful meaning in literature, through which it has, as in the case of Schumann and Berlioz, some actual contacts with music. When used more widely and contrasted with 'classical', it is one of the major nuisances of musical criticism. As in the middle of the eighteenth century music was ripening for the development of a dramatic style, so by the middle of the nineteenth century it had developed its full lyric possibilities. Critics have often commented on the time-lag between the appearance of great lyric poetry and the capacity of composers to express it in music. The tardiness of Mozart and Beethoven in finding expression for the lyric poetry of Goethe comes from no spiritual or intellectual defect. It is a natural result of devotion to musical forms in which harmony, especially in its larger aspect of tonality, had to be treated broadly and on a large scale. It has been said of Beethoven that no composer contributed less to the progress of harmony. His *Variations on a Waltz by Diabelli* show that, on the contrary, no composer since Bach was capable of contributing more, if it was advisable to confine the listener's attention to details. But in the large-scale handling of tonality not even Wagner covers a wider range than Beethoven, and to accuse Beethoven of restricted harmonic views is as inept as to assert that the designer of the Forth Bridge has contributed nothing to the progress of domestic architecture. Parry put his unerring finger upon the spot when he cited as a thing unattainable in earlier music the harmonically oblique entry of the voice in Schubert's setting of Goethe's 'Erlkönig'. Abstruse harmony is not the essential matter for song-writing, but powerful and long-experienced concentration. A musical lyric has no business to sound like a fragment that ought to have come from something larger. The association of romantic music with romantic literature is a natural fact; but its musical importance is less than one might suppose. The derivation of many of Schumann's finest pianoforte works from the writings of Jean-Paul Richter and E. T. A. Hoffmann is enthusiastically proclaimed in general and in detail by Schumann himself. But I frankly own that, though I know most of the music by heart, I have, like many of my contemporaries, failed to penetrate deeply into the jungle of those prose-writers, and have not found my efforts in the slightest degree necessary to my understanding of the music.

A more precise definition of romantic music identifies it not merely with lyricism but with the tendency to relate purely instrumental music to external subjects in life, letters, and art. As far as modern music is concerned, this tendency is at least as old as the *Fitzwilliam Virginal Book*. Moreover, the only report we have of purely instrumental music in ancient Greece is of a composition purporting to describe Apollo slaying the Python. Such programmes are often received gratefully by listeners who find the atmosphere of abstract music too rare; but Schumann himself (who with all his formal limitations was by no means scatter-brained, but belongs to the great race of attentive artists) goes far to demonstrate the flimsiness of all theories of programme music by confessing that he wrote his titles afterwards and expected the music to speak for itself. This does not impugn the depth of Schumann's poetical thought, whether in instrumental pieces with romantic titles or in genuine songs, in which his output was equally important and almost as voluminous.

With Schubert the current of song becomes a mighty torrent, unquestionably one of the major phenomena in musical history. Schubert wrote over six hundred songs, and Brahms asserted that something definite could be learnt from each one of them. This is as true as Beethoven's assertion that Handel was the master of all masters and that no other composer could produce such stupendous effects by such simple means. The trouble about these truths is that one must have made considerable progress towards being a Beethoven or a Brahms before one can learn the lessons correctly. Schumann is now coming into fashion again after a period of eclipse. The eclipse is in any case not as fatal as that which has overtaken all but a small selection of Mendelssohn's works; for Mendelssohn's was the kind of mastery which carries everything before it at the time and leaves to a later epoch the fatal discovery that it is superficial, whereas the defects in Schumann's art were not only obvious from the outset but self-confessed and turned to positive account as working hypotheses. Schubert is in a different position. Narrow pseudo-classical ideas of musical form, akin to those which regard Beethoven's later works as formless, have led to a gross underestimation of Schubert's greatness of conception and actual mastery of execution in larger musical forms. Musical critics are spoilt children by reason of the almost superhuman standards of perfection set by the masters of the Golden Age, and by Bach, Mozart, Haydn, and Beethoven. Schweitzer rationalizes the severity of current musical criticism by roundly stating that of all arts music is that in which perfection is a *sine qua non*. In literature and other arts critics have been compelled to take a more practical view; and they would assuredly have never dreamt of placing an artist of the calibre of Schubert in anything short of the highest rank. He died so young that his ripest work ought to be considered as early. And I question whether Shakespeare, up to the time of producing, say, *King John*, surpassed Schubert's attainments in the handling of large forms.

One more major event marks the development of the main stream of music. Perhaps some of us may be inclined to compare it rather with the flowing out into the ocean. At all events, that is the normal outcome of the main streams; and no amount of classical scruple, or of wish to retain our central position in criticism, should prevent us from facing the fact and its consequences. Throughout this discussion I have shown no patience with either of the terms 'classical' and 'romantic'. Following, with a certain respectful independence, Sir Walter Raleigh's lead, I am content to define the classical as what I always expected and the romantic as what I did not expect. Eminent critics can still be found to maintain that Wagner's style is entirely unclassical and will never become classical. If this is meant to imply that Wagner's art will ever become negligible in an account of the main stream of music, it seems to me to be frankly nonsense. Following the lead given by Bradley in his criterion of poetry for poetry's sake, I find no difficulty in regarding opera of all kinds as in its integrity an ultimately pure form of music. The main practical difficulty with opera is that its historic progress has by no means been essentially the progress of good music. Opera has continually subsided with full popular and fashionable acclamation into dead conventionality and bottomless vulgarity; but from the lowest depths it has shown a capacity to rise almost as high as absolute music can rise; and in Wagner we have the astounding phenomenon of its rise from downright bad music, such as is still painfully evident in *Tannhäuser*, to the loftiest and purest regions of *The Ring*, *Tristan*, *Meistersinger*, and *Parsifal*. Technically, the revolution effected by Wagner is not less important—or, as Kant might say, not less Copernican—than any previous event in musical history. It concerns the time-scale of music. All the conventions and difficulties of opera before Wagner may be regarded as resulting from the fact that classical music moved some ten times as fast as drama. Consequently, every classical opera was compelled to consist of between twenty and thirty separable musical designs fitted into the framework of the drama. Wagner's achievement consisted in refashioning the whole texture and form of music until it covered the drama on a time-scale measured by hours instead of by minutes. The process is not unlike that symbolized by Siegfried's refashioning of the sword Nothung. Mime, the cunningest of smiths, utterly failed to weld the fragments of the old sword. Siegfried ground the fragments into filings, which he melted down and cast into a new sword, before which the spear of Wotan himself was powerless.

Having thus sketchily traced the main stream of music to what we may regard as the ocean of Wagner, I can go no farther. At the present day all musicians feel more or less at sea, and not all of us are good sailors. Some day the ocean-bed may rise again, and the Thames and the Rhine and other rivers may be seen to reunite as they did in the days when bisons were painted by realistic artists in the caves of Altamira. I have laid before you enough material to provide a brief summary of the points on which our current musical culture and sense of proportion may be improved. First, then, I would wish all music-lovers to cultivate the habit of sitting round a table and singing the music of the Golden Age, from editions by Canon Fellowes, and whatever competent editors have produced in practical form. Second, I would wish every music-lover to acquire such mastery of the keyboard as to obey Schumann's advice to make Bach's *Wohltemperirtes Klavier* our daily bread. Third, I would urge all competent musicians to stimulate the printing in a decent score and to promote the performance of the thirty or forty middle symphonies of Haydn. Recent revivals of neglected works of Haydn fill me with exasperation by their perverse failure to fill up the biggest lacuna that yet remains in our public representation of the main stream of music. Haydn is an immeasurably greater and more central master than we as yet realize, but his development was remarkably slow and his work remains transitional and archaic and, in short, historically interesting, which is for me as a listener synonymous to 'boring', until the middle of his career. I am as ready as anyone to refrain from boredom when I want to learn or teach musical history, but I think it immeasurably more important to teach and produce mature works of art. And as long as some forty splendid symphonies in the middle of Haydn's career remain wholly inaccessible except to researchers of British Museum libraries, I feel nothing but irritation when early and archaic works of Haydn are enthusiastically produced and acclaimed, always with the aid of some title or anecdote. And I am roused to something like fury by the announcement that somebody has decided that a symphony which my beloved and learned friend Mandyczewski had relegated to the list of spurious works has been proved by some learned inquirer, on the strength of water-marks, handwriting, and musical vocabulary, to be genuine. I should be sorry to lose the first eighteen of Haydn's string quartets, opp. 1, 2, and 3, and am very glad that Miss Marion Scott has discovered and proved the authenticity of a still earlier quartet. But Haydn himself expressed a wish that his works should be considered as beginning with the quartets in op. 9, which is about where the middle symphonies begin. So long as I am hindered from performing, or even studying, the splendid symphonies of his middle years I can only be annoyed that anybody should waste time in disputing the authenticity of a work of which Haydn himself would probably say that he neither knew nor cared whether he had written it.

It is obvious that the achievements of Sadler's Wells and the Old Vic are assets of vital importance to our musical civilization, and that everything should be done not only to secure their permanence but to provide similar enterprises throughout the kingdom. The main practical cause of the universal musical culture of Germany was the tradition of local royal patronage in many small principalities. As I am always pointing out, we lost our musical prospects when we abolished the Heptarchy. As an experienced absolute musician, I do not believe that absolute music can be understood where opera is not also appreciated in its integrity as music-drama. Wagner as represented in the concert-room is one of the major nuisances in our musical civilization. The typical Wagnerian excerpt has trained both the public and the critics to be totally insensitive to whether any piece of music has a beginning, an end, or any meaning beyond that imputed to music by Lamb in his 'Essay on Ears'. Otherwise it seems to me that musically all is best in the best of all possible worlds. At all events, I am an optimist in my belief that this must be the best of all possible worlds, since it is the only one that exists. And in condescending to accept the universe I must agree with Carlyle that indeed I'd better.

A NOTE ON OPERA [1]

THE text and music of *The Bride of Dionysus* are conceived from the standpoint of Wagner's later operas, as regards the relation of the music to the words; that is to say, the words are set in a manner best described as realistic. Wagner himself created the technique of such a treatment of words, and, having created it, did not long remain bound by its strict limitations. In *Die Walküre* he confined his text to words as they would be treated in pure drama, and refused to let Siegmund and Sieglinde sing together in their love duet, because in real life when two people speak at once they can neither understand each other nor convey their meaning to an audience. Wagner had not finished *Siegfried* before he realized that if we can accept singing as a standard form of dramatic language, we have already accepted all that is implied by polyphony, and need not deprive ourselves of the possibilities which vocal ensemble presents for a sort of emotional composite photograph of a dramatic situation. And so Tristan and Isolde not only sing a real duet, but are joined by the voice of the watcher, Brangaene, in the background. Nobody complains that the effect is not realistic; and, in fact, nobody doubts that it is dramatic in a way beyond the capacity of ordinary drama. What is not permissible in opera of this kind is any convention by which words are repeated in order to complete a musical design. If there are not enough words for the musical purpose, the poet must supply more. If the musical purpose interferes with the poet's dramatic purpose, the musician must find a purpose which does not; and this must in the long run be a better musical purpose. It is not by accident that the greatest master of musical stage-craft before Wagner was also the great exemplar of symmetrical form in purely instrumental music. Conversely, we shall best understand a mature string quartet of Mozart if we begin by realizing that in every aspect its style is inveterately dramatic in direct proportion to the richness of its form.

The general formula for the solution of the problem of opera is that each step in the action must occur swiftly and culminate in a

---

[1] Sir Donald Tovey's opera, *The Bride of Dionysus*, with a libretto by Robert C. Trevelyan, was produced in Edinburgh in 1929, and again in 1931. The poem was printed and issued in booklet form, with an analysis of the music by the composer. To this analysis, there was an introduction, which is printed here under a new title.—EDITOR.

tableau which gives opportunity for highly developed music. This formula may be followed stupidly or mechanically. Metastasio (a respectable figure in Italian literature, though he devoted his whole life to opera libretti) handled it skilfully, and was by no means satisfied with the way in which the composers set his plays. With opera before Gluck the blame for failure lies neither with Metastasio nor with the composers, but is inherent in the musical art-forms of the time. Music itself was not dramatic. The supreme greatness of Bach and Handel makes us unwilling to deny their music any quality which we think good; but if language is to have meaning we must not apply the word 'dramatic' to sunsets and cathedrals; nor even to such soul-stirring contrasts as those of the duet and chorus near the end of the first part of the *Matthew Passion*, or the 'Et exspecto' of the B minor Mass. These are the contrasts which static musical forms can produce by mere juxtaposition. Their emotional force may be at least equal to that of drama; and obviously no stage representation could attempt them. But to call them dramatic is merely the opposite abuse of language to that by which newspapers call every murder discovered by the police a tragedy. It may be convenient to use words on that plane; and there is another plane, lofty beyond our ken, on which sordid lives and deaths are neither less nor more tragic than those of the most famous heroes. But terms of human art are a humbler subject, which is all that concerns the present essay. And on this humble plane it is important for us to realize that Gluck was no mere reformer of opera, but the pioneer in a total change in the nature of music, which thereby became dramatic for the first time in history.

There is nothing specially or conventionally musical in Metastasio's scheme of tableaux strung together by dialogue. On the contrary, it represents a tendency characteristic of all drama at all periods. Dramatic action is explosive, and each explosion changes one tableau into another. Now, which is the more important: the explosion, or the tableau? Were any dramatists profounder draughtsmen of character than the Greeks, and are any dramas more statuesque than theirs? Yet, who should know better than Aristotle when he says that the aim of drama is not character but action? Popular taste agrees with Aristotle in principle; but the practical difficulties of play-making confuse the issue.

There is a boys' school where the experiment has been tried of making the boys organize their work for themselves. The boys naturally embarked on dramatic efforts, and of course began with the useful experience that it was more interesting to read the adventures of Sherlock Holmes than to act them. They soon came to Shakespeare; and some of their experiences would be quite useful illustrations to a text-book on opera. Nothing can be more Wagnerian, for instance, than Shakespeare's habit of enumerating in a speech not only the gestures of the speaker but the 'properties' he is to handle. Dramatic poetry, and, *a fortiori*, dramatic music, must in the first place be histrionic. In the first place? Where, then, does rhetoric come? Demosthenes himself tells us that the three essentials of rhetoric are action, action, and action!

Now, many a chapter in the history of opera shows that success, in the sense of vitality and convincingness, depends on the existence of the right qualities in the right order of conception. The absolute aesthetic values are another matter; some operas with low absolute aesthetic values are still, a century and a half after their creation, living by reason of their operatic merits, while sublime music like *Idomeneo* is producible only at a Mozart festival. It is useful to arrive at the operatic qualities by separating them from the aesthetic values most nearly allied to them. Thus, rhetoric will not suffice to make either the text or the music live; but gesture, the histrionic suggestiveness of words and music, will carry almost any nonsense over the footlights. A fine story, such as that of *Fidelio*, may be so awkwardly set forth on the stage that it can hardly be understood. Even before such a drama is set to music we shall evidently find that theatricality is as necessary to drama as action is to rhetoric. On the other hand, nobody wants to make sense of the story of *Die Zauberflöte*. Histrionically and theatrically every incident in this pantomime is superbly timed by Mozart, working with a poetaster who knew the exact effect of every entry and exit.

One definite illustration from *Fidelio*, and a mere mention of points in *Die Zauberflöte*, will show the principle here involved.

Fidelio is the story of the heroic devotion of a wife who, believing her husband to be imprisoned in the dungeons of a certain fortress, disguises herself as a man, and enters the service of the jailer. The jailer's daughter falls in love with the mysterious 'youth', who reluctantly takes advantage of this to further the plan of rescue. The climax of the story is excellent; Fidelio, helping the jailer to dig a grave for her husband in his dungeon, reveals herself and holds the murderous governor Pizarro at bay with a pistol until a trumpet-call from a tower announces the arrival of a minister of state, who deals justice, poetic and political. It was this heroic

climax which attracted Beethoven, and which raises *Fidelio* above
the level of other pretty treatments of the political-prisoner-and-
heroic-wife theme that were in vogue as an artistic reaction after
the French Revolution.

At least three plays on this theme were written by Bouilly:
Fidelio, ou l'Amour conjugale; *Les Deux Journées*, Cherubini's
masterpiece; and *Hélèna*, a pretty little opera by Méhul, which
even has the rescuing trumpet-call in the overture and at the crisis.
In all three it is evident that Bouilly's main interest is to give the
adventures and dangers a background of sweet domesticity, not incompatible with a vein of gentle playfulness. *Fidelio* is no exception; the good old jailer's blessing is upon his little Marzellina and
his industrious assistant. Marzellina herself has substituted the
mysterious Fidelio for her faithful Jacquino, only to look forward to
the same sweet domesticity as the sum of human felicity; and when
the heroine is revealed Marzellina returns to her Jacquino as if nothing had happened. And so the climax of the first of the original
three acts of Bouilly's play is the plighting of troth between Marzellina and Fidelio under the blessing of Papa Rocco. Now, this is
obviously a good and sufficient occasion for music in an opera where
most of the story is enacted in spoken dialogue. But to Beethoven
and the first German adapter of the text this was inadequate to their
conception of the heroine. After all, the betrothal was only a step in
her sublime project of penetrating to her husband's dungeon. This
project must be handled in music, and in Beethoven's music!
Accordingly some of the previous dialogue, which discusses Fidelio's
betrothal in connexion with her prospective official appointment as
under-jailer, is now incorporated in the trio. The result is that the
music bursts into the middle of a prose dialogue, and continues the
subject thereof, without any discoverable reason. The story is good
and the music is Beethoven, but the resulting scene is a puzzle,
not a mystery.

Contrast a few incidents in *Die Zauberflöte*. A young prince is
lying on the ground, having fainted in flight from a serpent which
lies slain by three veiled ladies who appeared in the nick of time
and then departed to tell the news to their queen. The young
prince revives, and hears a singing and piping from a distance; the
singer approaches, sings his song, and plays his pipes. Then the
piper and the prince enter into conversation. Later, the three
veiled ladies set a padlock on the lying piper's mouth and tell the
prince that the Queen of Night looks to him to rescue her daughter.

They give him a locket containing her portrait. The orchestra heaves two sighs; the prince has fallen in love! In another scene the music begins with the entry of the poor padlocked Papageno singing *Hm, hm, hm, hm*, pathetically, until his punishment is remitted. And so at every point, whether the scene changes or not, the entry of the music explains itself as aptly as any fine detail in Mozart's style. And the merit is not exclusively Mozart's. Though the story is not only nonsense, but flatly shifts its ground and, after enlisting our sympathies with the Queen of Night, tells us that the wicked enchanter is the chief priest of Isis (*scilicet* Grand Master of the Freemasons), who, from the noblest of motives, took Pamina from her unscrupulous mother's clutches; though nobody ever understood either it or the music better for reading up the interesting lore concerning its political and Masonic allusions; though few people have ever read the sequel which no less a person than Goethe sketched for it; yet, *Die Zauberflöte* remains not only Mozart's sublimest work, but one of the most perfect operas ever written, because it is theatrically and histrionically in perfect co-ordination from beginning to end.

Now, strange to say, the use of spoken dialogue makes very little difference to the essential problem of opera. It vexes the *a priori* aesthetic theorists who complain that the human mind cannot enjoy a work of art that thus jumps from one plane to an incompatible plane. But human minds, confronted with anything so thrilling as the stage, generally prove as able to jump from plane to plane as Cheshire cats prove able to grin; in fact, 'they all can, and most of 'em do'. And the *a priori* aesthetics have, as we already see, no priority over the practical problem. The step from spoken dialogue to the perfunctory convention of secco-recitative satisfies the theorist's demand for unity of plane, but in practice leaves the gulf between dialogue and music almost as wide as ever. It makes, however, a step forward in enlarging the composer's responsibility for coherence in the general dramatic movement. Mozart was already taking trouble over his secco-recitatives at the age of eighteen in *La Finta Giardiniera*, and Gluck had at once begun his dramatic reforms with the deliberate elevation of all recitative to high musical importance, with aptly coloured instrumentation. Gluck, moreover, arranged with his librettists that whole scenes should be welded together by recurring stanzas for chorus or principal singers. Thus his action, though eminently statuesque and of the utmost simplicity, approaches that of Wagnerian opera more nearly than that of any other composer before Wagner. But, apart from Gluck and that wonderful triumph over impossibilities, *Fidelio*, the main resources of opera were worked out in comedy of manners by Mozart and in romantic fairy-tales by Weber. Afterwards, Meyerbeer and the Italians discovered the possibilities of blood-and-thunder, to the great hindrance of Wagner's propaganda. Wagner's effects came by causes; but Meyerbeer could produce them all as a box of tricks without any cause worth bothering about. And if Wagner had not been histrionically and theatrically, as well as dramatically, right, his reforms and his sublime music would have no more prevailed over Meyerbeer's well-staged shows than Schumann's *Genoveva* or Schubert's fourteen unproducible operas and fragments.

The advice of Wagner to young opera-writers is surely the advice of the most drastic idealist that ever brought his principles into practice. Yet he said, 'If you want to write operas, begin with *Singspiele*'. That is to say, the creator of the perfect co-ordination of music and drama advised composers to begin with works in which the story was acted in spoken dialogue with set pieces of music whenever a situation produced a good tableau. And this is obviously good practical advice. Begin with a scheme that gives the composer opportunities and does not load him with the kind of responsibility that inhibits his musical ideas. You cannot begin by trying to derive musical inspiration from those business affairs of dramatic presentation which must be made clear without being allowed to weaken the climaxes. The luxurious poet, e.g. the Shakespeare of *Richard II*, has exactly the same problem as the musician. Poetry delays action and action interrupts poetry. In pure music, the art of orchestration presents the same problem. Bach and Handel relegated the background-business of their orchestration to the continuo, the player at the keyboard who continually supplies the harmonic connective tissue and leaves the orchestral instruments in aristocratic freedom. Gluck, Haydn, and Mozart changed all that; their orchestra, whether symphonic or dramatic, must do its own domestic service.

The essential Wagnerian reform in opera is of the same kind, but has still wider consequences. The music must undertake all the 'business' of the drama. Now, this affects something more than its style from moment to moment. As long as there was a definite gulf between business-dialogue and emotional music, each musical section remained complete in itself. A motto-theme, a signal, or an ancestral ballad (such as conveniently narrates important antecedents) might foreshadow Wagnerian leitmotive; but any more extensive connexion between one musical 'number' and another would seem more like poverty of invention than like dramatic continuity. Wagnerian leitmotive is, in fact, a by-product of the Wagnerian time-scale, which is exactly that of Wagner's colossally statuesque dramas. The development of the music is not that of some twenty-four 'numbers', but that of the entire drama. Hence the most natural way for themes to be developed is for them to grow into fixed relation with dramatic elements—personal, psychological, and accidental. And yet this is not an inevitable result of Wagnerian continuity; Verdi's *Otello* and *Falstaff* are as continuous as *Tristan*, yet they each contain hardly two recurring themes, and these recur only once or twice. Weber's *Euryanthe*, on the other hand, contains thirteen, which is more than can be found in *Lohengrin*.

But a far more important aspect of Wagner's musical organization than any details of leitmotive is the matter of recapitulation. A leitmotive may be short enough to please the early official commentators on whom Wagner smiled playfully; but no classical symphony has larger slabs of exact recapitulation than those that hold Wagner's immense works together. Commentators have been known to analyse Isolde's *Liebestod* into its molecular figures without noticing that it consists of 100 bars of the love-duet in Act II, written in a slightly different notation. Wagner, when scoring *Götterdämmerung*, writes urgently to his publisher to send scores of the rest of the *Ring* which he has not at hand, so that he can get parallel passages to tally. Thus Siegfried, a moment before his death, recalls his conversation with the bird when the dragon's blood enabled him to understand all creatures, and thus he dies to the music of Brünnhilde's awakening. These are the obvious cases, but there are many that lie deeper; and perhaps the first necessity for the understanding of Wagner's music and drama is to realize that when he broke down the old classical organization of operatic 'numbers', he did not pulverize music into 'motives', but built it into symmetries tenfold longer in time and a thousandfold more voluminous than any that music had known before. How far smaller symmetries can co-exist with these is a profound and practical question which constitutes one of the permanent stumbling-blocks of criticism. Thus, Lachmann traced in the *Iliad* dozens of separate lays, one for each topic or person. The only puzzle was why these lays all began so clearly and all dissolved into obscurity.

To this the only answer was the obvious if paradoxical one, that the *Iliad* was not compiled by a committee of experts ranging from Pisistratus to James MacPherson, but was mainly a single work of art whose separable threads became interdependent because they really belonged to it. I can see no *a priori* reason why an opera on Wagnerian lines should not be equally full of promising beginnings suggestive of any features of classical form that can be turned to dramatic account. Of course a classical form that conventionalizes the words or hampers the action is unpardonable in relation to the Wagnerian time-scale. Only the mock-heroic style can be allowed anachronisms in its conventions. Classical forms are notoriously as likely to hamper the delivery of lyric poetry as to hamper dramatic action. The scope of lyric poetry in drama is also severely limited. To the musician its limitation can be summed up thus: that (except at the end, where we may side with Mozart and Beethoven in dwelling upon final happiness rather than with the French demand for a quick curtain) every expanse of lyric poetry or episode should rest on an underlying dramatic tension; as, to quote the work now to be described, when all on the stage doubt whether Theseus will return from his dive into the sea; or when we know that Ariadne is deserted, and are waiting to see how and when she will find this out.[1]

---

[1] Here follows the analysis by the composer of his opera, *The Bride of Dionysus*.

STIMULUS AND THE CLASSICS OF MUSIC[1]

WHEN General John Reid founded the Chair of Music in the University of Edinburgh, he, like all pioneers and prophets, was inspired by a vision the meaning of which grows with the passage of time. By this growth the truth of the prophet's vision is tested, and the history of the Reid Professorship has amply vindicated the foresight of its founder. I need not describe its experimental stages: they are past, and their monument is around us in this beautiful classroom with its fine organ, its valuable collection of instruments, both musical and scientific, and its copious library of music and musical literature. The name of Professor Donaldson must always remain associated with many of these excellent resources. To his predecessor, Sir Henry Bishop, the Chair owes the prestige of being held by a composer whose music was a household word; and after him, the name of Hugo Pierson is on record to show that this university had the courage to appoint a man of genius whose artistic outlook was one of open revolt against the musical orthodoxy of his time. After his merely nominal tenure, the Chair was held for twenty-six years by Sir Herbert Oakeley, whose fame as an organist survives in the memories of many of my friends. It is always difficult for a new-comer to take up an office which has been held for an entire generation by one man. Such a difficulty was faced twenty-four years ago in this place, and I have to face it now.

But my difficulty is not quite the same as that which Professor Niecks had before him when he came here. Twenty-four years ago, the fiercest of British musical patriots could hardly claim that our normal standard of musical culture had attained a level comparable to that which we instinctively demand in literary culture. The very activity in serious musical propaganda which had already so long distinguished Edinburgh proved that musical culture was still no matter of course, but an interesting and special phenomenon. Even if that had not been so, we must still honestly face the fact that our universities are not normally centres for training in music, or other non-literary arts, the solid foundations for which ought to be laid down in childhood by very special methods. In these circumstances a new professor could have only two alternative wishes for

[1] Tovey's Inaugural Address as Reid Professor of Music in the University of Edinburgh, delivered in the Music Classroom on 9 October, 1914.

the conditions of his task. He might wish to find a system already in working order which corresponded with his ideals. Similarly, the angels we see in pictures, having wings, might wish for muscles with which to work them. A practical man does not waste time on wishing for ideals which he sees to be Utopian: he will, if he is energetic, wish rather to be hampered as little as possible by tradition, even if he has to create an entire organization for himself out of rudiments and fragments.

This enviable task fell to Professor Niecks. All that had been done before him may, without any disparagement to those who had achieved it, be described as the collecting of apparatus. It was admirably done, and the time had not yet been ripe for turning the apparatus to its full account as a means of education. Professor Niecks knew that the time is never ripe until someone tacitly assumes that it is. He chose Musical Education as the theme of his Inaugural Lecture. His ideas had wings, and he developed the muscles with which to work them. Accordingly, his successor finds realized that most Utopian of wishes, a tradition which corresponds with his ideals; my ideals and Professor Niecks's. Another way of putting it is that Professor Niecks has done everything that man could do to make his post impossible for his successor. He has accustomed this University to his own standard, and never for a moment hinted that that standard is exceptional. It is a standard of development; it cannot be maintained by imitation. Professor Niecks is inimitable; the new Professor must do things in his own way or fail. There must be changes; for what is established here is a living tradition, and the right changes imply no criticism but the maintenance of its life. With the loyal co-operation of the University Professor Niecks worked in his own way; and that is how I must imitate him.

He did not use the prestige of his position to the advancement of his fame, though his musical powers would have sufficed for the reputation of half a dozen musicians. For some years Professor Niecks played the viola here in string quartets; thereby devoting far more executive skill to a true musician's task than many a violinist has devoted to acquiring the reputation of a virtuoso. On the other hand, a composer who produced an oratorio every year might show less self-criticism than Professor Niecks, without showing as much real experience of composition. It is admissible by a pardonable mixture of metaphors to say that in devoting to education so much that other musicians have given more ostensibly to mankind, Professor Niecks has rather hidden his light under a bushel. But, in the first place, education is meant for mankind; and, in the second place, when Professor Niecks hid his light the bushel began to glow: and every composer and every player who has warmed himself at that glow recognizes in Professor Niecks a colleague whose theories are throughout animated by experience. He retires for the benefit of his health. May the benefit of his health mean the enlargement of his sphere of influence; and may his leisure inspire him to collect from the vast stores of his memories his published and unpublished discourses, and his ever-fresh streams of thought, some volume or series of volumes that shall show the panorama of his mind to people who have not had the privilege of being trained by him, and shall come perhaps as a fresh revelation to those who have! For even here, as a lecturer, where his brilliancy was most impossible to conceal, he has taken more pains to make his ripest and deepest thoughts clear as the rudiments of musical common sense, than all the paradox-mongers in the world have ever taken to astonish by exploiting the grain of truth that can be shaken out of every inverted platitude.

With this I will, in appearance, take my leave of the subject of these introductory remarks; in reality my main theme, and everything else I can ever say about music, will remind you of my predecessor just in as far as I succeed in speaking accurately, originally, and clearly. Let me emphasize the point of originality. The very courtesy with which my predecessor always quotes authorities must often have minimized the effect of the freedom and vigour with which he differs from them. I am afraid of acquiring a reputation for originality by my cruder methods. I must confess to a certain pleasure in playing skittles with discredited theories: and one of the temptations of that game is that it is so troublesome to remember or discover the authentic origins of those theories that the player soon takes to setting the theories up for himself. This may lead to inventing bad new theories, imagining them to be old, and using a bad old theory to bowl them over under the impression that it is a good and original one. Well, I will beg you to believe that I am alive to such dangers when I now proceed to make short work of certain ideas about the claims of classical music—ideas which I believe to be widely accepted and which I am convinced are misleading.

It has been obvious for more than twenty years that all the fine arts, including literature, have displayed a growing tendency to revolt against everything that calls itself classical tradition. Some elements of revolt have always been traceable at one or more points in the career of every master who has ever become a classic. Cherubini, the most notoriously pedantic and discouraging teacher known to musical history, wrote some of the greatest operas in the French classical repertoire; and then dictated to his pupil Halévy (the composer of *La Juive* and other operas famous in their day) a treatise on counterpoint, in which he says that certain progressions which serious counterpoint strictly forbids may be found here and there 'in operas and symphonies and compositions of that sort'. For even asceticism is a revolt against 'the weight of too much liberty'. What is new in the artistic spirit of revolt at the present day is its bitterness and its universal range. Without entering into controversial questions, I may venture to assert that to-day it has, as it seldom had before, the aspect of a grievance. The mildest, and therefore perhaps the most serious, form of the grievance is that the load of classical tradition has long been so heavy as to repress further creative impulse, and that it is always increasing. And I am unable to see any lack of logic in those who, feeling thus, argue that they must shake off this load even at the cost of a violence that shall destroy, at least for themselves, the very record of what the classics have been. What I do believe to be fundamentally wrong is every attitude towards classical masterpieces which does not make them a stimulus instead of an oppression. Let me take this as an axiom: grant me that when a theory of music proves that a classical masterpiece has no stimulus for an active-minded musician, that theory has reduced itself to an absurdity. And where my assumptions seem too dogmatic, let me appeal to the whole teaching of my predecessor.

What theories of classical masterpieces are there, then, which are not stimulating? I have a recollection, which I regret that I have not been able to verify, that round a dome in one of our chief national centres of art is an inscription which reminds us that it is good to turn frequently to the contemplation of those imperishable masterpieces of the past 'which no modern efforts can ever hope to rival'. It is easy for us nowadays to see in such an inscription the well-meaning false modesty of a period in which current ideas concerning artistic masterpieces were utterly chaotic, when reverence inculcated boundless admiration but indignantly disclaimed the presumption of understanding, and when every young artist who ventured even to obey the advice to contemplate the great masters was practically warned from the outset that it was folly to believe a word they said.

It is hardly possible to exaggerate the depths of insensibility that have often resulted from this kind of reverence for great names. I can remember that a composition known to fame as 'Mozart's Twelfth Mass' was actually performed in London at a by no means insignificant festival on the centenary of Mozart's death. Now this 'Twelfth Mass' is one of a large series of forgeries which began to be foisted upon Mozart's name already during the lifetime of his widow. In the case of small works, an intelligent musician might perhaps have difficulty in detecting the forgeries; for instance, one well-known and typical spurious set of decently written pianoforte variations ascribed to Mozart betrays itself rather by too rich and full a pianoforte style than by its poverty of thought; for Mozart threw off most of his pianoforte variations so carelessly that they are almost certainly inferior to those he used to extemporize in his concerts, if indeed they may not be regarded as attempts to scribble a record after the event. But only the hypnotic suggestion of his mere name in an age of conscientiously unintelligent reverence can account for the very publication of such a work as this so-called 'Twelfth Mass' at all. It is longer than any of the genuine Masses, except perhaps the great unfinished work in C minor; it is therefore very ambitious. The genuine Masses show little of Mozart at his best. The Archbishop of Salzburg, for whom he wrote them, was a most unsavoury personage, and the time was in any case hardly a great period for Church music. It would be possible to quote passages from Mozart's genuine Masses which anticipate the notorious Rossinian crescendo, to say nothing of more classical if not less lively features of *opera buffa*. But it would not be possible to quote from Mozart, or from even any competent representative of a good school, such elaborate pointlessness and such grammatical and structural blunders as pervade every page of the spurious 'Twelfth Mass'. Its author, one Zulehner, has been identified; he was not without talent, for even the name of Mozart could otherwise hardly have hoisted no less than five of his Masses into a genuine popularity; but he was no master, and perhaps a motive for the fraud may be guessed from the fact that I myself have seen a stack of his manuscripts lying in the archives of the house of Schott in Mainz, where they still wait in vain for publication, since he sent them a hundred-odd years ago in his own name.

A reverence that disclaims criticism is as dangerous as no reverence at all. Classical masterpieces can tell us nothing if we remain at the mercy of any label that chance or fraud affixes to the clumsiest works of their period. These dangers are, no doubt, characteristic of the past: our present dangers come rather from lack of reverence. I have in mind a recent treatise on composition, which has extraordinary merit as a most practical embodiment of the experience of a brilliant composer who is eminently successful as a teacher, and who has followed the example of the classics, by always stimulating in himself and in his pupils an interest in contemporary developments. His book contains many illustrations from the great classics, and cannot be accused of any failure to stimulate enthusiasm for them. Yet I confess that for me the whole tone of the work is spoiled by one sentence in the preface, to the general effect (I quote again from memory) that, while it used to be orthodox to consider the classics infallible, the experienced musician knows that they are not. The attitude of mind which such a remark indicates does not, like its opposite extreme, seem at first sight to crush originality and all creative impulse, but it starves it, and can inflict serious damage on just that most priceless originality that would survive and react against old-fashioned methods of crushing. It fails to distinguish between wisdom and information; and it encourages the student to assume that everything he does not readily understand in a classic must be a blunder on the same mental level as his uncritical imitation of it would be. This assumption has really been just as characteristic of periods of unreasoning reverence, and it always produces much the same results whatever its manner of expression. Bach and Handel have a method of treating the orchestra which is radically different from, and obviously more primitive than, that of Mozart, to say nothing of more modern orchestration. Consequently, throughout the nineteenth century this primitive orchestration was unhesitatingly dismissed as merely inartistic by the spirit of reverence that admired 'Mozart's Twelfth Mass'; and though we have finally discredited the nineteenth-century practice of plastering Handel's oratorios with some six layers of 'additional accompaniments', beginning with Mozart and not quite ending with Sir Michael Costa, the musical scholarship that has learnt the practical methods of realizing Handel's own ideas in his own musical language is not yet so widely spread that performances without additional accompaniments can be trusted always to give pleasure.

These, then, are the two extreme errors possible in our attitude towards the classics: the indolent reverence that admits nothing in common between our minds and the minds of the great masters; and the irreverence that would reduce the mind of a great master, or, for that matter, any other mind, to the exact level of our own. Both these errors are forms of inattention and lack of sympathy. It is wrong to contemplate a masterpiece with the thought in mind that the present can never hope to rival the past. This thought would have extinguished every one of the classics themselves, except some solar myth whom we might conjecture to be the First Classic. But that is not the reason why it is wrong; and even a great master might be none the worse for the modesty it inculcates. The reason why it is wrong is that it is irrelevant to the contemplation of a masterpiece, and still more irrelevant to the creation of one. The contemplation of a masterpiece demands one's whole attention; and the act of creating so much as a decent piece of school-work demands a kind of athletic mental 'form' in which modesty has the place that it has in rock-climbing. Modesty comes before and after; it is the principle by which the wise man governs his resting-phases. No man, woman, or child ever did a good stroke of original work without feeling, for the time being, that it was the finest stroke that the mind of man could conceive. No sociable person wishes to retain that feeling after its function is accomplished; and though some very great artists have notoriously indulged it without scruple, in most healthy cases the experience of it and of the reaction from it soon become too familiar to produce any illusion as to their meaning. There is nothing more in it, for good or evil, than the ancient fact that the field of vision, whether physical or mental, is always of the same apparent size; and it is only experience that can tell us whether what fills that field is really large and distant, or small and near. Modesty will not make the field subtend a smaller or larger angle; and anything that professes to do so is mere double-mindedness and instability. The discovery, or even the first illusion, of capacity to do original work will always impose a severe strain on the mind which it suddenly floods; and nothing is of more vital and practical importance to the young artist than the attitude his disposition and environment may lead him to take towards classical masterpieces while his mind is at leisure to recover from the thrill.

Let us continue to play skittles with one or two minor false reasons for upholding the classics. The next doctrine that occurs to me is that the classics represent just what has stood the test of time.

I am not concerned so much with the truth or falsehood of all these current doctrines as I am with the difficulties of their application. The doubtfulness of this particular doctrine is very obvious, and more so in proportion to the time which has tested it. With Ancient Greece, time has no doubt been less capricious than earthquakes and volcanoes, but it has been quite as ruthless; and though we may have a pious opinion that the seven extant plays of Aeschylus really are the topmost tenth of his works, nothing is more certain than that the discovery of the other nine-tenths would profoundly modify that opinion, even if it confirmed it. On the other hand, to music, time has, in comparison with its treatment of almost any other art, applied hardly any real tests, fair or unfair. The whole art, as we understand and cultivate it, first assumes something like maturity after the invention of printing. Consequently, there is little or nothing to make its records incomplete; and as its real existence is not in writing but in performance, not in space but in time, there is no question of a musical masterpiece existing only, like a picture, as a thing unique and perishable, compared with which the best copies are to be regarded as self-confessed failures. Whatever may be the true definition of a classic, the musician, if he has used his opportunities as they would be used by a scholar in literature, will have a host of reasons for arriving at a conception thereof which differs markedly from any formed by connoisseurs of other arts. Apart from the exceptional completeness of his records, he is accustomed, as perhaps no other artist ever has been since the best days of Ancient Greece, to expect perfection from his classics: perfect authenticity, perfect form, and perfect style. I do not say that he always understands this, or even that he will often agree that it is the case. Stated as an absolute truth it will repel most people, and may even seem a mischievous doctrine; but as a rough comparison between music and other arts it proves itself easily and copiously.

As to authenticity, I have already spoken of musical forgeries; but they would have been far less gross, and we should have long ago become far less helpless in criticizing them, if they had not been so rare. A composer who should be as important as Giorgione, and whose most deservedly famous works should be of such doubtful authenticity, would not stimulate our present musical connoisseurship as Giorgione has stimulated the connoisseurship of painting, but would drive musical scholars into a state of despair which could hardly be relieved by any measure short of giving the degree of

Doctor of Music to every Baconian in the Empire. What are the usual difficulties in deciding upon the correct text of one of Bach's Forty-eight Preludes and Fugues? They lie in this, that we have sometimes as many as ten manuscripts, three of which will be autographs, and the rest copies made for and by Bach's own family and pupils with changes that may or may not be dictated or auto-graphed by him. These difficulties are often serious, but they make the musical scholar a spoilt child in comparison with the man who restored, to Mistress Quickly's account of the death of Falstaff, the line—

His nose was as sharp as a pen, and a' babbled of green fields.

Yet I must say that musical scholars have sometimes risen as nobly to the wealth of their heritage as any Shakespearean has ever soared from the squalor of the folios and quartos. Wilhelm Rust, in the 'sixties and 'seventies, more than once recovered modulations as priceless as they are abstruse from recitatives of Bach that seemed quite unintelligible, since the figured-bass part, which is the organist's only clue to the harmonic filling-out, was lost, or perhaps had never been written down since Bach played the organ himself. And, to go back to what we sometimes hastily regard as the Dark Ages of musical scholarship, that notoriously dandified eighteenth-century historian of music, Dr. Burney, can never be overpraised for the sympathetic ingenuity with which he deciphered one of the most touching works of the great early sixteenth-century composer whom a friend of mine has aptly called the Chaucer of music—the Dirge written by Josquin des Prés for his master Ockenheim.

The perfection of form in the musical classics is a subject that only the thorough analysis of entire works can even pretend to illustrate. To-day I must leave it as a dogmatic assertion, and can only pause to observe that it, more than any other peculiarity of musical history, is the cause of most musical fashions in fastidious-ness, scepticism, and revolt. The Church, the stage, the human voice itself, often invite music, as by royal command, to illustrate and absorb (as far as it can) ideas expressed primarily in words and actions. But have they ever seriously invited music to produce any-thing but art for art's sake? The Novel with a Purpose may have served its purpose and yet remain as a work of art. Or it may do either, or neither. But has anyone ever heard of an Opera with a Purpose? Yes, we have heard of *Die Zauberflöte*, with its special interest for Freemasons: and we know that nineteenth-century

Italian opera gave too much scope for anti-Austrian propaganda to be always acceptable to the police: but did the police have anything to say to the music apart from the words? And is the music of *Die Zauberflöte* as cryptic and formless as the libretto? Or has the research into it that identifies the Queen of Night with the Empress Maria Theresa and the nigger Monostatos with her clerical supporters cleared up any mysteries in the music? It has shown us how Mozart came to take an interest in such a pantomime, just as it shows us how such apparent nonsense could interest Goethe enough to induce him to write a sequel to it. But it does not show us how any interest Mozart took in it could make him compose it with success—he had twice before it failed to finish an opera because of the badness of the libretto. It was not the politics of *Die Zauberflöte* which helped Mozart to pull it through; it was the fact that this absurd and illiterate pantomime showed real musical stage-craft, and therefore could help the composer instead of hampering him.

There may, then, be music that has to deal with non-musical ideas; but there is no need for it to serve other than artistic ends. In the Church it is offered to the Deity, and if this condition limits the scope of its beauty, all the more severely does it demand that the scope shall be limited to the purest beauty, even if thereby it repudiates Mozart's genuine Masses.

Lastly, let us consider the perfection of style in the musical classics. Here we may hope to find some common ground between what is classical in music, and what is classical elsewhere; and so we may come to utter some truths about classical music which shall tally with the views of other artists and scholars, and shall prove to be essentially stimulating. I will take the point of musical style in which all modern musicians and students feel themselves to be most fastidious and most fully in the enjoyment of all their faculties: the treatment of the orchestra. Why, it is sometimes openly asked, should we retain any but a merely historical interest in Beethoven's orchestration, seeing that, even if his deafness had not led him into frequent errors in balance of tone, he wrote for string-bands whose members could not to-day retain their posts in any good orchestra, and for wind-bands furnished with instruments on which half the most ordinary types of passage were unplayable in all but a small and very haphazard list of keys, the trumpets and horns possessing an apology for a scale in which the gaps often seemed more relevant than the notes, while no experienced listener was so unreasonable as to expect the wind-band to be in tune with the strings until the middle half-hour of the concert (after which the wind-pitch would probably rise too far)?

Well, perhaps the performances of a hundred years ago were not always as bad as we have been told they were; and certainly if experienced listeners gave up grumbling at them, they, as well as the deaf composer, must have accepted Duke Theseus's philosophy that 'the best in this kind are but shadows, and the worst are no worse, if imagination amend them'. But I think that literary scholars could give us a more stimulating answer than this. The moment we begin to treat musical instruments and their resultant idioms as scholars treat language, all questions of the 'infallibility' or 'fallibility' of the great composer, of the equality or inequality of this master's output, the greatness or smallness of that master's range, and, most trivial yet most insistent of all questions, the nearness or remoteness of an older master's technical problems compared with those in evidence at the present day—all these questions fall into their place on the intellectual and artistic plane of, let us say, the relation between civilization and the speed of modern communications, or the relation between the means of life and the things that make life worth living.

These questions are not of equal importance, and none of them is unimportant. But they are all questions of relative terms, and that is what makes them so irrelevant to the understanding of great masterpieces. Even an historical view of art does not suffice to bring us in touch with a classic we have failed to understand without history. Whole periods of artistic history have never been and never will be called classical, though they may lie between two Golden Ages. To the historian such periods are actually more interesting than the Golden Ages, for history deals more easily with processes than with results. The musical historian can easily find ten times as much to say about the aims and characteristics of Monteverde and Philipp Emanuel Bach as he can say of Palestrina and John Sebastian Bach; so much so that most histories of music are very apt to leave the reader at a loss to know why Monteverde and Philipp Emanuel do not rank with the greatest masters, while Palestrina and John Sebastian do not fall to a lower plane. It is difficult to correct this impression by merely historic methods without adopting something like a schoolmasterly tone in criticizing the artists of the transition periods: and I believe that the only way out of the difficulty is to adopt towards music the scholar's attitude towards language. A classical period and a classical artist must imply an art-language in which all the means of expression—formal, technical, and rhetorical—are coherent. This qualification is in one sense quite independent of the range of the art. So long as that range is, to use a suggestive catch-word, *central*, then the mind will be filled by the art, and we know that its field of vision always subtends the same angle. But unless the range is central, the field of vision will not be filled.

Palestrina's art is comprised within a very narrow field at the very centre of the aesthetics of unaccompanied choral music. Now, I believe it can be shown that the aesthetics of the unaccompanied chorus lie at the very centre of what we know as classical music itself; and if Palestrina radiates evenly in all directions from this centre, his circumference will be to you the vaults of heaven, so long as your view has also started from the centre and not from outside. A very small step will put you outside: Monteverde took that step, and for a hundred years no man could build a new dome to contain the new music, or even guess whether the dome should be limited by the principles eventually attained by Bach, or by those of Gluck, Wagner, or, if you like, Strauss. Meanwhile, of course, outside the centre there are always ways of attaining a comparatively artificial perfection. Chopin is a wonderfully perfect artist: yet orthodoxy is justified in its almost instinctive refusal to regard him as a classic on so high a plane as Palestrina. His range of thought is incomparably wider than Palestrina's; and there is a sense in which his wonderful treatment of the pianoforte is as truly classical as it is original. But here we touch upon just what makes him a genius with a special province, instead of a spectator of all musical time and existence (to borrow Plato's character of the philosopher). The pianoforte is an exceedingly complex aesthetic phenomenon; and its peculiarities are very far removed from the centre of music. What is truly classical in Chopin's treatment of it is that instead of confining himself to its outermost and latest resources, he used it as a great writer uses language; he made its every utterance suggest the vocal origins of music, and never misjudged the amount of suggestion that its tones could bear. But he never attempted to leave this artificial medium, and interest himself profoundly in the real centre of musical aesthetics; and so his very suggestiveness has a note of exile in it which is not the universal note of the classic.

Well, you will say, Beethoven is supposed to be a great classic: he wrote a certain amount of very important choral music; how comes it that he is never supposed to have a good choral style? The question of what makes a good style is not quite the same as the question of what makes a good model. This is where we musicians are so often misled by possessing such an extraordinary number of very perfect works. We are not trained, like architects and Shakespearean scholars, to look for qualities of mind before we demand finished execution, unimpaired preservation, and undivided authorship. If Beethoven's choral writing were twice as uncouth as we find it, there would still be ample evidence that his imagination grasped every quality that choral writing ought to possess. It is not a merit that the writing is unpractical; but that, however deplorable and however much Beethoven's own fault, has no more to do with the quality of his imagination than the even more reprehensible habit of painting with cheap and perishable pigments has to do with a painter's sense of colour.

Can we, in conclusion, define an attitude towards classical music that shall satisfy every man of culture as being a stimulus to the art? It need not be new; and so I venture to suggest a very familiar argument. We should regard a classical masterpiece as a stimulus to our own activity, because it *generalizes* our special problems. It has solved them once for all in its own way, and that encourages our originality because its way cannot possibly be ours. Time may not always have preserved the greatest classics, or have exposed the hollowness of inferior favourites; but it preserves far too vast and heterogeneous a collection of undoubted masterpieces for us to have any justification in pleading their ever-increasing and diverging testimony in support of narrow doctrines, whether orthodox or revolutionary.

When critics adopt the eighteenth-century method of saying that such and such a classic ought to inspire us with noble feelings because its sentiments are edifying and its form perfect, we may legitimately argue that it is useless to tell us that we ought to feel this and that, when as a matter of fact we feel quite otherwise. On the other hand, we shall do well to beware of the exclusively subjective methods of criticism so much in vogue since the latter part of the nineteenth century; methods which may be but mildly caricatured as consisting in sitting in front of a work of art, feeling our pulses, and noting our symptoms before we have taken the slightest trouble to find out whether, as a matter of fact, the language of that art means what we think it means.

No one ever had a sane love of any art without a curiosity to extend his knowledge of it: and no one with a rational curiosity ever expects his appetite to be always in the same condition towards the same objects. Let the student and lover of music use every means to stimulate and satisfy his curiosity; and let no one be discouraged from playing or composing so long as those activities do not hinder him, instead of helping him to enjoy music. His neighbours, if not his teachers, will help him to form an opinion on that point. The future of music lies at the back of the young musician's head; let him produce it if he can. But his eyes are not inside his head; his widest field of vision looks out into the past, and it is for him to say how many centuries his gaze shall sweep. Whatever the range of his vision, it will always subtend the same angle. From this fact arise the illusions of conceit and of depression; in its right understanding lie their prevention and cure.

THE TRAINING OF THE MUSICAL
IMAGINATION [1]

GREAT harm has been done to musical education, and great discouragement inflicted upon the musical public, by ill-advised sceptical statements as to the possibility of reading music silently as we read literature. The scepticism has probably been provoked by foolish statements as to the imaginative powers of score-readers. At the turn of the century an article appeared in *Cosmopolis* in which the author put forward a new kind of poetry, in which a whole page was to be read in a single *coup d'œil*, as the musician reads a full score. The creator of this new art stated that every town in the kingdom possessed one or more Doctors of Music to whom the reading of full scores gave an immediate pleasure superior to that of actual performance, because it combined full information on technical matters and an immunity from accidental defects. The creator of this new art overlooked the fact that, if the score-reader is reading something that he has heard, he is retracing the memory of his own experience of sounds; and that he is none the less recombining remembered sounds when the composition is new to him. The inventor of scored poetry (I forget what he called it) did not, as far as I recollect, tell us whether his poetic symphonies were ever to be recited; nor how, if recited, their meaning was to reach the listener. Perhaps his favourite pastime in his youth had been the game of Shouting Proverbs.

The difficulties of arm-chair score-reading have been exaggerated, but they exist, and there is no reason for adding them to the difficulties of reading literature; but there is serious reason for protesting against the neglect of score-reading in the training, not only of professional musicians, but of all music-lovers. Some time ago, Sir Henry Hadow did great service to musical education by roundly stating that the arm-chair reading of music is not difficult. It is disappointing to find that more effect has not been produced by this statement by so brilliant a writer and so eminent an authority on all matters of education, general and musical. The neglect of score-reading by persons who ought to be musical scholars has for some years produced symptoms amounting to a major scandal. The critical editions of musical classics in the latter half of the nine-

[1] Reprinted from *Music and Letters*, October 1936.

teenth century had grave defects which Macaulay's schoolboy can easily detect nowadays, and which give delicious occasion for sneers from persons to whom they are pointed out by the inheritors of the despised old scholarship by which the pioneer work was achieved; but the worst blunders of those *Gesammtausgaben* are venial sins compared to the massive ineptitudes of much that has more recently been put forward as results of musical scholarship. Mr. Wotton has exposed the iniquities of the 'critical' edition of Berlioz's works; and, while I must enthusiastically join in the recognition recently given to Bach's *Kunst der Fuge*, I cannot refrain from insisting that the recognition has been accompanied by statements which show that many persons claiming to musical scholarship and to knowledge of the orchestra have never played from score in their lives. At the end of the nineteenth century we may have been more innocent, but we were more enterprising. The experiment was often tried, and in one case published at great expense, of putting fugues from the 'Forty-eight' into open score. Prout revealed by that process that Bach's part-writing was real and that Mendelssohn's was not. The *Kunst der Fuge*, prepared as far as it was finished by Bach himself for publication in score, and published immediately after his death, was, when I was a boy, accessible chiefly in Czerny's edition, which was printed as keyboard music with Czerny's often excellent fingerings; and no sane person had any reason to doubt that it was keyboard music until recent editors have stated that it was not playable, and have thereby proved that they never tried to play it. My own wish is to see it adopted in musical education as I use it myself. In score, without the distraction of an interlined pianoforte 'crib', it constitutes the finest possible school of score-reading in its first stage, the stage at which accuracy must be learned and can be achieved, before the student attempts the compromises of orchestral score-playing.

My present concern, however, is rather with the imaginative reading of music than with the reduction of scores to the limits of pianoforte-playing. What is at stake here is the whole training of the musical imagination. This should be the first and last concern of musical educators. As we do not live in Utopia, we need not be surprised to encounter famous musicians whose habits and training display everything that the conscientious teacher should regard as naughty. These great artists do not prove that the conscientious teacher is wrong, nor even that their habits have been harmless to them; though the critic would be rash as well as impertinent who should deduce *a priori* that their art must be defective because of their habits. We need not imitate the rabid apostle of temperance who prophesies delirium tremens to persons who are well able to carry their liquor. The ill-timed use of the pianoforte is foremost among the bad habits which not even the achievements of Haydn, Schumann, and Berlioz can turn into good habits. Sullivan committed an unpardonable blasphemy against the art of music when he set Adelaide Proctor's poem about the Lost Chord. The poetess may be forgiven for her sentimental description of the lowest type of musical maunderings, but no real composer ought to have confirmed his country in its self-satisfied ignorance of music by signing his name to a musical setting of those words. Fumbling for Great Amens on the noisy keys of an organ is a method of composition which ought not to be encouraged in students who have talent for anything better; and it is encouraged by people who talk sceptically about score-reading.

That which trains the imagination is good; that which starves or dulls the imagination is bad. Sitting at the keyboard and fumbling for lost chords is bad for the imagination. The poetess herself clearly tells us that the lost chord was struck by accident. Samuel Butler has already pointed out that it must have been two chords if it sounded like a great Amen, and my own theory is that the organist had stumbled into a plagal cadence, and probably often afterwards struck one or other of the chords without recognizing them, because he or she never got the first chord in a subdominant relation to the other. Obviously a little knowledge of theory would have given the organist's imagination the freedom of all the Amens in Berlioz's *Requiem*; which, by the way, ends with one now known as the 'Gounod' cadence. This, Charles Hallé tells us, Berlioz actually discovered by letting his fingers wander idly over the keyboard. What amused Hallé was that Berlioz should have thought the cadence particularly original.

Evidently it must be a bad habit that persistently substitutes accident for imagination. But the old-fashioned method of confining harmony exercises to paper-work is now discredited, and the teachers of it undoubtedly starved their pupils in precisely the food that the imagination needs. I have in mind the case of an excellent musician who gave up all hope of learning any musical theory because her teacher would never let her hear or play an unfamiliar chord before she had worked it out on paper in an exercise. Such discipline is nonsensical. Memory is the natural food of the imagination, and abstract calculation is a worse substitute for it than the idlest of wanderings over noisy keys. Dr. R. O. Morris and others have for some time past been leading a renascence of the real classical method of studying harmony from figured bass: not on paper (unless as a preliminary exercise in spelling), but at the keyboard, in accordance with the original purpose of the figured bass as a shorthand for the filling-out of the harmonic background of an instrumental ensemble. What the teacher must forbid is any confusion between keyboard-work and paper-work. The student at the keyboard must not write. The student who is writing must not use the keyboard as a 'crib'. Extemporization is a pastime which may lead to all manner of bad habits, but at least half the aesthetic resources of classical music have originated in it, and the wise teacher will neither close the playground nor supervise the games until they become a worse tyranny than the lessons.

Every musical activity has its proper part in training the imagination, and its danger of warping or starving the imagination by misuse. The orthodox rules of musical grammar are generalizations from the experience of composers. They are completely misunderstood if they are regarded as *a priori* principles to which the composers were bound by authority. Beethoven's fellow-students laughed at him for finding out by disconcerting experience what more docile people knew by rule of thumb; and Beethoven's own epigram that he learnt the rules in order to know how to break them has often been supplemented by the comment that he learnt them first and broke them afterwards. One of Walter Bagehot's most illuminating phrases is his description of Macaulay as a person of 'inexperiencing' character. A photographic and phonographic memory like Macaulay's must be a constant obstacle to growth, for it makes the recorded and immutable past nearly as vivid as, and much more varied than, the living and changing present; yet it would be better for most of us never to outgrow the pleasures of Macaulay's mental pantechnicon than to grow up into an aesthetic system in which music has degenerated into mental arithmetic. Such a consummation has more than once been attained through an orthodox training that was thought to be classical, and it is more likely to be attained through some of the *a priori* revolutionary systems of the present day.

As to the results of the orthodox training, I have seen them embodied in a printed exercise for the Doctorate of Music as achieved under the regulations of some fifty years ago. This exercise was a short oratorio in which an eight-part chorus was accompanied by a full orchestra. The whole composition from beginning to end moved in minims and crotchets, not only in the chorus but in the orchestra. In the days when this fabric was erected, the graduand had to conduct a performance of it at his own expense. Now let us consider the state to which the composing and producing of this work had reduced the composer's imagination. There could be no possible ground for refusing him his doctor's degree. The prescribed rules for the composition exacted a monstrous amount of skilled labour which the composer had thoroughly executed without a mistake. Strict obedience to the grammatical rules would, in fact, make it impossible for an eight-part chorus to sound bad. The rules are the equivalent of traffic regulations, and when the evidence before the court is that the alleged collision took place between two stationary cars each on its proper side of the road, the court can only conclude that there was no collision at all.

Now let us have no doubt about the fact that correct choral writing, whether for four or for eight parts, and whether or not reinforced by an equally correct full orchestra, produces an impressive volume of euphony. There is no question here of originality or of intellectual content. The fact remains that the plagal cadence at the end of a Handel chorus is not only like the sound of a Great Amen, but is precisely that sound, and is aesthetically worth more where Handel automatically puts it than when it was the solitary and accidental deviation into sense by the idle fingers of the weary and uneasy organist. Beethoven said that Handel was the master of masters in that no other composer produced such splendid effects by such simple means. Obviously the greatness of Handel depends, not upon his originality, about which he was notoriously unscrupulous, but upon the freshness of his imagination; and it is hardly possible to discover any technical symptoms by which his greatest work can be distinguished from his dullest. We still fondly apologize for the weakness of much of our nineteenth-century music by alleging that English music was crushed by the ponderous genius of Handel. It suffered no such fate. It was inflated by the dangerous ambition to achieve the Handelian naturalness and sublimity by composers whose talents might have made high instead of low art of light opera, and whose imaginations would have been greatly stimulated by the study of art-forms interesting for their own sake and unprovincially definite in technique.

To return to the case of our doctor's exercise. Its composer may at one time have had some imagination, but his handling of the orchestra showed conclusively that his whole training had been systematically devoted to destroying whatever imagination he had started with. He can never have had any ambition to handle an orchestra for its own sake, and now the regulations for his doctor's degree compelled him to handle it by rule of thumb as a support to an eight-part chorus constructed also by rule of thumb. The regulations themselves showed an infantile notion of the technique of choral writing. The Bachelor of Music was required to handle five voices. The Doctor of Music must show a higher accomplishment by handling eight. A moderate knowledge of the facts of classical music ought to convince anybody that the proper treatment of eight voices is much simpler than that of five. In any case, the technical difference is negligible if the music has any reality at all. The framers of the regulations showed no knowledge of why any composer should write for eight voices; and the eight-part writing of Handel himself would have been ignominiously ploughed if it had been presented in a degree exercise.

However, this Doctor of Music complied with all the regulations, and, having given incontestable proof that he had no previous orchestral experience whatever, had the costly but intense thrill of conducting his own work. My own imagination boggles at what the experience must have meant to him. He cannot have been very sensitive to the effect of works of art as wholes, and so the dullness and monotony of his composition can hardly have been evident to him. The work had cost him hideous labour, quite as satisfactory as that of an arithmetician evaluating π to a thousand places of decimals. And now the faithful labours of the graduand were rewarded by an hour's outburst of solid unwavering euphony— nothing more and nothing less. He had not imagined this: he had only kept the rules; but the work was his own, though he had not known that it was in him. For the rest of his life the whole past, present, and future of music were lost in the glory of his own realization that if you keep the rules nothing can prevent your choral harmony from attaining the sound of a Great Amen. There is, of course, a slight exaggeration in saying that the inhabitant of this fools' paradise had no idea of the sound of his work while he was writing it; but it is quite accurate to say that his training had systematically deprived him of the free exercise of his imagination, and that the glorious experience of hearing so much euphony created merely by his keeping the rules must have confirmed him in a state of mind to which any exercise of free imagination would seem painful if he could conceive it at all.

There is nothing destructive to the imagination in keeping rules. If everything in this exercise had been as imaginative as the most inspired works of Handel, the rules might still have been kept more strictly than by Handel himself. And it is not only possible, but sometimes desirable, to use an orchestra simply to double voices for a chorus. It might even be desirable, as happened once or twice to Bach himself, that such an orchestral support might be furnished for a whole choral work which the choir had not time to learn properly without such support. But here was a composer living in a world where the symphonies of Beethoven were in the repertoire of every decent orchestra and the scores of most of the orchestral classics were published at reasonable prices; yet every natural ambition to use an orchestra to proper purpose was so crushed out of him by his training that when he was actually compelled to provide an orchestra in a performance of his own work at his own expense, he could think of nothing for it to do beyond supporting and imitating standardized vocal harmony. The opportunity was far more rare than it is now, though I myself never heard my own orchestration until I was twenty-eight.

At the other extreme of a composer's opportunities we have a case cited by Richard Strauss in his edition of Berlioz's treatise on instrumentation. A man brought to him a concert overture in which the four tubas specially devised by Wagner for the solemn purposes of his *Ring* danced throughout the score in the simplest of waltz rhythms. When Strauss pointed out the futility of this procedure, the composer said: 'But goodness me, every orchestra has them nowadays: why shouldn't I use them?' Such people, says Strauss, cannot be helped.

The problem then is this: first, to train the musical imagination; and, secondly, to keep it fresh. I shall now venture to go into some details of my own experience as a reader of music; there being nothing immodest in choosing an experience which nobody can know so well as myself.

I began the study of harmony at the proper mental age—that is to say, when I was ten. The correct resolutions of the dominant seventh, the dodge for avoiding forbidden consecutives in a scale of four-part chords of the sixth, the ruling by which a sequence can or cannot justify a rough progression: all such matters belong to the mental age of the inky schoolboy and are a ridiculous diet for the mind of the sceptical undergraduate. I frankly do not know a satisfactory solution of the undergraduate's problems if he has not had the right education; unless the solution is to endure the martyrdom of Berlioz as a man of genius and character. The breezy solution of omitting the elementary training altogether has not been accepted by such men themselves. Even Beethoven felt that his early training had been defective, and his grievance against Haydn was not that Haydn advised him against publishing the best and boldest of the three trios of his first opus, but that Haydn had not the patience to correct his counterpoint exercises thoroughly. I am not comparing myself with any such great men, but am dealing with educational conditions that should be open betimes to all musicians. My first master in harmony and counterpoint was Parratt, whose glorious sense of humour enabled master and pupil to see the fun of admitting frankly that drudgery was drudgery. The authors of the text-books he found it convenient to use might have been disconcerted if they suspected how he spoke of them; but perkiness towards great music was not a weed that could flourish in his climate, though it pervaded large tracts of the technical articles in Grove's *Dictionary*. The one great lost opportunity of my early years was that, under the mistaken idea that organ-playing would be bad for my pianoforte touch, I never learnt the organ from Parratt; but I did form all my notions of that instrument from hearing and watching him every Sunday in the organ loft of St. George's Chapel at Windsor, and I grew up in the happy and stimulating delusion that the organ was a rhythmic instrument, and that the use of its stops was analogous to good orchestration. In Parratt's hands both these propositions were true, and many significant evidences of this are still to be found in his contributions on organ-playing in Grove's *Dictionary*, where he laid down principles which no changes in the modern instrument can make out of date. My disillusion was great when I first heard organists of coarser fibre on the Continent and elsewhere; and as a teacher I have since accumulated a long experience of the difficulties of syringing out the mental ears of organists who never know how many sounds they are producing with their mutation stops. I was not conscious in my childhood that there was such a thing as a special 'Parratt school' of organ-playing, and to this day the expression makes me see red, because for me Parratt stands for music, and you might as well talk of the 'musical school' of musicianship, or describe such and such an astronomer as belonging to the 'scientific school' of astronomy. Parratt's organ-playing was, like the whole of his teaching and personality, a continual stimulus to the imagination because it was perfectly clear. Experience is a good school only if it is the experience of what ought to happen, and I am thankful that my early experience of the organ was so strictly confined. I have a great disbelief in the experience of the grandmother who confidently takes charge of the sick grandchild because she has buried six of her own children.

Another great advantage of my early experience of music was that I lived neither in London nor too far from it. The 'eighties and 'nineties were the great days of the Saturday and Monday 'Pops' in St. James's Hall, and excursions from Eton to hear Joachim and Clara Schumann were neither too rare to accumulate into a general experience nor too common to remain memorable. Moreover, Payne's Miniature Scores[1] had just begun to come out, and were on sale at these concerts. Not only did they become infinitely more valuable records of the treat than the analytical programmes, which merely infuriated me, but, apart from concerts, these scores were within at least fortnightly reach of a boy's pocket-money of sixpence a week. Most of the Haydn quartets were sixpence each, while Mozart and Beethoven ranged from ninepence to a shilling.

The acoustics of the old St. James's Hall were so good that it was a positive advantage to me that the hall was really too large for chamber music. I looked with awe at the fortissimo opening of the Schubert D minor Quartet, and received a stimulating shock when I found that as a listener I must learn to appreciate the gradations between the grasshopper energy which reached my ears in this opening and the awe-inspiring pianissimo of the *Tod und das Mädchen* Variations with their appalling pathos.

At about the same time, somewhere about 1886 or 1887, I had what I still believe to be the most stimulating possible experience of orchestral music. Whether it was my first experience of an orchestra I cannot say, but it was the first that made a vivid impression on me. Lady Hallé was playing the Beethoven Violin Concerto. I had already begun to find score-reading the most exciting of my diversions, with the exception of actual composition, which was too absorbing for me to think whether it was exciting or not. I had no orchestral score of the Beethoven Concerto, but during the forty minutes' railway journey I read the pianoforte

[1] Now known, for many years, as the Eulenberg Edition of Miniature Scores.

score. My expectations of large musical form were based on the experience of sonatas, and I was very much puzzled by what seemed to me the patchiness of the long opening tutti, and especially by the fact that after the first fortissimo irruption in a remote key the whole enormous procession of themes remained flatly in D major. I was held up at the tenth bar by the mysterious D sharp which so obstinately refuses to explain itself; and I had great difficulty in imagining the sound of it, both in itself and in its effect upon the context. As to tone colour, I suppose that I must have imagined it more or less as pianoforte music, though I had already begun to feel suspicious of the style of pianoforte arrangements of orchestral music. Moreover, to this day I find that my imagination is as lazy as Nature in following the line of least resistance. I am bored by reading pianoforte music, because if it is not monstrously difficult I can do so much better by playing it; and if it is too difficult to read at sight it is also probably difficult to construe, so that in any case to practise it technically is as quick a way to know it as to read it in an arm-chair. And so, what with one thing and another, I did not get far beyond the entry of the solo violin in reading the pianoforte score of the Beethoven concerto on the way from Windsor to Paddington. I cannot say what difference it might have made to my experience if I had had the full score to read. Probably not much, for I did not associate the names of oboe, clarinet, and bassoon with definite tone colours, and I remember reading Mozart's three great symphonies in 1889 while uncertain whether horns transposed upwards or downwards.

On the whole, I think it was an additional stroke of luck that I had no means of foretelling the orchestral sound of the opening of Beethoven's Violin Concerto. A more vivid first experience of orchestral sounds cannot be conceived. The facts are both elementary and intensely surprising. Widor, in his delightfully stimulating work on instrumentation, has wittily traced the young musician's progress in the appreciation of orchestral values. It begins with what is known to English musicians as the 'kitchen department', an exquisite refinement of Bottom's favourite 'tongs and bones', ranging from the big drum to the glockenspiel. From this it passes, let us hope quickly, to an extreme veneration for the harp, which detains the student more or less according to whether he has an inexperiencing or an experiencing nature. It then dwells for a while, as it did in Beethoven's own case, among the wind instruments with their fixed and vivid differences of tone colour, and it becomes ripe only with the growing consciousness of the inexhaustible and unfatiguing beauties of string tone. I had already had the advantage of being awakened betimes to the transcendental light of common day diffused by the string quartet; but what further enlightenment was needed the Beethoven concerto supplied with a systematic efficiency which I can find in no other work of art. Consider the facts as they presented themselves to my ear almost in the exact order traced by Widor, with the exception of the harp, the presence of which would have been an unmitigated nuisance. (No sane composer would introduce into a violin concerto an instrument so distracting to the attention, and I cannot help it if the harp is prominent in a well-known half-witted violin concerto by a virtuoso eminent in his own day.)

Well, here begins Beethoven's Violin Concerto with a mysterious summons to attention by means of a simple rhythmic figure on a drum, a musical note completely detached from all other orchestral experiences. On the top of this, Parratt's pupil suddenly heard a mass of organ-like harmony that sounded as if the organ had become as alive and human as Parratt himself. I believe there are people who have discovered that if the conductor allows the wind-players to play like pigs, this opening can be made to sound quite nasty. Classical orchestration is severely criticized on these lines nowadays by bright young men and dull old men who will certainly bury six of their own children by way of qualifying themselves for seeing their grandchild through an attack of croup. All scoring can be made to sound bad if you do not know the composer's style. In the 'nineties it was assumed that Brahms could not orchestrate and that Tchaikovsky and Dvořák were infallible. Brahms will not sound well in the hands of a conductor to whom Wagner is the only normal composer; and composers as reckless and untidy as Dvořák and Tchaikovsky will sound as magnificent as Brahms only if the conductor is brought up to believe that it is his duty to make them so. Beethoven is an untidy artist, though not as untidy as many people seem to think; but he is uncannily accurate in his Violin Concerto, and I had the good luck to begin my orchestral experience with a first-rate performance of it. After the shock of hearing the radiant tones of these wind instruments extended over the mysterious bass of the drums, how could the subtleties of orchestral string tone be more impressively put before me than by the mysterious D sharp with which the violins enter? And what could be more lucky for me than the fact that the D sharp itself had already aroused my curiosity, so that there was no danger of my losing the effect of the strings in a general dazzle of new experiences? Children must be allowed to lose definite impressions in such a dazzle; and nothing could be worse than spoiling their chances of enjoyment, as well as their hopes of constructing their own impressions, by submitting them to the equivalent of a Fairchild-family examination on the contents of Sunday morning's sermon. I remember that either before or after my experience of the Violin Concerto I heard Beethoven's *Missa Solennis*; and that, although I had been much excited by what I could make of the vocal score, I came away from the performance over-ready for bed and made the illuminating comment that 'it was a curious drum-part'. This did me no harm, and the comment was obviously correct, though I did not see the point of Beethoven's drums of war in his 'Dona nobis pacem'.

Returning to the Violin Concerto, let me point out that my best chance of early appreciating the beauties of string tone was supplied by the fact that the composition is a violin concerto, and that the long-deferred entry of the solo violin gave me the most vivid possible experience of the contrast between the tone of one violin and the tone of an orchestral mass of strings. In his admirable treatise on instrumentation, which follows Widor's line of experience and begins with the 'kitchen' department, passing gradually to the higher and more universal ranges of the orchestra, Mr. Cecil Forsyth observed that in a concerto an absurd effect is often produced when the solo violin has given out a phrase which is afterwards taken up by the strings of the orchestra, who seem immediately to demonstrate: 'this is how it ought to sound'. This is the sort of experience that ought not to happen, and I was lucky in beginning with the experience of a concerto in which nothing of the kind does happen. Some of the difficulties in training the musical imagination come from two facts: first, that the glorious normalities of the classics are rare in comparison with the commonplace errors of most composers, ancient or modern; and secondly, that we take the classics for granted by accepting them as commonplaces before we have really allowed them to be granted to us at all. My early experience was lucky in that I was carefully protected from the experience of bad music, and that the experience of first-rate performances of great music was never so common as to cease to be a treat. Through no fault of Mr. Forsyth's, a great many students will read his wise remark about the difference between solo and tutti tone with the tacit assumption that Beethoven and

Brahms were capable of blundering in that matter. It is not so easy to learn from the classics as you might think, for most of the lessons they teach are negative. A riddle which I always propound to my students is this: *Q*. What is it which we all wish to learn from the Great Masters, and why can we never learn it? *A*. How to get out of a hole. Because they never get into a hole.

My experience of arm-chair score-reading began with a natural discovery that the notes of the printed page recalled to me what I had heard with a vividness in proportion to that of the original experience. Children do not, or at all events need not, start upon such adventures either with an undue expectation of pleasures in store or with a damping scepticism; nor are they much depressed or resentful if part of the experience is boring. I soon found that in reading scores the difference between a score that I had heard and a score that was new to me became less and less; but I have always found that the pleasure depends on my memory of experienced sounds, though that memory naturally becomes generalized. There is no essential difference between the vividness of reading music and the vividness of reading literature; and most of the difference is in favour of music. I became very jealous for the reality of my musical imagination, and I was surprised to find myself laughed at for reading repeats, a habit to which I can at all events ascribe certain clear ideas as to what repeats and da capos are important and what are not. I was shocked to find later in life that many musicians do actually read music far too much as if it was ordinary literature. I read prose extremely fast, far too fast to find it worth while to skip; and the consequence is that, if I wish to read poetry or any literature where rhythmic movement is important, I must read it aloud. With music I have from childhood assumed that the tempo is absolutely essential to the musical sense; and it horrified me to discover that there are musicians who are satisfied to take in the sense of an adagio by a quick glance along the printed lines. To me this procedure is not reading at all; it is merely looking to see if the stuff is worth reading. If I were thus to read with attention such an enormous proposition as the first sixteen bars of the slow movement of Beethoven's D minor Sonata, my imagination would definitely hear it as a minuet or scherzo. I cannot separate the general sense from the tempo, because I do not think there is any sense without the tempo. To understand those sixteen bars as a grammatical proposition which can be taken in at a glance, while a generalized instantaneous notion of the slow tempo subsists at the

2E*

back of one's mind, seems to me as useless as to say that the soul is either blue or not blue. Moreover, I am convinced that a large category of errors, not only in students' compositions, but in second-rate works by composers of some standing, comes from failure to imagine the simple fact that if a passage that has been played at a fairly fast tempo is played four times as slow, it will take four times as long.

In the 'eighties and 'nineties it was commonly supposed that young and otherwise reprehensible composers who might do well enough in scherzos always broke down when it came to slow movements; and their failure was ascribed to lack of sentiment and to the attempt to replace it by a display of ingenuity. The effect of these warnings against being young and otherwise reprehensible is that not even the most reprehensible of us has often shown the slightest need for them. I believe that in the majority of amiable, if unconvincing, school-works at the end of the nineteenth century the slow movements will be best, and that the worst and most artificial movements will be the scherzos. Good finales are the rarest of all, and their deficiency I believe to come from lack of training in any sense of movement whatever. The commonest cause of failure in slow movements is that the composer has never imagined a slow tempo, either in his own works or in his reading of other music. I should be inclined, even in the absence of more interesting evidence, to regard it as a sign of promise in a young composer if he had the patience to play me a slow theme in a slow tempo. Composers' playing is proverbially bad and misrepresentative in its sketchiness, but I firmly believe that the sketchiest composer-player who presents a correct tempo in strumming a slow movement has the root of the matter in him.

Early in my adventures in score-reading I encountered a useful but disconcerting experience. Playing from scores, as distinct from reading them, is a practice to which I owe much; and it was wisely controlled by being assumed to be rather a naughty diversion destructive to my legitimate pianoforte technique, but to be officially ignored on much the same principle according to which Eton masters considered that a boy was not out of bounds if on emerging from the tuck-shop he concealed himself, ostrich-like, from the master's eye by holding a teaspoon before his own eye. Now some scores are easier to play than others. Beethoven's Serenade Trio, op. 8, almost instantly became a favourite pianoforte work for me, but I was disconcerted to find that I could hear nothing but pianoforte tone in it when I tried to read it to myself. This might seem too obvious to be worth recording as an experience, but it applies to the whole field of the musical imagination. Imagination will always follow the line of least resistance.

If you can overcome the difficulty of assembling its facts, the printed page will convey to you almost as vivid an impression as you have had from the actual sounds of the music. What is feeble in this impression may even be over-compensated by your discovery of details that you missed in listening to an actual performance; and these details are also those of remembered sounds, though the memory is of generalities not confined to the music before you. No two performances will bring exactly the same details vividly to your ear, as no two days or times of day present the same lights and shadows in a scene or building. But a well-imagined composition, like a well-imagined building, will make sense in every reasonably good presentation. The musician's capacity to imagine new combinations of sound is in no way inferior to the reading capacity of lovers of literature; and the data given to the musician by a full score are incomparably more exact and adequate than those given by the most readable printed presentation of a play.

Of course you must not expect from the musician feats of imagination which would be manifestly absurd to expect from the reader of literature. You may contrive to learn much of the grammar and vocabulary of a language without knowing the sounds of it. It is doubtful whether the finest and most philological of scholars can get nearer to the sound of classical Greek than the equivalent of an Englishman pronouncing French according to the phonetic chaos of English spelling. On such conditions, not even the most insular of Englishmen would be satisfied with his enjoyment of French literature, even if he mastered the arithmetical rules of French prosody. But we are not justified in concluding that the enthusiasm of classical scholars is a mere affectation. If I am confronted with a score in a language so private to the composer that I know no more of its sounds than an English scholar, or a modern Greek without a classical education, can know of the sounds of Homer, my impressions of that score will be vague and its construing too difficult an exercise to give me much pleasure. But one experience of an actual performance will, if the composer is a master, give me the freedom of his style once for all; and if he is not a master I shall probably have seen unmistakable symptoms of the fact in the mere appearance of the score.

It is notoriously unsafe to diagnose rashly from such symptoms. Berlioz is, with all respect to his more fanatical worshippers, not an advanced or adventurous master of harmony, except sporadically and capriciously; and the difficulties in imagining the effect of his scores mostly come from the fact that they look all wrong to a reader who has never heard Berlioz's orchestration. Some of the details are certainly wrong—as wrong as split infinitives or Malapropisms—and these will naturally attract a disproportionate attention from the score-reader who does not know Berlioz's style, and who is perfectly justified in refusing to believe that such features in the style of any of his own pupils indicate anything like Berlioz's talent. But if you have heard, or still more have conducted, one representative score of Berlioz, there is not much in his orchestral resources that will not reveal itself to you by the printed page. Some things you cannot foresee, and I am not so very sure that Berlioz himself always foresaw them. The effect of six pairs of pianissimo cymbals in the 'Sanctus' of the *Requiem* is incomparably more mysterious than anything that can be produced by a single pair; and the pedal notes of trombones in unison in the 'Hostias' is not a thing the sound of which can be guessed by its appearance on paper. But it is ridiculous and mischievous to discourage the musician's imagination by citing details that are *ex hypothesi* quite outside the normalities of music in which every musician should keep himself fit. The experienced musician can recognize Berlioz's scoring at a glance, and Stanford tells us that he can also recognize at a glance its unfortunate influence on students who are not getting on with their proper work.

Once more to cite my own experience, this time more recent, I can assure the reader that the scoring of Sibelius, which looks almost as wrong-headed as Berlioz's, seemed to me not only obviously masterly, but almost impeccable, long before I experienced it in actual performance, and that I have not found much trouble in discriminating between its occasional miscalculations and its chronic necessary difficulties. With Strauss there is, of course, the difficulty of assembling the details of a complicated 'skyscraper' score, and of determining how much may be neglected of the all-pervading grit that results from his road-hog procedures through the rules of musical traffic; but I have found my experience as an ordinary concert-goer quite adequate to the purpose of guessing the general effect of a tutti by Strauss or by any modern master whose works are not too unpractical to be performed at all.

The experienced musician appreciates many qualities of tone and matters of musical sense at a glance, even with the most paradoxical and difficult scores. Sibelius is difficult to read only to those who have never heard his musical language, for his scores are drastically simple, and *Punch* has commented acidly on the scandalous overwork of the word 'bleak' by Sibelius's critics, whether friendly or hostile. The difficulty of reading very complicated scores is merely the difficulty of assembling them. It is nothing like the difficulty of reading literature in a foreign language of which your knowledge is in the travellers' phrase-book stage. Musicians themselves will doubt their own capacity to read modern scores if they compare their capacity with what is alleged in pious opinions instead of comparing it with the manifest difficulties of general reading. But I have already remarked on the possibility that some musicians have never discriminated between reading and glancing. What I have said about the duty of reading a slow movement slowly does not bind me to spend a whole minute over forty ticks of the slowest metronome measuring a paragraph which I can see at a glance to be rubbish; nor am I obliged to assume that every score that displays the grammatical blunders of Berlioz is inspired by Berlioz's genius.

There are well-defined circumstances in which a musician will genuinely prefer reading a score to hearing it, and there are few in which he will not derive from a single reading vivid impressions which only a large number of actual performances could attain. Conversely, there are impressions which a single performance will convey immediately, but which would take form only after many silent readings. And, of course, you cannot expect to imagine the sound of an instrument which you have not actually heard; though Wagner took the risk of composing the whole part of his bass trumpet throughout the *Ring* before the instrument had been invented, with the result that the makers of the instrument had to devise something almost cheap and nasty in principle and in quality of tone.

Over-indulgence in *a priori* scepticism will soon leave us unable to discriminate between Wagner's practical miscalculations and the ineptitudes of a composer with no imagination at all. It is unfortunate that we happen to know that Beethoven was deaf. This knowledge has led to a terrible perkiness in the orthodox attitude towards his scoring; a perkiness which Weingartner has nobly relegated to the limbo of 'things that are not done' by his exhaustive discussion of the retouchings that are necessary to bring Beethoven's scores into the condition in which the composer would have left them if he could have controlled the rehearsals. Beethoven's deafness would have been an irreparable disaster if, and only if, it had come upon him before he had accumulated a more intimate acquaintance with the actual sounds of an orchestra than Schubert attained in his whole lifetime. Practically, Schubert must be considered far deafer than Beethoven, for he never heard his own greater orchestral works at all. Brahms always refused to publish any work, whether for chamber music or orchestra, until he had heard a public performance of it. But none of the difficulties and limits of the score-reader's imagination are as serious as those of a general reader of literature. It is true that the time-element in music forbids anything analogous to a *coup d'œil*; for, as I cannot too often urge, to glance is not to read. The *coup d'œil* is perhaps the crowning glory of architectural joy, but its nearest aesthetic equivalent in music can exist only in the memory, fresh or remote, of a finished performance that cannot have been short. As a person ignorant of architecture, though perhaps not incapable of enjoying it, I confess myself quite unable to understand in what sense one can know a cathedral, either as a whole or in detail, unless by the accumulated experiences of a lifetime. Accumulated experience is necessary for knowing any work of art whatever. The *coup d'œil* is a fortunate asset to architecture, but it can never deal with more than one aspect of a building at a time, and the eye has no such guidance for assembling the impressions of architecture in a proper order as is given to the ear by the time-sequence of music.

On the whole, then, I come to the conclusion that to those who can enjoy it at all music is not more difficult, but easier, to enjoy than most arts, whether in performance or in silent reading; and that the chief obstacles to the enjoying of great music and to the composing of enjoyable music come from habits that dull the imagination. My first and last advice to students of composition, even in the humblest of exercises, is that they should write what they can hear. If anyone, whether inexperienced or experienced, tells me that he wonders how such and such an experiment will sound, I can tell him that, if his wonder is an ordinary doubt and not a Socratic irony, his passage will sound fluffy and hollow, these being the almost invariable qualities that result from unimaginative breaches of rule. Nobody is ever in doubt about the sound of a passage that keeps the rules. If it has not been imagined, it will be dull, though cleaner than ditch-water. If it has been imagined, it may be as vivid as the opening of Beethoven's Violin Concerto, even if it is as unoriginal as Handel's Hallelujah Chorus.

Neither as admirers of nor as critics of Berlioz must we be misled by him. His grammatical solecisms will always loom disproportionately large in the imagination of even the most experienced score-reader, because it is hardly possible to be a score-reader without wondering how such blunders are compatible with a sensitive ear; and, as a matter of fact, Berlioz has left abundant proof in his criticisms that his capacity for reading harmony was very small. His crusade against appoggiaturas and his detestation of the chromatic style of Wagner are not manifestations of academic prejudice, such as he himself was the first to ridicule, but simple demonstrations of what he could not read. Charles Hallé tells us in this connexion that, when Berlioz was scoring Weber's *Invitation à la Danse*, Berlioz came to him in great bewilderment at Weber's quite ordinary enharmonic return from C major to D flat, and was surprised and relieved to find that when Hallé played it it sounded all right. But in spite of limitations and solecisms, the experienced score-reader can see at a glance that Berlioz imagined with uncanny accuracy the sound of everything he wrote. It is not true that the solecisms sound well; and though it is true that every attempt to correct them will sound commonplace, it is not true that Berlioz's style would not be better without them. His ear is simply defective on these points, exactly as Mrs. Browning's ear is defective in 'her inability either to achieve or to avoid rhyme'. And there is no wisdom in inventing special theories of assonance or of 'apostleship of the fundamental bass' in order to glorify such defects. The Berlioz hagiology has gone so far as to express regret that Cherubini did not grant Berlioz's application for the Chair of Harmony at the Paris Conservatoire. The tyranny of an orthodox pedant is bad enough without being aggravated by Cherubini's bad temper; but it would be enlightened liberty compared with the tyranny of an unteachable composer of genius who built infallible doctrines on every result of the defects of his own education. The average student shows a healthy spirit if he is puzzled by a teaching which imposes upon him the orthodox rules of strict counterpoint without telling him that, while they are true of unaccompanied vocal music, there are conditions of instrumental scoring in which they become false. He must be trained to recognize very fine distinctions of harmonic progression, true for all qualities of tone, just as Shaw's Eliza Doolittle must practise her natural talent for recognizing and imitating every nuance of vowel and consonant in Professor Higgins's thousands of phonograph records before her Pygmalion can present her at a royal garden party. But the well-trained elocutionist does not believe that every correctly placed aspirate can blow out a candle; and the musician with a delicate ear for harmony is not he who is in danger of lock-jaw whenever it is possible by a counting of intervals to detect that two parts have moved in forbidden consecutives. Unfortunately, there are such people. I remember that some thirty years ago one such musician contributed to a learned musical journal an article on Bach's breaches of rule. He himself had written fugues in quadruple counterpoint which looked impressive enough on paper to produce glowing testimonials from eminent musicians who ought to have known better. His quadruple counterpoint was wrong from beginning to end, because its themes all moved at the same pace and were not transparent to each other; whereas every example that he cited as licentious in Bach happened to illustrate perfectly the real principles which the rules attempt to codify. I owe to this innocently terrible person much of my impulse to investigate these principles for myself; and at the time I began a detailed article by way of rejoinder. But I had not proceeded far before I felt that the doctrines to be refuted were too silly to be associated with the difficult demonstration I was projecting; and I was very glad when in the next issue of the journal a *Musikgelehrte* dismissed the attack on Bach in three snorting sentences. It is a pity that one cannot say that the day for such controversies has passed. All that has happened is that the ground has shifted, and I am not sure that the present state of things is not worse than in the times when orthodoxy was impenetrable. But the impenetrable orthodoxy and the present chaos are equally amenable to treatment by score-reading.

Let us, then, follow the line of least resistance and quickest progress, as the classical masters did; but remembering, as they did, that the line of least resistance must be that of our own progress and not of mechanical transportation through tunnels and over clouds. Gramophones and broadcasting will do much for us, but only if we do still more for ourselves. Let us learn our vocabulary by achieving fluent figured-bass playing and score-reading at the keyboard, and let us stock our imaginations by using printed scores to remind us of what we have heard and enable us to learn many times more than we can hear in a lifetime. There is as much sense as satire in Mr. Belloc's pseudo-scientific aspiration: 'Oh, let us never, never

doubt What nobody is sure about!' In his treatise on novels Mr.
E. M. Forster has devoted a chapter to proving that nobody can
read a novel. But he has written many readable ones himself. I am
quite certain that I shall never know a cathedral, though I enjoy
assembling my impressions of it. I claim a conductor's knowledge
of Wagner's *Ring* as a whole, though the occasions when I have had
time to read the four operas continuously, even in the enforced
leisure of cross-continental railway journeys, are as rare as my
leisure for hearing actual performances. Such passages as Mime's
fit of terror after the exit of the Wanderer must be known before
they can be read: at all events a reader who has not heard them
would have a long labour before his assembling of the facts could
lead him to a coherent guess at their effect. And scores that consist
mainly of such passages do not often convey ideas worth the labour
of arm-chair reading without the help of remembered performances.
A reader whose musical diet consists of what Stanford called 'fish-
sauce' may perhaps get vivid impressions from them, while the
scores of Tallis and Palestrina convey nothing but grammatical
abstractions to him, as he never listens to pure polyphony in a
vaulted building. Familiarity is the root of the matter, and its first
condition is that it must not be of the kind that breeds contempt.
A person for whom the bed-rock elements of Beethoven's Violin
Concerto, or the pages for strings and a few occasional wind instruments in the first scene of *Die Walküre*, have lost their vividness,
will impart to the most modern fish-sauces the same dullness that
pervades my poor old exercise for the Doctorate of Music. But at
any stage, early or late in one's musical experience, a sceptical
analysis of one's imaginative powers may paralyse them as effectively as the centipede was paralysed by being asked which foot he
put down first.

THE MEANING OF MUSIC[1]

It is hardly reasonable to expect that all lovers of music will agree in their attitude towards instrumental music that professes to describe things outside itself. But to the non-musician, there is something intimidating in the severely uninformative titles of the purest musical compositions; and Beethoven himself did not object to his publisher giving the title *Appassionata* to the powerful work which would otherwise have been known merely as 'Sonata in F minor, op. 57'. Yet there must be some cogent reason in the nature of music that has prevented Beethoven and other great composers from giving descriptive titles even to their most emotional and dramatic instrumental works, although Beethoven himself said that he always composed according to a *Bild* in his mind. It is misleading to translate *Bild* as 'picture', for it is a much more general term, which a scrupulous translator could easily whittle down till it amounted to 'idea'. Thus, if Beethoven had been talking Greek, he would have told us simply that he had some idea of what he was writing. But he was as churlish as Brahms in his response to intrusive inquiries into so private an affair as his *Bilder*.

The dislike of external titles for purely instrumental music is as ancient as the use of them, and has probably always been a trait of musical orthodoxy. We know of the famous piece of programme music which represented Apollo slaying the Dragon, mainly because it was cited by philosophers as a flagrant instance of the abuses to which art can descend. On the other hand, pure musical orthodoxy becomes fanatical pedantry when musicians and critics object to vocal or stage music that illustrates the words of the poet and the situation of the drama. Plato, who never mentions absolute music, is really on the side of the musical illustrators. Where voices are used, words must be used. To Plato the only thing more degraded than making the human voice imitate the cries of animals is for it to imitate inanimate noises, such as the sound of wind. The human voice should not be wasted on less than human speech, and when the musician has to deal with words his natural duty is to illustrate them. If he dismisses this as a nuisance he is repudiating a normal condition of his art. The human voice is the oldest and most perfect of instruments, and Medtner's vocalized sonata is

[1] From *The Listener* of 16 September 1936.

a more difficult proposition to defend than any musical mis-handling of words or conflict with an intrusive programme. (In parenthesis, may I hope that Mr. A. P. Herbert[1] will not range me on the side of the enemy in his Word War for pointing out that 'vocalize' is the necessary and only possible term for the art, legitimate within its limits, of singing without words?)

I regret that I have not Mendelssohn's letters within reach, and that I have been too lazy to learn by heart an excellent reply which he took the trouble to give to a correspondent who asked him the 'meaning' of some of his *Songs without Words*. The gist of that reply is a demonstration that, at all events to the musician, it is music that has a definite meaning, whereas the meanings of words are at the mercy of the personal equation. Mendelssohn says that to one man the words 'Praise the Lord' may be associated with the same emotional thrill as another man would receive from the words 'Par force Jagd'; an expression which I take to mean something like a *grande battue* or other Continental mode of sport. He expects nothing better from words than the ridiculous discrepancies that are shown when different people try to give titles to pieces of pure music. He used titles himself more often than Beethoven, but he shows the two possible extremes in the relevance of these titles.

At the age of seventeen he reached the summit of his powers in the *Midsummer Night's Dream* Overture, which is a perfect piece of absolute music and, at the same time, a miraculously accurate illustration of the main features of the play, not as a sequence of events, but as the world that Shakespeare's imagination had built up therein. I, for one, have learnt a good deal about Shakespeare from that overture, and still more from the later incidental music with which Mendelssohn accompanied large areas of the play as accurately as Mozart ever translated his libretti into music. On the other hand, I took the trouble to read Victor Hugo's *Ruy Blas* in order to find out what was in Mendelssohn's mind when he wrote his effective and popular overture to that title; and my research amply bears out Mendelssohn's assertions in his letters that Victor Hugo's play was an abomination to him, and that the overture might just as well have the title of the charity for which it was written. Accordingly, I snatched a fearful joy both from Hugo's play and from Mendelssohn's peevish inattention to it.

Obviously, no light can be thrown on programme music by seeking a common ground in all the reasonably masterly instrumental

---

[1] Now Sir Alan P. Herbert, M.P.

compositions that have titles. The use of titles for absolute music will always meet a natural public demand. If our more abstract painters not only reduced the art of painting entirely to abstract elements of line and colour, but insisted on describing their master-pieces merely by the dimensions of the canvas, they would not hasten the coming of that glorious time when their art shall become as popular as Beethoven's C minor Symphony.

The public will remain starved of informative titles; but every reasonable lover of music will welcome Mendelssohn's paradox that words convey miserably vague information as to the meaning of music. Indeed, they often mislead precisely where they are most appropriate. Beethoven would have been foolish to deny the illus-trative elements in his 'Pastoral' Symphony. But there are probably few great classics that are more grossly underrated and more unin-telligently abused by wiseacres than that work. I have not space here to defend its integrity as pure music, but I take the opportunity to point out one of the chief fallacies in comparisons between pro-gramme music and absolute music, as exemplified in what Mr. Ernest Newman has quoted from Wagner, who adduced the regu-lar recapitulation of the Overture *Leonore* No. 3 as an example of how abstract musical form compels the composer to falsify his pro-gramme. Wagner not only missed the point but quite incorrectly described what happens. The trumpet call is not, as he assumes, the climax of *Leonore* No. 3. It was the climax of *Leonore* No. 2, and was there followed by a coda which wound up the overture as quickly as possible, and made thereby, as Weingartner points out, an admirable prelude to the rise of the curtain. No person in musical history was less likely than Beethoven to sacrifice dramatic and emotional fitness to an *a priori* musical form, and Wagner's criticism dates from a time in which it was already assumed that the laws of sonata form had been established as things to which, in Rockstro's pious phrase, 'The Great Masters lent their loving obedience'. Who established these forms we are not told, except that we are led to suppose that orthodoxy was represented by Mozart and Haydn. But at the beginning of the nineteenth century Mozart and Haydn were as recent as Richard Strauss is to us. They differ from each other widely in their habits of form, and, as far as technical analysis can disclose, most of Beethoven's enormous extensions in form can be defined as an integration of the different habits of Mozart and Haydn. Such an integration is a very different matter from an average; it raises Beethoven's resources to an incalculable power. Instead of being the climax in *Leonore* No. 3, the trumpet call is a halt in the middle of the development; after which the real excitement begins. The return to the main key is now no matter of perfunctorily winding up the illustration of a story. It is a thing, far more dramatic in itself, to which all the rest has been a prologue; and the regular recapitulation gives the natural relief of spacious leisure during which the music stores up energy for one of the most tremendous of all Beethoven's codas. To anyone who can feel something like Beethoven's emotion at the thought of the heroism of Leonora, this is the music that can adequately express it. But such music entirely kills all that can be achieved in stage drama, and when Beethoven finally revised his opera neither *Leonore* No. 2 nor *Leonore* No. 3 could be retained at all.

The whole of Beethoven's exasperating experience with his opera taught him a truth which underlies many of the dangers of programme music. Music for the stage is not, as is popularly supposed, distinguished by a higher emotional tone from absolute music. It is music under conditions where unsophisticated and simple indications of emotion produce an immediate effect, just as stage scenery, viewed by stage lighting, is much more effective than easel pictures, though its colours and forms can be splashed on out of pails. Accordingly, one reason why programme music incurs the suspicion of being bad is that, if its composers are experienced writers for the stage, their habits may be stagy. If, on the other hand, they are not experienced writers for the stage, they may be inexperienced in other ways as well, for there is a strong presumption that great mastery of purely instrumental music will fill a composer's mind with things for which he feels words to be inadequate.

But no such *a priori* theories will prevent artists from using what they have found to be the shortest way of disposing themselves to work and of refreshing their energy and courage during the labour of planning and writing. Both for listeners and composers the temptation to appeal to external ideas probably varies according to the extent and power of visualizing. My own visualizing powers are feeble and my eye has never been trained by the study of pictures or architecture. Consequently music does not call up to me any visual associations, unless I am surprised by some peculiar quality of sound. Then, indeed, I have sometimes been startled by an intense visual impression: as, for instance, when the use of an unexpectedly bell-like stop in an episode of one of Bach's organ fugues made me seem to see every note as a shining globule of quicksilver;

or when in the early days of broadcasting the sudden intrusion of a pianoforte crudely 'cued-in' for a passage in the *Tannhäuser* Overture caused a sheaf of leaves and stalks of honesty to dance before my eyes. These impressions were not only spontaneous, but irresistible. If they were normal in my musical experience I might be too much accustomed to them to notice whether they enhanced or spoiled my enjoyment of the music. But a powerful and habitual visualizer is probably much more ready than I am to associate instrumental music with literary and pictorial ideas.

I do not myself experience any difficulty from conflicts between instrumental music and the programmes imputed to it by the composer or foisted on it by others. If the music fits the programme it will tell me more of the programme than the programme will tell me of the music. No illustrative element can make bad composition good: and the merits of good composition are not reducible to rules of abstract musical form. Liszt's Symphonic Poems are more weakened by his mechanical theory of thematic development than by his programmes. Berlioz tells us that the public has no imagination, and that, therefore, some parts of his *Roméo et Juliette* will be intelligible only to those who are thoroughly familiar with Shakespeare's play with the *dénouement* of Garrick. Berlioz's *Roméo et Juliette* contains some of his best music and some of his worst. The best of it is quite intelligible without Shakespeare, and the 'Queen Mab' Scherzo is untrammelled by the necessity that compelled Shakespeare to kill Mercutio. What is not so intelligible remains unilluminated by any ray from Shakespeare or Garrick.

I am glad that Mr. Newman has mentioned Elgar's *Falstaff*, because for me that work will always be a *locus classicus* for perfect relation between matter and form. Unlike Berlioz, Elgar is one of the most attentive artists who ever lived. His knowledge of Shakespeare was as profound as that of many professed Shakespeare scholars. I am in a position to give evidence as to the musical integrity and intelligibility of his *Falstaff*, because I ventured to send him the analysis I wrote of it for one of my concerts, not knowing, as I must confess with shame, that his own analysis had been published some years ago in the *Musical Times*. He kindly sent me a copy of it, and permitted me to correct my analysis by footnotes quoting his descriptions wherever I had gone wrong. I did not find that I had gone seriously wrong, certainly not in any matter of aesthetic importance; but I can certify that, while my own analysis went into considerable detail as a result of careful reading of both parts of *Henry IV*, I had at no time felt the slightest need for explaining Elgar's form by his programme. Of course, if I had started with the idea that there were laws of abstract musical form which must be reconciled somehow with the sequence of dramatic events, I should have been involved from the outset in inextricable tangles and mendacious terminology to justify Elgar's music; but as I do not regard even the strictest sonata form as an external framework, I simply took this music as I would take a Haydn quartet, first as a whole, then phrase by phrase, and read my Shakespeare after I had enjoyed the music. Then, indeed, it was thrilling to see the splendid independence and integrity of Elgar's mind; to realize the musical convenience of a view of the character and kingship of Prince Hal that was more sympathetic than my own, if not more sympathetic than Shakespeare's; and to realize that though Shakespeare gives us only Mistress Quickly's account of Falstaff's death, Elgar views its pathos, not through poor Quickly's eyes, but through Shakespeare's. Such is the power of absolute music.

INDEX

(NOTE: Entries in this index refer only to musical works mentioned in the author's text. Several essays deal specifically with certain composers—e.g. those on the chamber music of Haydn and Brahms, on Schubert, Gluck, Elgar, and Beethoven's art forms. No work by the subject of the essay in question mentioned in that essay is included as a separate entry in the index, though such works, if quoted in other parts of the book, occur in their proper order, and so do works of other composers cited in those pages, which are generically listed *s.v.* the composer's name.—ED.)